Sign up for our newsletter to hear
about new and upcoming releases.

www.ylva-publishing.com

Other Books by Lola Keeley

A Roll in the Hay
Slammed
Major Surgery
The Music and the Mirror

HER *Royal* HAPPINESS

LOLA KEELEY

Acknowledgements

First and greatest thanks must go to Astrid and Daniela for their patience and faith even when I wasn't at my best as an author. They were kind enough to ever take a chance on me in the first place, and all of this is about repaying that kindness.

A debt of gratitude to C.S. Conrad, not just a thoughtful and brilliant developmental editor, but also a wonderful sensitivity and authenticity reader.

Further, to Sheena on copyediting for her detailed work. Any lingering mistakes are my bad, but we really tried to stamp on those. My new beta reading team are phenomenal, they picked up so many tiny details and saw the big picture in ways I could only have dreamed of. Big thanks to Catherine, Órla, Leslie, and Ann for their thoughts and brilliance.

Sensitivity readers are out here saving us from ourselves, and I'd like to thank Sarah, Molara, and Jo in particular, for their advice on the topics and perspective raised in this book. I have tried my utmost not to let them down in writing about women of colour and autistic people, but any misses there are my fault entirely. I will try to keep learning and doing better. I'm so grateful for resources like the National Autistic Society and books such as *How to Write Autistic Characters: An Incomplete Guide*.

Being amazing above and beyond the call of duty is my wife, Kaite. She shares my home, my life, and the rota for cuddling our four cats. Kaite is a wonderful novelist in her own right, always in demand, and yet she always makes time to let me plot out loud or argue about character decisions. Just one of the many ways in which I'd be utterly lost without her. Also, she knows about posh things far beyond my own experience.

My best friends have been their usual awesome selves, so thank you to Lande and Lisa-Marie for the advice, the great company, the space to vent, and the constant supply of memes to stop us all losing our minds.

Special shoutouts to Natacha, Jo, Judy, Adam, Michael, James, Lesley, Lisa, JD, Orlá,Annie, Kayla, Laura, Olivia, Bianca, Ashton, Molly, Emily, Gane and Erin for being hilarious, lovely, and supportive in various ways. I hope I've been returning the favour, and if not: feel free to call it in!

Also, stupidly, at least a bit of credit has to go to none other than Taylor Swift because this pandemic year has been utterly soundtracked by Folklore and Evermore. They kept my brain working when the world got very small indeed.

Finally: to my parents, Isobel and Raymond. There was a time long ago when I wouldn't have believed I would be writing sapphic romances as an out lesbian and sharing that reality with them, but it just goes to show that there's always hope and sometimes things really do get better.

For Laura,
Who makes me laugh and makes me think!

Chapter 1

HER ROYAL HIGHNESS, PRINCESS ALICE was prepared for any reaction when she spoke in public, but a small girl bursting into tears wasn't one of them. The whole room seemed to freeze, adults and children alike, as one tiny person started to sob. Each shuddering sound echoed against the mostly bare walls of the school gymnasium.

On sheer instinct, Alice stepped back from the podium decorated with children's artwork and made her way across the low staging area to comfort the child. She hunkered down in front of her and laid a calming hand on the girl's shoulder, with the very lightest of touches. Her hand, evenly tanned from a recent sailing trip, was still pale in comparison to the dark-brown hair and brown complexion of the little one. Alice brushed her own short blonde fringe out of her eyes.

"Hello there." She kept her voice low and friendly, a chat just between the two of them.

"H-hello."

"Is everything okay? Did I say something that upset you?"

The girl shook her head.

"My name's Alice. What's yours?"

Wiping her tears, the girl gave Alice a long, appraising look through wet eyelashes. "Libby. My name is Libby."

"Excuse me—" said a voice over Alice's shoulder, but she dismissed the person with a wave of her hand. It was a moment of the utmost delicacy, one she'd experienced more than a few times with her young niece and nephew. More adults were not what the situation required.

"Now Libby, I'm sorry you're feeling upset. Do you want to talk about it?"

"Well…" Libby looked up at whoever stood behind Alice, considering her options it would seem. "I'm quite stressed, actually."

Stressed? Stressed? The girl couldn't be more than seven years old. She barely came up to Alice's crouching height, although admittedly Alice was a tall specimen by anyone's standards.

"What has you stressed, Libby?" Alice kept her expression warm but serious. Letting a smile creep in would be unforgivable. Everything was very serious at seven. Not to mention Alice's unapproachable reputation. Smile at a few children and people would start to wonder what she was plotting.

"I'm supposed to be playing my violin now. After your speech. But you just kept talking and talking and I worried I was going to be late. Or that I wouldn't get to play at all. I practiced really hard. Every day!"

It took all of Alice's reserve and stiff upper lip not to dissolve into laughter. Kids could be so dramatic, but there was no doubt that this sweet little girl also meant every word. How refreshing it must be, to simply express one's feelings so openly. She rather envied her.

"Your Royal Highness, we're so sorry." The prim and proper head teacher who had greeted Alice on arrival came bustling out of the front row. She reminded Alice of every teacher she'd had at boarding school—all blind devotion to the rules with a large dash of self-importance. The moment's peace was shattered, the reality of the situation seeping back in like cold puddle water through a leaky boot.

"No, don't apologise for her," that voice from behind came again, only then did the woman stepped into Alice's sightline. Average in height, subtly curvy, and frankly, a bit bloody gorgeous. The family resemblance was apparent, though this woman had a much lighter complexion and hazel-coloured eyes. She was sharply dressed too, not quite runway style but everything about her well-tailored skirt and blouse suggested an eye for fashion, and it was all tastefully offset by minimal jewellery and a silk scarf artfully knotted at her throat. Alice returned to standing, bracing herself for a protective mother.

"It's really no trouble," Alice said, extending a hand to shake in her practiced, brisk way. The woman didn't take it. "Libby was quite right,

I was rather waffling on a bit. One can just get so excited about music programmes like this. Such a gift for all the children involved."

"Ms Marteau, if you could remind your daughter that we don't speak out of turn at this school, no matter how things are done where you teach." The head teacher was bristling beside Alice, almost vibrating with the need to take control of the scene.

Alice didn't mind the disruption. It broke up the monotony of event after event, all so similar in their formality and people stiff with nerves. Despite her very best efforts to put people at their ease, they only heard 'Her Royal Highness Princess Alice, fourth in line to the Crown of the United Kingdom of Great Britain and Northern Ireland, Duchess of Dumbartonshire and Wessex, daughter of Queen Caroline.' Alice was fairly sure most people still left off her father, the queen's late husband and former England rugby captain Cameron Hardcourt. It was one of the few things that upset her on a regular basis.

None of which mattered, in the grand scheme of things. Yes, it brought a chance to raise money for charities and bring media attention to important causes, but more and more Alice found herself craving the anonymity that so many, more average, people seemed to enjoy. She was certainly getting a taste of it from this Ms Marteau, who seemed unimpressed by Alice's title, her station in life, or her attempts to calm an upset child.

"I don't teach. I'm a Special Education Needs consultant. Libby has been raised to speak up if there's a problem," Ms Marteau replied to the head teacher. "And you assured me that the children wouldn't be put under additional pressure to perform for the event today. She says she's stressed. That shouldn't be the case."

"Perhaps now that I've said my piece, the children can play their music? I'm sure they've practiced very hard." Alice found herself trying to win the woman's approval. Why it mattered, Alice had no idea. Any other time she would be halfway out of the door by now. "Would that be okay, Libby? If we grown-ups went to sit down and you could play your violin?"

Libby nodded, a little smile flickering across her lips. This was a kid used to bending the world to her will. It was hard not to like that about her.

"Only if you're sure, Libs. You don't have to do things just because someone with a fancy title is here." The easy rapport between mother and daughter was evident in the way Ms Marteau didn't have to bend to make eye contact, her hand on Libby's back for constant reassurance.

"Well, it is quite important to learn to honour one's obligations." Alice found herself speaking before her brain could catch up, relaying the lessons from her parents and grandparents without thinking. "And there's such a thing as a sense of duty. If we make a promise to an audience or our friends, it is always best to keep it. If we possibly can."

"Easy to say when you don't have to work for a living," Ms Marteau replied without missing a beat, hands on her hips. Alice felt a little dowdy next to her, and that usually only happened around the actors and models she crossed paths with. The odd foreign princess too, since a lot of those hewed much closer to the Disney versions than she ever had. Still, the one thing they all had in common was a lifetime of learning to be utterly diplomatic, even in the face of rudeness. "No offence, of course. I'm sure it's very important that all those ribbons get cut. I just don't think the experience is relevant to my daughter. I'm not a big believer in royalty, so please excuse me."

"I'm sorry, but we're not the tooth fairy. I'm afraid we exist whether you believe in us or not."

"Well, I hold out hope that one day this country will see sense just like France did, and become a republic." Alice noticed a faint accent on the way she said France, correctly rolling the 'r'.

"Oh well, as long as you don't mean to offend." Alice could give as good as she got in passive-aggression. She glanced around and saw at least one camera phone pointing their way. Best to control the situation. "Shall we sit down? We seem to be making a bit of a scene." Alice found her placid temper fraying around the edges.

Ms Marteau looked as if she was ready to argue about that too, but Libby tugged at her wrist, gaining her full attention in an instant.

"I do want to play, Mummy. It'll be really good, promise."

"I know it will be, *chérie*," her mother said.

"Wonderful, now let's all turn our attention to the children where it belongs." Alice opened her arms to the other adults, ushering them across to the waiting seats. One perk of the title was that people deferred to her physical presence, and a few years barking orders at pilots in the Royal Air

Force hadn't hurt on that front. Most situations could be resolved with a clear head and a determined bearing; everything else was just detail.

As they found their seats on the front row of hastily assembled chairs, the children took up position with their instruments. It was rather adorable, Alice had to admit. She'd seen every configuration of these events while opening schools, community centres, hospitals, and a thousand other buildings besides. She'd lost count somewhere in her mid-twenties and had never bothered to get an exact figure since. Someone would know. The palace staff specialised in arcane trivia.

"Actually… I apologise, I didn't mean to be so rude just then. I'm Sara, Sara Marteau, by the way." Sara had been left to sit next to Alice, for lack of other spaces.

Alice turned in surprise. "I'm Alice, although I suppose that was announced at the start."

"It was, but it's still a nice touch dropping the 'princess' part, though." Sara smiled at her for the first time. "It's very 'one of the people' to do such a thing. Anyway, my daughter is sensitive. I try not to jump in at every turn, but it's the job of my life to protect her."

A teacher had stepped in to organise and calm the children, although it seemed closer to herding cats than conducting a symphony.

"She seems very bright. And a musician already? You must be very proud."

"I am. She's the best thing that ever happened to me. Do you have children?"

Alice shook her head. How unusual to speak to someone who didn't already know the intimate details of her life. Then the music began, and well, Alice had to admit it wasn't the worst concert she'd sat through. At least nobody had a recorder. Or was called Ed. The short repertoire was jaunty and upbeat, and Alice found herself watching Libby most of all. Gone was the stressed little girl from before, and for three songs she was utterly lost in the music, eyes closed and swaying as she played with considerable skill for her age.

When the music concluded, the small crowd clapped with enthusiasm but stopped short of an ovation. A typical British audience that way. Sara proved the exception, leaping to her feet and thundering her hands together as tears welled in her eyes.

Alice caught her herself staring, but as soon as she averted her eyes, she met Josephine's knowing glance from over by the doors. Damn. That just earned her at least a week of mild teasing. All for some overprotective mother that Alice would never see again, and for whom this entire bizarre experience would just be another story to tell after yoga class or bumping into a friend at the supermarket.

"I think this is my cue to go," Alice said, standing up next to Sara. "Let the children enjoy all the attention."

"Thank you. And you don't seem so bad, you know. For the representative of an ancient, undemocratic institution."

Alice blinked once. Twice. "You really do just say what you think, don't you?"

"I do. Saves a lot of time and dishonesty."

"Well, I doubt I can convince you otherwise on the value of the monarchy in the time I have between this and my next appointment, but I think I deserve a fair shot at it all the same." Where had that come from? Alice fussed with the sleeves of her blazer, straightening the cuffs. "If you would indulge me, Ms Marteau, I have an invitation for you. And your daughter."

"What are we being invited to?" Libby said, violin case in hand. The heavy looking thing was as long as Libby was tall.

"In the summer we have garden parties. Well, my mother does. At Buckingham Palace. On the grounds. And we get to invite all sorts of people from the charities that we're patrons of, and people who make a difference in their community. That sort of thing. If I got my private secretary, Josephine, to come and take some details, I could arrange for you both to come. See it all up close and maybe that will change your view on us a little. Or make it even worse. Always an option."

Sara tilted her head slightly as she watched Alice speaking, appearing to listen intently. For all her protest that she was no teacher, she certainly had the bearing of one. Perhaps a Special Education Needs whatever was something similar enough.

"My daughter interrupts your speech, I insult you in the heat of the moment, and your response is to invite us to lunch?"

"Well, yes. I suppose it is." Alice could feel her face warming beneath the minimal make-up she always wore. Great, blushing was now adding insult to injury. "I can assure you this is not something I do every day, but I know I prefer to see something up close before sitting in judgement on it."

Sara smiled. For the first time since Alice laid eyes on her, Sara dropped her shoulders an inch or two, and let her half-pursed lips relax into an easy grin.

"I don't meet a lot of princesses. Maybe I haven't kissed enough frogs."

"Mummy, that's for princes." Libby looked between them as if she was watching a tennis match played with an invisible ball. "And you haven't kissed anyone for ages. Except me and *Mamie*."

"Libby!"

"From the mouths of babes, eh? Sorry, but I really must dash. Look out for that invitation."

Alice turned and made her way towards the exit. In their usual seamless way, her small team activated at the first nod. Protection officer flanking on the right, Josephine staying behind to follow up with the headmistress, and at Alice's discreet gesture, with Sara.

"All okay, ma'am?" Josephine was the first to speak once they were safely back in the car. The dark blue Bentley pulled away from the school car park with not enough haste for Alice's liking.

"Always a good sign when the subjects are crying, Josephine."

"It all worked out, though. I spoke to Ms Marteau and she mentioned your invitation to the garden party."

Alice made a point of looking out into traffic. "I thought it might smooth things over. Don't want her talking to the press, or worse ranting on social media about today. Isn't that the kind of thing you're always encouraging?"

"It is."

"You'll arrange the invitation? Don't forget the child should come too. Preferably without her violin, though. There was mention of a grandmother? Grannies love me."

Josephine tapped at her phone screen a few times. "Consider it done, ma'am. Now, should I check social media to make sure nothing comes of that little scene in there?"

"I'm sure that won't be necessary," Alice replied. "Who could make a story out of a child crying?"

DAILY BUGLE, 30TH APRIL

A RIGHT ROYAL UPSET

There were tears in the eyes yesterday at Ryeham Primary School, south London, when a concert given to celebrate the school's groundbreaking new music hall and gymnasium caused some royal embarrassment.

In attendance was the Princess Royal, HRH Princess Alice, to officially open the new space and congratulate the school and community on their fundraising efforts.

But her congratulations went on too long for one tearful child, and despite the princess offering comfort, she was subject to an anti-monarchy rant from a concerned parent. The shouting match made the rounds online, and the viral success means this school concert played to an audience most professional bands could only dream of.

When asked for comment, Buckingham Palace said only that: HRH Princess Alice attended a wonderful concert today, and wishes the children, teachers, and their families every future success.

Chapter 2

"MUMMY!"

Sara closed the front door behind her and leaned back against it with a smile. No matter how engrossed Libby got in something: her homework, her music practice, baking with her grandmother, she always dropped everything to come running when Sara returned home.

"Who's that shouting in my house?"

"It's me!" Libby said, well, it was more of an excited shriek as she collided with Sara. They almost matched, Sara in her grey shift dress for a serious day at work, Libby still in her grey pinafore and white polo shirt from a day of school. Most days they'd get home together, Sara collecting her for the bus journey home, but her new job brought longer hours, leaving her mother to kindly step in. "Who else calls you Mummy, silly?"

"Oh, lots of people," Sara replied, splaying her fingers on top of Libby's head and gently turning her around. Taller again, she was sure of it. The girl was growing like a weed. A bright, funny little weed. "Now, where's *Mamie*?"

"She's here," Inès said, coming out of the kitchen at the back of the small house, wiping flour from her hands with a well-worn tea towel. "And *mademoiselle* here tells me I'm to be called 'Granny' because that's what all her friends do."

Sara sensed the generational clash in that familiar complaint and decided she didn't have the energy to wade into it again.

"Well, I still call you *Maman*. To your face, anyway."

"Very funny. There's post for you. *Un café*?"

"Tea?"

Inès sniffed at the rejection of her beloved coffee but retreated into the kitchen all the same.

Taking a seat at their plain, wooden dining table, Sara prodded the stack of envelopes with little enthusiasm. Bills, circulars, people wanting her time and money as always. After a day of arguing with school governors and teachers about funding for her department, there wasn't much energy left in the tank.

"Aren't you going to open them?" Libby said, taking the seat opposite and plopping her elbows on the wooden surface, chin clutched in her hands. Sara felt her smile return at the sight. No one could accuse her of having anything other than an adorable child.

"Post isn't very exciting when you're a grown-up, Libs. Just bills and trying to sell me things I don't need. I'll get to it later."

"I never get any post," Libby said, pout firmly in place.

"Be grateful. Once it starts coming, it never stops. And oh—this one's addressed to both of us."

Libby perked up instantly, scrambling around the table to see.

"Lord Cham…ber…who?"

"Lord Chamberlain," Sara supplied automatically, her attention drawn to the crest next to the postage: CR I with a little crown on top. Caroline Regina the First. Or Queen Caroline to most of her subjects. Royalty. Fantastic.

"What is it?" Her mother returning with a steaming mug of tea picked up on Sara's distraction right away.

"You remember how Libby crying at her concert got all over the internet a couple of weeks ago?"

Inès nodded. "Not how I thought my baby would get famous. You got it taken down, though."

"Well, at the time that princess what's-her-face said she wanted to invite us to some party, to show me that royalty is oh-so-great. I can't believe she meant it."

Libby squealed, grabbing the envelope, and finishing the job of opening it.

"Are we going to a palace? Can we go in a carriage? With horses?"

Sara pinched the bridge of her nose.

"We'll see. I don't even know the date; we might already have plans."

"Mummy!"

"Libby, come on. How's that homework looking?" Sara held out her hand and gestured for the invitation to be returned. "Go bring your book down and I'll sign it."

Without arguing for a change, Libby went running upstairs. Sara turned to her mother with a shrug. "Just when I thought that little incident was done with."

"Let me see." Inès took the invitation, her face lighting up as she read it. "Ms Sara Marteau, her daughter Elisabeth, and Mrs Inès Marteau. How do they know about me?"

"I don't think I—oh, Libby mentioned you. To the princess. But it's not as though she sat and wrote the thing herself. They have staff."

"Lots of staff. It's a busy job, all they do for charity. You should be more respectful, Sara." Despite the mild scolding, Inès pulled her daughter into a hug. "Long day?"

"Hmm. I'm making some progress, though. The school finally accepts that if they want to really support children with additional needs, they have to spend some money. Still going to make me fight for every penny, though."

"You're doing a good thing. I know people think only teaching matters, but nobody stands up for the kids more than you."

"Thanks, *Maman*. I think I needed that. So, shall we play princess for the day and take Libby to the palace? They say it's a once in a lifetime opportunity..."

"Of course we're going! I'm going to need a new hat."

"What is it with mums and hats? You don't need to go to any trouble. It's just a cup of tea and shaking hands, I'm sure."

Inès swept up Sara's cup of tea before she could finish it, retreating towards the kitchen. "Nonsense. Queen Caroline will be there. And that handsome boy of hers, Prince Jamie."

"James. Prince James."

"You know who I mean. That wife of his seems very nice, very polite. I don't know why you dislike them all so much. Even going to Cambridge with all the posh kids, it didn't change your opinions. This is your country, your royal family, and more than that, it is mine."

"I was born here, but that doesn't mean I need to like everything about it. And trust me, Cambridge is not the kind of place that makes you want more of the upper class. It's practically an immunisation against them. Do you love everything about France? And what about Iran?"

"It's not as though leaving Tehran for Paris was entirely my choice, hmm? But lucky you, you get the best of both worlds from me. Dinner's almost ready," Inès replied, avoiding eye contact. "And *oui*, maybe we are not so fond of royalty either."

"I'll go and get changed into something comfortable, clean myself up. I'll find out what distracted Libby as well. Thank you for dinner. You know you don't have to do that every day."

"It keeps me busy. But okay, just until you get used to your new job."

"You're the best." Sara kissed her mother on the temple before jogging upstairs, taking the rest of the post to flick through as she went. Nothing interesting, just as she predicted.

She changed out of her formal work clothes for much more comfortable sweatpants and a long-sleeved T-shirt, both a well-washed navy that felt as natural to wear as her own skin. Content that Libby was happily playing in her own room, Sara detoured to the house's only bathroom and washed the minimal make-up from her face. Keeping her hair back off her face with a hairband, she wandered into the next room to retrieve her daughter.

Libby seemed to have forgotten the homework retrieval already, but a quick glance at her workbook on the tiny desk showed it had at least been completed. Sara realised the furniture was getting too small for her almost eight-year-old, which meant another weekend sometime soon would be given up to finding and building a taller desk and chair. Would the bed follow suit? Sara put it on her mental to-do list for later. It was a list that never seemed to reduce, no matter how many tasks she completed.

"Hey, little monster. You coming down for dinner?"

"What?" Libby looked up from the comic she had been engrossed in. "Oh, my homework is there. I just started reading."

"I still need to check my calendar, but Granny thinks we should go to the palace. Are you sure you want to go? These things can be very boring and grown-up. Lots of queuing and fussy little sandwiches."

"But it's special, isn't it? Not everyone gets to go?"

"That's true," Sara said.

"And that princess lady wanted to show us that they're nice. It would be rude not to give her a chance."

"Oh, I doubt we'll see her again. Maybe from a distance. But it will be a nice day out for us all, and something you can tell everyone about at school."

Libby unfolded herself from the beanbag and put her comic book back in its correct pile. "Will there be horses?"

"At the party? I don't think so. Maybe we'll see some outside the palace, though."

"Because I know we have to wait before I can do lessons—"

"Libby, sweetie. Let's not have this conversation again." Sara tried to shield her kid from the realities of living in London on one salary, but there was no wiggle room for an expense like horse-riding lessons with everything else they had to cover. "I promise, if and when it's possible, I will book lessons."

"I know."

"I don't like saying no or having to wait. But that's just how it has to be. Now, shall we go down to dinner before Granny has to yell?"

Libby agreed, leading the way to the door. "But Mummy, I think she likes shouting sometimes."

On the way out of the room, Sara noticed one of the picture frames turned towards the wall. Usually, it sat with pride of place on top of the drawers.

"What's wrong with this photo?" she said, before Libby could disappear down the narrow staircase. Frozen against the pale blue wall for a moment, Libby almost looked as if she was in mid-air.

"Nothing. I just don't always like to look at it. I'm only a baby in it, not like me now."

"But this is your photo with your dad." Sara didn't move away from it, refusing to let either of them change the subject. "Has someone been saying something?"

"No! No, but school this week was all about family trees again. We have to do this stupid picture, and I don't want to."

At that, Sara relented. She set the photo back in its proper place and crossed the short landing to hug Libby where she stood at the top of the stairs.

"I'm sure you're not the only one in class who has a parent missing, or with gaps on their tree."

"It's not that." Libby rubbed the tip of her nose against the hem of Sara's T-shirt, seeming to draw comfort from the overwashed and faded cotton. "I just don't like when people ask questions. Like why did you and Daddy make a baby if you knew he was going to die? And you weren't married, and he wasn't your boyfriend and—"

"You don't have to explain all of that to anyone."

"Right, but people always ask, and I don't want to tell lies, Mummy."

Sara patted the top of Libby's head. "You don't have to lie, sweetie. Or tell people more than you want to. Your daddy was my very best friend, and he loved you so much. He wanted to be a dad more than anything, so we did what we did, and you came along. That made him so happy."

Somewhere along the line, the story had become easier for Sara to tell. She had loved Jayesh as the best of friends did, and his tumour diagnosis had rocked their last year of university. One minute they'd been planning a post-university trip around India to visit his extended family, and the next life was full of doctors' appointments and too much bad news to handle.

"Okay. It would be nice to have a daddy, though. Or another mummy."

"Maybe one day. A step-mummy." They'd had that conversation more than once. Sara was confident that Libby understood dating women was the only option on the table.

Libby's scoff was a moment of sheer genetic inheritance, as though Inès had levitated through the floorboards to make the sound herself. Maybe they were spending a little too much time together. "How are you going to get me a step-mum if you never even date anyone? Honestly, Mummy. I get asked out more often than you do."

Ouch. The accuracy of the statement didn't make it sting any less. From the mouth of babes indeed, just like Princess Alice had said.

"You two take forever to get ready," Inès said as they returned to the table, Libby taking her usual seat and setting out the waiting plates as Sara detoured to start helping with the last stages of the cooking. "Does it really take so much time to look like you crawled out of the laundry pile?"

"We're here now," Sara said, bumping her mother with her hip as she passed the cooker. "I'm on rice duty, huh?"

"Even you can't ruin my rice, baby girl."

"No, but I can order a good pizza. That's what I'd have to do if you weren't so good to me and Libby."

Inès made a pleased sound as she stirred the pot on the hob. "What else is a mother for?"

"I'm just sorry we don't have room here for you permanently. I don't like you going back home on your own."

"Shush now, we all need our spaces. I spent long enough throwing your father out of mine, I'm not giving it up yet." Tasting the chicken straight from the wooden spoon, Inès frowned. Sara made a silent bet with herself, and sure enough her mother picked up the cumin a moment later. She loved the spice in abundance, and Sara missed it when other people did the cooking in her life.

"Well, at least you get to go to the palace. Consider that my latest thank you. In fact, maybe you and Libby go without me. That could be your gift to me."

Inès tutted, the click of her tongue muted as her lips pursed. "I didn't raise you to be ungrateful. One afternoon isn't going to kill you. Besides, there are worse things than catching the attention of a princess. This one is even gay."

Sara laughed out loud at that. "Only you, *Maman*. Only you could see a dating opportunity from a PR exercise. I bet you anything she doesn't even remember us. It'll be a vague smile and a handshake, just like all the other guests."

"You need some romance in your soul, *ma fille*. You're too young to have given up on so many things. It can't be just work and Libby, no matter how much time they both take up."

Sara lifted the rice pot, transferring the contents to a bowl and nodding at the light, fluffy texture of it. Perfect every time. "Fine, fine. I'll download a dating app or something. But I'll set my sights a little more realistic than the world's first queer princess. Like she's going around to look for commoners to date. Honestly!"

"According to the papers she's about as good at dating as you are, so never say never. Come on, let's go feed this child of yours so she grows up big and strong."

"On my way," Sara said, carrying the large bowl of rice out of the kitchen.

She caught sight of the invitation again, this time laid out neatly by Libby's plate. It did look quite personalised, but then again, they probably had a fancy way of making it look so relaxed and genuine. Some underpaid intern would be stuck with such a meaningless task, no doubt. Oh well, it was something unusual in a life that had become really quite routine. Maybe in ten years they'd still be talking about the day they all went to the palace.

"Ready?" Inès said as she brought the deliciously scented pot of stew to the table.

"I think so," Sara said.

Chapter 3

ALICE NODDED TO THE STEWARD as she entered the private dining room at Buckingham Palace. Although she'd spent half of her life nominally living there, she still felt the weight of history bearing down on her from the walls. The dark oil paintings and heavy tapestries at every turn were familiar but a constant reminder of how much history, money, and expectation came with every step taken within the building and others like it.

"Good morning, Mummy."

Queen Caroline looked up from her copy of *The Times*. Dressed for a day of engagements, she looked regal as ever in her cerise pink dress, sleeveless in her preferred style, a matching bolero jacket for it waiting draped over the empty chair next to her.

Alice slipped into the other seat opposite, unsurprised when the steward seemed to materialise at her elbow without actually moving across the room.

"And for Her Royal Highness?"

"I ate at St James's, thank you. Though might I trouble you for a cup of tea?"

"Of course. Anything else for Your Majesty?"

"No, thank you, Robin." Caroline picked up her fine china cup, sipping from it pointedly. "I'm surprised to see you here so early, Alice."

"I asked when you had a moment today, this was all they could give me. I'm on the train to Manchester shortly."

Caroline buttered a slice of toast with slow, precise scrapes of a knife. "I heard about your little concert kerfuffle week before last. Making children cry for sport again?"

"You know me, I just love being part of these viral videos." Alice accepted her teacup gratefully, adding sugar just to draw a tut from her mother's lips. "It all smoothed over rather well in the moment, I thought. At least until I offended the child's mother. That was my first real mistake."

"I'm surprised she gave you such a telling off. You must have deserved it?"

"I did. And she was simply being protective, as was her right. It was nothing other than what you might have done for James or I."

"You did look quite excited about the whole encounter. Get the blood pumping, did it? Getting someone to argue with you for a change?"

"Mummy—"

"One is merely stating the facts, Alice. It's been quite some time since you had a young woman on the radar, and this simply reminded me of the fact."

Alice scoffed. The last thing she wanted to discuss was her love life.

"It has been some time since we discussed finding you an appropriate match." Caroline took a bite of her toast, waiting for a response. "Not this girl, of course. But it has put the idea back on the agenda. To think about bringing someone in. It would all be kept under the radar until you were sure about a match."

Alice stood and began to pace, hands behind her back in that practiced way she'd learned as a small child. She could feel her mother's appraising glance up and down her pale blue skirt and black blouse, and the instinct to defend the choice rose up in Alice's throat. Her shoes, as always, were downright sensible. The one benefit of being tall for a woman was that Eugenia, in charge of Alice's extensive wardrobe, rarely foisted heels on her.

"Into all this?" Alice gestured towards the trappings of the palace around them, stopping by the ornate fireplace. "That would hardly be fair on some unsuspecting girl, would it?"

"Oh, come along, darling. We have given you every support, just like we did James when he started stepping out with Annabel. I know you were let down badly before—"

"I have no wish to talk about Kristina." Alice regretted snapping at her mother almost as soon as the words left her lips. There was no denying the truth of what she said, though. She really had no wish to discuss that part of her past.

The queen stood then, crossing the few steps it took to reach out and pat Alice on the arm. "Just because she felt unable to cope with the demands, that hardly means no one else will ever be able to. And even the newspapers are starting to feel sorry for you, all alone."

Alice closed her eyes for a moment, accepting the comfort from her mother by patting her hand in return.

"You say that, but it is still different for people like me. I know the press have been better, that they broadly supported me coming out, but they still have ways of digging at anyone not pale, male, and stale. It would take the hide of a bull elephant not to be affected by all that attention."

"That is how your father always described it."

"And why you nicknamed him Nellie."

They shared a smile at the fond memory. For the first time in years, Alice felt a real temptation to suggest they cancel their day of handshakes and ribbon cutting and curl up in the family room with some old movies.

"I married a commoner, Alice, and we both knew there would be a price. That is why we did all that we could to improve things for you and James, to protect you both. And it has rather paid off, you must admit. You went to quite regular schools, to university. You even served in combat, for goodness sake, against my own wishes. That is progress, by any measure."

"Perhaps. Anyway, I doubt it will make much impact in the grand scheme of things, but I have invited the woman from the video to one of the garden parties. Josephine thought it was the correct PR move, and I am inclined to agree." Alice made sure not to meet her mother's gaze, looking firmly out of the window instead.

"Well, Josephine is usually right in these matters," Caroline said. "Although one feels a nice bouquet of flowers might have been enough."

"Better safe than sorry." Alice felt the need to change the subject. "James and Annabel were talking about schools last time I saw them, and how much intrusion it will bring into their lives. Rupert and Anne will be off to prep school soon, but there's been no announcement of where they're enrolled. Before, when Rupert would have been automatically next in line by being the male heir, his schooling would have been rather set in stone. But since the rules changed and Anne is next in line after James, I suppose the right fit for her is the priority?"

"Arrangements were made..." Caroline turned away, back to the table where she took her seat once more. She picked up her toast and took a dainty bite.

"But those are changing? James looks panicked anytime the question comes up." Alice followed her mother back to the table, taking her seat once more.

"You should speak to your brother."

"I shall. Whenever our paths next cross. Isn't he off somewhere?"

Queen Caroline glanced at the printed schedule next to her plate.

"Wales, I believe."

"I suppose he is prince of it." Alice did her best not to grin.

"Alice, my dear, have you considered that it is this sense of humour that stops you getting women, rather than the glare of public attention?" The queen made no attempt to hide her own smile. If only the British public and the tabloid hacks could see this side of their monarch; they would hardly recognise her.

Taking her cue, Alice stood to leave. "Have a good day, Mummy. I shall see you at the garden party."

"Bloody hell, look at you: dressed like a girl." James gave Alice a playful shove. He had two inches on her in height, and the same broad shoulders and back that had served their father so well in his rugby career. Despite all that, Alice didn't flinch, shoving back every bit as hard. It earned them a glare and a soft tut from their mother's private secretary.

"I could say the same for you. I saw the pictures of you in a kilt. You do know you were in Cardiff and not Glasgow, yes?"

"There speaks someone jealous that I got the better legs. Ready for this year's old-farty-party?"

"I assume you mean the garden party, you absolute arse? The highlight of the year for some of these people."

"Don't be pious, 'Lice."

"Do not call me that. Not today, where people might hear."

That, unfortunately, caught her older brother's attention. An amateur mistake, Alice realised too late.

"People overhear everything we ever say...so someone special in today? Thought you had sworn off the old meat market?"

Alice punched his arm, but it didn't even wrinkle his pale blue shirt.

"Nothing like that. I had a tiny PR situation, so I have to make nice with a teacher and her daughter."

"That's right! Good old 'Lice, visited the kids and made them cry. Annabel played the video for me; we had quite the chuckle."

That only earned him a roll of her eyes; Alice had endured far worse public events and so had James. "You take the school visits from now on then. Might help you and Annabel hurry up and decide where you're sending the twins. They are going to board, yes?"

Alice hadn't expected a proper reaction; her brother had a much better poker face than she ever had. But his restlessness gave him away instead, as he shifted his weight from one foot to the other, and back again.

"Thinking of getting a governess," he said, into the silence Alice had stretched out for him. "Better than some draughty old dungeon full of young earls and the kids of oil barons, surely?"

"A governess? Instead of going off to school? I seem to remember ours was quite 'normal'. Finger-painting and everything. At least until you buggered off to Eton and abandoned me."

James gave her a warning look, scrubbing a hand over his hair, cropped close these days to pull focus from his receding hairline. "Normal is the problem. This whole country has a mania about the bloody word, and yet no one can agree what 'normal' even means. Never understood that."

"Jamie—"

"Don't call me that."

"Consider it payback for 'Lice. Now tell me. What's wrong?"

James glanced over his shoulder again. "Nothing major. Late on a few developmental milestones, or whatever you call them. Plenty of schools are willing to overlook it just to get the royal heirs on the books. And this is just Rupert, to be clear. Annie...well, that makes it worse. Absolute prodigy so far, bless her. Just as well, since she's next in line. But Rupes, he's really struggling. We thought he was just being an obstinate sort of fellow to begin with, but the doctor suggested there might be more to it."

"I must say, I have noticed the occasional issue. I know he can be fussy over his food, there was that screaming fit at Christmas that you both tried to hush up. He's not the chattiest soul, certainly not compared to Annie. But does that really add up to some kind of condition? Could it not simply be a difference in personality?" Alice knew she was underplaying it, but she had a residual sensitivity to being labelled that made her reluctant to see one slapped on any member of the next generation, not without considerable thought first.

"Very much the tip of the iceberg, I am sorry to report. You know as well as anyone that we have plenty of help, but the nannies have been tricky to retain so far. These episodes, or 'meltdowns' as Annabel has been calling them, can be set off rather easily it seems. The wrong food, the wrong type of clothes, being taken away from one activity and asked to focus on another...one rather feels like it is impossible to do anything right. We pressed the doctor, but he seems reluctant to come to any conclusions."

"Surely The Firm doctors don't have any experience—are there specialists to call in? People who know this sort of thing?"

James winced as Alice went straight into helper mode. She tried to hold back, but it had always been her role. If she could have solved the issue herself, she would volunteer in an instant, but it was clear this situation was beyond her expertise.

"Rupert is not a new skill to master, or a bit of conversational Italian to pick up. I don't think we need medical help, as such. The key from what I've read is in how we teach and socialise him. What we really need is someone who teaches somewhere not so mainstream, someone who can really assess what he needs. But I don't want rumours following him all his life if it's not anything too serious. The thought of some of those tabloid rags using it to mock him...no, I can't stand the thought of what they might print."

Alice pulled her brother into a quick one-armed hug, about as affectionate as they got as adults. James leaned into it, a sure sign he was stressed.

"What if I got involved? If I spoke to some people through one of our charities, or Josephine found the right people to ask...no one would jump to conclusions surely? Actually, I think I just met someone who's something of an expert in this area. At least I think she is."

"Wait, that teacher woman who shouted at you? The one who doesn't 'believe' in royalty? Doesn't seem like she'd be much inclined to do any favours for our sort."

"Not a teacher, exactly. But she's some kind of consultant in special needs education. If you were concerned you could run some checks, but she did seem a very dedicated type, despite the calls for bloody revolution and our heads on spikes." Alice smiled at the over dramatisation of it all. "Just a suggestion. It seems you're in a bind, and I want to help. If not her, perhaps she would know the right people to speak to."

James pulled away, scrubbing a large hand over his face. He reminded her so much of their father in that gesture. "I feel like anything we do will be lighting a torch paper under poor Rupert. It might be nothing, but he doesn't deserve a whole country speculating on his learning abilities."

"Of course. Goes without saying this will be utterly confidential. Trustworthy sorts only, whether it's this Sara Marteau or someone else. We will find the solution, and I'll get Josephine on the case before we make any moves."

"You're a good egg. Right, shall we brace ourselves for the unwashed masses? Hope you've got some hand sanitiser in your pocket."

"Jamie!"

"Kidding, kidding!"

They went their separate ways, out to the respective receiving lines that had been handpicked for them to greet first. As Josephine reappeared at her side, Alice leaned in for a quiet word about what she and James had just discussed.

"I'll see what I can find out, ma'am. You got my notes for your guests?"

"I did, thank you. You're a lifesaver as always, Jos." Alice fiddled with her father's ring on her left hand for a moment before launching back into the social fray.

Their mother emerged from a small crowd of courtiers, radiant as ever, and began to tackle the more substantial line in front; she was always the main event whenever the family gathered.

Alice made her way from person to person with the usual slow stride. She'd learned a long time ago that if she kept a minimal sort of motion as she greeted each one, they didn't expect her to linger for long. It felt a little crass to be so business-like about it, seeing so many excited faces, but for Alice this was just one major event in a day stuffed full of them. Everyone wanted a piece, and she made sure everybody got some.

The queue of invitees looked much the same as every other time. The elderly and the well-behaved children, a mix of races and ethnicities that reflected the make-up of the country rather well. Alice murmured platitudes and smiled as broadly as she could, shaking hand after hand and apologising that she wasn't supposed to stop for selfies, even if they did have the phone right there and ready to go.

She recognised Libby right away. That the name had registered was impressive, but for the first time in the long line of people, Alice stopped entirely.

"Well, hello there. Before we start, I really ought to ask: any tears on their way?"

Libby gave a delighted little laugh, music to Alice's ears. She could sense people around them start to notice and put the pieces together. Camera shutters from the official press photographers went into a miniature frenzy.

"No!" Libby gave an energetic curtsey, complete with a sort of bounce as she touched the ground and looked the picture of angelic youth in her light green dress. "No crying today, your uhm, Royal Highness?"

Alice nodded. That was the correct form of address, even if she rarely insisted on it. "Why don't you introduce me to your fellow guests, Libby?"

"This is my *Mamie*," Libby said, gesturing to the older woman next to her, who was in the process of nudging Libby's mother with her elbow.

"Inès Marteau, Your Royal Highness. It is such a pleasure."

"That's a wonderful accent. Do I detect a note of *Français*?" Alice silently thanked her almost eidetic memory for retaining the handful of facts Josephine had popped on a card for just such a moment as this.

"*Oui*, ma'am. I moved to Paris in '79. And you remember my daughter, Sara, if you remember young Libby?"

"Of course. Ms Marteau, how lovely to see you."

Sara raised an eyebrow, but still extended a hand in politeness. Despite her aforementioned disdain for royalty, she had certainly dressed for the occasion. Alice found it difficult to look away from the spotless ecru trouser suit, the emerald blouse beneath it complementing Libby's outfit very well. The same tones could be found in the bold patterns of Inès' dress and her hat was wonderfully dramatic too. Altogether they made a lovely little matriarchy.

"Thank you for inviting us," Sara said, her voice low but friendly. She sounded faintly amused by the whole situation. "As you can see, the rest of my family are big fans of your family."

"How nice of you all to believe in us. Now, I have a lot more handshaking to do, but usually after all this I like to hang around the smaller drinks tent just over there. If Libby had any questions."

"You don't have to—"

"Just in case. Must get on. Hello there, thank you for coming today." Alice moved seamlessly to the next man in line, an elderly veteran with his medals proudly displayed on his pressed and starched uniform. Why had she made that offer? Surely the handshake and free cucumber sandwiches were peace tokens enough? What was it about Alice's traitorous brain that seemed insistent on keeping this story alive, viral videos and all? Was she setting herself up for another humiliation on social media?

As she glanced back to see Sara looking at her, Alice found herself fervently hoping not.

Alice continued her rounds with the usual handshakes and small talk, taking a break only when her wrist began to twinge, the legacy of an old hockey injury. As soon as she stepped into the private tent, Josephine appeared with her usual silent magic.

"I did some preliminary research, ma'am. And I hope you don't mind me taking the liberty, but I did check in with the staff at KP who work with that branch of the family tree, as it were. I thought it best to know exactly what we were dealing with."

"I am nobody's idea of an expert, but are we talking something like autism?" Alice looked around as she asked, confident nobody was close enough to overhear. This small enclosure was off-limits to anyone but family and palace permanent staff. "There must be other conditions, other learning difficulties, but what James told me rang a bell."

"Yes, from what I can gather we should be at least looking at testing for autism, though there are other possibilities. I did overhear a little of your conversation with the Prince of Wales, ma'am, and well, it turns out that one of the country's foremost experts is the woman you invited today, Sara Marteau. Although she doesn't have a doctorate yet, she has been working in some of the south London schools with complex needs, and has written a number of papers that are being held up as the new standard for education throughout England. Ms Marteau is a seriously impressive figure in her field."

Alice nodded at the information, trying not to get carried away. "But we also have other names?"

"Yes, a few. Not all are as readily available and obviously there's no personal connection, but we can make it work with any of them." Josephine consulted her notes, ready to rattle off more screeds of information and qualifications, no doubt. "Though the new school year isn't far off, so there's something to be said for Ms Marteau being right under our noses today. Some might say it was a sign."

"A sign of something, perhaps." Alice could hear the grumbling in her words and forced herself to shake it off. Of course the universe wanted her to ask a favour of the woman who had made a fool of her and hated everything she stood for. Asking for some sort of favour might only turn Sara even further against them, but for some reason Alice found herself hoping that wouldn't happen. Something about this Sara woman intrigued her, made Alice want to seek out at least another conversation. "Should we keep my brother appraised on this?"

"I already have. I assumed that was the plan. Forgive me, ma'am."

"No need to forgive," Alice said. "Just good anticipation on your part as always, Jos."

"Would you like me to sound out Ms Marteau before she leaves today? Or get you both in a room together perhaps?" There was something mischievous in the way Josephine raised one immaculate eyebrow.

"No, if we cross paths then so be it. I did tell her where to find me. She really is an expert in her field, then?"

"Her name popped up everywhere I looked, yes. She knows her stuff without a doubt." Josephine consulted her notes. "And for the record she has never been married, has just the one daughter, and seems to date exclusively women. Not that we've had the full background check done yet, of course."

"Jos—"

"Ma'am. I believe there's a group of military widows waiting to meet you." Josephine darted back towards the tents with her usual subtle speed, leaving Alice to shake her head.

Well then. Onward and upward.

Chapter 4

"Ah, might want to stay away from the salmon. Trust me."

Sara stopped mid-reach for the tray of salmon-topped blinis. After doing a wide circuit of the immaculate lawns with Libby, they'd sort of drifted towards the tent that Alice had indicated. It was certainly much less crowded than the huge one that most people had defaulted to for tea and sandwiches.

"Thanks for the tip. Oh!" She looked up to see who was giving the advice. "I mean, thank you. Uh, Your Majesty?"

Prince James shook his head, but he smiled at her while he did it. "Only Mummy over there gets the M-word. If we really must do titles, it's simply Your Royal Highness for little old me. Same as my sister. I saw you were talking to her before?"

"Of course. Princess sister, I mean your Alice…oh, dear. I did get this right before, I swear. I apologise. I'll get the hang of it eventually. Probably just in time for when we get kicked out."

James shook the hand of an older man who stopped on the way past, acknowledging his deep bow. "Don't worry. I've been at it my whole life and there are still days when I don't know my baronets from my second cousins."

He really was charming. Sara couldn't think of a less princely word for it. The prince had a lovely—if practiced—smile, just a little lopsided in that way white boys had; like they didn't have to put the work in for a smile to go all the way across their mouths. Taller than his sister, he shared her sandy blonde hair and peach-pale complexion. Other than his heavy cufflinks on his crisp blue shirt and the chunky sovereign ring on his left pinkie finger, he could have been just another good-looking man at a garden party.

"It's a lovely event," Sara said, mostly to fill the silence. She watched as her mother and Libby danced in the struggling sunlight to some sort of swing music. "You must get tired, always going to all these things."

"Quite used to it by now, I'm afraid." James tucked his hands behind his back in that effortless way. He stepped further from the crowd, indicating with a jerk of his chin that she should follow. "Not that I mind, although it can be tough on the offspring in the early years. Especially the long trips."

Finally, the small talk was on familiar ground for Sara. "Children are very resilient. You'd be surprised. I find both with my own daughter and the children I work with that feeding their curiosity makes up for a lot. Keep them interested and try to keep some routine. That gets you pretty far."

"Oh yes, Josephine over there—she works for my sister—mentioned you are something of a super-teacher. After the little scene with Alice and all. Sorry, but I did find the video rather hilarious. Not many people can stop our Alice in her tracks, you know. It was really quite something."

"Not a teacher, exactly, but I do work with children with additional needs. It's not the same as being in a classroom every day, but I like to think I'm helping even more children get the education they need this way. The system has been improved, yes, but it has to keep adapting and improving to include every child. I apologise, I'm rambling on. You can probably tell it's something of a passion project for me."

James laid a gentle hand on Sara's elbow, guiding her away from the onlookers to a quieter corner by some empty tables. It was strange that no part of her seemed to think about not allowing him to steer her like that. Some kinds of authority just imprinted themselves on a person. Even one who didn't give two hoots for the idea of royalty.

"That does sound like just the thing. And I am sorry to ask you to talk shop on a day off, but would it be possible for someone in your job to be, well, a consultant of sorts? Do a bit of work on the side? Privately?"

Sara straightened up at the question. That sounded just casual enough to be premeditated. "I'm sorry, I don't quite understand."

"Right. Of course. Say a family had some schooling concerns, about mainstream versus something more specialised. Are you the sort of expert that could jump in and assess what ought to be done? To help things along with the learning?"

"No, not as such. I mean, it doesn't really work that way..." Sara trailed off as she saw James's shoulders slump. "Usually if we're talking about additional needs, any testing would be done by a psychologist, perhaps alongside a speech therapist. I'm familiar with how it works, and I've assisted many times, but I doubt I would be anyone's first call."

He ran a hand through his hair, suddenly looking older. For the first time she could see that his hairline was starting to recede a little.

Sara felt the urge to reach out and pat his arm but held back. "Still, I suppose it wouldn't do any harm for someone with my experience to take a first look. There will still be a need for formal assessments, just to keep the records accurate. "

James lit up at her change of heart, suddenly the charismatic man who'd welcomed them all to the event again. "We'd be more than willing to jump through every hoop, I assure you, Ms Marteau." He said her name with the correct French inflection, suggesting he spoke the language with some ease. "I suppose I am being a little ham-fisted about all this. Normally we would have someone reach out to someone through channels, that sort of thing? But this is incredibly sensitive."

"And from what I'm assuming," Sara said, "it would require the utmost discretion?"

James raised an eyebrow at her, fussing with the open collar of his shirt as though he missed wearing a tie. "It would, rather. My dear sister would probably be a sort of liaison, as it were. I've only just tasked her with finding someone, and then I saw her talking to you. It all fell into place in a moment. The idea though is to keep me and my wife out of it, publicly, just gives it that extra layer of deniability that our children are the ones involved. Well, child. With twins we expected everything to be roughly similar in the early years, but already there are marked differences between Rupert and his sister. They're both wonderful, of course. But there are difficulties for him that don't seem to affect Anne."

Sara took a sip of the crisp old-fashioned lemonade, swirling the ice at the bottom of the glass. "My first instinct is to help if I can, of course. But the one thing I suppose I have to ask, is, why you have not had it checked sooner? There are experts, excellent schools who could do discreet testing...

all the diagnoses or lesson plans in the world won't help a child whose family deny their situation, or treat it as some shameful secret..."

For the first time, James let the affable demeanour slide. His hands clenched briefly into fists and he squared his shoulders. "No, not at all. Quite the opposite in fact. My wife and I want to do all that we can, but every decision we make for our children is weighed against how it might play out in public—whether we're risking their privacy—compromised as it already is by the very accident of their births. A simple enquiry from the palace can attach a lifelong association to my children, and they deserve a choice in that, at least. It's one thing to support a cause, it's quite another to become the public face of it without your consent."

Sara took a deep breath. "I hadn't thought about it that way. I apologise. But if I can help, then I'll do what I can. I warn you though, that may not be much in the grand scheme of things."

With that, his smile returned, reaching his eyes that time. Prince James looked five years younger again as he clasped Sara's right hand between both of his, shaking it effusively. "Thank you. Thank you, Ms Marteau. I can see why you made such a splash at my sister's event. But I must get on, make the rounds and all that," he added. "I shall have someone reach out to you, get some plans in place. Don't worry, we'll cover all the expenses and anything else you deem appropriate."

Frozen in place, Sara stood exactly where he'd left her. What had she just volunteered for? She didn't know these people, and she certainly didn't owe them anything.

But in that same moment her thoughts turned to the young prince; he couldn't be more than six or seven years old. Seven, in fact, even in her first few months as a mum to Libby, Sara had been aware of the new royal arrivals. The very event of their birth had dominated the entire news cycle for a full week. Being twins, with the elder of them a girl, had sent the media into a special level of frenzy. Still, every state occasion had featured him front and centre. Every sneeze and every step were reported for both children, but always in that bit more detail for the queen's only grandson. How was a child supposed to identify and get help for his educational needs under that sort of scrutiny?

Sara tried to imagine other people paying such close attention to Libby, and it made her feel queasy. It was bad enough when people stared on the bus in the morning, as though trying to work out the equation for how Sara's daughter came to be darker than her. The only people who cared about that were usually the last people she ever wanted to hear from about it. Speaking of her daughter, Sara braced herself as Libby came running over.

"I saw some horses!" She said. "The guards out by the gate are up on horses and they're huge. Nineteen hands, Mummy! Easily nineteen."

"That sounds big," Sara said. What a surreal day. From mixing with royalty to talking horses with Libby. Sara would have to do some research to keep up with the latest obsession. Maybe that would be something the princess could help with while Sara helped assess Rupert for his school needs.

Had she really agreed to that? Never mind the royals and their royal problems, with the practiced mother's eye, she could see that Libby was flagging for the first time all day. "Still having fun?"

Libby nodded, but her grip on Sara's leg through her ecru trousers was tight.

"Tired?" Sara pressed her a little.

"Maybe a bit," Libby replied, smiling up with a smear of white icing on her cheek, from the delicate cupcake she'd just taken a bite from. Her brown eyes had lost some of their earlier sparkle. Sugar crash? Probably not far off. "Can I sleep when we're on the train?"

"Of course, Libs. You want to go now? We can round up Granny and slip out while it's quiet."

"Please."

For a moment, Sara contemplated tracking down Alice and trying to say goodbye in person. Maybe she'd have more to say about this whole secret-schooling plan. But a tired Libby was frequently an emotional Libby, and the last thing they wanted was another online video of sobbing.

Instead, Sara tracked down Inès, who had fallen in with a group of women her own age, sitting around a small table and swapping tales of their children. Sara knew a gossip fest when she saw one, so she gave her mother a quick kiss on the cheek and explained they were going home.

"You need me?" Her mother said right away, but Sara had no intention of interrupting this kind of fun for her.

"No, you stay. Get your whole day's-worth." Sara passed the invitation, now a little crumpled, across the table for Inès to keep.

"It's a lovely day. Thank you, *ma chérie*."

Sara departed knowing her mother would be showing off about her and Libby to the new gang of friends. Some things were as reliable as clockwork.

With that, Sara took Libby's hand again and steered her towards the discreet signs for the exit. The lawn was huge, but they made good progress across it without interruption. On the stroll back to the tube station at Green Park, Libby perked up at a brief detour to see the majestic horses up close. As brushes with royalty went, the day had definitely been a much more successful one.

Sara was just surprised that it wasn't going to be her last one, and a small quiet part of her was excited about that fact. Not that she'd be admitting it to Libby or Inès any time soon. Anyway, perhaps someone more qualified would be found, or plans would change. No point getting too invested.

Sara closed her office door behind her as she completed her unscheduled dart across the school yard during first break. Usually, she reserved her wandering around the school for class time, drawing far less attention and fewer distractions in doing so.

"Hello?" She answered her ringing phone, the reason for her rush to privacy.

"Ms Marteau? This is Josephine from St James's Palace. Could I ask you to hold for Her Royal Highness, Princess Alice?"

Oh. So they did have her mobile number. Of course they did. It had taken them two weeks to call, two weeks in which Sara had become certain she had been forgotten. When she was busy again, the call came for a favour.

"Sure. Yes. I mean, I only have a few minutes, but sure."

"Much obliged."

The line went quiet, and Sara hummed under her breath, a snippet of something she'd played on her headphones that morning. It wouldn't be such an imposition, really. Not with the prospect of really helping a child in need.

"Hello?"

"Hello," Sara said, trying to keep the irritation out of her voice. Of course they hadn't factored in that she worked. Of course they hadn't arranged a time to call first. These were people who expected the world to revolve around them, so they just interrupted. "I'm afraid I don't have long."

"Right. Understood." The princess sounded so brisk, it wasn't hard to picture her a bit younger, in her military uniform. Sara might just have searched the internet a time or two to find out more about Alice, Princess Royal. Most of it had been vaguely familiar, seeping in through the media's obsession with all things royalty. A few new facts had leapt out, brand new to Sara. How had she missed that Alice was an Olympic gold medallist, or that she'd flown planes in two separate warzones? "I just wanted to touch base, as it were. I understand my brother rather jumped the gun on a favour he asked me to do, and I simply wanted to let you off the hook. Sometimes people get overwhelmed by the title and feel obliged to say yes, and James can be very overwhelming. So I wanted to let you know that I am quite happy to track down the relevant specialists and have them come in-house to help."

"Are we talking about the issue your brother mentioned to me about at the garden party? He said you'd be involved somehow, to make it less obvious to outsiders I suppose. I think you know I'm not a big fan of constitutional monarchy, but when I consider the risks of approaching multiple people about this situation… well, let's just say I'm happy to be a first port of call. For the little boy's sake. I'm sure there's a lot of noise and fuss in his life, and if I can give him the calm to start a diagnosis, then I'm happy to help."

"Just like that?"

"Yes. And as for a specialist, you'll still need medical appointments of course, but assessing the needs for someone in that situation is part of my job. You won't find many people better suited. I do have considerable experience and stand among those with authority in the area of expertise."

Was that bragging? Sara decided in the same moment that she didn't care. It happened to be true. Not to mention it had stopped Princess Haughty right in her tracks with her offer of a way out.

"Well, anyone who was properly asked and who was brought into the family's confidence would have to sign some serious paperwork," Alice said, still sounding a little flustered to Sara's ear. "Non-disclosure, all that sort of thing. It is utterly tedious, but for various reasons it is necessary."

"Not a problem. Though there's nothing I could sign that would matter more to me than protecting the child in question. That's also part of my job, whether it's written down or not. But if you have doubts, I have no issue with you going elsewhere."

The pause seemed to crackle over the line between them, before Alice came to some kind of decision. "Very well. Then there's the question of how to play this and deflect attention. We'll pick a day when big headlines are being made elsewhere, and then if it's not too much of an imposition, I wondered if you might bring young Libby along."

Sara's answer was interrupted by the bell signalling end of break time.

"Do you have to go?"

"No, not yet. I don't teach regular classes. But bringing Libby? That's hardly professional. I mean, it's not how I usually work," Sara said.

Alice covered the phone for a moment, at least that's what Sara assumed from the muffled sounds.

"No, but the thing is that Annie and Rupert are pretty much inseparable at the best of times. We thought if Annie had someone else to play with for a little while, it would be the least disruptive way of getting you some one-on-one time with Rupert. After all the paperwork and such. We just don't want this to be upsetting for him."

"You can send that over in advance, I'll bring it with me all signed. The focus should be on the child." Sara wasn't always this bossy, but she found she rather liked it when talking to an actual princess. She wasn't about to start bowing and scraping to some title now. Not to mention the backhanded slight about her trustworthiness. Didn't they know how extensive the checks were to work with vulnerable children? Surely no royalty needed more protection and privacy than that. "And I won't take Libby out of her school for it, so it would have to be on the weekend."

"Does next Saturday work?"

Sara ran through her mental diary. Only an optician's appointment that she was keen to put off. All they ever did was try and talk her into designer frames, even when her prescription hadn't changed.

"I'll have to check a few things, but I think so. You know, there are alternatives we can offer your brother and sister-in-law. Maybe a visit to my school, or something else that looks perfectly innocent."

Alice gave a hollow little laugh. "You have much more faith in the press than I do. Even putting the words in the same sentence is enough to set them off. They never quit."

"It shouldn't have to be this way. I haven't even met your nephew, and already I feel terrible that this has to be treated like a secret."

"You and me both. There was a time the children were rather considered off-limits. But anything that gets a click is fair game now. Which, again I really must stress, is why this must be utterly confidential. Just children playing together, if we absolutely have to tell anyone."

Sara clicked her tongue against the roof of her mouth. "I understood the first time. Can you send the details of where to go and who to ask for with all the paperwork?"

"My private secretary will make all the arrangements, yes. I believe you spoke to Josephine before?"

"I did. Then I really should get back to work."

"Right. Yes. Only…Ms Marteau?"

Sara had almost hung up.

"Sara?"

For that, she pressed the phone back to her ear. "Yes?"

"Thank you. For doing us this great kindness. It really shan't be forgotten."

"Let's see if I can be any help first, okay? I'll see you next Saturday."

Ending the call, Sara was surprised to see her hand trembling just a little. Maybe she wasn't as bold about speaking truth to power as she thought. Or maybe Princess Alice was an exception to some of Sara's personal rules, including being neither impressed nor intimidated by someone just because of their station in life.

It was certainly nothing to do with the princess sounding so sincere and concerned for her niece and nephew, being quite personable, and looking smart in a suit. Nothing to do either, with her being the only openly queer member of the royal family.

No, she would have to be mad to think these things made Princess Alice quite a bit more endearing than Sara had expected. And Sara had no interest in doing anything mad. She would help out a child in need, maybe provide a few unforgettable memories for Libby, and get back to her life with her family, and her successfully growing career she had worked so hard for.

Nothing had to change.

Chapter 5

Alice paced the receiving room just off the official entrance hall at St James's Palace. Once the working home of the monarch, these days it housed her own apartment, and those of her various aunts and uncles who shared the burden of official royal duties. Her mother, the queen, had lived at Buckingham Palace officially since ascending the throne, but in reality, spent most of the year shuttling between Balmoral, Sandringham, and Windsor Castle, when not travelling to Wales, or other countries on official State Visits.

Finally, the car pulled up with the tell-tale crunch of gravel. Alice didn't have to look to know that the staff had sprung seamlessly into action; these people were consummate professionals who never let her down. The hushed tones of Sara and Libby took a moment to reach her, but Alice was ready with a smile and a handshake as soon as they stepped through the door.

"Wow!" Libby got the first word in. "Is all of this your house?"

"Not all of it," Alice said. "Quite a few of us all live under this one roof. In apartments."

"It must be nice, having your family so close," Sara said, fishing around in her handbag and producing a sheaf of papers which she handed over. "Especially the twins."

"Oh, no they're based at KP with their parents." Alice hated drawing attention to the many opulent properties in the royal portfolio, even if some were draughty old relics held together with gloss paint and the collective hope of the National Trust.

She passed the papers off to Josephine without even glancing at them. Checks had been done and no one was particularly worried. "That's

Kensington Palace, sorry. And of course, until we went off to university and military service, James and I stayed with Mummy over at the House."

"The 'House' being Buckingham Palace?" Sara failed to hide a little smirk. "I don't know how you keep track of it all but having enough houses to need nicknames is quite something."

"Definitely something." Alice rolled her neck just a little, trying to crack the tension out of both her body and her voice. Why did this little family always get her instantly on edge? Sara especially. "Anyway, we have a sort of playroom just upstairs. That's going to be our base of operations for today. James has stepped out to do a joint event with our mother, to maximise the press focus on them. But I can introduce you to my sister-in-law, Annabel." They made their way upstairs on the rich navy carpet. "Ah, speak of the devil."

Annabel couldn't have looked much further from the devil, dressed in a flattering sundress with those Liberty artistic floral prints she favoured so much for press events, and strappy sandals to match. She looked ready for another fancy garden party more than a playroom with sticky-fingered children. Alice's own staff were always hinting that she should look in that direction for fashion tips, but Alice was quite confident that copying Annabel's style would just make her look like a thoroughbred horse in a dress.

"Ms Marteau, what a pleasure to meet you." Annabel extended her hand in greeting at the top of the stairs, impeccably briefed as always. "Thank you so much for giving up part of your weekend. I'm sure you've had a busy week."

The woman was charm personified, and Alice frowned at the slightly star struck expression on Sara's face. Oh, so now she was impressed by royalty, when it had the figure of a supermodel and the flowing auburn hair to match. Alice knew how much effort Annabel had to put into her appearance, and still the pang of jealousy flared up like an oddly specific spot of heartburn.

And damn, why had no one mentioned formally hiring this woman for her expertise? There should be a contract, a consulting fee of some kind. That would keep everything comfortably in the realm of business. Alice wondered why they hadn't organised that with the paperwork.

"Of course, if you consider this freelance, I'm sure someone from the office could sort out a fee and—"

"It's a favour." Sara cut Alice off, with a nod towards Libby. "After you said how much you thought your niece and Libby would get on, she insisted we come. I think she'll be disappointed that you don't keep horses in the house, though."

Libby turned around from where she'd fallen in step with Annabel, confident and upbeat as ever. "Of course, there are no horses in the house, Mummy. The only horses at the palaces are working ones, and we can't distract them from their jobs."

"Silly me," Sara said, muttering under her breath. Alice did her best not to laugh.

She led them all into the sitting room of her apartment, transformed into a mixture of playroom and classroom for the day. Amongst Alice's furniture, mostly antiques that had been shuffled from one house to another over the years, brightly coloured bean bags and small chalk boards livened up the space. The staff had wheeled in a dry erase board and markers for Sara, and there was a table laden with the contents of a small stationery store as well.

Alice didn't really know where to start. Her indecision was saved by the doors opening once more, Anne and Rupert barrelling through like little tanks cresting the hill.

"Mummy! Aunty Alice!" It was easy to see the children were twins, their appearance like a masculine and feminine miniatures of their mother. Alice swore she could see something of her father in their noses and jawlines, but nobody had ever agreed with her on that. Anne led the way as always, and she was doing all the talking as the children joined their little group.

"Rupes, Annie, we'd like you to meet some friends of Aunty Alice. This is Libby, she's come to play for a while today. And this is Ms Marteau, Libby's mummy."

"You can call me Sara," she said, but Alice couldn't tell if it was just her way of being friendly, or a push back against the stuffy formal nature of all things royal. "Are there any favourite games you'd like to show Libby?"

Anne and Rupert gave one of their colluding looks, before Anne strode across in her sweet pink dress and cardigan and hooked her arm through Libby's. Although barely seven years old, they had the determined profile of middle-aged women on a mission. Rupert held back, retreating to Alice's side and leaning against her hip in his usual way.

"Girls, you start," Alice said, ruffling Rupert's hair. "Rupes, do you want to go with Mummy? She and Sara have some fun things for you to try as well."

Rupert nodded, but even when he pulled away from Alice he avoided eye contact. She didn't mind in the slightest, knowing it had no relation on how close they were. Whatever Sara concluded today, it would only help Rupert to get the support he needed. Everything else could go hang.

Between the energetic games the girls dreamed up while chattering nineteen to the dozen, and an early break for the steward to roll in snacks and juice for all, the first two hours absolutely flew past. Alice found herself a willing accomplice to most of Annie's schemes, but both niece and aunt alike were clearly distracted by keeping an eye on Rupert and Sara. Annabel came over to join in an energetic spell of decorating paper masks, and she gave Alice a nod of reassurance in the process. She thought it was going okay, then.

"Do you like being a princess?" Libby turned to Anne as they sat side by side on the floor, cutting out shapes to stick to their masks.

"It's lovely," Annie replied, all grace like her mother. "Although it is strange that everyone knows who I am. All the time, everywhere we go."

"You should wear disguises," Libby said as she traded her scissors for a glue stick. "That's what I would do."

"That's good advice," Annabel said, meeting Alice's eye over their heads. "But you have to pick really boring costumes, otherwise you catch even more attention. No dressing up as a unicorn, for example."

"My mask is a unicorn," Libby replied, holding up her sticky, half-finished masterpiece.

"Did you know that the unicorn is the national animal of Scotland?" Alice asked the children.

"But they're not real!" Anne was wide-eyed at the news.

"Well, some people say Scotland isn't real. It's just like Narnia, you can only visit by going through the wardrobe," Alice replied. "Isn't that right, Annabel?"

"Don't listen to Auntie Alice. She knows fine well we go to Scotland every summer, don't we, Annie?"

Anne nodded and went back to her mask, quite content. As she did, Sara and Rupert came over to join the rabble, and Alice felt her heart skip a beat at the sight of him holding Sara's hand. Whatever first impression she'd made, it had been one hell of a positive one.

"We'd like to make a mask too, if that's okay?" Sara let Rupert pull away, automatically drawn to his mother's side. When she took a seat on the floor cushions, the obvious space for Sara was next to Alice, their knees almost touching.

"Here you go," Libby said, taking charge in a way that suggested it was not the first time. For a child with no siblings, she was a natural little leader. Rupert looked to his mother for reassurance and then accepted the cardboard from Libby. "We were just talking about unicorns. Do you think they're real?"

Rupert shook his head.

"I suppose this could be a horse instead," Libby said, holding up her own mask. "But I can't get the nose right."

When she laid it down, Rupert leaned over with his marker and drew a neat, accurate representation of a horse's nose, making the whole thing look quite three-dimensional in the process. Libby clapped her hands softly in delight.

"Can you show me how to do that?"

Alice looked to the other adults - was this part of the plan? Should they intervene? Her gut said to let it play out, with the children interacting quite naturally. Sara gave her a discreet thumbs up.

They all watched as Rupert showed Libby a step-by-step way to draw the circular shapes and link them all up. He didn't talk through the process, but he paused after each new line to see if Libby was following along.

"Do you like horses?" Libby sat down right next to him. For a moment, Rupert froze, but then he relented and kept his spot around the low table.

"I like *my* horse," he said eventually, watching Libby attempt to copy what he'd shown her. "He's the best horse."

"Is he really?" Libby didn't seem overly impressed. That clearly ran in the family. "What about the other horses?"

"Well, Auntie Alice's horse, Pickle, is my horse's mummy. She's quite good too." Rupert flushed red after saying so much out loud at once, and Alice watched Annabel give his shoulder a reassuring squeeze.

"The horses live out in the country," Anne took up the thread, effortlessly as always. "We go there at the weekend, and in the holidays."

"Yes, at Sandringham," Alice said, as though it mattered. "That's home for this mob really, and I've always stabled my horses alongside James's. Old habits and all that. Are you a rider, Libby?" Alice doubted it, from what the cursory background details had thrown up. Where did one even manage such a feat in the urban sprawl of south London?

"No. Not yet," Sara stepped in to reply, shooting a glance at her daughter that Alice had no idea how to decipher. "It's on the list for when she's a bit bigger and taller."

"Oh, she's old enough," Alice said without thinking. "We were rolling around on fat little ponies since before we could walk. It was something my parents had in common, their love of the outdoors and animals."

"Your daddy's dead too, isn't he?" Libby stunned the room into silence for a moment, not least of all Alice.

"Er, yes. He passed a few years ago. I miss him very much. As you must miss yours?"

Libby shrugged. Alice noted the look of unease on Sara's face and decided to get the topic back to safer ground.

"I have an idea. What if we were to arrange for you to come riding sometime? That way you could try it with some very safe, very experienced horses. And we all know our way around, plus there are stables staff too."

"We couldn't impose—" Sara began. "Although if it meant some more time to talk, that might be good." Her gentle nod towards Rupert gave Alice a surge of hope and a kick of despair at the same time.

"You can ride with me," Anne said, squeezing in between Rupert and Libby once more. "My horse is the actual best. And she lets me put ribbons in her mane."

"Looks like we'll all be spending some more time together then," Annabel said, getting up to fetch the teapot and freshen the cups of the adults. "Won't that be just lovely?"

"Are you sure that's okay?" Sara hated sounding so insecure, but she was far outside her comfort zone. "I mean, I suppose you both know how all this works, you and Princess Alice. But can you really just invite people along to do things? I would have thought security was an issue."

"Oh, we always have plenty of people coming and going," Alice replied. "Especially outside of London. Special Branch do their checks, of course they do, so it's hard to be completely spontaneous."

"Is it Special Branch or MI5?" Annabel interrupted, handing out fresh cups of tea to Sara and Alice. "I rather thought it was MI5 now."

"Whomever keeps the files, I suppose." Alice watched Sara out of the corner for a reaction. She wasn't disappointed.

"Wait, are you saying the police have a file on me? Or wait, the spooks at MI5 do? Like James Bond and spies?"

"I believe Mr Bond was MI6, in fact," Annabel replied, keeping her smile contained. "I don't believe the checks are any more detailed than the ones you would have to work around children or vulnerable adults, if that's any comfort. And you all passed the test to come to the garden party, so as long as you don't try to overthrow any governments while we're all making friends..."

"No overthrowing. Got it," Sara said. "I don't know how you ever get used to all this. Did you find it quite challenging at first?"

"Definitely." Annabel checked that the children were still occupied before continuing. "I was obviously very blessed growing up in the country as I did, and of course I went to the right sort of schools. But I met James in my gap year after university, doing voluntary work in Central America, and I suppose that was that." Annabel had a patience for retelling the same story that Alice lacked. Perhaps it came with living the fairy tale of marrying an eligible prince and having two beautiful children.

"The things we do for love. How do you cope with the press? Does it ever scare you?" Sara seemed more interested in Annabel again. Alice resisted the sudden urge to pout. What did she care, so long as Rupert got the help he needed?

"Those first years it did, how they were everywhere. And sometimes it gets so tempting to read what people are saying online or pick up a newspaper and really let all the cruel comments get to you. But mostly life is too busy for that. These two keep my hands full at all times, and then there's the work of it, of course. My charities are very dear to my heart."

"Sounds like any other working mum to me," Sara said, taking a sip of her tea. "Never enough hours in the day."

"No, not even with all the tremendous help we have. As long as you have multiple responsibilities, something will always make you feel as though you can't quite keep up. But I look at these two and how could I trade it for anything else?"

"I know that feeling well," Sara said. "What do you say then, Libby? Would you like to go riding with Anne and Rupert some time?"

Libby's squeal was answer enough for all of them.

"Seems you're making yourself popular there," Alice said to Sara once the commotion had died down. "Do you ride?"

"Not even a little bit," Sara said. "And you needed a promise from me to come here and help Rupert, right? Well, I have a condition for us coming out to play at horses."

"Name it." Alice finished her tea and set it aside. She was braced, though unsure for what.

"No one, under any circumstances, makes me get on one of these damn things. Oh, I'm sure they're lovely and patient, well-trained even. But these two feet are much happier on the ground. There's no point trying to convince me, I tried often enough in my Cambridge years and we're not a match."

Alice considered arguing, but that would be much more effective once they were around the horses. For the moment, it was a concession worth making.

"You have yourself a deal, Ms Marteau. But Libby can have some time on a pony?"

Sara nodded, setting her empty teacup aside.

"Excellent," Alice said, dusting herself off and shuffling over to where the children had just discovered some face paints in the overflowing toy box. "Now, who here can make me into a tiger, do you think?"

That set off a fresh round of squeals, and as the first brush landed on her cheek, Alice offered a silent apology to Eugenia and all the other staff who spent their time keeping Alice's hair presentable and her skin cared for. At least face paint was bound to wash off. Right?

"Aunty Alice, what if you were half tiger and half monster?" Anne said, holding her little brush with the seriousness of Picasso.

"Do what you must," Alice said, resigned to her fate. She risked a glance towards Annabel and Sara, and while her sister-in-law had already resorted to tidying away their dishes, Sara was watching Alice more closely than she had before. There was a warmth in her eyes that was certainly quite new, a slight crinkle around the edges of them too.

Being the focus of Sara's attention was something like basking in the sun, however briefly. Alice rather suspected she could get used to a feeling like that.

Chapter 6

SARA WAS HAVING AN ALMOST perfect Sunday. With Libby off spending the day with her paternal grandparents, she had a stretch of hours to herself that felt almost decadent. With all her chores completed and the house empty, she took advantage of the early afternoon sunshine and sat out in the tiny garden with her sunglasses on and a juicy thriller of a book that she'd been trying to finish before someone spoiled her on the ending. Three pages in, she was interrupted by sound of the doorbell.

"Jasmin!" Sara threw the door open and enveloped her best friend in a hug. They hadn't seen each other in almost a month, nearly a record in the twenty years they'd known one another, and that made her a sight for sore eyes.

"Hello, Duchess Sara. So glad to find you home and not hobnobbing with royalty. Unless the carriage is parked round the corner?"

"Ha ha. That was last weekend. Come in, come in. Shall I put the kettle on?"

"Give over, I brought some rosé."

"Isn't it a bit early?"

"Oh, like you never have wine with lunch."

Sara considered a moment, before reaching for a family-size bag of popcorn stashed on top of the microwave. "Look, I found lunch."

They made their way out into the little paved patio and sat either side of the metal table, Sara's book set aside and forgotten.

"How's life in investment banking?" Sara poured them both some sparkling wine into clean mugs. For Jasmin, there was no need to get as formal as rooting out the good glasses. In their university years they had drunk out of anything available, including a vase. "No wait, I wouldn't understand even if you told me. What about that hot new Vice President of…something? Is she still there?"

"Yup, she was supposed to be moving to our Hong Kong office but she told the big boss last week that she's found 'some things that appeal to her' about London."

Sara snorted a little laugh into her mug. "And you're hoping you're one of those things that appeal? How many after work drinks have you spent crushing on her now?"

"Too many," Jasmin said. "I know, I know. All I need to say is, 'Hey, Kathleen, that's a great story about living in Chicago but any chance you could shut up and kiss me?' I just don't seem to have any game around this woman. She's my kryptonite."

Sara made a scoffing sound. "Oh please. No woman is all-powerful. You're gorgeous, intelligent, and great at your job. She's not so special, Vice President or not."

"I *am* gorgeous," Jasmin said, stretching out her long brown legs clad in ripped skinny blue jeans. She flicked her thick, dark braid back over her shoulder, managing to avoid it catching on her gold hoop earring. "But we can't all be stone cold like you, Sara. Still giving side-eye to royalty? I forgot to check the internet and see if you got Princess Alice to go viral again."

"Bite me."

"I'm worried I'd chip a tooth. When's the half pint coming home? I thought I'd tag along back home and have dinner with my mum and dad. But I wanted some favourite auntie time first." Jasmin would have been given the title even if she hadn't been Jayesh's sister, but she and Sara had become even closer as they both grieved for him. Aside from Inès, Jasmin was the person Sara trusted most with Libby.

"They usually bring her back after lunch. No doubt talking about horses and helmets and boots like she has been for the last week, solid. That child is going into politics, Jas, I swear down. She's only gone and wangled an invite to Sandringham to ride horses with the heir and the spare."

"Sandringham is where Queenie and co spend Christmas, isn't it? You see them going to church and that."

"I thought they were all mad for Wales?" Sara knew that a few hours on the internet would answer so many questions, but she had no intention of falling down that rabbit hole. Not with funding applications to write and lesson plans to correct. Besides, that would imply she cared. This was a random encounter—okay two, no, three—and would make a cool anecdote for Libby someday. It was absolutely nothing more.

They'd had a talk about whether to tell people about it, and what to tell them, and Sara was still surprised that Libby wanted to keep the royal visits private, even without prompting. "It's nice, isn't it, Mummy? Having something that's just ours."

It saved a lot of time and trouble, at least. Sara wasn't thrilled about spending another precious weekend day running around with princelings, but it was better than taking Libby to some indoor soft play centre or hanging around a park and hoping no teenagers showed up to make it unsafe for the little ones.

At least there was no chance of having to reciprocate the playdates as she did with Libby's school friends. The trading of children back and forth gave overworked parents much-needed respite some weeks, but Sara was pretty sure the second and third in line to the throne wouldn't be introduced to the wonders of Peckham Rye anytime soon, unless it was possibly waving from behind some bulletproof glass in a fancy car.

Sara realised in that moment she hadn't been listening.

"So yeah, that's why Wales is just for summer, but Windsor and Sandringham are like, the weekend boltholes. You know how rich people are—they're the only ones who can afford to live in London and they don't even live here full time." Jasmin topped up her mug and did the same for Sara.

"Good to know. Oh God, I have no idea what to wear to Sandringham. Will I have to take changes of clothes?"

"You said for the party thing they sent a protocol guide?"

"Yeah, but this isn't all official. It's...you know, the kids hit it off and they're spending some time. I'm sure it's just a photo op to show they have the common touch or something. Or maybe they want the children to meet a regular person every now and then."

"Won't get much common from you and the Libster, will they? That girl is a one-off."

"Rude. Don't suppose you have riding gear I could borrow? Not that I'm getting on any kind of horse, but I'm picking up some pieces for Libby and that's kind of wiping out the clothing budget for the month. If she's going to finally get to go riding, I want her to look the part. And I don't want to embarrass her by wearing yoga pants or something."

"You're in luck because I never throw out anything that still fits me. You can wear jeans but go for the forgiving kind—think mum jeans and not low-rise pop star style."

Sara rolled her eyes. When had she ever gone for that kind of style? She had conveniently skipped the Britney phase. Not to mention she was a mum.

"I've got a riding helmet, couple of cute gilets you wear over a long-sleeved top, and my boots are somewhere in the back of the wardrobe but I'm a size bigger remember."

"I can double up on socks. Knee-high boots are not in the budget right now, unless you count my glitter ones from going to the Rocky Horror Show."

"Gotcha. How are you getting to Sandringham?"

"I thought we'd make our own way, but apparently there's some kind of royal train? Or at least a train the royals use, anyway. We're meeting at Liverpool Street and travelling together."

"Wow." Jasmin sat forward in her chair, serious for a moment. "You'd tell me if something was going on, right? Only Princess Alice is, y'know... one of us. And it's not like you don't have form when it comes to those jolly hockey sticks type girls. You left a trail of broken-hearted posh girls at Cambridge before you and Jayesh hatched your baby plan."

Sara snickered into her mug, only to find it was hiding quite a genuine smile. Where had that come from? "Oh please. I insulted her on first meeting, and if not for Libby I'd probably be up on charges by now. I'm just playing nice so I don't get beheaded for treason, leaving my child an orphan."

"Sometimes I forget Libby gets her sense of drama from you. But you could do worse than catching the eye of a princess. Not exactly lighting up the dating scene lately, are you?"

"There's dating and then there's...whatever that would be. Can you imagine all that press attention? Going viral for a hot minute was bad enough, I'd never cope with all the shouting and stalking. No way."

Jasmin shrugged. "Maybe the lady protests too much. Maybe you're right. Mind you, must be even tougher for someone like her to get a regular date. Or do they just open *Tatler*, pick a girl, and have her sent over to the palace?"

"I don't think it works like that, but I'll be sure to ask. Before they throw me out, anyway. And I do have dating options, thank you. Just no time for them."

Sara drained her mug. A moment later the distinctive sound of the front door opening reached them. Rapid footsteps rattled through the house until Libby found them.

"Auntie Jas!" She hurled herself right into a hug.

"There's my Libster. I've just been hearing all about your new royal friends. Will you remember me when you live in a palace surrounded by horses?"

Libby laughed, wriggling free and coming to give Sara a hug in turn. "The horses will be in the stables, silly. They're not allowed in the palace. You might be; if I invite you."

"See? The power is already going to her head. We're in trouble."

Libby took off back into the house as Jasmin chased her, leaving Sara to slip the wine bottle back into the kitchen before greeting her teetotal... in-laws. She'd never really found a great term for them beyond Jay's parents or Libby's grandparents. All the same, they'd been devoted to their first grandchild from the moment Sara fell pregnant, and their regular offer of hosting sleepovers or weekend activities were often a great help when things got chaotic.

"Hello, hello. She wasn't any trouble, I hope?" Sara greeted both Somesh and Deepa with brief hugs, all their attention focused on Libby as always.

"She could never be trouble," Deepa said with the indulgence only a grandmother could provide. "We hear she will be out riding horses. Not too dangerous for her?"

"No, all very well supervised," Sara said. "By professionals, not by me."

"Did you enjoy your trip to the palace?" Somesh said, quietly playing peacemaker as always. "It must have been quite an honour for you all."

Before Sara could answer, they were interrupted by the arrival of Inès. The usual merry-go-round of hellos and how-are-yous began again in earnest. The moment the palace was mentioned in front of her mother, Inès was off and running. Sara knew her most important job now was to retreat to prepare tea for everyone.

Of course, her mother did not leave such a task unsupervised for long, even though Sara was technically hostess in her own house.

"I can manage, *Maman*. You should go compare notes on our lovely girl."

"Yes, our Libby is lovely. Not even in high school and already she's making friends with princesses. We all have to pull together, Sara darling. Make the most of these opportunities."

Sara didn't have the energy for another argument, nor did she want to spoil the easy going atmosphere of the day.

"I ordered some riding things for Libby online, they're coming Tuesday. Are you okay to be here, to sign for them?"

"Of course."

"Good, that's one thing off my list." Sara smiled at the sound of happy squeals from the living room. "I think you're all going to need the caffeine to keep up with her."

"Either that or the rest of your wine," Inès said with a smirk.

Chapter 7

ALICE FOUND HERSELF PACING ON the platform, watching the porters load cases and bags as her private protection officers watched over her. With the queen already on board, and James and Annabel bundling the kids into their private carriage of the royal train, Alice was at something of a loose end as she was waiting for her guests.

Usually she would just take a seat in her carriage, after all it had a perfectly comfortable sitting room and work area, as well as a small bedroom and bathroom for her private use. The train had barely been updated since not long after her parents got married, but like most things part of the royal estate, hardworking staff who took pride in every detail kept everything spotless and working well.

A steward could round up Sara and Libby, bring them to her or seat them in the staff carriages in back of the train, but something had Alice determined to make more of a 'woman of the people' impression by doing it herself.

Then, keeping perfect time, Sara and Libby were revealed as a small gaggle of staff cleared a path down Platform 10.

"Hello! Don't you both look smart?" Alice cringed a little at her formal tone. She never had entirely got the hang of 'human'. She could only hope it didn't show too badly.

"Thank you," Libby said, her smile absolutely beaming. "I'm so excited to meet your horses."

"I didn't realise that, uh, the whole family was going?" Sara's eyes darted around the platform, landing anywhere but Alice as she took in the organised chaos. "Are we dressed okay? The email just said to bring a change of riding clothes."

"Yes, perfectly. That dress is like something Annabel would wear, and such a lovely shade of yellow on you. And Libby, when did you start modelling?

"I don't."

"Her Royal Highness is just teasing, Libby."

"Please," she said. "Alice is fine, when it's just us. Now, would you like to see my carriage? You'll be travelling in with me, if that suits?"

"You have your own carriage?" Libby barely contained a squeal. "We don't have to ride in the last car with the luggage?"

Alice laughed. Children really had no filter. Clearly that joke had been bandied about near her.

"Of course not," Sara said. "Although I did think we'd be in with the staff."

"You can if you prefer, but as my guests you're welcome to travel with me. I've had a spot of breakfast laid on. It's also right next door to James's compartment, so you'll be able to dash off and play with Annie and Rupert."

Sara gave a tight smile, finally meeting Alice's gaze. "Then we'll do that. Thank you."

It didn't take long to get settled in the end, but Alice found herself a little flustered over the simple act of getting everyone seated. Only when the train chugged away from the platform did she lean back in her armchair and relax a little.

As soon as they were up to speed and rattling towards Sandringham, Anne appeared in search of her new friend. With a promise to her mother to behave, Libby disappeared into the body of the train with her little accomplice. The staff would be watching them like hawks, not least Anne and Rupert's newest nanny.

"That's a lovely ring."

Alice was startled from her silent vigil looking out the train window by Sara's voice, soft and increasingly familiar to her now. Perhaps fourth time would be the charm for them being friendly. Making a fist of her left hand, Alice showed off the ring on her index finger a little more. "This old thing?"

"I suppose it's some family heirloom, or like a thousand years old." Sara bit her lower lip after saying it. Was she worried about crossing the line somehow? It hadn't been a huge concern for her before, a quality Alice found downright refreshing.

"No, I'm afraid not. Which is not to say that there is any shortage of jewels with interesting histories hanging around, naturally, but this here is just a standard gold sovereign ring."

"It's unusual, but it suits you." Sara wriggled out of her chair, moving to the window and looming over Alice for just a moment. Alice was suddenly aware of how little space there was between them in the narrow confines of the train carriage. She stood too, putting them back on an even footing.

"My grandmother used to complain about me wearing it, right up until she passed, long before I came out to The Firm, but I think she had her suspicions even then. She said it looked rather manly."

Sara gave a little snort. "Rings have genders now? People are so obsessed with that neat little binary."

"True. Although in a sense she wasn't wrong. It belonged to my father. James wanted his watch as a memento, and I thought this was something discreet to carry with me. Granny always thought it should be on a chain around my neck instead."

"Oh." Sara nodded, as if urging Alice to continue. For once, she did.

"I usually say 'my late father', but I suppose knowing the age you are, and from Libby mentioning it last time out…it would be what one calls a safe bet to assume you know what happened."

"I do," Sara said. "I mean, I remember the news coverage. I can't imagine what that must have been like for you. I'm so sorry for your loss."

Alice allowed the moment of sympathy to curl up inside her chest, warming her for a second or two. "Thank you. No one really says that anymore. I suppose it has been too long."

Sara took another step, until they were fully side by side at the window. "What's too long, when you miss someone? Libby's dad, he and I weren't a couple, in any conventional sense. But he was dying, I was losing my best friend…he wanted a legacy to live on past him. It made sense at the time."

Did that information lurk in the security files Josephine held? Alice still hadn't read them, although they had been available to her since inviting Sara to the garden party.

Alice closed her eyes to the fields rushing past and let herself picture her dad. The images had a faded quality, as though the light had been different. Details were blurry, but she could steal see the whiteness of his crooked smile, feel the bristles of his bushy moustache as he had kissed her on the forehead to say goodnight. She could never think about going riding without picturing him.

"I do. Miss him, still. I think of him every day, one way or another."

"I'm sorry if I brought up something that upsets you. I hate making anyone sad." Sara took her seat, but closer to Alice this time.

Alice smiled, placing the hand with its ring lightly on Sara's shoulder nearest to her. They both stared at it for a moment.

"No, remembering now is just...bittersweet. But it feels like getting to visit him for a moment. Makes the empty spaces where he should be...feel full again. He would have loved to be a grandpapa. I think of that every time I see Rupert and Annie running around."

Sara reached across and gave Alice's hand a gentle pat. "Is that okay? With my friends, when we get into the difficult stuff, I always feel like they need the contact."

Alice found it hard to concentrate on Sara's words, the world having reduced in an instant to where skin was touching skin. So much of her days were spent in brief, inconsequential contact—handshakes and air kisses and salutes from a distance. How rarely, Alice realised in that moment, did she touch someone just for the human contact of it all. She had never considered herself to be lonely, but Sara's natural gesture prodded at something deeply-hidden in Alice.

"Okay. Definitely okay. My lot are terribly good at handshakes, but it can be a stretch to do this kind of thing. Not the way one is programmed, you see." Alice felt almost disloyal to say it, but why lie about something she missed so much? The simple touch had been a pleasant thing for Alice as a person, instead of a princess for once.

"Then I'm glad we talked about it," Sara replied. "You shouldn't have to clam up about these things just because of who you are. When Jayesh passed, I cried on every stranger who stopped to ask if I was okay. Although hormones had a lot to do with those public displays."

"Never really been my way." Alice looked away, withdrawing her hand from under Sara's. She regretted moving it almost immediately. Would it be ludicrous to seek out another few seconds of contact, to bask in the comfort a little while longer? Perhaps. In the battle between her pride and her needs, Alice chalked up another round to her stubborn need to always seem perfectly fine. "But it sounds like it helps others. Do you never think about meeting someone else, finding another parent for Libby? Not that she needs that, of course. You're clearly doing an excellent job."

"Well, I wasn't really expecting a performance review," Sara said, but with a smile on her face. "But I'll take the compliment. She's the best of all of us, of both families really. I hope she stays that way as she grows up."

"I'm sure she will. One can tell she has good role models."

"My mother will take credit for that, I'm sure." Sara jumped as the carriage door opened and an older woman wheeled in a tea trolley. "Oh, how nice."

"Hello Gillian. Any chance of an Earl Grey?" Alice was relieved to be back in easier conversational waters. "Sara, what can we get you?"

"Tea would be lovely."

"Got those sultana cookies you like so much, Your Royal Highness," Gillian said, presenting a small plate of them. "I thought I'd give you first refusal before the kiddies descend on me."

"By 'kiddies' she means my brother, who is almost forty and should know better," Alice replied, taking the plate and offering them to Sara first. It pleased her when Sara didn't wave them away or make some excuse about watching her weight. She certainly had no need to, but so many women defaulted to that.

As they settled to their tea, Alice heard a knock at the carriage door. Only one group of people would be coming from that direction, so she wasn't surprised to see James appear, smart as ever in his suit and tie.

"Ladies. Gillian, are you giving away all the good biscuits before you come to us? My heart is breaking here."

"Plenty more where they came from, Your Royal Highness. I'll just head through for the kiddies shall I?"

James nodded, and Gillian passed through the open door.

"Welcome aboard the old clunker that passes for a royal train these days. Just wanted to thank you for giving up another precious weekend day to all this. We all appreciate it, especially young Rupert."

Sara looked down at her cup for a moment before replying. "You're welcome. Rupert is a lovely boy. A credit to you both. To you all."

"He is. Thank you," James said. "Now, not that I care in the slightest, but thought I should give you the heads up. One cannot get on the train without a press pool, as you know, 'Lice. Seems they had a whip round for some extra brain cells and have recognised Ms Marteau here. Might be something to do with that little video. Probably means there'll be some coverage. Just another day for us, but Annabel mentioned you will not be used to it, Sara." James leaned across and stole the biscuit from Alice's plate, popping it in his mouth with a wink at Sara.

Oh, he was going to pay for that. More importantly though, how would Sara take the prospect of more press intrusion? Was this the moment it all blew up in their faces and she refused to get any further involved with Rupert's education? Alice had to admit, she felt her heart rather sink at the prospect.

"Right," Sara said after a moment. "I suppose that was inevitable. It was, right? I mean, I'd be mad not to expect it. Didn't expect anyone to recognise me amongst all of you, but still."

"You really do get used to it," Alice said, aiming for reassurance. "They usually don't get too close these days, especially if the children are in the party."

"I really wasn't looking for any attention," Sara replied, setting her teacup aside with a trembling hand. "I mean, I hope you noticed at the time that I didn't lose my temper about Libby crying. I didn't shout or make a scene on purpose."

Alice exchanged a glance with her brother, who seemed unmoved. "I did notice that. No one is accusing you of anything, Sara. Or Libby for that matter. The public eye is a strange place to navigate."

"I have no idea how anyone does it and stays sane. How could anyone possibly be interested in me, based on about forty seconds of video?" Sara wrung her hands as she spoke.

"Most of us were far from sane to begin with," Alice replied. "The one good thing is that they'd much rather make fun of the Princess Royal than a normal person. We can call in some favours to keep them away from you the rest of today. We will most certainly be safe at Sandringham itself, though. They have no access to the grounds. Does that help?"

Sara nodded.

"Thing is," James said after a moment. "There is also the distinct possibility they consider you to be...well, you know. If someone thinks to check the palace visitor logs, it could paint a picture of you two deliberately spending time together. And with dear Alice here being royalty's answer to Billie Jean King—"

"That's the best example you can come up with?" Alice wasn't sure why she objected to that most, but out the words came anyway. "Kristen Stewart was right there as a reference, or hell, I would have taken Sue Perkins."

"There might be speculation, is all one is saying, dear sister. Best you both put your heads together over that and come up with a better story for them. One that, sorry to ask, does divert attention away from Rupert and his needs. At least until decisions can be made." James stood and took his leave, an uncomfortable silence in his wake.

"There really is no story," Alice attempted some bravado on the point, even though she knew the tabloids would be ready to pounce. "Not least because you have a child, and why would they assume you to be anything other than perfectly heterosexual?"

"Perfectly heterosexual? That sounds like a cologne that's trying too hard," Sara replied, and Alice did her best to suppress an unexpected smile. "And it wouldn't take them long to dig up that I'm anything but."

"Right." Alice remembered Josephine's early mention of Sara only dating women. More information was no doubt tucked into the dossier Josephine had been leaving all over the office and apartment to tempt Alice into reading, but so far she had resisted. It felt like an intrusion too far, or maybe some kind of unfair advantage. "So, that is to say, that you would identify as…?"

"A lesbian. Gay. Queer. All of the above? I never slept with Libby's father. He was gay, too. We were just the closest of friends."

"You certainly have no need to justify or explain any of this to me. Although I am glad you feel you can be so open. Even ten years ago, a conversation like this seems like it might never have happened for me."

Sara stood, smoothing out her dress. "I should have said. It was incredibly brave of you, coming out like you did. All this attention, all the history you're part of. That took real guts. And probably helped more people than you know."

"Hardly brave," Alice replied, standing too. "Just more public than what most queer people go through."

"Still." Sara hesitated, as though she wanted to say more. She thought better of it, gathering up her handbag. "I should go and find Libby. Make sure she's playing nicely with the twins."

"Of course. You might want to start up front. They're fascinated by engines, and the driver usually teases that he might let them drive the fast stretch."

"Libby will love that. Anything that means getting in somewhere she shouldn't, or finding out how things work. Horses are just as fascinating as a great big train."

"Quite right. Do let the staff know if you need anything. And I will be right here. Should I be needed."

"Thank you. I know it's just another day to you, but for Libby this is something properly special. She'll always remember it." Sara moved towards the carriage door. "And so will I. Surprising, but there you go."

Before Alice could conjure any kind of smooth reply, Sara was gone, the door clicking shut behind her. Her steady confidence was no less impressive when she wasn't picking a fight. Just which type of women did she date, Alice wondered? But no, that way madness lay.

"Josephine?"

"Yes ma'am?" She was never far away.

"Can I get the highlights from our departure please? And we need the press backed up a bit at destination. No need to spook our guests, hmm?"

Josephine came in with her tablet ready to go, handing it over even as she placed a call on her phone.

"Consider it done. What are you smiling at? If you don't mind me asking, ma'am?"

"Am I?" Alice prodded at her cheek. Sure enough, she was grinning. Usually she got a headline a week about her naturally dour expression, or 'resting bitch face' as some sites preferred to label it. "Must be the prospect of getting out in the fields."

Josephine's reply was interrupted by her call connecting, and Alice turned away to read the social media coverage, including a short video of Sara and Libby boarding the train with her.

It made for quite a pleasant picture.

THE LONDON HERALD, JUNE 4TH

ALL PALS (NOT) AT THE PALACE

A familiar face joined the royal family on their regular family trip to Sandringham this weekend. Waiting on the departure of the royal train from Liverpool Street was the star of a recent viral video, in which HRH Princess Alice got something of a tongue-lashing from a protective mother.

The woman, named locally as Sara Marteau, was in attendance as a guest of the Princess Royal. Sources confirm that her daughter, whose tears sparked the scene with Princess Alice, was also invited. Photographs show them on the platform together, and it is understood this is not their first meeting since that concert gone wrong. As the photo opposite shows, Ms Marteau was also a guest at the queen's annual garden party, held on the lawns of Buckingham Palace.

Coincidence? A very prolonged apology? Or could something more be going on under our very noses? Princess Alice famously came out as a lesbian a number of years ago, and while she has never formally introduced a romantic partner to the public spotlight, rumours abound that she's dating every eligible bachelorette from European royalty, to sports stars and Hollywood actresses.

Has the famously single princess finally met her match?

Chapter 8

Sara clutched Libby's hand in relief as they stepped out at the quiet country train station to zero photographers, just a line of Range Rovers all in dusty black. Unlike the yummy mummy tanks that were routinely driven around London to show off status, these were mud-spattered around the wheels and discreetly dinged up in all the right places. Working vehicles that belonged in the countryside.

As they were shown to a waiting car, Alice peeled away from a small group of people to join them. The driver seemed to wait for her nod before tossing the keys her way. He wandered off without a word being exchanged, and Alice swung the driver's door open for herself.

"Ready, troops? Libby, there should be a booster cushion in back for you."

Sara got her daughter seated and belted in with minimal fuss, impressed that they'd already been accommodated for. She considered slipping in beside her, but it felt more adult to go around and get into the passenger seat. As soon as she did, Alice revved the engine and they pulled out of the car park, leaving the rest of the convoy behind.

"Best to get a head start," Alice said, eyes on the rear-view as they roared along a country lane. "As you can see, moving a bunch of us is quite the operation. Best to make a dash for it or spend all your riding time in a queue to escape the car park."

"You look almost as excited as Libby to be getting out of the city," Sara replied, bracing herself a little with the door handle. The car felt like it could drive through brick walls, but it was a bit of a bone shaker all the same. "I suppose days to just be out in nature are rare for you?"

"I try to support a lot of outdoorsy charities, and I still get out for the odd game of polo or hockey, despite my advancing years." Alice gave a little wink at that, before fixing her attention back on the road. "Of course, it's not so much the sport at the time, as it is recovering the next day."

"I just have my gym membership, but it's really not much more than a card to carry around in my purse. Oh, and somewhere to get a smoothie when I pick this one up from swimming lessons." Sara was surprised to hear her own confession, but something in Alice's easy company was bringing it out of her.

"Well, it's not too much of a drive. You're welcome to try the radio, but there's always the risk of something boring, like the news."

"Ew, not the news," Libby said from the backseat.

"Agreed," Alice replied. "So why don't you tell me what you're most looking forward to with these horses, Libby?"

By the time they entered the stables, Sara realised she had made a serious mistake. Changing had been simple, their bags stashed in a little cottage right by the stables that took up more ground than the entire school Sara worked in. She felt comfortable, at least, in riding boots and jeans that stretched in all the right places. With the long-sleeved top and quilted waistcoat, she almost looked the part of the country gentlewoman. Unlike everyone else, she didn't have a helmet tucked under her arm or already strapped to her head, but she was glad to see Libby's firmly in place, over her braids.

Libby had run on ahead with Rupert and Annie, Alice jogging behind them like a bodyguard. For the first time in the royal presence, or whatever they bloody called it, Sara noticed no security nearby. Clearly, on this massive country estate, there was more than the average level of safety. All the same, it was hard to shake entirely that prickly feeling of being watched.

But there was no amount of protection or distance that could make the hulking beasts Sara found in the stalls to be manageable.

No way, no how.

She had racked up her share of daredevil experiences over the years, from riding a mechanical rodeo bull at a graduation party, to diving off cliffs into the sea and calling it fun. It had been fun, mostly. But these huge, smelly horses? That was another problem altogether.

"Are you going to let the children on these things?" Sara blurted out the question before she could censor herself. The panic had gripped at her chest by then, even though nobody else in the stables seemed remotely intimidated by what they had to handle.

"Not on Pickle here, gosh no!" Alice patted the long nose of the brown horse she was standing in front of, looking at it with undisguised adoration. "They'd never reach the stirrups for a start, she's over nineteen hands. That is to say, she's a tall one. Like me."

"Right."

"Ponies are much more the thing." Alice gestured to a few stalls down, where Annie was deep into explaining something to both Rupert and Libby. "Although you never did mention what sort of experience you had?"

"Watching. Observing. Just watching is fine by me."

"Are you sure? We have some darling old girls in back, terribly patient with new riders."

"I did try before, while I was at Cambridge." Sara cringed at the memory. She had never found a way to relax around the huge animals, and she knew it was showing.

"No pressure, of course," Alice said. "The important part is that we'll all keep an eye on Libby, she doesn't seem to share your reservations about riding."

Sara laughed at the earnestness of Alice's words. "There might be no stopping her at this point. Just remind her she can't bring a pony home on the train?"

"Deal." Alice agreed with her usual ease, before heading off to another stall and greeting a huge horse by patting its forehead.

Sara watched on in quiet awe as the respective royals got their horses ready for a ride. Although staff buzzed around, none came to interfere beyond passing over the occasional bit of leather kit or to greet the children. Libby was practically vibrating with excitement as she was introduced to her companion for the afternoon, Alice returning with her saddled horse to lead the group.

"This is Cricket," Alice explained to Libby, stroking the horse's neck to demonstrate. "She's not too big, just over eleven hands, which is just about right for your size. Annie used to practice with her, so she's used to being a teaching horse."

"The horse teaches me?" Libby repeated back. She was adorable with her sturdy navy helmet, her polo shirt and jodhpurs still neat along with her waterproof jacket.

"Oh yes. Humans can teach you good manners for being around horses: how to sit, how to greet them, how to be gentle. But the one who teaches you how to really ride? Well, that's the horse herself."

Sara wrinkled her nose even as Alice's words reassured her. No amount of good breeding and expense could remove the fact that stables were not the nicest smelling place in the world.

"Where will you be, Mummy?" Libby took the reins from Alice as though she'd been leading horses her whole life, and the group made their way out into the huge courtyard.

"I'll be cheering you on," Sara replied, before turning to Alice. "Are photos okay? Just of Libby, I mean."

"Take any you like," Alice said. "I know you well enough already to know you'd sooner die than sell some snaps to a grimy Sunday tabloid."

Sara laughed. "Say what you really feel, princess. But you're right. It's of no interest to me."

"Annie, you show Libby how to mount and then we're off." Sara smiled about how it sounded like orf, no matter how normal Alice tried to sound. The intense poshness of royalty was just baked in, and not a complete turn-off.

The closest they'd come to real riding before today was on a holiday to Portugal, with an ancient, grumpy donkey. Here the majestic horses towered over them, and Sara felt that familiar bubble of panic that any parent experiences when their child tries something unknown and potentially dangerous.

But in that moment, Alice stepped to the fore. Taking Libby by the hand, she walked her carefully from one side of her horse, around the front to the other, explaining the whole time, and pointing out parts of the horse tack.

Sara couldn't help but be reassured as Alice patiently explained the correct way to mount and dismount without startling the horse. Once she had helped boost Libby up onto the horse—oh, that looked so much higher than it had when Libby was still on the ground—the same careful attention was paid to how to hold the reins. Sara smiled as Alice demonstrated how to keep a firm grip, but also made sure that Libby knew how not to hurt the horse's mouth by pulling too hard on the bit.

"I'll ride beside you at first," Alice said, seeing Libby fidget in the saddle, impatient to get started. "And we'll try everything we have just talked about. Once you feel confident, you can follow Anne and Rupert around the paddock, okay?"

"We'll take it slow up to the paddock, walking pace," Alice said to Sara, the sun behind her making her into a talking shadow as she spoke down to Alice from her own horse. "Then we can let the horses really run, but all in a contained space. No scares or surprises that way."

"Thank you."

"Really, this has all been my pleasure."

And there was something so genuine about Alice's soft smile that Sara had very little trouble believing those words were true.

"Wow."

"I swear, if I catch you laughing—"

"I would never laugh in such a serious situation I assure you," Alice replied, offering a hand to Sara where she lay in a considerable patch of mud. Cold, wet, liquid seemed to be seeping through every crease and seam. Her so-called riding boots had been about as much use as a chocolate teapot, with absolutely no grip on the slippery paddock grass. While the horses had covered the ground without incident, one wrong step from Sara had left her entirely flat on her back.

"Laughing at someone this muddy would probably justify treason, I'm just saying." Sara surveyed herself in dismay as she got back to her feet. At least she had a change of clothes with her. It wasn't much comfort for the clammy, chilled sensation that seemed to go all the way to her bones.

This was why she had never been an outdoors woman. Sofas didn't pull this kind of crap on a person. A nice footstool could be trusted not to soak a person's clothing without warning. Her humiliation was compounded by the arrival of the Prince of Wales and his wife, looking young, wealthy, and clean atop their huge horses.

"'Lice, what have I told you about pushing people into bogs?"

"Are you okay, Sara?" Annabel slipped down from her saddle, a picture of grace in her jodhpurs and plaid shirt.

"Just my pride that's hurt, don't worry. I might head back for something dry, though?"

"Of course! I can take you."

"No, you get some time with James and the kids," Alice replied. "I can take her back to the cottage and we'll be dried off in no time. Might even have a medicinal brandy. For the shock. Then Sara can still spend some time with Rupert, yeah?"

"Good shout," James said. "We shall keep an eye on the youngsters, don't worry. Alice, can I have a quick word?"

He steered his huge black horse around in a semi-circle so he could lean down and talk to his sister. Sara took an instinctive step back as the animal got too close. Whoops of laughter came from the children, and Sara recognised Libby's giggles in amongst the noise. It seemed fine to leave her in safe company, and Sara was hardly much help on the horse front anyway. Annabel got back on her horse, leading James over to the paddock with a shout of encouragement for the kids. That left Alice behind, holding her horse by the reins with a pinched expression on her face.

"Everything okay? I can find my way back. I don't want to ruin your day off to ride."

"Not at all. Saves you getting lost on this sprawling old place. We'll hardly lose any time, trust me."

Sara didn't have the energy to argue, and so she fell into step with Alice as she led her horse back along the bumpy path they'd travelled barely an hour before. For the first time, Alice made no attempt at small talk, leaving Sara to fill the void.

"Everything okay? Prince James seemed quite serious. I should still spend time with Rupert, after the riding and all. I was going to run through a more formal assessment today, give them the start of the answers they need."

"Ah yes. About that..."

Alice brought the horse to a halt, moving around to the same side of it as Sara. It was quite sweet how she never moved anywhere near the horse without a reassuring pat or a few murmured words. This Alice, in riding gear and talking to the animals, was a million miles away from the stiff, formal person presented in the press.

"About that?" Sara squinted a little in the sunlight. She should have brought sunglasses. Alice had a pair of aviator style ones tucked in the pocket of her shirt, seemingly prepared for anything.

"It turns out the press have rather latched on to your presence today. Speculation is running rampant in a way none of us anticipated."

"Do you need us to leave?" Sara found herself surprisingly reluctant to do such a thing. Some part of her wanted to see how this day would play out. For Libby's sake, of course. This was a once in a lifetime riding class she was getting.

"Nothing like that. But James is uncomfortable that they've already found out some things about you. Your job as a special needs consultant, for a start. He thinks it might not take long for someone to put two and two together."

Sara shook her head. "It's nobody's business. That isn't fair on Rupert."

"No, but there are only three people between this boy and being king. People seem to think that buys them the right to comment, no matter how young or vulnerable he might be."

"You do know I won't say a word. Even aside from signing those papers, I have no interest in—"

"James had a suggestion that he thinks might fly better than outright denial. My preference is not to make any comment at all, but he seems to think that will only increase speculation. In the interests of giving them some kind of narrative... Oh hell, this is ludicrous."

"Ludicrous how? He's not trying to pass me off as your new girlfriend is he?" Sara laughed, a real eruption of a belly laugh that seemed to come all the way from her toes. It soon died off when Alice didn't join in.

"Clearly that idea is too hysterical to consider."

"No, wait!" Sara reached for Alice's arm as she moved off, grabbing hold a little more firmly than she had intended. She glanced around, half expecting some protection officers coming to swoop in. "It wasn't the idea, not at all. If anyone should be laughing right now, it's you."

"His idea was that if we present you as some sort of, yes, girlfriend, but try the 'early days, respect our privacy' angle, it might buy a few weeks of them only focusing on that. He does know, of course, that it is too much to ask of either of us. But he always has been a cheeky bugger."

"It must be bad if you're busting out the mild curse words, Your Royal Highness."

Alice groaned. "You should hear the salty language when it's just family. But that is hardly the point. I should put it off until you and Libby go home, but I will absolutely tell James to go hang with his preposterous ideas."

"That's probably for the best. Not least because the press probably won't buy you dating some single mother from south London. Who works in the public sector, no less. I mean, no one would say it outright, but they would have a field day, wouldn't they? And that's before they find out I'm part Iranian and part French."

"I think the French part would cause more of a stir than anything else, even the gay thing," Alice said. She gave a quick smile to show she was teasing. "But this is the twenty-first century after all, and they were mostly benevolent when I came out. A few remarks crossed a line, but that was more out of ignorance than anything approaching hatred."

Sara pinched the bridge of her nose. "With all due respect, that's exactly how every privileged person describes it. Those things aren't over just because they don't happen as much to rich people. I don't want to be some kind of social justice whatever here; but trust me when I say that plenty of people still don't feel safe out there in the world."

"You don't?"

"Not all the time, no. And I've had to talk to Libby about some of that, young as she is. And you've seen that she's darker-skinned than me. I pass for white, mostly, but with an Indian father she never has. I don't want her seeing headlines about the princess and the 'terrorist', you understand? Because they will be that blatant."

"I'm sorry. I do see some of what you're talking about, through the charities I help with. Not remotely the same, I know. I just don't want you to think I'm indifferent."

"I might not have spent much time with you, but the last thing you are is indifferent. If anything, you care much more about things than anyone would ever guess. Look how devoted you are to your niece and nephew for a start." Sara hadn't intended to be so complimentary, but the truth had a habit of spilling out.

"Most kind of you to say."

"Now, what you say about press attention is probably all true, and my first instinct is to want no part of all that. But I can't help thinking what we said before about the press prying into the children, and maybe making a splash out of whatever diagnosis might be settled on for Rupert—and my first best guess is that he will need some adjustments, at least in these early years."

Alice considered for a moment, stroking the horse's long nose when it started to fuss. "What are you suggesting?"

"I'm not exactly what someone like you would be looking for, and I can't promise it won't get too much. I might bail so fast you'll wonder why I offered. But if it protects Rupert for us to steal focus for a few weeks, then I suppose that's just part of helping out."

"Are you sure? For what it's worth, I rather think I'm the one punching above her weight here. My silly title—does it count for much in comparison to someone who dedicated her life to helping educate children? The ones who need her help most, at that? Perhaps no one reminded you in a while, Sara, but you are one impressive woman. One that I, for one, feel very lucky to be spending time with. I cannot think of a better person to help Rupert, and the fact that everyone else seems to have taken to you right away is testament to that."

"It's been easy to get along with everyone. For Rupert's sake if nothing else."

Alice let go of the horse and came closer again, taking Sara's hand in both of hers and shaking it in a huge, enthusiastic handshake. It drew another rumbling laugh from Sara, and she could have sworn for a moment that the skin on her hand tingled.

"This is truly above and beyond, Sara. Please be assured I will find some way to make this up to you. And if anyone, anywhere, ever so much as attempts to slander you or Libby where I can read or see it, trust me when I tell you there will be hell to pay. I gave up fighting them on my own behalf, because there is an argument that it comes with the royal title. But you and your daughter will be strictly off-limits for any of their lies or prejudice. Please know, on this you have my word."

"You don't owe me anything, Alice." Sara felt a pang of hesitation calling the princess by her name and seeing the look in her eyes as she did. "Just a friend helping another friend." Could they be? Friends? A princess and a nobody? But Alice didn't think Sara was a nobody. Or so she'd said. "You've already made Libby the happiest little girl when you got her on that pony."

Sara shook her hand where it still rested in Alice's grip. "Just as long as you promise me Libby will not have her heart broken over any of this and the children come first." She felt a long-drawn shiver shake her entire body, "And that we can get me out of these muddy things." And a blush.

"That I can do." Alice didn't smile but she squeezed Sara's hand one last time before letting go. "And I shall come up with a plan for the rest of it." Alice straightened up and snapped into what Sara recognised as her business mode. "Make a statement first asking for privacy. Then work out what the minimum disruption would be to your life, while making it look convincing for…well, everyone else. Will Libby be okay with this? With me?"

Sara felt her smile falter a little. Libby always was her biggest concern.

"She is always pushing me to date someone. She likes you, and she's certainly loving a chance to be friends with Rupert and Anne. I always said I wouldn't lie to her, but I don't think asking her to lie is any better. So, for the sake of what we're trying to do here, she can think we're really dating, too. If it even gets that far."

"Right. They may well see the press release and wander off to something more interesting." Alice might be a lot of things: a princess, a Olympic medallist in field hockey, and a fast driver, but she was certainly not one of Britain's great actresses. They wouldn't be recasting Downton Abbey with her any time soon.

"It won't take much, will it? We'll be seen in public once or twice, they'll take some photographs…" Sara said, following Alice as she urged the horse back towards the stables. "I mean, when that's all it is, how bad can it really be?"

Chapter 9

Changed into a fresh pair of jeans and a borrowed blue jumper that Sara had the sneaking suspicion was actual cashmere, she was at least presentable again, Sara set down the bag full of toys and books she'd brought with her, but a cursory glance around the room saw that the playroom was well-stocked with everything a child could need. The space was light and airy, with tall windows that looked out over the immaculate lawns, and even though it wasn't the sunniest of British weather, it all felt quite lush and late spring-like as she watched the activity of the estate workers hurrying to and fro.

Before long there came a knock at the door, revealing Annabel, James and Rupert. The boy had opted for the shelter of his much taller father's leg, clinging to the grey material with small fists. Annabel betrayed no sign of having been out riding besides the slight flush on her cheeks, her riding gear traded for deep blue overalls and one of those striped tops beneath that just screamed yummy mummy. In his shorts and dinosaur T-shirt, Rupert really could have been any little boy, but then how did anyone look like third in line to the throne, exactly?

"Hello," Sara said, and, summoning all of her concentration she put the very idea of royalty to one side. Two parents, one child, and a gentle discussion to find out what they all wanted to know. This was something she could help with, and she was determined to do exactly that.

"Rupert, you remember Sara, don't you?" Annabel urged him forward, offering her hand to him. It took a moment, but he gave up his hold on James to take it.

"Hi, Sara," he said, not quite making eye contact as he clutched his mother's hand. "We did drawing."

"That's right, so we did. Now, if you're okay playing with me for a little while, shall we ask Mummy and Daddy to go have a cup of tea and come back later?"

Annabel and James exchanged a look at that, but Sara was more than used to it. When Rupert made no objection, she gestured with her head back towards the door. "We'll see them in a little while then."

James was mumbling some form of protest, but thankfully Annabel took him by the elbow and steered him out of the room. No doubt they wouldn't go far, and there may even be cameras in the 'nursery' as they all referred to it, but Sara felt her chest expand fully on her next breath. Now she could relax into the work itself.

"What would you like to play first?"

Rupert didn't need time to consider that question, making a beeline for the train set on a low table in the corner. Clearly, he had his favourites, and started the trains in motion with a practiced hand. Sara came to sit cross-legged on the opposite side of the table.

When she had done this before, Sara had worked in a team of two for assessments, but since a lack of paper trail worked in their favour here, she was happy to keep track in her head instead of letting someone take notes.

"Would it be okay if I played with the trains too, Rupert? Is there one that you don't mind sharing with me?"

Sara watched his responses carefully. Using the standard developmental markers, by this age a child would be comfortable flicking attention back and forth between the person talking and the task at hand. She was wary of relying too much on standardised scores, but as part of a broader assessment with lots of factors, it didn't seem so restrictive.

Rupert handed over a small blue train in the end, and Sara smiled while thanking him. At least her presence didn't seem to be unduly stressing him so far. She watched his method of playing, noting that he stuck to just one part of the train set, repeating the actions with just two trains over and over again.

"Can I have my train back?" Rupert spoke up after a short while. "If you're not going to play with it."

"Sure. Would it be okay if we did some reading together? Maybe you could pick a story you like and read some to me?"

Rupert huffed at that, but he set his trains down and scurried over to the nearest bookcase. He pulled out something bright with an elephant on the cover, and Sara clapped her hands in excitement. Although he moved closer to her, when he sat down on the floor Rupert was mostly turned away from her. He dived right into the book and started to read aloud, not struggling with the vocabulary at all, but delivering it all in a sort of monotone. The reading seemed like just another task for him, and she didn't get any sense he was picturing what the words told him, or imagining the characters and events to be something real or tangible.

"You're doing great," she assured him when he paused between pages. "After this I'd like to show you my bubble machine."

As she predicted, when Sara opened the nursery door to check for Annabel and James, they were leaning against the wall just opposite, in quiet conversation with each other. Sara's sudden appearance startled them, but Annabel was the first to regain her composure and ask if they were needed.

It was momentarily bizarre to see such well-known figures arrange themselves into bean bag chairs in the centre of the room, but Sara thought it made things less formal than the high-back couch under the window.

"Rupert's going to have another turn with his trains while we catch up," Sara said by way of explanation. She was pleased when Rupert stopped to give her the requested high five before rushing back to his beloved train set.

"How is he?" James never took his eyes from his son. "Were you able to look at the particular concerns we raised?"

"The important place to start is what I mentioned back at the garden party, Your Royal Highness. There is no one medical test for autism. We can't take a swab or a blood sample and point to some definitive symptom or reading. The best we can do is make an assessment based on some of our most reliable tools and talking with the family who know Rupert best."

"You might still prefer a formal assessment based on what I've discovered, but I've stuck pretty closely to the ADOS, which is the Autism Diagnosis Observation Schedule. Normally that would take place over a few home and clinic visits, with a psychologist or speech therapist as the second clinician."

"Testing sounds…difficult." Annabel spoke up first. "Will it upset him? He seems fine now, but does it get worse? We're used to managing meltdowns, but we'd prefer to avoid them if we can."

"There's no stress involved, if at all possible," Sara said. "The main thing I'm doing is comparing Rupert to the usual development milestones for his age. If there is a delay—and in this case I can see signs already that there is—then it's a case of working out whether that is a general delay. That would come under different learning difficulties, each with their own treatment or management plans. But if there are specific markers, more concerned with social skills and communication, that's when we're talking about autism spectrum disorders. Although some of that terminology is changing, this area is evolving constantly."

"So you think that's what it is?" James rubbed a hand over his knee, like he was scratching some irritation. "What's that going to mean going forward? Mostly for school, yes, but what about public events and all the other expectations?"

"James. Let Sara explain. She doesn't need the third degree." Annabel placed a hand over his, whether to soothe or in warning it wasn't entirely clear. Sara was relieved that so far, they'd presented a mostly united front. A lot of the difficulties she'd encountered in her career came from parents who were at totally conflicting levels of acceptance.

"Last time out we talked about his sensitivity to crowds and loud noises. That's easily managed with ear defenders - there are more subtle ones now that cancel out all external noise. As for schooling, he would get something out of a mainstream education because he's terribly bright. With twins we often find they compensate for each other too, so that could help. But honestly? If you want to do the very best for him? You'll look at a school with more catered individual learning plans. Rupert shouldn't have to bend and struggle to adjust. Not when we're able to give him an environment where he can thrive."

"I wasn't the best student," James said, with Annabel squeezing his hand. "I know a lot of marks were nudged upwards, and a few quiet words were had behind the scenes. Nobody wants to think their next king is a bit thick, you know? But is it possible…has this come from me in some way? That I didn't put in the effort, and now poor Rupes is paying for it?"

Sara shook her head. "That's not how it works. This isn't something that needs blame or tracing back to a source. It's just a difference, one that means a new approach. I've got some recommendations I can give you, smaller schools where Anne and Rupert could still go through primary education together at least. He'd have some additional support and a few curriculum changes to manage areas where he needs it most."

"You make it sound so simple. We were worried all this would suffocate him." Annabel gestured vaguely to the building around them. "That the institutions wouldn't be able to adapt or adjust. It broke my heart to think we wouldn't be able to help him."

"It's a decision for you both, and for Rupert, but I think you could make a very big positive out of this situation. Any number of families juggling these responsibilities would feel seen and understood to know that even for royalty, this is just reality. Not to mention the charities who would appreciate raising awareness of autism." Sara felt a little crass mentioning the opportunities, but if she didn't make the case then who would? The last thing she wanted to be involved with was hiding Rupert away like some fragile flower or shameful secret.

"We don't want to use him," Annabel said. "But we do take your point. Of course we love him exactly as he is, so it's very good news that we can focus on supporting him and not trying to change him."

"That's very much the spirit." Sara stood then, a little less than graceful getting out of the low beanbag. Annabel and James stood to join her. "Have your doctor handle any further referrals you might need, and I'll provide a brief report just for you both so you know what next steps are available. You've done right by seeking out advice, now you just look after him as any parent would."

James stuck out his hand, and Sara shook it. "I knew we were right to seek you out," he said. "As soon as Josephine found out you were an expert right in front of us, I rather think it was kismet. We won't soon forget this kindness, Ms Marteau."

"Think nothing of it." Sara was surprised that Annabel skipped past the handshake and drew her into a hug. It was no polite press of bodies either, it was a genuine bone-squeezer that seemed to express a lot of relief and thanks all at once. "I should probably go and track down my own beloved daughter, before she talks Alice into giving her a pony for the trip home."

"They're just at the end of the hallway, in the sitting room," Annabel said.

"Bye, Rupert," Sara said. "Thank you for hanging out with me today."

Rupert looked up from his trains, waving the red one in her direction. "Bye, Sara."

She set off down the corridor with a smile on her face, pleased at a job well done. A moment later, Sara felt a tap at her shoulder as Annabel caught up with her.

"They told me what they've asked of you, James and Alice. I know there are a few more meetings to come, but are you sure you know what you're letting yourself in for? Using dating as a cover story can be a risky business."

Sara couldn't deny being surprised that Annabel had even brought up the subject. "I don't mind. I know it's about protecting Rupert, and as far as I'm concerned, that is absolutely my job too. More of a duty, really. When it comes to keeping any child in my care safe."

"That's very noble," Annabel said with a smile. It failed to reach her eyes entirely. "We truly are so grateful, but I wonder sometimes if they forget what an ask it is—to bring anyone new into this circus."

"I'm sure you're used to it by now. I mean, you seem very good at it all, the press and appearances. They seem to like you, at least."

The laugh Annabel gave was a little stilted, too. "Some days I wonder about that. I got used to the intrusion eventually, but it's one hell of a commitment. James and Alice, being born to all this, they can't always see what an adjustment it is for someone who isn't. They get peeved at the people following them, and sometimes lines are crossed, but for the most part being photographed and written about is as natural to them as breathing."

"Hopefully if I'm not actively looking for attention the paparazzi won't be all that interested in me. I won't be falling out of clubs at 4 a.m. and dragging a princess through the mud with me, you know? It's just walking to and from cars and buildings mostly."

"What kind of clubs have you been going to that have mud outside?" Annabel looked relaxed for the first time all day as she teased. "And I wish that theory held true, but as much as we appreciate your invaluable help, I completely understand if you want to end our association here…before the madness can descend and upend your whole life. We can always ask someone else if you think it's too much."

Sara could hear the sincerity in the warning, and it certainly overlapped with every concern she'd had since first setting eyes on Alice at Libby's school. It would be as simple as thanking Annabel, collecting Libby, and never seeing any of these people again, outside of a laptop screen or a newspaper stand.

They would find some other way to protect Rupert while also getting him a fine education. Money, resources, none of the usual barriers would apply to these people. But something that Sara couldn't put her finger on had already shifted inside her. The same sense of responsibility that had made her volunteer as a Brownie leader, and had made her confident without any proof that she could cope as a single mother, was already locked and loaded on the prospect of helping Rupert.

Sara was one of the best in her field. If Libby needed this kind of help, someone exactly like Sara would be her own first choice. And if it did all come out at some future date, well, surely the publicity would only help an important cause that was constantly trying to raise awareness and understanding. The red flags weren't reasons to stop, exactly. Just sensible warnings for Sara to consider.

"No, we're in it now. Rupert is making progress even from one session and the exercises I left with you and your husband—in a positive and safe way. You could start all over with someone new, but it feels like my responsibility at this point. One that I welcome. Rupert really is a lovely boy, and he's going to flourish even more once he gets everything that he needs."

"Then I suppose I should just thank you again," Annabel said. "This really is above and beyond, even if you understand as a mother what we're all going through."

Sara didn't hesitate, "That's what it comes down to, in the end. Even in a palace, you're just parents trying to do the best for your child. I can understand that, and what's more, I respect it. I'm glad you're able to let me help. We'll see this through."

"Mummy?" Libby appeared from a doorway at the end of the long corridor.

"Duty calls," Sara said, and she left Annabel watching on as she jogged over to reunite with her daughter.

Chapter 10

Alice groaned as she drove the Range Rover into the private car park. Any hopes of this first, hastily arranged date flying under the radar had disappeared into the clamouring pack of paparazzi that greeted her when she parked. Thankfully, Josephine had arranged for Sara to be picked up and brought in separately, because this unwelcome sight might have made her turn on her heel and run.

Which she might still do, once she realised what Alice had planned for their day out. It had seemed so simple once they'd decided on no kids in the picture, all the better to sell the fake romance, but then Alice had come to the startling realisation that she hadn't organised a date of any kind in over five years. The few women she had seen socially had been so casually arranged, either through mutual friends or worse, through Josephine and the office. Stilted dinners and nights at the opera had seemed wrong, now, somehow.

"Princess! Alice! Princess! Your Royal Highness!"

The shouts went up as she jogged across the car park. Every time they seemed to think that if they just hit the right combination of names and titles, Alice might break with longstanding habit and go over for an exclusive interview. Not bloody likely. She kept her head down as best she could and entered the clubhouse where Uncle Jock was waiting as always.

"I was beginning to think you'd lost our address," Jock said, pulling her into a bone-crushing hug. Well over six feet tall, and as broad as a wardrobe, he had the beard of a seasoned Hamley's Santa and a twinkle in his eyes to match. "The girls are thrilled you wanted to drop by."

"Safety in numbers and all that," Alice said, fussing with the zip on her tracksuit jacket. "Can I suppose I have a guest waiting?"

"You do. A most punctual young woman, and lovely manners to go with it. I've set her up at the bar with a pot of tea. Don't worry, I haven't warned her what you're all like when you get out on a hockey pitch."

"That's why you're my favourite uncle."

"Says the niece who never visits these days. How's that brother of yours? He's around here even less. Your dad would be sad to see his activity level drop."

"James still gets out for some polo now and then, but I think his back protests too much after hockey now. I keep telling him he's getting old."

"He always was the soft one. Will you be wanting a drink? Or shall I leave you to your company?"

"If I could have a moment with her? Time for a quick introduction to the hockey gang and all that."

Jock nodded into the members' lounge and made himself scarce through the kitchen door. Every inch of these buildings was familiar to Alice, decorated in muted colours with the odd bold splash of tartan or some surprising modern photography. She had often fallen asleep on the sofas in the lounge, and never paid for her drinks at the grand old-fashioned bar. Jock had chased off every photographer and spying journalist since they were children, and it had become something of a haven for James and Alice alike. Their school friends had certainly enjoyed the complete lack of checking for ID when they were still underage, too.

Alice strode through to greet Sara and was rewarded by the sight of her lost in a book, sipping at an oversized mug of some fragrant tea. For a moment she forgot the whole day was a construct, a little ruse to keep the press outside from thinking too hard about Rupert's well-being and educational options.

And it ought to be said, if Alice were had been meeting Sara for a real date, she could have done a hell of a lot worse. Hair in loose chestnut curls and pulled together with a silk scarf wrapped around them at the base of her neck, Sara looked far more comfortable dressed in jeans and a leather jacket than she had in full riding gear. Her low-heeled ankle boots and fitted wool sweater weren't quite something Alice would have worn, but what didn't suit her she could certainly appreciate on other women. And Sara was worth appreciating.

Not that she was doing that. Of course not.

"Do you come here often?" Alice opened with the cliché, betting successfully that it would make them both laugh.

"I bet you say that to all the girls," Sara replied. She gave a few darting glances around the empty bar. "Should we...uh, might be worth establishing some protocol? Before we're around other people? Just so we both know how to act and what to expect."

Alice had offered a hand to shake as Sara spoke, but then she realised that girlfriends would do no such thing. Even ones dating a boring princess who spent all her time cutting ribbons and giving little speeches.

"I hope it goes without saying," Alice said, leaning in to brush the very faintest of kisses against Sara's left cheek, "that this is entirely based on your comfort level. It might help to sell it if we held hands in front of the cameras, or a little smooch like that to convince them, but you don't have to do even that. Your presence alone is what fuels them."

"Well, the same goes for you. This clearly wouldn't be your idea of a suitable date if it didn't help out your family, so I can respect whatever boundaries you might have. Not everyone likes to be pawed at—or have a partner hanging over them like draped fabric."

"No matter the reasons for our spending time together, Sara, I hope you realise that you make a more than suitable choice. Indeed, anyone should count themselves incredibly lucky to have a woman like you on their arm. Real or not, I am certainly proud to be seen with you." Alice felt her face flush at giving the unexpected speech, but she would simply not stand back and let Sara put herself down.

"The man, Jock, he showed me in here. He seems very nice. Very fond of you," Sara said, changing the subject with a deftness Alice hadn't expected.

Alice took the seat next to her at the bar, leaving one foot firmly on the floor. "He's practically my uncle. My father's best friend. They go right back to prep school, you know. Anyway, this has always been our little haven in the country. Our house, our proper house that is not an actual palace, is about twenty minutes down the road. This was always a safe place to come and be...well, just like other people. Be teenagers without it ending up in the tabloids."

"Is that why he's so twitchy about letting the press on the grounds today? It looked like he wanted to chase them away with a big stick."

"Thankfully we have a lot of those."

"You do? Oh wait, you never did say what we'd be doing here."

"I thought, to take the pressure off, a group sort of thing might be nice. Also, I think being around friends presents the best version of a person, certainly in my case. So, I thought a quick hockey match and then some drinks with my team. Is that utterly boring?"

Sara topped up her tea from the pot. "It's very... lesbian? It's a pretty good pick. If this were a real date I'd be impressed. Assuming you've bribed your friends to say nice things about you."

"And let me win, yes," Alice replied, getting back to her feet to show off her navy Olympic team tracksuit and smart white trainers. Sara had seemed suitably impressed with mention of all that back at Sandringham, and it wasn't as though Alice had done anything so gauche as to wear her medals with it. "It's also why I'm dressed like this. Let me just check in with the squad and then I can show you where the...well, where the guests watch from. Introduce you to a few of them."

"Sounds lovely."

Alice lingered just a second or two longer than necessary, before loping off in the direction of the changing rooms. She saw the hockey pitches through the huge windows in the hall, crisp and green and gleaming. A perfect day to run around and let off steam. As long as Sara managed to not entirely hate it.

She shoved the changing room door open, braced for the cheers and whistles that always greeted her presence. As Alice tried her best to throw her things in a locker, she had to navigate a barrage of hugs, back slaps, and something approaching a rugby scrum by the end of the row.

"All right! Get off me, you brutes!"

"Come on, ladies," Esther said, in her best mock stern voice. She sounded like a Northern Irish schoolteacher. "Please mind your manners while you handle our national treasure. Nice to handle, nice to hold, but if you drop her, consider her sold!"

That just set off another round of roughhousing. By the time Alice fought her way back to the door, they were all red in the face and ready for the match ahead. A friendly against another local club, and there would be very little friendship involved.

"Now before you all start to embarrass me out there, I am trusting you all with the knowledge that I have brought along a date." Alice had often addressed them as captain when she played full time, but this was considerably different.

The whoops went up again, this time mixed in with a few, "Yeah right"s and even a sole, "Poor cow!"

"Her name is Sara and I told her you lot were good fun. So don't let me down, eh?"

"Oh course, HRH," Esther said, with a deep and mocking bow. "It will be just like we're back on base, all on our very best behaviour."

Alice rolled her eyes but gave Esther a fond fist bump anyway. Stripped down to her vest and shorts to play, Alice only had to retrieve her hockey stick from her locker. She kept a rotation of her favourites in there, and she opted for her most faithful. A mix of carbon and fiberglass, it was designed for 6-foot plus players, which she skirted just below height wise, but the bow of the stick was extra low to allow for more advanced player. As someone who'd made her career on fast dribbling and accurate shooting, it was a perfect fit for her.

"Where are you going?" Esther called after her as Alice slipped away in the corridor.

"To fetch Sara. I'll be right out, come on. It's not like I'm captain anymore or anything."

"Two minutes or it's a fine," Esther replied. "And I am your captain, so don't even think about messing me about. I will bench my best players, you know that."

"I do."

Esther continued on after the rest of the team, and Alice waved to Sara from the door of the bar.

"You're just over here," Alice said, leading Sara out towards the huge garden and the playing fields just beyond. "The seats aren't the most comfortable, but I brought a little picnic basket to keep you going. Ah, there it is."

Alice had staffed it out, of course, but they'd left it thoughtfully by the spectator gallery benches. She left Sara to fuss over the contents, jogging into the centre where Esther had handled the coin toss.

"Ready to show off for your new lady? She's gorgeous."

"Just try not to trip me every five seconds, okay? Remember we're on the same team."

Esther pulled her long red hair up in an even higher ponytail, making her eyebrows look quite startled. "It's every girl for herself out there, you know that. And this Sara girl is quite a looker. If you can't woo her with all your titles, maybe I'll be more her cup of tea."

"Don't you dare." Alice gave a warning glare, waved to Sara, and set off in pursuit of the game ball.

"Well," Alice said as she collapsed onto the wooden bench next to Sara, fully twenty minutes later. "I suppose this makes us even."

"The fact that you look like you just waded through a swamp to come over here?" Sara was fighting a losing battle not to laugh, and Alice found she had come to enjoy the sound. Okay, so two weeks before she had liked it a lot more when Sara had been the one covered in mud, but at least Alice had scored a goal or two before landing in the marshy side of the pitch.

"They'll swap me out at half time—means everyone gets a game. I'll get cleaned up and we can spend some time with the girls."

"I look forward to meeting them properly. I confess, I was expecting Duchesses and Viscountesses, but so far I believe I've spotted two CEOs, a Cabinet Minister, and that politics woman from the BBC."

Alice was impressed yet again at how unfazed Sara was by impressive people or fancy titles. "Not bad. The rest are just Olympic medallists, some pilots, and we're not technically allowed to tell you what Janie does for a living."

"MI5 or MI6 then," Sara said, raising an eyebrow in challenge.

"You did not hear it from me. Now, I should warn you that they like a drink. Don't feel obligated to keep up."

"I'll bear that in mind. School friends, are they?"

"A couple of them. It's a nice mix. Being out here has always been a home away from home. We spent most school holidays and weekends here.

Then when I joined the RAF, my base wasn't far. A few friends from the service settled around here, even once they came out of it all. Esther was at uni with me too, and in the Olympic squad."

"You should get back in the game. I'd best get working on my girlfriend chants. The only sports songs I know are from football, though."

"Good enough. If you get stuck, there's always 'God Save The Queen'." Alice patted Sara on the thigh, quite without thinking about it. The photographers on the far side of the field went into a frenzy. "Oh, I almost forgot those buggers were here."

"Do you think that's enough to convince them?" Sara leaned in close to ask the question. Alice shivered, nothing to do with the breeze that had picked up, and everything to do with the tickle of Sara's breath against her cheek. "Or do we need to do, uh, other things?"

Well. That was the question, wasn't it?

"Entirely up to you, Sara."

Sara's response was to press those full lips, impossibly soft and almost pillowy, against Alice's cheek for a second. No, two. Alice was already red in the face from running around on the hockey pitch, but a fresh flush raced up her cheek. Without thinking, she ducked her head.

"That did it," Sara said, nodding towards where the paps were practically climbing on top of each other to get more shots. "Be sure to come celebrate with me if you score another goal. It is called a goal in hockey, right?"

Struck without the power of speech, Alice simply nodded and did as she was told. She forced her feet to move one in front of the other and jogged back across to join the restarted game.

The whack of stick against ball brought her back down to earth in a hurry, just in time to evade the left back charging towards her. Concentrate, Alice told herself. Faking a romance for the papers was no excuse for losing a friendly game. Besides, it suddenly felt more important than ever that she score another goal.

Alice looked back over her shoulder to confirm the growing realisation brewing in the pit of her stomach. Just a glance of Sara's beaming smile, and her hunch was confirmed.

Great. She had a crush on the woman risking all sorts of public attention to help out Rupert. What a fundamentally stupid thing to do. But as Sara waved at her, Alice found she couldn't seem to mind that much at all.

DAILY BUGLE 13TH JUNE

CHICKS WITH STICKS

With HRH Princess Alice releasing a rare press statement this week requesting 'privacy in her private life' and making allusions to not interfering with the business of private citizens who might happen to be around her, everyone has been primed and ready for a splashy event where she shows off her new girlfriend.

But the days rolled past without a single movie premiere, charity ball, or royal appearance with Ms Sara Marteau in tow.

Imagine our surprise, then, when the big debut turned out to be at a quiet sporting club in the Surrey countryside. Owned by Jock Hardcourt, a close friend of her late father the Prince Consort, the unnamed facility has long been a favourite with the younger royals and their set.

No designer gowns or helicopter rides for the princess and her date. Instead, a rowdy game of hockey with her closest friends from university and her time in service. She might have medalled with some of these players at the Olympics almost twelve years ago, but there was more evidence of fun in their play than any serious sporting competition.

Ms Marteau, reportedly an educational specialist born and raised in south London, cheered on the princess from the sidelines, but didn't pick up a hockey stick and get herself muddy. As official first dates go, it was the definition of low key.

Will we see something more glam from the newest royal couple next time?

Chapter 11

SARA SQUARED HER SHOULDERS FOR the usual march along the north end of Oxford Street. She was at least fortunate to be above ground and walking to her post-work post-shopping-trip dinner with Jasmin, who would have to brave the jam-packed crush of the rush-hour tube to Bond Street. Although the street was thick with commuters on both sides, Sara found herself making good progress and only two men collided with her, surely a record for late night shopping on a Thursday.

"There you are!" Jasmin met her outside the tube station exit. "I thought you'd be getting followed and stuff."

"By whom?" Sara looked around, just in case.

"I dunno, the paparazzi, innit? Or like, have the palace assigned you a bodyguard?" Sara had half expected that to become her life after the day of hockey with Alice and her girls, but aside from rampant internet speculation and a handful of tabloid stories, the press seemed to be holding back.

"Ssh!"

"What? I'm just asking!"

"Can we not draw attention to any of this? And please do not mention any of them by name. God knows who might overhear."

Jasmin gathered herself, back to her most professional face as she linked arms with Sara and led her down the street. She was still dressed for the office, in a sharply tailored skirt suit and killer heels.

"You got it. Did you get your shopping done?"

Sara clutched her bags a little tighter.

"Yeah, mostly. But tell me what's up with you, it's been weeks since we had a proper chat."

"Not since you borrowed my riding gear. You can return that anytime, by the way."

"Damn, I forgot. I have at least cleaned it all up. I'll drop it round. "

Jasmin waved away Sara's pang of guilt. "Please, when do I get out of the office long enough to do anything like that lately? My American VP lady will be the death of me."

"Yeah, but is that from all the extra meetings she makes you go to, or the fact that you have to stare at her legs for most of them?" Sara nudged Jasmin with her elbow.

"Kathleen did ask me if I wanted to play some squash at her gym. At least I think it's squash. Is that the same as racquetball?"

"It's all hitting things at the wall, yeah." They waited for the traffic lights to change and crossed the road arm-in-arm. "Either way, you have to be good at ducking."

"Sorry I couldn't get away sooner," Jasmin said. "But at least you didn't just click at something online for once. Don't you miss proper shopping days out?"

"Single mum working full time? Trust me, when I have free time I don't want to spend it shopping. Buying things is way more fun done in the bath, with a glass of wine in the other hand."

Jasmin gave a snorting little laugh. "Okay, that's hard to argue with."

"So where are you taking me for dinner? Libby has a mania for chicken nuggets lately and I'm losing my mind along with my taste buds."

"I made us a reservation, but if you want to change it up and just go to town on a curry, you know I can always handle that."

"Nah, let's be West End girls at whatever trendy place you picked," Sara replied. "But it better not be, like, little drops of mousse and one spinach leaf. I don't want to have to stop for chicken and chips on the way home, yeah?"

"Wow, someone got picky since she started hanging around palaces." Jasmin was the one to nudge this time.

"They don't really go in for spicy, shockingly enough. It's all white-people levels of seasoning. They don't even throw in a bit of garlic most of the time. So you-know-who told me, anyway." Sara hoped Jasmin's choice of restaurant wasn't too much further. Her appetite lacked the patience for all these bustling little side streets heading towards the old American Embassy and Soho. It seemed like every time she came back into the centre of London, some other landmark she took for granted had changed or moved.

"You can't call her that, she's like, not a villain in some cartoon? Or is she? You never know what to believe in the papers. But you're the expert now, invited into the inner circle. You must have made some impression." Jasmin said it in a knowing sort of way, and for a moment Sara forgot the whole thing was just a cover story.

"I think Libby is mostly to blame. And I'm sure it's good PR for her to be seen hanging out with someone who's not, like, an actor. Or someone who's also royal and basically her second cousin. I don't think that makes me Cinderella somehow."

"You're not the ugly stepsister though, are you babe?"

"One thing that worries me is that I'm just being steamrollered here. I mean, I made it quite clear that I think monarchy is old-fashioned and we should probably get rid of it. But because they want something, my whole little family is swept up in the royal slipstream. I want Libby to have nice experiences, but am I giving in too easily? I like to think I have principles, Jas."

Jas laughed and patted Sara's arm. "There's my full-time worrier. You're not doing anything wrong by letting Libby see how the other half live, you know. Now come on, you are going to love this food. Then you can show me what you bought to wow her. It better be hot enough to make her want to risk it all, including the Crown jewels."

"You're mad, Jas." Sara followed her best friend into a small, nondescript restaurant with the windows steamed up and the welcome scents of chilli and ginger hanging thick in the air.

"Oh don't worry, payback is listening to me whine about my love life for the rest of the evening. And I don't even get a pony in mine."

They settled into a booth and ordered their usual favourites without much debate. Everything brought out would be fair game for sharing—they had done it that way ever since school.

Sara sipped at the green tea that had been served up without them having to ask, and leaned back against the leather of the seat to take in the buzz of another London evening. Nobody in the place except Jasmin knew her name or her face, or who she went to see playing hockey. The city had a wonderful gift of anonymity, and after her first recent brushes with a tiny moment of fame, Sara pulled that sense of privacy around her like a cloak.

"So real talk. What's she like?"

"She's everything you think she is. Posh. Polite. Loves horses. Really solid with her family, despite the stuff you've read over the years. She's just another person. Like I've said about that lot all along, they're not special, or better than anyone else."

"You say that but even my dad does the bending and scraping routine when it comes to the queen and all that. He's basically a Communist about everything else, but it's like something flipped when her husband died, back in the day. Like all our mums and dads, people their age, they feel responsible for Queen Caroline. They think they owe her looking after or something."

"Public grief must be so weird. I looked up the funeral on YouTube, because I kind of remembered it but not really. They all look like totally different people."

"I remember the fuss when Princess Alice came out, though. Everyone was like modern Britain rah-rah-rah, but we know different. This country loves to pretend it solved all its problems, as long as you ignore those bigots marching in the streets and shouting at football matches every weekend. England's no more solved its homophobia problem than it has gotten 'past' racism and colonialism. But they like to tell themselves that to sleep easy at night."

Sara nodded along with Jasmin's words. She was far from the most political of her friends, but even she had attended more than her share of protests and rallies, signed petitions and raised money for countless charities fighting racism, homophobia, and other injustices. It was just a fact of life, growing up with her background. Her rights, her safety, her ability to work and live, and raise a daughter, all of those had been impacted by misogyny, and homophobia. She'd seen Jasmin run into countless instances of overt racism too and feared when it would strike in Libby's young life, since they were similarly dark-skinned.

And yet, here she was. Fake-dating a princess, not that anyone had realised the fake part. Lying to Jasmin had been a difficult choice, but in the end Sara wanted to keep the risk small. Only her mother knew that the whole thing was a cover for helping out with Rupert, and she had been sworn to secrecy on pain of death. Or at least Sara getting a nanny instead of letting Inès help with Libby, the greatest threat in her arsenal.

They paused to welcome the arrival of their food, baskets of steaming prawn dumplings and rich, salty bowls of chicken and noodles.

"This was a good idea," Sara said around her first mouthful. "I'm not used to getting out this much without Libby."

"If you need some babysitting from her favourite auntie, I'm open to negotiation," Jasmin replied. "Consider it my way of crowdfunding your way back to a love life."

Sara stuck her tongue out at that. "I've hardly been hiding in the nunnery, Jas. But you know how it is with women. They want to commit after three dates, but then when the kid is in the equation… I'm just dipping my toe in the pond, ready to get thrown back out any minute."

"Pfft, I don't care what she's born as, this girl is lucky to have you, Sara. I don't know why you don't have the confidence of a supermodel, girl—"

"We can't all be like you."

"Even so, you know you're a fine-looking woman. You're smarter than any three other people I know, and you've got the best, dirtiest laugh in south London. Don't tell yourself this is some charity move from the pals at the palace. You're the one doing them a favour."

Sara hid a frown at how close to the truth that was. "Mate, you've always been my biggest cheerleader, so thank you. This is just one of those random things we'll laugh about in ten years."

"I don't know, maybe in ten years you'll be dropping Libby off at some fancy polo club with her step-mum."

Sara rolled her eyes. "Oh yes, just to start the weekend before we drive down to Windsor for dinner with the Duke of Brigadoon. I can see it now. Just me and the King of Norway, hanging out in the tapestry room and talking about who the best singer in Eternal was."

"If he says Louise, we break off diplomatic relations. But I'm serious. Did you at least have fun?"

"You know what's wild? I did. They're all really normal when they're chasing stuff on the grass. The drinking games? Well, they got pretty hardcore. But singing, jokes, some of the stories they could tell about flying, about going to the wildest places you've ever heard of…it was really nice. Different, anyway."

"And she's asked you out again, so you must have made a good impression," Jas said. "Bet her friends are no different to us. If you were a dud, they'd tell her to bin you off. Just like I will after we go to brunch at Windsor Castle and become insta bezzie mates."

"You do know you can't just drive up there and drop by for lunch, right? There's a whole massive park before you even get near the place."

Jasmin shrugged. "We'll borrow a helicopter. My work has a helipad. Sorted. I can even use the brunch to dazzle Kathleen, get her to admit she does fancy me."

"You've got it all worked out, haven't you?" Sara took another sip of her tea, glad she had a friend in her life like Jasmin. "Let's see if I can get through a second date first."

"What's the big plan for that?"

"Well," Sara replied. "This time she wanted to include Libby, which I thought was nice, so that changed the plans a little bit."

"Hold on." Jasmin placed a protective hand on Sara's forearm. "Don't look over, okay? But a bunch of people have been snapping pics, and now it looks like there's proper paps outside. Big flashes, whole deal."

"What?" It took all of Sara's self-control not to whip around immediately. "Please tell me we're accidentally having dinner with half the Chelsea team or something?"

"It's all pointing this way, mate. Shit. What do you wanna do?"

Sara started down at her plate for a moment, chopsticks pinching a prawn dumpling hard enough to split it.

"Sod it. I came here to have dinner, and that's what we're doing. Maybe they'll get bored and piss off by the time we're done."

"Maybe." Jasmin didn't sound convinced. "This doesn't mean you get the extra dumpling, by the way."

THE LONDON HERALD, 22ND JUNE

ROYAL NON-EXCLUSIVE?

Sara Marteau, a rare public addition to the dating roster of HRH Princess Alice, was spotted out in London's trendy West End last night in the company of another woman.

Sara and her unnamed gal pal were spotted at Flying Lotus restaurant, in swanky Mayfair. The two seemed cosy in a private booth, sharing food from each other's plates and chatting intimately for most of the evening. They were surrounded by bags that suggested a recent shopping spree.

Neither women commented to reporters as they exited, hailing a taxi and speeding off into the night. According to public schedules from the palace, Princess Alice spent the evening at a charity gala for one of her pet causes, the RSPCA.

Was it a case of new girlfriend doesn't make the guest list? Or has Princess Alice not tied her new woman down to an exclusive relationship yet? Perhaps the monarchy is more modern than we thought, if they're out here having open relationships.

Chapter 12

SARA HAD ALWAYS SAID SHE would do anything for her daughter. Give her a kidney? Without a doubt. Run into traffic to save her? Sara wouldn't even blink. She had even endured those first six months of shrieking violin lessons before Libby really developed some skill, although most of that had been from under some noise-cancelling headphones. That reminded her, she had some recommendations to send over for Rupert. Maybe it would be easier to just give the information to Alice rather than leave an email trail.

But on that Sunday, faced with a huge interactive media experience called Spidertown, Sara had officially found a limit to her endless love for her child.

The second date with Alice had been arranged at the movie studios that dominated the western suburbs of London, the buildings making up a small village all by themselves. Huge aircraft hangars held sets, tanks, vehicles, and costumes. It all went on for miles and miles. Countless famous films had been shot there, and part of it had been turned into a very big, noisy and popular tourist attraction. One especially favoured by screaming children.

"Everything okay?" Alice said as they stood in the enormous plaza outside the Spidertown exhibit. From a queasy glance at the sign, Sara understood it was a replica village from a movie where spiders took over. Not to terrorise humans, oh no, but to warn them about the dangers of deforestation and global warming. Very noble goals, and particularly cute animation in places, but there was no escaping the fact that it was a big room full of scrabbling, jumping, web-spinning spiders. Sara's brain didn't seem to care that they were as fake as her current relationship.

"Just wondering how I spawned a daughter who loves creepy-crawlies as much as she does horses," Sara replied, aware of how tight her chest was and how strained it made her voice sound. She startled further as Alice reached for her hand, enveloping it in her own with a squeeze.

"Is that…?"

Sara nodded. She did feel better, small comfort though it was. "I don't like to show Libby when I'm scared. Her world view is that I'm here to protect her."

"I don't think it's a bad thing to know grown-ups can be scared sometimes too. When you think she's ready for that."

"You make a good point. All those fancy schools taught you a thing or two then?"

"That and some therapy, I suppose," Alice replied. "Not that I would ever admit to such a thing in public, of course."

Sara watched Libby race back and forth between giant spider statues, suppressing a shiver. "It's a shame. I understand the reasons for shielding Rupert, but things like normalising therapy might help a lot of people."

Alice stiffened but didn't drop Sara's hand. They kept walking, going deeper into the exhibition space. "Or it might become another stick to beat one with. I assure you, Sara, I consider all these things very carefully. What might seem like reassurance for people who struggle with mental health can also send a signal that there is something wrong with how I am, that I need treatment for it. That was the tightrope I had to walk."

"I'm sorry. I didn't think. And you really should not have to feel like this."

"Thank you. But don't worry, no average person would think of it that way. Just one of those quirks of royalty." Alice squeezed Sara's hand again. "Shall we catch up with Libby before she crawls inside one of these things and tries to hatch herself?"

"Okay, but only if you never call me average again." Sara looked her in the eye before she took the lead, charging into the throng of people and picking Libby out with the ease of a mother. "I have a reputation to maintain."

"This is nice, thank you for sharing even more of your precious spare time with me," Alice said once they were in a quiet stretch with nobody close enough to overhear. "Especially since we're apparently in an open relationship! James mentioned that you saw Rupert again too, and you think there's a workable plan?"

"There is, although we will need to consult at least one other expert. He's a wonderful boy, and he's going to thrive with everything adjusted correctly."

"Of course he is. I'm just sorry you get stuck with the public embarrassment of dating me in the meantime. And I must apologise, not even thinking to ask if you were seeing someone before we hatched this little scheme. I do hope the attention caused no disruption to your date."

"I try to avoid the papers, and I'm not one for social media. Do you really think I was on a date? Why would I do that when it jeopardises the cover story for helping Rupert?" Alice blushed faintly at the question, intriguing Sara further.

"I suppose we never said that was off-limits."

"I wouldn't have agreed to this if I weren't single." Sara didn't care to think about exactly when her last genuine date had been. Changing jobs and looking after Libby hadn't left much time for jumping back into the dating pool. "Jasmin is my best friend, and she also happens to be Libby's aunt. Her brother, Jayesh, was Libby's father."

"I think there are plenty of people for whom an existing girlfriend would not have been a consideration," Alice said. "Just another way in which you are something of a breath of fresh air. I only knew you dated women because Josephine mentioned it, back when we were vetting people who could help."

"And why would she do that?" Sara didn't know she would be so invested in the answer, but she practically held her breath in waiting for it.

"A permanent case of matchmaking-itis, is the medical term." Alice laughed, charming as ever. Then she abruptly changed the subject. "Perhaps the initial statement was too vague, now I think about it. Might need a clarification. Are you sure you still want to go ahead?"

Sara was surprised how much she didn't want out. Her sense of duty to a child in need was one thing, but there was a growing part of her who had come to look forward to messages from Alice, and these rare days out with her. Slowly but surely the person underneath the princess title was starting to show, and Sara found herself unable to look away.

"I'm sure. Maybe we're overestimating how interesting we are?"

"I've been trying to do that my whole life, I'm afraid. They always get involved," Alice replied. "But I have to believe we can control it, keep the focus off Rupert just a while longer. Shall we do some proper photos on the way out of here? I'll have my protection officers keep Libby out of the camera line."

"Only if you think I look okay? This dress and jacket, they're new."

"You look wonderful, Sara. You always do. Bold colours look fantastic on you."

"That's quite a smooth line you have there, princess," Sara replied. "You've obviously had some practice with flattery."

"Not enough, I'm sure. Ready for the final stretch of spiders? I am reliably informed these ones glow in the dark."

Sara groaned at even the thought. "Okay, but this is one visit I am never repeating."

They took a bracing step forward together and faced the dark tunnel ahead. As they did, a shout came from across the space.

"What was that?" Sara turned around sharply.

"You two make a cute couple!" A woman shouted again, and they traced her to a small group waiting in the entrance line.

"Thank you!" Alice called back, giving one of those little half-waves that seemed to come so naturally. The group dissolved into giggles. "Well, that was a positive start."

"When I heard raised voices, I thought…" Sara trailed off. "Anyway, that was better. Shall we brave these damn spiders?"

"Here goes," Alice said, trading her hold on Sara's arm for an arm around her shoulders. "Don't worry, I shall let them get me first."

"Now that," Sara replied. "Is noble."

Chapter 13

FACED WITH A RARE DAY off thanks to the bank holiday, Alice was luxuriating in her bed at Sandringham with a fresh cup of tea and the morning paper. The clear spaces on her calendar had been something to hold on to these past few weeks, especially with the additional demands on her time to see both Sara and Libby.

Except it never quite felt like a demand. Even then, with peace and quiet and no obligations, Alice felt her fingers twitch towards her phone. Perhaps if she sent a nice general sort of message, find out what Sara had planned, then they could still contrive to spend the day together. They were officially making headlines after all, so how better to keep adding fuel to the fire?

Before Alice could decide, her bedroom door slammed open, loudly enough to make her jump. None of the staff would ever dare, not even if the old place was burning down, so that left only a handful of suspects. Sure enough, it was her mother who came striding in, dressed for another day of work, right down to the mint green handbag over her arm that matched the rest of her ensemble.

For the first time in quite a while, Alice took a proper look at her mother. Usually they nodded at each other from opposite sides of large rooms, or their respective places at dinner. Quality time was rare, apart from the weeks away over the summer, and that had been almost a year ago already.

She had stopped dyeing her hair since turning sixty a couple of years before, not that anyone dared comment on such a thing. The usual severe bob had gone from a vibrant chestnut to something rather more streaked with salt and pepper, but it suited Caroline very well. Alice wished, growing up, that they had looked more alike, thinking it unfair that both she and James were so similar, and so like their father. What she hadn't gained in looks, Alice had definitely inherited in temperament and sense of duty, at least, but it also meant she knew well enough to brace herself and set her cup of tea aside.

"Good morning, mother." 'Mummy' was reserved for expected greetings, ones that took place after breakfast.

Protocol did dictate that Alice should curtsey to both her mother and brother on first meeting, but since she hadn't made it out from under the covers yet, it seemed unnecessary to do so much as a simple neck bow.

"Alice, what is going on with this woman? I go to a Commonwealth summit in Barbados for a few days and come back to, what? You suddenly playing the field?"

Oh. Was that all?

"Believe it or not, this is all to do with Rupert and his schooling. We talked before, about how James was dragging his feet on choosing a place? Obviously the home schooling everyone had to do bought him some time, but after the holidays the twins really should be enrolled. Sara, she is something of an educational guru. Annabel and James have noticed some delays with Rupert in his development, and Sara has helped to confirm that our little fellow is most likely autistic."

"James started to tell me as much, though this is more information than he gave me. What on earth does any of this have to do with you dating the woman? And splashing it all over the tabloids? That is most unlike you, Alice. Even your more serious relationships you've been able to keep under wraps."

"The dating is to divert attention from Rupert having someone in to help. It was James' idea. My role is merely as willing accomplice."

Her mother walked over to the large window that cast its light over the bed, opening the curtains another inch or so. Alice propped herself against the pillows, waiting.

"Have we not talked about this exhaustively, darling? This notion that you can simply make the acquaintance of some girl and start dating her? There are procedures in place. Safety considerations. Not to mention... well."

"Mention what, mother?"

"You know I am all for modernising the monarchy. Your father was a great support in that, but we have to handle the reality of the country we live in. The world."

"My being a lesbian is hardly a secret. I seem to recall it made the front pages a few years back. With your blessing, I might add."

Caroline came over to sit on the bed, setting her handbag aside for once instead of brandishing it on her forearm like a shield.

"Please, this is no time to be naive. I thought it was understood by now. A lesbian, in theory, is fine; people can choose to ignore that so long as nothing is thrown in their faces. But a lesbian princess with a partner, with a name, who is in all those official photographs...?"

"And I suppose this has nothing to do with Sara being Persian and French? And that she has a child? A brown-skinned child whose father was British-Indian on top of that?"

Alice refused to wilt under her mother's glare. That stern queen face might look the part on a stamp, but it no longer intimidated the adult princess.

"Do we really need to get into all that? This is simply about the pressure of being involved with this family, and not everyone has the stamina for that. I should think your dating history proves my point."

It was difficult to resist the urge to wriggle away from discussion of her exes, but Alice recognised the tactic for what it was. Forcing herself to stay the course, she lifted her chin a little as she addressed her mother.

"So, which is it? That I oughtn't date anyone because of the attention and hate it might bring? Or that I should only date people who are listed in the peerage and used to being in the papers every week?"

"You have to understand, Alice." Her mother reached out, patting Alice's hand for just a moment. It was a million miles from when Sara had offered the same comforting gesture on the train weeks ago. "When I say these things, I have to consider them as the Crown, not as your mother. As your mummy, who loves and protects you, I only want you to be happy. But as Queen, my job is quite different."

"This is a lot of hand-wringing for a relationship that—I might remind you—is not even real. Sara could not be less interested in dating a princess, and since she checks out with security and is helping Rupert, can we not just call this a...well, a test balloon? In case I were to meet someone serious. I have been thinking it might be about time."

That got the attention of both parts of her mother.

"Really? I thought you had sworn off romance forever? Or is it the fact that forty is knocking on the door?"

"Hey!"

"Well, thirty-seven is close enough, darling. I am so proud of how well you do all this...really. It takes such a burden from my shoulders. But I don't have to tell you again how lonely all this is without a partner, without someone at your side. If you really do want to go ahead, we can use this as a practice run and find you a tabloid-proof real prospect. Someone appropriate."

"Excuse me, there are few people more appropriate than Sara Marteau. Not only is she kind and intelligent, but she put herself through Cambridge and has dedicated her career to helping children with special needs. She speaks fluent French, decent Farsi, is well-read and cultured, and she is raising her daughter to be a fine young woman in her own right. If Sara is not up to our standards, then I am afraid our standards are simply unrealistic." Alice caught herself in full defence mode, and forced her shoulders to drop a little.

"And might I remind you, you married someone that plenty would have called 'inappropriate' too. Is that how you think of my father?"

"That was different. Times have changed, but the gay thing will still trip people up. We must represent the whole country, even the ones who dislike us or who think differently than we do. We have to find someone who works with you, of course, but who manages not to draw any additional attention. Above all, you must think of the risks you expose this woman to, and her daughter. The press coverage alone...one shudders to think."

Alice grimaced at the delicate wording. She knew exactly the privileged, inoffensive type of woman that would provide. She had attended the finest schools with hundreds of them. "Like I said, it's nothing real. So we agree that I can continue this charade with Sara? Trust me, it is doing no harm."

"Yes. Your aunts and I will discreetly start the search for someone more long term. I have another blasted trip, but we can start some informal meetings after that."

"I really thought all this arranged marriage nonsense would be confined to James, as the heir."

"Well he spoiled all my fun by meeting Annabel and falling for her all by himself. That just leaves you, unless Rupert and Annie start looking for a partner in primary school."

Alice took a deep breath, weighing her options. A life of service to the Crown, when for most of the years that had been her mother, and her grandfather before that, meant she defaulted to agreement and a life of keeping the peace. No charity was too small, no event too long; she simply stepped up and did what was asked of her as long as it was physically and mentally possible. Do well in school, get a nice little degree in something non-threatening like Classics, and serve the requisite time in the military to do everyone proud. To go against any of the grand plans, to deviate from the preordained path was something Alice had only tried once before, by coming out in the first place.

"No, mother. Thank you, but no. Take me off the list, don't waste time on trying to find me a match. If I am to meet someone, I want what you had, and what James has. Someone whose path I was meant to cross, and whom I can love for exactly the right reasons. I would rather be alone than pushed into some kind of transaction."

"You say that now…" Her mother stood to leave. "We can check in with each other after my trip, see how you feel. I see Josephine has been keeping your calendar full."

"You say that like work is all there is in life. Did we not just establish otherwise? What about you, mother? Should we be vetting the aristocracy to find you a suitable widower with his own fortune?"

"No, dear. One love was quite enough for me. Try not to waste the whole day in your pyjamas?"

"I have a tennis match with Esther after lunch."

"All the better. Give her my best, when you pick her off the floor. See you during the week no doubt." With that, the queen was gone, back to her waiting public. Alice sank deeper into her pillows, luxuriating in the sunlight just a moment longer.

The end of their third set found Esther lying on her back on the grass court, refusing to get up.

"You're supposed to shake my hand even if you lose, you absolute ham."

"And you're supposed to let me win, since you were born to a life of privilege that made you weak, woman!" Esther's Northern Irish twang only got stronger when she was worked up.

"Those are a lot of words from someone who can barely catch her breath," Alice said. She stepped over the net and yanked Esther back to her feet with one hand, both of their tennis whites looking worse for wear.

"Don't remind me, I am absolutely choking for a cigarette over here. Exercise is bad for you. When are you going to launch a charity to tell people the truth, hmm?"

"Drinks are on me, does that help?"

"It does." They collapsed onto the bench at the side of the courts, and a club waiter appeared as though summoned by incantation.

"Two very large gin and tonics, I think," Alice said.

"Sold," Esther said, her pale skin flushed pink everywhere it was exposed to the sun. With her jet black hair and big blue eyes, her petite frame looked like a doll dressed up to play sports. "So no Sara this time? I thought you'd be suggesting a doubles match by this point."

"Two dates hardly make us joined at the hip," Alice replied. "I still get to see my friends, go to Firm stuff—you know how it goes."

"Not really. Been ages since you spent more than a night with someone, Princess Casanova. Love 'em and leave 'em, I thought that was your philosophy."

"A handful of flings does not a Casanova make, Esther. Although the very idea of me dating has set Mummy off. She's quite determined to have me married off before forty."

"To a woman?"

"No, to a chestnut gelding. Of course to a bloody woman."

"I know. Your mum is great and all, it's just sometimes she can be a bit tone deaf on the gay stuff. Like that time she asked Leonardo DiCaprio out on your behalf. And David Beckham."

"Don't remind me," Alice said. She groaned and covered her face. "I suppose that is one upside to being back in the dating pool. I remembered how nice it is to have proper company."

"But Sara isn't a long-term prospect?" Esther seemed confused. "If Queen Mummy is already looking for more suitors, like you said."

"I don't know. She says she has no interest in royalty. Or publicity," Alice said casting her head down with what she knew was disappointment, before realising she was almost giving the game away. She changed tack, sharply. "So while this is nice, stepping out together, I doubt I can convince her to stick around long term."

"And yet you still made a public statement. Very unlike you. Hell, you and Kristina were practically engaged and you still refused to confirm or deny—"

"I don't want to talk about her."

"I think she's relevant here, old chum."

The waiter returned with tall, frosty glasses. Alice felt her mouth water at the sight of the chunky lime wedge alone. It had been a hard-fought match, despite Esther's dramatics.

"Kristina hating the spotlight was an excuse. As a princess in Norway, she was used to so much of the same treatment. Not maybe on the same scale, but she was no shrinking violet. The truth is she got cold feet. Or she got bored of me. Either way, it made the prospect of giving it all up for Blighty and the hounding press no longer worth her time."

"But you came out publicly for her."

Alice took a long sip. "That was what I planned. But I went through with it for me, even though we split. I came out for my own good, for my health and happiness. And yes, partly in case it helped other people out there."

"It did," Esther replied. "But even if you only did it for selfish reasons, I'm still proud of you."

"Do you think it would change the acceptance levels, me being with someone in public? Mummy seems to think it changes things from theory to reality. That there would be threats and whatnot."

Esther considered the question for an endless moment. "I think…it could. But it could also be that your mother is a little behind the times. Sometimes you just have to present things as a fait accompli. Then people accept it right away. Don't give them room to argue."

"I hope you're right. Sara will be a useful test of it, anyway."

That prompted a nudge in the ribs from Esther. "Ah come on, is that all she is? Or are you not trying to get one up on the palace?"

"Excuse me?"

"Bringing her to meet the girls, doing theme parks with her kid. Plus you're both like a bloody Jane Austen novel with all that hesitant, terribly polite touching. Keep taking sneaky looks at each other too."

"It's just a casual thing, I don't know what you're talking about."

"Sure you do, princess." Esther snorted using the term. "Now come on, the sooner we hit the showers the sooner we can have lunch in the clubhouse."

Waiting for Esther, who always took an entire Ice Age in the shower, Alice took advantage of being freshly dressed to step outside and make a quick, private call.

"Hello?"

"Hi, Sara. It's Alice."

Alice heard the distinct sound of footsteps and then a door being closed.

"Hello, you. Having a nice bank holiday?" The warmth in Sara's voice struck Alice every time. So different from their first meeting.

"Very. Just got some tennis in, and now a bit of a boozy lunch I think. Thank God I'm not driving."

"Is everything okay? I know I'm seeing Rupert on Friday during school hours, but did you want to attach a date to that?"

Alice nodded, before realising Sara couldn't see that. "Yes, although I'm all the way in Gloucester on Friday, so would have to be a separate, weekend thing."

"Libby has a birthday party with a sleepover, so I have all of Saturday free."

"Good." Alice smiled into the phone, a pleasant warmth springing in her chest at the idea to spend some time with Sara. "That fits perfectly. Do you, uh, mind it being a surprise? I know we're just pretending, but it might be good for me to really put the work in. Bit out of practice."

"Fine by me." Sara gave a soft chuckle. "It's easy to get caught up in all this. I might have to pinch myself, like they do in books."

"I doubt I qualify as a fairy tale. That said, if I send over the draft of the statement I was going to make, dropping that Thursday night will keep attention on me all of Friday, and us at the weekend? Unless that's too cynical."

"That's...what I agreed to." Sara's hesitation made Alice long to hear what her first thought had been, her gut level response. Still. That was something a girlfriend could expect. Not a co-conspirator in a grand old scheme. "I'm sure the statement will be fine, but I'll keep an eye on my email."

"Thanks. And thank you again, for all this. You might be helping in more ways than you know."

"I suppose that makes me a loyal subject, huh?" Sara gave a soft little snort of a laugh. "Maybe you're winning me over after all. Just took some pony rides and hockey with your 'average' friends."

"I think it takes more than that to really win over someone of your calibre, Sara Marteau. But I can show you my A game on Saturday." Okay, where had that bragadoccio come from? Alice pulled a silent screaming face into her phone, glad it wasn't a video call.

"Then I look forward to it. I should go, I have a garden full of seven-year-olds."

"Have fun."

They ended the call and Alice shoved her phone into her pocket as Esther approached.

"Why are you grinning like the cat that got the cream?"

"Oh dear, already forgotten how I destroyed you on court? That is why, dear Esther."

"Just for that I'm ordering two desserts, but don't think you're off the hook."

Alice held up her hands in surrender as they headed towards the restaurant, part of her wishing she could tell her friend about Sara in ways she knew wouldn't be wise.

Chapter 14

BUCKINGHAM PALACE
Statement by Her Royal Highness
The Princess Royal, 27th June

Due to recent speculation in the press about my personal life, I wish to state at this time that no further details will be forthcoming on this matter.

As your princess and as a working member of the royal family, it is always my intention to give everything that is asked of me. This was also true of my time in military service, when I proudly flew for the Royal Air Force, and when I had the honour of representing Great Britain as an Olympian.

Subject to future announcements, I politely request that my privacy be respected, as well as that of any acquaintances that I may be spending time with over the coming weeks.

As agreed in the Royal Rota, I will continue to discharge my public duties and be available to the authorised royal press correspondents at events when representing Her Majesty the Queen or this United Kingdom.

With many thanks for your co-operation in this matter.

HRH Princess Alice.

Sara grabbed the little handle above the car door as the Range Rover took a bend in the road quite sharply. Clearly this driver—Stuart, as he had introduced himself—was used to more difficult terrain and was trying to make some country lanes just as interesting. He didn't have the suit-and-tie look she had come to expect around the royals, but then it was the weekend. He looked every bit the off-duty soldier, in cargo pants with a fitted T-shirt that suggested he had the physique to handle most physical threats. His dark-brown skin glowed in the summer sunshine, his bald head catching the light in an almost distracting way at times. With a quick glance to make sure he was watching the road—he was—Sara also checked her seatbelt for the fourth or fifth time since the journey from the train station started.

"Now approaching, ma'am," Stuart said a few minutes later, startling Sara from her reverie of watching the countryside rush by. The trees were lush and green, glistening in the early summer sunlight, and it was one of the parts of living in Britain that Sara had always enjoyed the most. She loved visiting France every year and jumped at any chance to travel further that was possible with a little one in tow, but a part of her soul seemed to be fused with the country of her birth, in all its grey, rainy, and blustery glory.

The tree-lined lanes and low stone walls abruptly gave way to open fields, and Sara almost missed the low grey buildings until the car was driving right up to them. A long strip of tarmac stretched beyond the buildings, and only a few people were in evidence, no matter which direction Sara looked in.

She hopped out of the backseat, ready for the day's adventure. When she turned to close the door, she felt an overwhelming urge to ask Stuart whether he'd brought her to the right place. The last thing she wanted was to be stranded in the middle of who-knew-where in the suburbs of Greater London.

The question was saved by the sudden appearance of Alice, emerging from the nearest building as if she was fresh out of a Tom Cruise movie. The jeans looked a little too new, but the carefully distressed denim made Sara's fingers itch to reach out and touch them, just like the leather jacket above, although that felt more…grabbable, somehow. With a checked shirt underneath, Alice had mastered the royal-about-town look.

So much for not being attracted to the princess.

"You're right on time," Alice said, waving to Stuart. "I knew I could count on Stuart to make up for the train delays, he always got us around Kabul in record time. He could have been in Formula One, don't you think?"

"Oh, I think. It was quite a drive." Sara watched the car pull away, gravel spitting from under its tyres on the turn. She shoved her hands in the pockets of her padded jacket, glad of its warmth. "Can't say I've been here before."

"It's so nice of you to do this," Alice said. "I know you don't get much time to yourself without Libby. How is our future prime minister?"

"She's great, as always. Only this week she thinks she might want to be a singer again. Apparently, they do more to save the world."

"She might be right on that." Alice leaned across to greet her properly, a brief kiss on the cheek that Sara mourned the moment it was over. It probably meant nothing to Alice, a formal move that she learned at the same time as learning to walk. Sara had been raised with constant affection, always brimming with feelings, and she couldn't help but blush gently at the brief contact. She hoped her cheeks hadn't darkened too obviously. She glanced around and noticed there was no one to witness their moment of easy affection.

"I took the liberty of loading up already, so ready when you are," Alice said, gesturing towards the huge shed that she'd come out of.

"So what are we really doing?" Sara fell into step and noticed how well matched they were in their sturdy boots. She liked that Alice was taller than her, and those broad Olympian shoulders were reassuring in ways that Sara didn't dare dwell on for too long. "I thought horses when you brought me to the middle of the countryside, but it doesn't smell like stables."

"I do love my horses, so that's a fair guess. But you don't."

"And if we were driving, I suppose you could have collected me at the station yourself for that."

Alice jogged ahead, opening the heavy metal door and holding it for Sara to catch up.

"I think you were wasted on education. Never consider a career in the police? Detective Sara Marteau, CID?"

"I've never seen myself as the cop kind," Sara said. "I'm not exactly a rebel, but you know, more of a reform-the-justice-system type of girl."

"That makes sense," Alice said with a nod as she grabbed the large handle on the door. "Well, let me put you out of your misery about today. Through here."

Sara stepped into what turned out to be much more than a large shed. A hangar—that was the word. Lined up in front of a huge doorway were a cluster of small, private planes. One looked like something straight out of a war movie, down to the British flag painted on its tail.

"Are these all yours?" Sara had to ask.

"What? Gosh, no. Not even close. Well, technically one is partly mine. I share it with a dear friend, her papa owns the airfield you see. Her family goes way back with The Firm, so I think we sold the land off cheap to them after the war. My dad came out here a lot for lessons, and I've been using it to keep my hand in since leaving the service."

"The service?"

"Ah yes, I forget not everybody knows the old biography by heart. After uni—Classics, deathly boring and not at all worthwhile compared to your studies—it was straight into the RAF for me. They even let me fly a few planes, so I suppose I wasn't totally incompetent."

"We're...going up?"

"I suppose I should have asked if you're good with heights or flying in particular. Sorry, foolish of me to just assume. I would have been sure to ask, if Libby had been coming, but I thought you might prefer a surprise all told and—"

"Alice—Alice, it's okay. I love flying. I mean, I love regular, boring flying on a big old jet. This kind of thing is new to me, but I'd love to try it."

Alice just about bent double in relief, blonde hair falling in her eyes. "Oh, thank God. We don't have to spend too long on it, but I've arranged to be 'accidentally' snapped when we land. Then a bit of a picnic in peace, and I'll fly us back. If that works?"

"Sounds fun. I think you're spoiling me. I wish some of my real dates put in as much effort as you do for a fake one to help out your nephew."

"Well, they say one will do anything for family. Ready for your safety briefing?"

Sara stopped in her tracks. "Really?"

"I'm kidding. Here, let me help you up. The safety briefing, by the way, is: Don't touch anything unless I ask you to."

"That I can work with."

Sara took a long look at the plane before climbing up the little ladder. Alice moved around the small cabin checking things and giving them a thump before getting into the pilot's seat. It was a cute, sleek machine. Bright yellow on the outside, with an impressive wingspan, as far as Sara could tell. It just seemed a little flimsy for something as dangerous as flying.

"Ready?" Alice was grinning from ear to ear.

"I hope so!"

"Welcome to the cockpit then."

Sara tried her best to suppress a snigger, but that teenage part of her brain had never truly gone away.

"Really? Go on then, get it out of your system," Alice said, but she was still smiling. "And there's just one last safety consideration: if anything should happen to me, use this handle here to keep the plane level, and press the button on the radio here saying Mayday, Mayday!"

That shut up the giggles in a hurry. Sara stared at Alice, wide-eyed.

"Seriously?"

"Yes. But it will absolutely never come to that. This is a fun little outing, and a flight I could do in my sleep. Just sit back and relax."

Being in such a small space to fly felt alien, though Sara had to concede the co-pilot chair was much more comfortable than any plane seat she'd taken in economy before. Most of the flights she'd taken in her life had been to and from France, with the odd holiday in Spain or Portugal.

Alice looked every bit the confident pilot as she slipped on the big headphones and started speaking into the microphone with short, sharp commands. Lots of 'niner' this and 'Roger' that.

It was, Sara had to admit, downright hot.

Which was a complication she did not need. Shifting in her seat a little, she cursed herself for wearing tighter jeans with that bit more pressure on the central seam.

The plane rolled out of the draft hangar and as they taxied to the runway. Sara watched in awe as grey rainclouds started to part and blue skies started to creep back across the lush English countryside.

"Okay, that's not you controlling the weather, is it?"

Alice just laughed in response, flipping some switches and checking gauges in a quiet, methodical way. The gold ring on her left hand glinted each time it caught the sun, and the watch on her wrist was something different today, a chunky leather strap and more dials than Sara could read on its face. It only drew attention to the way working the controls made Alice's forearms flex, tanned and defined as they were.

Sara applied the brakes on that train of thought. There was no need to be objectifying the woman like that. Maybe it was time to invest in a better vibrator, like Jasmin always joked.

"It's going to get louder now," Alice said, making Sara jump just a little. "You might want to put your headset on. That way we can hear each other without shouting."

"Roger," Sara said, with what she hoped was a relaxed grin. She fumbled the heavy pads over her ears, the engine noises instantly reducing to a dull background hum.

"Golf Bravo Niner, you are cleared for take-off on runway 2-4," a male voice crackled like an old-fashioned radio.

"Runway 2-4, taking off Golf Bravo Niner," Alice replied, her voice clear and almost melodic in Sara's ears. The closeness of her voice seemed unbearably intimate for a second or two, until Sara forced herself to, once again, settle down. She hadn't suffered like this on their previous dates. Was this all the fault of Jasmin planting ideas in her mind? Or all the photos and articles people had been waving in Sara's face at work, at the school gates collecting Libby, and even in the supermarket? Had Sara become caught up in her own useful lie?

She kept quiet, the chatter between Alice and the flight tower petering out as the plane rattled, gathering speed by the second. This part? The wheels leaving the earth and suddenly feeling weightless part? That had never been Sara's favourite. It felt like the part where humans crossed over into things they didn't fully understand, taunting gravity, or God, or something elemental and beyond their control.

But like every other time, after that stomach somersault of panic, Sara took a deep breath and let the exhilaration of flying really take over.

"Okay there?" Alice's voice was more honeyed over the plane radio.

"Oh yes." Sara looked to the side, seeing the countryside roll out beneath them at a tilted angle as they climbed and climbed. "This is amazing. Nothing like commercial flying at all."

"How so?"

Sara laughed. "Not something you'll ever have to worry about, Your Highness."

As the plane levelled off, the sun spilled over the patchwork of green and brown fields; a pleasing lack of symmetry to it all. The countryside seemed to stretch for miles in every direction, and Sara found herself leaning toward like the glass, like a child eager to drink in every detail.

"This is magnificent," she said, reaching out blindly and patting Alice's arm. It was impossible to tear her eyes away from the view. "How lucky you are. This seems like a wonderful kind of freedom."

"This way is certainly more fun than doing it in the military. No guns and missiles to worry about. And dare I say, better company."

"Really?"

"Infinitely better than a co-pilot nicknamed, Cheesy, yes. I shall let you guess as to how he got such a descriptive name."

"Oh dear." Sara inhaled sharply as the plane dipped and then righted itself under Alice's careful guidance. "They really didn't go easy on you in the RAF, did they?"

Alice huffed through her nose at that, and it wasn't hard to tell she was holding back a laugh. "Oh, where were you when I was dragging myself through basic training? There were times, I confess, usually in the pissing rain in the middle of the night, where I thought I had gone wrong. I could be like some of my uncles and other relatives, just take the medals and shake hands at the ceremonies. Once you meet your first injured veteran, though..." She trailed off, clearing her throat. "Well, to be able to look them in the eye, it helps to have at least faced something of what they have. Some would call it the least I could do."

Sara looked at Alice properly then, hearing the gravity in her words. She might be a pacifist at heart, but Sara respected anyone who could volunteer for a war zone, especially someone with every excuse not to. On her bravest day, Sara couldn't imagine going where the bombs were, and it said a lot about Alice that she would do something so dangerous to honour the sacrifices made by others. At the same time, however, Sara carried her family's past traumas of fleeing unrest and falling regimes, and so was always on edge at the mention of war and conflict.

"Plus, now you can do this whenever you want. Does it usually go over well with the ladies?" Sara wondered as she said it if she was going too far.

"This is something I rarely share with other people, in fact. Flying can be the most wonderful alone time. At least until they get camera drones sophisticated enough to stalk us up here as well. They are working on that, I'm sure."

"Thank you. This might be, dare I say, the most wonderful date I've been on, fake or not." Sara reached over to pat Alice's forearm, where it was still flexed as she operated the controls.

"The least you deserve is some privacy."

Sara looked away, hiding her smile. "There's that smooth talk again."

The laugh through the headphones was soft, tinkling. "Okay, duly noted. Just enjoy the scenery, and we can save the talking for solid ground."

Leaving the outskirts of London behind, Sara realised she still had no idea of their actual destination. Only when she saw the coast come into view did she finally crack.

"Are we leaving the country? I don't have my passport."

"Oh, no. That won't be necessary. I thought while the weather is nice, we could visit somewhere I spent a lot of time growing up. I suppose you know my mother was always tied to Wales, and to Cornwall, before becoming queen?"

"Yes. And now your brother is the Prince of Wales. This much I know, even if you're not my specialist subject." She couldn't help but tease.

"And my father came from this part of the world, so it was a natural bolthole for us. Ever been to the Scilly Isles?"

Sara shook her head. "Don't think I've even heard of them, I'm afraid. I'm sure they're lovely."

"They are. We shall be landing at St Mary's shortly, I thought it was one way to control the number of photographers, and also get a jolly nice lunch with a walk on the sand. Assuming you like that kind of thing?"

"I do. The flight alone has me impressed, but I never turn down good food."

Alice laughed, looking away. "That is just the right attitude. I think you would fit in quite well, if we ever did this for real. Not that you would want to, of course."

"Of course," Sara said, but even she could hear the lack of conviction in her voice; she couldn't help but wonder if Alice did too.

"Sara?"

"Nope."

"Sara, you can uncover your eyes now. We are back on *terra firma*, I promise you."

"I don't care what we're on, I'm not moving one inch."

Alice put her fingers around each of Sara's wrists and tugged her hands gently from her face. "I'm sorry about the steep landing. I thought you'd find it exhilarating."

"Flying headfirst towards the ground is not that. It's damn scary, is what it is. Do people know you're a lunatic, or do you always save it for the third date?"

"Depends on the date. Come on, let's undo this seatbelt and you can be content on the ground again. And I promised you lunch. This picnic will make it all worth it."

Sara took a moment to consider her options. Seeming to take that for defiance, Alice unclipped her seatbelt for her, hand grazing Sara's thigh in the process.

"I'm sorry."

"It's okay. I'm okay. Let's go."

"You are not, but as you wish," Alice said.

Sara stood up without taking Alice's offered hand, and they made their way down the steps onto the tarmac. Alice carried an elaborate wicker basket over one arm.

"Now, once we get around this building, there will be a few people with cameras. They'll want to sell those and file stories right away, so we should get a chance to outrun them. Ready?"

"Guess so." Sara was distracted by the sensation of her stomach finally settling for the first time in an hour. "We should hold hands, right?"

"Might stop yours from trembling," Alice said, not unkindly.

They walked around the small terminal building with hardly anyone paying attention to them. Apparently arriving royals didn't register as anything particularly unusual. Only when they stepped through the glass doors did fawning employees appear, providing car keys and loud welcomes.

"Here goes," Alice said, squaring her shoulders and squeezing Sara's fingers with her own.

The group was much smaller than Sara had built up in her head. Three or four men in jeans and jackets, cameras stuck in front of their faces and others hanging around their necks. Had they travelled here especially? Or was this what passed for a day's excitement in the Scilly Isles?

"Princess! Princess Alice! Over here!" The cries went up in their usual way. Sara didn't feel the panic rise in her chest this time. It was planned, anticipated. They had car keys and a clear escape route. She simply stopped for a moment when Alice did, sort of posing but not really as she placed the basket in the back of the car. A vintage Jaguar this time, lower to the ground and quite sleek too. It looked like a James Bond car, and Sara couldn't help but blurt out exactly that.

"I think I might have made a good spy," Alice said. "Not sure about 007, though. And I never did like martinis."

"Shame."

"Alice! Sara!" The photographers had found a way past the temporary barriers and had come a lot closer. "What about a kiss?"

"Oh for the love of..." Alice's complaint was probably heartfelt, but Sara found herself caught up in the moment, her fright at their landing fading in memory. Hadn't Alice greeted her with a simple kiss on the cheek not so long ago? Where was the harm in returning the favour?

She leaned in, surprised at how natural it seemed, and made to place a quick kiss on Alice's cheek. But somehow, at the same time, Alice turned her head to say something more, and when Sara's lips landed, they were squarely on Alice's mouth.

The kiss lasted a second or two, an unexpected meeting on both sides, but Sara swore that under the light pressure of her mouth, she most definitely felt Alice kissing back. Just the press of her mouth back against Sara's, but enough to make her lips tingle in anticipation of more.

"Oh," Sara said as Alice pulled back. "That was..."

"I'll drive!" Alice said, just a little too much cheer in her voice. "Ready?"

Sara nodded, a little hurt that Alice was acting like the kiss hadn't happened at all. Still, there was a picnic and a whole day ahead of them. Who knew what might happen next?

Chapter 15

"IT DOES SEEM THAT THE kitchens thought at least six of us were coming on this date today." Alice smiled as she plucked another strawberry from its simple white bowl, bypassing the cream and popping it in her mouth whole. Sara enjoyed seeing her so relaxed.

"Everything's delicious," Sara said, leaning back against the tree they'd picked to shelter under. The sun was high and though the heat was bearable, a little shade saved them squinting at each other. Alice had her usual sunglasses stashed in her pocket but hadn't reached for them yet. "I suppose the standard must be pretty high to work at a palace."

"Well, most of the time. There was a brief spell when my father insisted on teaching us to cook. That was a trying time for all involved. Still, it meant that all the palaces finally got new smoke alarms."

"Was he a good cook?"

"No, he could have burned salad," Alice replied, smiling at the memory. "But he was always coming up with these grand schemes to keep us 'in touch', most of which were a bit more successful. How are you in the kitchen?" To Sara's ear, it sounded almost suggestive.

"Oh, I was a helper as soon as I could stand on a stool. It wasn't even a question. My mother would have been ashamed by a daughter who couldn't cook, sew, and keep a spotless house. Those are her standards. Passing on her favourite Persian recipes and methods was important to her, it kept her memories alive. And the French side of her couldn't bear for us to be anything but chic. So I had little choice in the matter."

Alice shifted on the blanket, stretching her legs out a little more in front of her. Sara wondered when the last time was when she had just been outdoors like this. It was hard enough to find downtime in a life like Sara's, never mind one so public. Maybe that could be the upside for both of them, to this falsehood of a relationship.

"And you're passing all that on to Libby?"

"Actually, the nice part of her spending regular time with her grandmother is that they do it directly. We're so lucky to have that, even if my mother refuses to come and live with us full time. I suppose for the sake of my love life she might be doing me a favour."

"Well, that's why I don't live with my mother."

Sara waved her hand at Alice. "That and the having a bunch of palaces to choose from, right?"

"That helps. And they're not all palaces. Some of them are merely mansions."

"I like that you can laugh about all of it," Sara said after a moment. "There's nothing I hated more—university was the worst for it—than people with all those advantages talking like we'd all grown up in the same boat. You know?"

"Someone told me once that it's not about being the in the same boat, but rather the same storm. Some of us are in canoes, some are in luxury yachts or giant cruise ships, and some are just trying to swim as best they can. Something like that. I think it's a more realistic view of the world. Less patronising, anyway."

Sara shrugged off her jacket, balling it up into a makeshift pillow and laid out on her side of the large tartan blanket, relaxing in the sunshine like a pampered cat. She felt Alice watching her, and looked over to catch her smiling as a reward.

"I think you're right," Sara said once she had settled into place. "When people lose sight of the differences between us, it does more harm than good. Like when people tell me they don't see colour, or class."

"There was a time, back in my twenties, when I might have been one of them. You know the sort of thing. 'I have black friends, so I know all about it.' Embarrassing, I know. But if an old institution like ours can learn, nobody else has an excuse. Speaking of differences, how are things with my boy, Rupert?"

Sara looked over at Alice, whose expression was inscrutable. "You haven't spoken to your brother?"

"James can be elusive when it suits him. Our paths don't cross that often most weeks. We tend to save things up rather than talk on the phone. Well, I suppose I don't have to say why..."

Sara had noticed that Alice never made any mention before of the phone hacking scandals that had dominated the news for well over a year. Royals were far from the only victims, but they had been the most relentlessly exposed. Alice had got off lightly in comparison, just some embarrassing messages from an ex, but James and the queen had both suffered considerable public mortification.

"That was so wrong, what they did. I'm glad people got fired for it."

"Not enough of them, unfortunately." Alice picked at the grass by the side of the blanket, sprinkling it back over the ground. "There was the inquiry and all these promises about a code of conduct, new laws to protect privacy...but nothing really came of it. It won't take much for some other editor to think crossing the line is worth it just to sell a few more newspapers. Still, we were talking about Rupert. And how very glad we all are that we trusted someone like you with his privacy." A little compliment never hurt anyone, and Sara received it gladly.

"What do you want to know? He's very bright, and very kind. You can tell that right away." Sara smiled, genuinely fond of the little boy.

"Well, I suppose I wondered if we're talking about a definite condition, whether regular school will do the trick. That sort of thing?"

Sara propped herself up on her elbows, switching to a sort of professional mode despite the circumstances. "That will take a doctor to be sure about, but yes, Rupert's learning style is consistent with that of an autistic child."

"Ah."

"That's not some impossible hurdle." Sara hurried to reassure, nudging Alice's foot with her own as they sat and lay side by side on the blanket.

"I have heard the terms. About the spectrum, about functioning, all that. I will do my homework, rest assured. Prince or not, Rupert is going to get all the accommodations and help he needs as a child with autism."

Sara shook her head. "You might find that he prefers to use identity-first language –autistic person—rather than being a person 'with' a condition. For a lot of people, being autistic is a central part of who they are, not something that happened to them, or something that needs to be cured. In fact, it's often a matter of pride that they can see the world differently and approach things in new ways. As he gets more comfortable, Rupert will let you know what he prefers."

Alice moved the empty basket that sat between them, setting it aside. Under the guise of moving out of the direct sunlight a little, she shifted closer to Sara, who made no move to restore the distance between them.

"You're good at talking about this. You should be in fundraising. Certainly a lot more effective than some of the boring speeches I get to sit through for various charities."

"That is a small part of my job, but mostly I'm out there trying to get changes made where they're urgently needed. Whether that's helping to write new training for teachers, or lobbying MPs, or talking to parents about what help they're not getting." Sara wanted to laugh at her own enthusiasm. Despite years of working at that difficult job, she still had a genuine passion for her work.

Alice seemed to like it. "When you talk about it, all things seem possible, Sara."

"I don't know about that, but it is satisfying to get creative about education. Kids are so adaptable, and schools can be too. Did you like school?"

"Not overly," Alice said with a snort of laughter. "When I was little it was fun, and I had no idea why the teachers were always so nice to me. It got difficult for a while there in the middle when we went off to boarding school and Daddy was gone. Then by the time I was thinking about university, being an athlete and training, thinking about the RAF, those girls at school were the few I could trust. As close as I ever got to ordinary I suppose. I trust them more than anyone. What about you? You must have loved being in education, to dedicate your life to it..."

That was Sara's cue to laugh. "Oh mercy, no. Nuh-uh. I was an unholy terror for a while there. Not badly behaved, not like the teachers in a Peckham comprehensive were used to, but a real handful."

"Then how did you terrorise them?"

"I was a bit of a militant. You know how it is, you find out so much about the past, about your heritage and your history at that age. And even knowing all that, it's like injustice was invented just for your generation. I didn't get sent to the head teacher for smoking or fighting, but I did get put out of classes for arguing about our rights or trying to start petitions. I did not agree about much with my history teacher either."

Alice chuckled. "That is... well, you would barely have made the detentions list at my school. Mind you, a lot of them were expected to act like politicians in training. Not that I ever got involved in the real hijinks, of course."

"You weren't tempted?"

"Horribly. I wanted nothing more than to act out, most of the time. It was a constant temptation. But then every time I almost got involved, I would picture the blaring headlines about the spoiled princess doing something illegal...and it never seemed quite worth it. James got away with a lot, but I never dared."

Sara sat up properly then, squinting into the sunlight behind Alice's head. "That's a lot of pressure to live under. Something tells me it hasn't gone away. Has it?"

"Oh, don't cry for me," Alice said. "There are worse things than having to behave. And make no mistake, I did still manage to have plenty of fun."

"I suppose I would know more about that if I'd gone back and done some old-fashioned internet stalking. You would be a dream for anyone who's ever obsessively scrolled their new girlfriend's social media. Only instead of locked profiles and friends of friends, they could just pick up the newspaper on any given day." Sara felt bashful about admitting it. She started reloading the empty packets and glasses back into the picnic basket to avoid Alice's gaze.

"It really is quite easy to ignore them, but it can be weird," Alice said, joining in by gathering up their cutlery. "Sometimes it seems like one is at a permanent disadvantage; in every conversation the person knows me a little better than I know them. Not that I mind, but it really would be nice to start from scratch now and then. No preconceptions. And certainly none of the outright lies."

"At least they would mostly be positive ones," Sara said. "Other than the odd lefty single mother taking you to task in front of a crowd, anyway."

"I did mean to take your temperature on that. Formally, of course. Would you say, Ms Sara Marteau, resident of south London, that your opinion of the British monarchy is now more, or less, favourable than it was a few weeks ago?"

Sara pretended to mull over her answer, tapping one finger against her chin.

"I'm not sure I would put it in writing, but I suppose I can admit that for a staunch anti-royalist, my views have certainly evolved on some members of the family."

"And for our records, are there any family members in particular that you have a positive opinion of?" Alice sounded for all the world like a bored pollster with a clipboard, but she never dropped eye contact with Sara as they talked.

"Well, the children are adorable. Polite. They've obviously been raised properly. And I suppose there's always—what's her name?"

"Which one?" Alice moved a little closer. Sara pretended not to notice. "If you could name anyone that you have changed your opinion on?"

"There is that woman, you know. Works very hard, does so many events for charity. Dresses nicely, always has good hair. Despite all the money, power, and fame, she works very hard to put her privilege in check…"

"That does sound good. And her name, just to be clear?"

"…Annabel." Sara held Alice's gaze for a whole ten seconds before they both dissolved into helpless laughter.

"Oh, well played," Alice said when she caught her breath. Where they could have moved further apart to laugh, instead they had all but closed down the space between them. She found her hand resting on Sara's shoulder for balance, the blanket beneath them all ruched up.

"If you really must know, I think you're my favourite," Sara said. "But obviously I would never be able to admit that publicly. I have my reputation to think about."

"A shame," Alice said. "What if we both were to think about it? Or think about you? I confess I find myself doing that a lot, even when we are in different places. Perils of a grand deception, do you think?"

"Faking it, you mean?"

"If you must. Never been one for faking it, personally."

"No?" Sara was watching Alice's lips as she talked.

For a moment Alice felt an unusual self-consciousness, wondering if the strawberries they had just shared still stained her lips. "No, I prefer the real thing," Alice said. "And I would always ask politely first, before starting something."

Luckily that was the end of the sentence because Sara's lips were pressed against Alice's as she finished speaking, swallowing the last word or two. One of them—Alice couldn't be sure which—made a startled sound as their mouths seemed to fit together instinctively, the kiss developing into something deeper almost right away.

And hell, anti-monarchist or not, the woman could kiss. Alice felt a tingle all the way from her toes to the roots of her hair as they kissed, Sara's fingers brushing her cheek as Alice tightened her grip on Sara's shoulder.

For a moment the world seemed to stop entirely, reduced to just the two of them, the faint taste of strawberry, and the sound of their breathing in the rare moments when the kissing paused.

Then just like a radio shouting back to life after a power cut, everything came racing back. Alice saw the realisation hit Sara in one awful second, like a physical force. She pulled back from Alice, looking as if she had just uncovered some cruel trick.

Alice braced herself for the rejection she knew was coming.

"Sara?" Alice stayed right beside her, unable to ignore how Sara's face was flushed and her eyes were sparkling. She was incredibly attractive. That glossy brown hair fell in her eyes and with a slightly shaking hand, Alice reached out to push it back. Only then did Sara find her words.

"That was..." Sara seemed unable to find her words. She got up on her knees first and then stood. Alice scrambled to follow but Sara held out her hand, as if to stop her. "I apologise, I just got caught up for a moment." She turned around, her back to Alice. "In the charade. In this." Sara made a hand gesture, and with her voice a whisper, she said, "In you."

Alice stood after her, "Sara, we both did. That rather suggests there might be something more to—"

Sara turned around, conflicting emotions playing out across her face. Alice wondered what it must be like to let feelings show so deeply, so readily. She had never had the opportunity. "Your Royal Highness, with all due respect—that is a tempting proposition. Very tempting. But I cannot."

Alice felt the force of the words like a slap. She fumbled for a response, but Sara carried on.

"You would make a wonderful date for someone, but I don't have room in my life for a proposition as wild as what you have to offer. I have to think of Libby, above all else. Dating is complicated enough without...well, without all these complications. Maybe at another time I could have made it work, but I can't afford to throw my whole life open like that. I can't afford to be in every newspaper and magazine. The things they would write, the terrible things that people would assume... It's all very well saying we can ignore it but those records are permanent. Libby being targeted for her skin colour, our heritage, or because of my sexuality...I can't bear the thought of any of it. You know what I mean, too, because you've suffered plenty of that. Your whole family has."

"Of course." For a painful moment Alice considered arguing her case, but instead she started to gather up the blanket, the last item left to pack away. This was the price one paid for putting herself on the line and ignoring what the cost of a relationship with her was for anyone else. Sara deserved grand promises, absolute assurances that Alice couldn't make. How could she risk causing any of that pain or humiliation to someone as good and as charming as Sara? Add sweet young Libby to the equation and Alice knew she wasn't prepared to have that on her conscience. With deft motions, she folded the blanket and set it on top of the basket. "I am sorry. The last thing one wants is to impose further, especially after you have been so very kind to my family."

"Alice wait, I didn't mean to—"

Sara had turned to face Alice during her verbal withdrawal, but it was Alice's turn to walk past her and turn her back to Sara. The closeness that had thrilled moments ago had turned claustrophobic along with the conversation.

"No, it is quite appropriate to establish clear boundaries. I apologise for ever overstepping them. Quite unforgivable on my part. Shall we head back to the airport?" She didn't wait, the tears stinging in her eyes.

"I—yes, if you don't mind. I think it's time I headed home."

"Right. Jolly good." Alice picked up their things. "Back to the car then."

"Alice?"

"Hmm?"

Sara moved around so Alice would have to look at her. Her own eyes shone with tears just as surely as Alice's were. "You don't have to apologise.

That was on me, okay?" She took Alice's hand, squeezing it tightly. "You're right about boundaries and keeping things simple. This is for Rupert. For the children."

"Of course." Alice swallowed hard.

For a moment the air seemed to charge with the intensity always between them again, as Sara's touch was gentle, and Alice leaned into it. But Alice forced herself to walk away, marching towards the car with more purpose than she possessed.

People kissed. These things happened between people who liked and respected one another. No reason why anything had to change. At least, that's what Alice kept telling herself as she started the car for the drive back to the airport, her heart just as wounded as her pride.

Chapter 16

DAILY BUGLE, 10TH JULY

NOT SO SCILLY NOW?

The proof was in the pudding—or should that be the picnic basket—this weekend. Rumours have been swirling, fuelled by rare missives from the palace, that HRH The Princess Royal, or Princess Alice, as most affectionately know her, has entered the dating pool. Her alleged companion? None other than Sara Marteau, a schoolteacher from London.

Some weeks ago we brought you exclusives about the one-time viral shouting match opponents taking a cosy train trip to Sandringham, and since then the potential lovebirds have been spending time playing hockey in the countryside and chasing spiders at the theme park. Is that a perfect date for a single mother and her child? Ms Marteau certainly seemed to think so, accepting cheers and compliments from a small crowd.

Now the royal pairing has been island hopping by private plane - jet set or what? Of course, as a decorated RAF pilot, Princess Alice knows her way around the controls. Did she advise her passenger to strap in? Only time will tell, but we have all the shots from their outdoor lunch date on pages 3-8.

"Mummy?"

"Hmm?" Sara looked up from her coffee mug, realising she had forgotten to add milk.

"I asked if you had seen my swimming costume," Libby repeated. "I'm going to the pool with Grandma after school."

"Yes, you are. Check the clean laundry pile." Sara hadn't technically forgotten, but it had certainly slipped from the top of her internal to-do list.

Libby scurried down the hall to do that, school bag bouncing against her back. Had she grown overnight again? Sara had arrived home just in time to put her to bed the previous evening. Already she was getting up and getting ready for school mostly by herself, with just a knock on the door from Sara to wake her.

"I bet Rupert and Alice never have to go and look in the laundry," Libby said, returning with her swimsuit and stuffing it into her backpack. "Did you have a nice time with Princess Alice?"

"Actually, they both help with chores," Sara said, having been surprised to learn as much herself. She also had no intention of talking about her fake-real date with Alice. "Like with the horses, they can't just ride them. They have to know how to clean out the stables and look after the ponies too."

"Muck out." Libby corrected her mother while reaching for an apple from the bowl in the centre of the table. "Did you see the men outside?"

"Men?" Sara got up and walked into the short hallway. Was there some kind of work planned for the day? She always ignored the various leaflets about gas works and waterworks access. Whatever they dug up, she was always able to get in and out of the house, and they had no car to worry about moving. She pulled back the net curtain that hung over the glass panels of the front door, something she'd been meaning to replace since moving in.

And jumped right back.

Outside, a cluster of men with huge camera lenses had gathered like trick or treaters at her front gate. Even the simple lift of the curtain had set them off, barking and shouting her name over and over. Sara! Sara! Sara!

She backed against the wall as if she was trying to press herself through it. How had they found out her address? It was one thing to be photographed when entering a palace or standing with actual royalty, but who in the hell came to a south London residential street on a Monday morning?

"Libby! Are you ready?"

"Yes?" Libby appeared in the kitchen doorway, munching on the apple.

"We have to go out through the back, okay?"

"But Mummy—"

"Libby, not now sweetheart. Listen to your *Maman*, hmm?"

Sara's heart thudded against her ribcage as they made their way to the back door, grabbing her jacket and handbag on the way. Their back garden was tiny but it had the benefit of a side gate into the lane that split their modest street in two. Motioning for Libby to stay, Sara edged past the front hedge to see how many paparazzi laid in wait. At least six or seven, two on the pavement outside their house and the rest spilled into their small, paved front garden.

Even though it took them further from the bus stop, Sara steered Libby back in the opposite direction, checking over her shoulder with every few steps. If anyone noticed her strange behaviour once they made it to the main road, they didn't show it. Sara supposed Londoners had seen stranger sights on its streets than a slightly paranoid woman with a young child in her care.

"Mummy, what are you doing?"

Sara had pulled out her phone, standing back from the rush-hour crowd at the bus stop. Were these the same people as every other morning? She recognised a few faces but years of commuting had dulled her senses to familiar strangers. Sometimes she nodded at other parents wrangling their children into their school uniforms, but for the most part that Londoner code of never talking to strangers held fast.

"I just need to make a quick call, sweetheart. Can you watch for our bus please?"

"Are you calling Granny? Is she going to tell those men to go away from the door?"

That earned a curious look from a woman in the bus queue. Sara turned away from her. "No, but I will let her know. You might go to Granny's house after school today."

"But I've got swimming—"

"After swimming."

"But Mum—"

"Libby, not now, please. Mummy is a little stressed and I need you to go with the flow today, okay? I know you're a big girl now, and you can handle this sort of thing." Sara wasn't sure that she could, never mind Libby. She stabbed at her phone screen with her thumb, selecting Alice's name from near the top of her contact list.

The phone rang out. No response. Only a generic voicemail message, nothing to confirm she'd reached Alice herself. Remembering their conversation about phone hacking, Sara ended the call before saying a word.

A moment later, a call came through from an unknown number.

"Sara? It's Alice."

She sounded brisk and business-like despite the early hour. No doubt already up and smartly dressed, on her way to some official event or other. Sara ignored the pang of recognition in the pit of her stomach. It had barely been fourteen hours since they parted. Surely Sara was not missing the very person she had rejected on their third fake date after their only real kiss.

"Thank you for calling back, I uhm, I don't want to bother you. Sorry, I should have called Josephine, I wasn't thinking. It's a staff sort of thing for you—"

"No, no, I'm always glad to hear from you. But I sense this is not a courtesy call. What's wrong?"

"Photographers. Paparazzi." Sara said, relieved Alice didn't seem angry with her, but rather, was intuitive, a characteristic she rather appreciated in Alice. "They're everywhere. When I went to leave for school just now, there were a pack of them waiting in my front garden. The neighbours hadn't come out to look, but I'm sure they saw. I thought I would let you know."

Sara heard Alice suck air in through her teeth, a faint whistle of impatience passing over the line between them, even over all the background noise of traffic and people.

"Sara, listen to me. Are you safe? Is Libby safe?"

"We went out the back, we're fine. I'll have to let my mother know, she's supposed to be bringing Libs home from the pool later."

"Those absolute fuckers," Alice said. "This is unacceptable."

"Alice, it's fine—"

"No. It is far from fine. I put up with this nonsense because it happens on public property. Or at least they have the excuse that taxpayers have the right to know what we do. You are a private citizen, and they should not be scaring you and your daughter by showing up uninvited."

Sara had to admit, the righteous anger on her behalf was not unattractive. She dismissed the image of Alice on her horse, charging into battle like some old-fashioned knight. That was too much of a period drama romance, even for her.

"They were just a little loud. And since we've gone, they'll give up soon, I'm sure."

"I suppose this rather proves your point," Alice said, her voice tight. "One of these days I will learn that you're always right, Sara. Listen, I can speak with Josephine and the gang here. It might not require private security, but we will have to let the police know."

"Oh no, it wasn't that serious."

Alice sighed. "Regardless, they consider that sort of thing a potential point of access. To me. Part of the deal with our security is we let them know anyone within our circle who might be targeted. They won't intrude. If anything they might just intervene and remove any trespassers."

Sara felt her pulse pick up again. "It's not that I don't appreciate it, but you have to understand that I don't want police around my house either. I know you have to trust them with your safety, but that's not the relationship I have with them. I have to raise Libby with the knowledge that the police might not always be on her side as it is."

"Not on her side?" Alice sounded genuinely confused.

Sara waited a moment for the penny to drop. She wasn't about to lie to her biracial daughter about the reality of what the police could be like. And yet, here Sara was calling an actual goddamned royal, not doubting for even a second that Alice would be on their side. What did that say about what Sara had come to expect? It certainly suggested changes to her life that she had neither noticed nor approved.

Alice continued after the loaded silence. "Fuck. Of course. Can you leave it with me? As you say, they might give up now you've escaped them. Well done on that, by the way. Most people would just panic and walk right into it. You really are made of sterner stuff, Ms Marteau."

"It doesn't feel that way."

"Mummy, the bus is coming!"

Sure enough, the next red bus chugging along the road was the one that passed Libby's school and carried on to take Sara to work. The crowd at the bus stop shifted and rippled in preparation, and not for the first time Sara realised they might be waiting for the next one to avoid being pulled into a crush of bodies.

"I have to go. Thank you for listening, and I'll let you know if they're there later I guess? It's not a big deal, swear down."

"That sounded so south London," Alice said, the tension finally leaving her voice. "But yes, please keep in touch. I do hope this is the last inconvenience to your Monday."

"Me too," Sara said, before adding her goodbye. "Me too," she repeated quietly, shoving her phone back in her bag and leading Libby towards the waiting doors of the bus.

Any hopes Sara had of the intrusion ending there were wavering after the number of second glances she received on the short bus journey. Those hopes were downright rocked by the nudges and whispers at the school gates, and all but obliterated by the time she arrived at work to find two men in denim jackets with huge cameras being moved away from the teachers' car park by a pair of police officers.

Ducking the morning assembly, she jogged down the main corridor to her office, closing the door behind her. After a moment's thought, Sara pulled the blinds down on both windows, shutting out perfectly nice sunlight in favour of the harsh overhead lighting.

Finally. She was alone. No one could stare or whisper or point. Sara sank into her office chair, dropping her handbag at her feet. The phone on her desk started ringing, along with her mobile. She silenced both.

Deep breath in… Deep breath out. She hadn't tried yoga breathing since giving birth to Libby, but Sara was ready to clutch at just about any straw to avoid a panic attack.

Her mobile kept lighting up, and so she gave into the inevitable and answered her mother's call. Inès wasted no time on greetings.

"Have you seen the papers? *Zut*, have you seen the photos on six pages here—six!—in *The Sun*!"

"*Maman*, please. Don't buy *The Sun*, we've talked about this. I don't mind what else you read, but that tabloid has a history of lying and breaking the law. We don't give them our money."

"Don't you start with your student politics at me, young lady. *The Bugle*, *The Herald*, you even made *The Guardian* but not the front page."

Sara pinched the bridge of her nose. Just get through this, she told herself. Everything else would be easier than her mother.

"It's a storm in a teacup, nothing more. But after swimming today, can you take Libby back to your house please?" Sara knew that there would be no relaxing until plans for Libby were in place. "I'll get her from yours."

"Why? What's wrong? These photo men following you around my girl? Are they giving you trouble? You tell me, and I'll come down there and show them nobody bothers my baby, I don't care who she's dating."

"*Maman*—"

"You must think about these things, Sara. If these *connards* can get to you, they can get to Libby. What if they're hanging around her school?"

Sara's blood ran cold in her veins. She'd looked, hadn't she? There had been no sign as she dropped Libby off. That added another awkward call to her list, growing by the moment.

"They weren't. She's fine. I've warned the school, and we're dropping her off and picking her up. It's all perfectly safe, *Maman*. I wouldn't put her at risk, you know that."

"I see this princess of yours is nowhere on the scene when the real trouble starts, hmm?" Inès had none of her usual warmth as she spoke, and that was the most troubling part of it all. Inconvenience was one thing, but the last thing Sara wanted was to properly upset her mother.

"She had no idea. I had no idea, until I was about to leave for work."

A knock came at her office door.

"*Maman*, I have to go."

The door opened and Dennis Pritchell, the head teacher and her boss, stepped into the room. Not waiting for her invitation was a bad sign. Sara hung up without letting her mother respond.

"Dennis! Good morning." Sara stood up, smoothing out her suit jacket before extending her hand.

"Did I hear correctly? Were the police called to remove freelance photographers from school property? Paparazzi," Dennis said, pronouncing the word like it physically pained him. "Stalking an area full of vulnerable children...in search of you?"

Sara moved around her desk, the better to plead her case up close. "I can explain—"

"I'm sure you can. I do read the morning papers, Ms Marteau. I see you had an eventful weekend. At the taxpayers' expense, no less."

"Actually—"

"Is this going to be a problem? For the school?" Dennis put his hands on his hips, which, given his all-black suit and shirt, and slight build, just made him look even taller and thinner than he already was. His beard was trimmed to utter precision, and he had a fastidiousness about his appearance and his office that Sara had never been able to match.

"No, I won't allow that. I don't know what you read, I haven't even been online yet, but I can assure you that it won't keep happening. I've already started to deal with it."

"Yes, I'm sure you have. And what about your...friend? I hope you remember we've never made an issue of any teacher's sexuality at this school—"

"And you have no reason to. Not least because that kind of discrimination is illegal, Mr Pritchell." Sara had sworn to keep calm but the hackles on her neck rose all the same.

"Right. Of course. But are they—is your royal acquaintance dealing with it on her end? Since they have all that police protection and whatnot? Surely it should extend to you, if you're involved?"

"I don't have any control over the police."

Dennis looked her up and down, apparently lost in his own thoughts. He seemed to come to some decision at last. "Very well then. At least you're not in front of a class most of the time, which does make it easier. Maybe keep a low profile for now?"

"Gladly." Sara wanted to tell him exactly where he could shove his low profile. The only reason she was even anywhere near royalty was because of her excellence in this particular job, but Dennis had never seemed to appreciate the asset he had inherited on his staff when he had taken over as head. Men like him only noticed the people around them when they were looking for a scapegoat, or trying to take credit for their achievements.

"Budget meeting after lunch. See you there."

"Certainly," Sara said, biting her tongue to say no more.

Dennis walked past her to the door but hesitated before opening it. "Dating a princess, eh? You kept it quiet, the fancy circles you move in."

"I don't see how that's relevant," Sara said.

"Still, I guess we know who to ask next time we need a guest for the school fayre. Ha ha." Dennis exited on that fake laugh, and Sara resisted, just, the urge to hurl the nearest object after him. At least she hadn't ruined a perfectly good stapler.

Sitting back down, she opened her work email, and personal, in neighbouring windows. The unread stared back at her in their hundreds.

Great.

The phones kept silently ringing as she took a deep breath and started scanning for the most urgent that truly needed a reply, ignoring the blatant attempts at fishing for gossip, including from people she hadn't spoken to since school.

Remembering what Inès had said, Sara picked up her mobile to call Libby's school and put them on guard. The alternative didn't bear thinking about. While it rang, she let her mind wander for just a moment to kissing Alice, that brief but exhilarating moment she had initiated.

If her day had proven anything so far is that she was right. It wasn't worth it. Or was it?

Sara forced her attention back to her call, spine straight as she sat in her chair, resolved to get her suddenly derailed life under control.

Alice left Josephine to make apologies, storming away from the event she was due to give a speech at, and heading straight for the car instead. Stuart, not expecting her back so soon, was leaning against the driver's door, sipping at a coffee as he read a newspaper.

"Ma'am?"

"The second Josephine gets in this car, I want you to take us to…where are they based? Not Fleet Street, not anymore. Is it Wapping?"

"I'm not sure I follow," Stuart said, disposing of his coffee and the paper before opening Alice's door for her. "Don't you have another event back at the House?"

"That can be cancelled as well. I want the editor of every tabloid in this country gathered into one room within the hour."

Josephine came scurrying along just in time to hear that last part. "Ma'am? There's just no way that will be possible. We can get one at a time short notice, but it will cause a media firestorm if you yank all those powerful people out of their days."

"I do not give a single damn, Jos." Alice got in the car, punctuating her point with a slam of the door. Stuart and Josephine scrambled to join her. "These hacks have had too much leeway for too long. They can say what they like about me—and we all know they have—but to be stalking Sara already, like some kind of prey... No, I cannot and will not allow this to happen."

"Your Royal Highness—" Josephine began, but Alice silenced her with the ferocity of her warning glare. She was in no mood to be talked down.

"Make the meeting happen, and Stuart, get us on the road to wherever Josephine tells you."

Josephine sighed. "I suppose in the circumstances we should invite them to the palace. It will pique their curiosity if nothing else."

"Good. St James's then. One hour. Stu, step on it."

Alice sank back into her seat as the car revved into life, Stuart steering them back toward main roads with his usual efficient driving. Josephine typed frantically into her phone and then answered as soon as it began to ring. Used to tuning out conversations, Alice ignored the muttered words, focusing on the lecture she would have to give to the tabloid editors.

A few minutes later, Stuart met her gaze in the rear-view mirror while they were stopped at traffic lights.

"Ma'am... Alice...you can't do this. You know that, don't you?" He licked his lips quickly, before carrying on. "If you go in to these people and say she's special, tell them to leave her alone, give her special treatment... that's painting a target on her back. It's a few rogue paps now, but if you make an issue of it then the entire industry will devote themselves to finding out why you don't want Ms Marteau in the spotlight."

"What did I say about not wanting to discuss this?" Alice didn't mean to snap, but that was how it came out.

"I heard you. And you know that I respect you as both my boss and my commanding officer. So think how bad an idea this must be for me to speak up anyway, ma'am. It must be important enough to be worth me doing that."

Alice thumped her first against the arm rest. Damned if Stuart didn't have a point. In all the years he'd worked for her, since six months after they returned from Afghanistan, they'd enjoyed plenty of conversations and laughs, but he had never spoken back to her or challenged an order.

"I just..."

"I know, they're bang out of order. But you charging in there becomes the story. This is a boat you don't want to rock, and you'd say the same if your mum or your brother was suggesting this plan to you." Stuart eased the car back into moving traffic, eyes back on the road.

"You're right," Alice said finally, with one more thump of the arm rest for good measure. "Jos, call off the meeting. Never mind. I'll go do my events."

"Are you sure?" Josephine put the phone down right away. "I really do think Stuart is right, saying nothing is best. We're working on some perimeter security for Ms Marteau, though."

"Good enough." Alice watched London slip past outside the window, and tried to tell herself she wasn't just letting Sara down a second time. "Let me know when the security is in place."

Chapter 17

As the week rolled on, Alice was relieved to see no further pictures of Sara appear in the press, but equally sorry not to hear from the woman herself. Hardly unreasonable given the circumstances, but it seemed especially cruel so soon after the moment where they had first had something genuine between them.

Alice was only too aware of her own shortcomings when it came to all things romance. Her sheltered existence left her at a near permanent disadvantage in that one particular area.

Returning from a slightly tedious day opening a hospital wing in Leeds and seeing a new youth centre in Hull, Alice was looking forward to a rare free evening without a formal dinner or any kind of performance being put in front of her. While she usually enjoyed a night at the opera or ballet, or even the odd football match, it was pleasant to have the working day end before sundown. Not getting dressed up and made up was just another bonus.

As they approached the familiar streets of Westminster, mostly deserted now the evening rush hour had wrapped up, Stuart let down the partition between them.

"Your Royal Highness, we've just had a request from KP to take you to dinner there."

"Oh, really? Can you tell them I'd rather not?"

"Your brother apparently said that any refusal was to be met with a 'get your lazy backside over here.' Just the messenger, ma'am."

Alice nodded and leaned back against the leather seat. She had been so close to peace and solitude, and with it a chance to call and check in with Sara. Oh well. Maybe this way she would make less of a fool of herself.

Kensington Palace always did feel more residential once she got inside. It had been their home before Queen Caroline ascended the throne, succeeding her own father and Alice's grandfather when Alice was already eleven. Before that they'd been left mostly in peace, with most of the press attention falling on Alice's parents, with both herself and James shielded from anything but the most official of photographs.

As soon as Alice stepped inside the family quarters, she was tackled by the small hurricane that was Anne.

"Auntie Alice! You came at last!"

"I only saw you on Monday, scamp." Alice had indeed been at the same afternoon event over at the House. "Is that tummy rumbling waiting for me to serve up dinner?"

"No, Rupes and I ate in the nursery. This is too late for us, silly. We have homework and baths to take before bed."

"That's right, I can smell you from here! That must be what happens when you only take one bath a year…"

"I do not!"

"What, not even one?"

"That's not what I mean!" Anne was at her most indignant, hands on her hips and little foot stamping to make the point. Alice struggled to keep a straight face, and she was saved by Annabel arriving, Rupert close on her heels.

"Are you tormenting my child?" Annabel greeted Alice with the customary kiss to the cheek.

"No more than usual. I was summoned?"

"Sorry, I have told James not to do that, but he does enjoy messing with your plans. Something about pulling rank I think."

Alice scoffed. "Typical army boy, trying to throw his weight around while the real parts of the forces get the job done."

"I heard that, you insufferable blue job. You all think you're so special just because they let you have a joystick. We fly our own choppers, you know." James came to join them with his usual long and confident strides. Her brother had a way of always seeming to be in a hurry.

"I'm surprised you remember the slang, since you enlisted and then got out of there as quickly as you could, big brother." Alice bumped James with her hip as he came to stand beside her. "Now why was I dragged from an evening of catching up on soap operas and a long bath to eat at your table?"

"Come through, we'll get the plates filled and then talk about it," James replied, leading them into the small dining room with its table for eight. Alice shook her head, realising for most normal people nothing about that would be small, let alone having a separate dining area in the first place. She could just hear Sara mocking her for the assumption.

They sat to something that smelled delicious, heaped plates of rice and vegetables and some kind of chicken that had Alice reaching for her fork right away. Then she noticed another place was set at the table.

"Are we waiting for someone?"

"That sounds like my cue," her mother replied, entering in a flurry of motion where she handed off her coat and bag to one of the household staff. "How are we all?"

"Very well, Mummy," James replied, seemingly for them all. "Thanks for coming."

"I simply go where the staff tell me I am needed. And apparently tonight, my grandchildren need me. Now, where are my cuddles? I am the queen, you know. I can command them." There was no need to, as Anne launched herself from her seat, soon followed by Rupert. They snuggled into each side of their grandmother, producing her first genuine smile since she had joined them.

"Granny, Granny, are you coming riding with us this weekend?"

"Unfortunately not, Annie dearest. Granny will be all the way in Inverness. Do you know where that is?"

"Far away?"

"Yes, it is." Caroline turned to James. "Should we not be looking at maps in her lessons by now?"

"Speaking of lessons," Annabel said, all smiles as she took charge of the conversation. Alice never liked her sister-in-law more than when she was soothing the sometimes choppy waters of family conversation. "We wanted you both to know that we have a school choice for both children, thanks to the help from Ms Marteau...from Sara. Dr Naylor helped, too."

"This is the woman in the papers with you?" Caroline said, addressing Alice directly for the first time.

Alice reached for her wine glass. "Yes. The very same. She has been quite invaluable, and very kind to Rupert throughout."

"Well, you can let her off the hook now, dear sister," James replied. "This terribly modern little school is just across the river, and they can accommodate individual teaching plans, which is just the ticket for different learning styles. We'll visit as a family soon to seal the deal, but it seems to suit our purposes very well without having to make anything a matter of public record."

"I still do not see why it was necessary to distract the press with some imaginary romance," Caroline said. Then she flagged down the server and requested her wine be replaced with a double Scotch. "Other than to remind us all that it is quite beyond time for Alice to be settling down with someone appropriate."

"You could do a lot worse than someone like Sara," Annabel said, her voice soft. "She has a way of seeing through the nonsense that is quite refreshing to be around."

"Nonetheless, I had my staff liaise with Josephine in your office about some suitable introductions. There are some names for you to consider. A few that surprised me, I confess. I had no idea that the Duchess of Glamorgan was that way inclined."

"Elizabeth? Is she not my third cousin?" Alice had run through the family tree quickly in her head.

"Yes, but that is hardly unheard of in our circles. Very practical sort of girl, good at public speaking I seem to remember." Her mother gave Alice an encouraging nod as she said it. As though that was the kind of thing a person looked for in a romantic match.

James snorted, barely suppressing a laugh. Alice resisted the urge to kick him under the table.

"I did tell you that this was a colossal waste of time," Alice said eventually. "Not one of these names so far can hold a candle to someone like Sara, and that is the benchmark right now."

"Did we not already dismiss this silly notion about dating a commoner?"

"Come along, Mummy," James said, interrupting for Alice. "That is one area on which you have little room to talk. I, for one, was quite impressed with Ms Marteau. Knows her onions, and she has handled the royal circus so far like a pro. 'Lice here could do a lot worse."

"That's true." Alice found herself in the rare position of agreeing with her older brother. "Whatever happens going forward, Sara or otherwise, one is quite capable of arranging one's own dates. But enough about my love life, how was your week, Mummy?"

"Oh, it was quite lovely," the queen said, settling back with her drink into storytelling mode. Alice heaved a sigh of relief and leaned back in her chair to listen.

She might have lost any chance with Sara, thanks to the paparazzi proving exactly why they were not to be trusted, but that didn't leave Alice any more inclined to be fixed up with some acquaintance of her mother's. No, she had survived all these years outside of a relationship, and Alice would continue to do so. Unless Sara had a sudden change of heart, perhaps. But there was surely no chance of that happening.

"You like her, am I right?" Annabel said, sneaking up on Alice as she settled into one of the large leather sofas in the sitting room. James had disappeared to read bedtime stories to the children, and Caroline had returned to her solitude at Buckingham Palace. "All this 'Sara or otherwise'... you really do like her."

"Say what?" Alice stalled by taking a sip of her brandy. She used to loathe the stuff, but had built up a tolerance having been offered it after dinner so often. Now the sharp and smoky taste was a comfort on her tongue.

"Sara. This may have been a favour to us, but somewhere along the line you ended up smitten, I think. I can see it whenever we talk about her."

"Just the novelty of someone out of the ordinary." Alice refused to make eye contact, knowing she would give herself away. "How often do we get to know anyone beyond a handshake and some small talk, really?"

"Even so. A few dinners in London would have kept the press happy, but you went all out. Spending time with Libby, that impressive little flying date. You were rather bringing your A game, and now that you can walk away... I suspect you don't quite want to."

"Don't you have anything better to do than speculate about my love life? Besides, you heard Mummy. She's scouring the peerage for a forgotten lesbian daughter somewhere. The token queers of the aristocracy are about to be foisted on me like piano lessons were, and probably with just as much success."

"Does Sara know you might be interested?"

Alice felt her cheeks flush. Damn.

Annabel cackled on noticing. "Well, that answers that question. Has anything happened between the two of you?"

"Perhaps. Nothing significant. But all it led to was a conversation about how she has no intention of being in the public eye, which the fucking paparazzi followed up perfectly by deciding to stalk her this week."

"Have you tried calling in a favour? Warning them off?"

"As much as humanly possible, yes. But you know they're a law unto themselves. They always make just enough money for the risk to be worth it, even more so if the decent ones have been scared away."

Annabel took Alice's glass and topped up both of their drinks from the decanter on the table. "And have you thought about convincing her?"

"What do you mean?" Of course, Alice had thought about convincing Sara. It was all she could think of. She leaned forward, waiting for Annabel to arrange herself cross-legged on the other end of the sofa. With her hair pinned up and make-up faded after a long day, the princess looked quite like a regular mother-of-two relaxing before bedtime.

"You cannot imagine how reluctant I was to join this circus when James started chatting me up. I was quite content to be the university girlfriend that was kept on the hush-hush, fully expecting him to ditch me as soon as we graduated, and he had the world at his feet."

"Still took him long enough to get serious about it all, though." Alice had given James considerable grief during those years for stringing Annabel along. It had been a relief when he finally saw sense and proposed to her.

"We were young, neither of us were ready. I wanted some kind of career, even just for a little while. Even now I'm still pushing to be able to have some real work outside of The Firm. I might finally have convinced your mother, by the way."

Alice raised her glass in salute. "Well done you. What sort of thing?"

"Running a charity, of sorts. Not just being the patron. Helping LGBTQIA+ youth who want to work in fashion and media. There are so many barriers if you don't go to the right schools or have parents who can support you through internships... Since so many still have issues at home or none at all, this is a way to level the playing field and give them access." Annabel spoke with real conviction, not just regurgitating from some press release. It was clear from the gleam in her eyes and the broad smile that she was genuinely proud of the idea.

"Sounds wonderful. And necessary." Alice drained her glass and set it aside.

"You could always come on board as patron. It can only help." Annabel turned that glint in her eye on Alice.

"Shall I say yes now, since we both know you always get your way in the end, Annabel?"

"Probably wise. Now, about this paramour of yours... Are you really going to give up so easily? Settle for whichever horsey distant cousin can be shaken from the tree for you?" Annabel fetched the bottle, refilling for both of them.

"I suppose I could make my case more strongly, but how? What would show her that I want to really try dating, and remove all the hassle?" Alice had been puzzling over that central conundrum right from the start. Whatever she thought to try, real life was bound to find a way to intrude and ruin it all.

"Take her away from it all; see if you can talk her into the idea of a bubble together, drowning out all the noise. Far from the baying packs of press, far from the people who think they own a portion of you. Pick somewhere miles from anywhere and get to know each other. Then you'll know for sure you really tried."

"She has a child. I can't just whisk her away. There's her grandmother, I suppose..."

"Take them on the trip if you have to, show them you are serious about the whole package. Then leave them on a beach somewhere pretty and get some quality time alone with Sara. That's what the balancing act is always going to be, until Libby is grown and off to university." Annabel leaned back against the couch cushions, closing her eyes for a moment. "Just be sure how much you do want her before you turn her world upside down. Don't just break things and run."

Alice finished her drink and stood, ready to be alone with her thoughts. Annabel stood to see her out, giving her a hug as they approached the door to their apartment.

"Be happy, Alice. You deserve to be."

"Well, I can try. When did you get so wise, anyway?"

"Must have been while I was getting my hair done. Goodnight, I'll give James your love, and the children."

"I'm so pleased the school issue is sorted. If nothing else comes of this, I will always be glad to have helped even a little."

"We are grateful." Annabel kissed Alice on the cheek. "Rupert is going to get to be all the support he needs so he can truly be himself."

"Goodnight." She headed downstairs to the waiting car, wishing it was easier to turn down the chauffeured escort, to be able to walk through Hyde Park and head home that way. That kind of freedom didn't exist for Alice, certainly not while in London. Maybe with some planning, dressing down, and a couple of inconspicuous protection officers some evenings, but usually it was more trouble than it was worth.

Instead, she was left to her thoughts for just the few minutes of driving, and then the walk up to her own apartments when they reached St James's.

As soon as she stepped into her private office, she felt her resolve settle on Annabel's suggestion. Sitting down at the sturdy desk that had once been her grandfather's, Alice pulled out a sheet of her personalised letter stock and picked up her favoured fountain pen.

If she truly wanted Sara, it was time to stop hiding behind excuses.

Chapter 18

Sara woke up to a busy Saturday as always, the tasks neglected during the week all waiting for her. Even more so than usual, since this weekend was her turn to host the playdate for Libby's little posse of friends. It rarely required more than providing food and a clear space to play, but first and foremost came the shopping, which Sara did not have much time for. She'd been dragged around markets and cute little food stores by Inès growing up, because to her shopping and cooking were competitive sports. However, these days, when she could get away with it, Sara simply ordered her groceries online.

When they arrived home Libby busied herself with looking for some game or other that she wanted to share with her friends, leaving Sara ample time to get organised in the kitchen. The pizzas slotted into the oven, and she started chopping up vegetables for a kid-friendly arrangement that used fun animal shapes to disguise the healthy nature of it all. Inès had made no such accommodations for Sara as a child, because the French did not accept criticism of their cooking even from their own children, or so it always seemed to her. Still, Sara had learned a lot about the sensory and visual presentation of food when it came to children, and she was happy to bring that part of her work home with her.

It had been quite nice, the past few weeks, to finally be something other than Libby's full-time mum. Dating a princess might be something out of a cheesy Christmas movie, but it had awoken a part of Sara, the part of her that longed for a grown-up person to share her nights with, as well as all the little joys and stresses of regular life.

That was before she even got started on sex. Ever since that mistake of a kiss with Alice, a certain hunger had clicked into gear for the first time in too long. A faint ache had settled in, and despite her best attempts during stolen time in the shower or lying in bed late at night, Sara hadn't been able to successfully scratch the itch. Seeing Jasmin, clearly fresh from a night of misbehaving with her latest fling, only served to set Sara's teeth on edge even more. Not that she was jealous. Not about Kathleen, certainly. But just the prospect of that intimacy, it tugged at her like an invisible fishing line.

When the doorbell rang, Sara had just finished putting everything out for their guests, but they were still early. She wasn't used to that, since getting young kids out of the door was normally enough to make everyone slightly late for everything. Parents tended to spend half their lives apologising.

"Come in, come in," she said, opening the front door. "You know you don't need an invitation..."

Sara trailed off when standing in front of her was one casually dressed member of the royal family, and her familiar protection officer hanging back by the gate.

"Alice?"

"Sorry to drop in unannounced, but I was rather hoping we could talk about my letter."

"Your letter?"

Alice shot a nervous glance back over her shoulder. "Would it be okay if—?"

"No, come in. Of course. Does he—?"

"Stuart will keep watch out here. And don't be alarmed, but I believe his colleague is already around the back. In case he startles you at the kitchen door."

"Right." Sara didn't know whether she was coming or going. "Sorry, come in properly," she said, ushering Alice past her with a wave and closing the front door behind her. "Uh, welcome to our home... I guess."

"Mummy?" Libby peered around the top of the stairs, her face breaking into a grin. "Hey, it's Alice! Are you coming to my playdate too?"

"You didn't invite me!" Alice called back, hands on her hips in mock indignation. "Maybe next time; I just need a quick word with your mum."

"Okay! Tell Rupes and Annie I said hi and I can't wait to play again!"

Sara gestured towards the kitchen, her home feeling like a doll's house after seeing Alice in palaces, most of which could fit this entire property into one of its medium-sized cupboards.

"I didn't know you could do this sort of thing. Unscheduled visits, I mean." Sara perched on the stool at her simple breakfast bar, wishing it was a bit tidier. "Wait, did you say something about a letter?"

"Yes. I think it possibly arrived yesterday. Or today, even. First class is not what it was."

"Plus, in this house we have something of a mail magpie. Libby?" Sara called out, knowing the thud of footsteps would follow almost instantly. Sure enough, Libby appeared with envelopes in hand. "Is that the mail you picked up yesterday morning and today too?"

"Yes," Libby said, handing it over. "I didn't open any of it."

"I see that. But I also need to see the post in case there's anything important. This can't just disappear into your room for days, Libs. Thank you for these, you can go back to setting up your room."

"Something smells nice," Alice said as they waited for Libby to fully beat her retreat.

"Pizza. Lots of pineapple. Already allocated for guests, sorry. So, this letter?"

"I realised I forgot to really specify how you should reply. Should you even want to. We were heading south today anyway, for some cricket thing James wants me to go to in his stead, and I thought I would swing by for initial thoughts. Sorry, seems more of an ambush now that I know you haven't read it."

"Texting was still an option. Or email," Sara said. "Sounds to me like someone got impatient. This isn't anything to do with Rupert and his schooling, is it? Do you need me to sign more things now a school is settled on?"

Alice took a step closer, moving in from the kitchen doorway. "No, nothing that important or official. The letter was, well, personal in nature."

"I'm not sure I understand." Although Sara did, in fact understand. It would be impossible not to, with Alice firmly in her personal space. The sensible thing would be to restate their boundaries, to run from the room if need be, but once again Sara felt that magnetic tug of Alice's presence.

Some low-level vibration that made her want to stay as close to Alice as possible.

"We discussed, in the abstract, why dating for two people like us was probably not the greatest idea," Alice said, holding Sara's gaze the whole time. There was something utterly disarming about her. Had Alice's eyes always been such a steely blue? They almost seemed to shift colours from grey to blue, brightening as she talked.

"And I thought we had settled on that." Sara glanced towards the door, making sure they were still alone. "Kiss or no kiss."

"Ah, but there definitely was a kiss," Alice said. "A very pleasant one, if I recall. The sort of kiss that might tempt a person to want to do that again."

"But then I wake up to intruders at my door."

Alice nodded. "Yes, and that was not acceptable. Do you trust that I will do everything possible to prevent that happening again? I mean, at the moment there isn't anything more to report on, is there?"

"Not at the moment." Sara had wondered about that, when the paparazzi disappeared just as readily as they had appeared in the first place. Was that the silent power of the palace at work? Or something more personal on Alice's part—a threat, a favour? Either way, it sent a little thrill down Sara's spine that such a move would be taken on her behalf.

"Unless I can persuade you otherwise. Which I mean in the most noble, respectful way possible. This is not about nagging you to give in or pushing past boundaries. I suppose I just hope that the fact that you kissed me—twice, technically—means there is interest on your side?"

Sara looked away, pretending to be fascinated by the plastic cups she had set out for the children. How was this happening, in her tiny, everyday kitchen? Had Alice ever had to take the tram to IKEA after work for party supplies? Sara was willing to bet her life that she hadn't.

"I'm not going to pretend I'm not attracted to you," Sara said. "I did make a move when I had no excuse. I mean, you are...you. Gorgeous, confident, powerful. A princess."

"Which is just something I was born into," Alice said.

"But still very much reality. One that doesn't overlap with mine. I know, I know that I'm more than what that reduces me to, but as far as the press are concerned that's all I'll ever be. A single mum to a biracial child.

Daughter of immigrants. Middle class at best because of my career. Living in south London. Which is to say that I'm not someone the people would pick for their princess. Or your family for that matter."

"Aside from the fact that I do not care in the least who the people, or my family, would pick for me, what if I could show you another reality?" There was that hint of a swagger again, the easy confidence that Sara found more and more attractive, much to her annoyance. "The good side of all this? Where we do get some privacy and have ridiculous amounts of fun. Or all the experiences you could have with me that aren't available to just anyone. That would be something, no?"

"I've never been big into that whole Cinderella idea," Sara said. "I know most people might be waiting to be swept off their feet. But I like my life the way it is. I'm not sitting around expecting a fairy tale to arrive someday."

"And I am no Prince Charming, but I do try now and then. Think what issues we could bring attention to, the charities we could help. The children we could console and inspire, simply by being in the conversation."

"That's your big pitch? We should date to do charity work?"

"Is that such a bad idea when you've dedicated your life to public service? Surely you deserve the little luxuries too, and if that lets other people dream that it might be their turn one day, well..."

"You're impossible." Sara folded her arms across her chest, then thought better of it. "I can't believe you're standing here, like this, in my house."

Alice didn't smile, but her look was intent, focused. "It's all you have to do, isn't it? Believe, just a tad."

The doorbell rang at the worst possible moment.

"Just coming!" Sara called out.

"I should go," Alice said, with a reluctant glance at the back door. "Do I have your permission to make a real go of it? No more faking the dating?"

Sara bit her bottom lip. For as much as she had tried to convince herself that Alice's world would only bring her pain and hassle, some part of her cried out for the thrill of that kiss, of once in a lifetime chances that never came around. Who in their right mind rejected a princess? Who in their right mind rejected a woman like Alice?

"Fine. Make your case, but it better be a good. I have a busy job, and a daughter who comes before anything. If you can convince me that seeing you is viable along with all of that? Then you deserve a chance."

"God, I love that confidence. I wish I could bottle it, for difficult days."

Sara scoffed. "You're pretty cocky yourself, strolling in here because I didn't reply to your handwritten letter fast enough. Anyway. My guests."

"I'll see you soon." Alice moved towards the kitchen door, but the only route to it meant passing right in front of Sara. She hesitated as their bodies came into close proximity, catching Sara's eye. Alice gave a cheeky grin. "Goodbye. For now."

"For now," Sara said, and as Alice leaned in Sara let her eyelids flutter closed. Instead of the friendly kiss to the cheek she expected, Sara was suddenly aware of Alice's fingers clasping around her hand. Looking down, she watched as Alice drew in Sara's hand and gently kissed her right on the curve of her knuckle. The subtle woody tone of Alice's perfume tickled at Sara's nose, even over the pizza scents, but just as quickly she had moved past.

Oh, damn. Sara rubbed her hand, where her skin was still tingling.

Alice opened the door with a nod to her waiting officer, and in just a few strides of those long legs, she was gone.

Conscious that people were waiting for her, Sara only lingered a moment longer to savour the brief contact. Had she just set herself up for complete mortification? Somehow, she didn't seem to mind. She pocketed Alice's letter, sure that she would read it more than once, and went to greet her guests.

Chapter 19

LONDON HERALD, 22ND JULY

LIKE ENGLAND'S CRICKET DREAM, IS IT OVER?

Perhaps it's hard to find time as busy working women, especially with a child in the equation, but our royal reporters confirm a definite cold front in Princess Alice's romantic life.

Did we expect too much from the perennially single royal? Or has her next big prospect simply got cold feet? Even if they haven't been spotted together, there's still hope that HRH might get HERS. No news is good news, even in royal circles. Have they slipped off the radar on purpose? Or is the game over before it ever really began?

"You really think this will work?" Alice fussed with the baseball cap for the tenth time, flicking at the bobbed dark wig that peeked out under the brim. "And you're sure I don't look like a footballer sneaking home from his mistress's house?"

"That's oddly specific," Esther replied, watching the Saturday evening traffic in the rear-view mirror. They had parked outside a row of clothes shops, already closed for the day, but the rest of the street was lit up with bar fronts and kebab shops, some kind of supermarket dominating one side of the road. If she had ever been in this part of London before, Alice had no recollection of it.

"Is the protection car deathly obvious?" Alice was unable to see it without turning around in the backseat and staring out of the side window.

"Nope, just another Ford on a street full of them. How did they take the request?"

"Stuart says his car is more reliable than our stock anyway. He's happier behind the wheel of his own car anytime."

"All this to go to the cinema?" Esther fiddled with the radio in her Land Rover. "You're a better girlfriend than me."

"Girlfriend is a ways off," Alice replied. "A goal, of sorts. This is about proving we can be regular folks."

"I would have thought that's the last thing anyone wants to be, dating you."

"Yes, well. Sara's not like the grasping social climbers we see out in Chelsea every other weekend. No merging of the family estates or whatever else. But once we get over this hurdle, I do plan on dazzling her with all the benefits of my position, since you asked."

"And the benefits of a few positions too, right?" Esther snorted with laughter at her own joke.

Alice rolled her eyes, but with great fondness. "Remind me why we're best friends again?"

"Because I have all the juicy pictures of your RAF initiation and haven't sold them all these years?"

"Fair." Alice squirmed in her seat, eager to get out and stretch her legs but not wanting to draw a second's more attention than necessary. "This isn't too dressed down, is it?"

"I don't think white tie goes with the cap, pal."

"Ha ha. I just don't want to look out of place. This is all about blending in, but I don't want Sara to look right past me."

Esther turned in the driver's seat. "You look great. Not eye-catching, but lovely. She's daft if she isn't glad to see you."

"Speak of the devil." Alice nodded to where Sara was crossing the road, a few cars down. "I'd better go head her off then. Wish me luck?"

"You do realise you could probably issue a proclamation ordering her to date you, right? And that you already are? I don't know why you're suddenly going all James Bond about it now."

"Maybe I just realised she's worth it," Alice replied. "Anyway, thanks for the ride. I'll head back with the protection officers, so you're off the hook."

"Just get back to their car before you turn into a pumpkin, yeah?"

"Always."

Esther grabbed Alice's forearm. "Be careful. No girl is worth your safety, you know that? You have nothing to prove to anyone about what a good catch you are, Al."

"Careful, might remember that you care about me. Thanks, though. I've done worse, remember? With your help usually."

Esther gave a nod, and Alice let herself out of the car. Checking both ways, she jogged after Sara, catching up to her in the small crowd milling around outside the cinema.

"Hey."

"What?" Sara barely glanced up from her phone. She looked pretty and relaxed in her fitted black dress, a denim jacket over it to keep things casual. Instead of heels, she had opted for slightly worn-in Converse, letting Alice comfortably keep her height advantage. "Oh," she said, on second glance. "Oh, that's good. Very sneaky. Hello, you."

"Not bad, huh?"

"I wouldn't try and get through passport control or anything, but yeah. Now I know who to call for my next jewel heist."

"No need for a heist, I can just ask for the keys, remember?" Alice risked a joke. The sooner they got fully comfortable with their status, the easier it would be. "Now, what kind of movie have I trusted you to pick?"

"I was tempted to see if you'd suffer through the latest Disney cartoon, but honestly it's not that often I get to see something above a PG rating."

"I trust you," Alice replied. "Usually when I see the film it's at some premiere, and I always miss the start thanks to all the handshaking in the foyer."

"That's a hard life, right there. Popcorn?"

"Is it even a cinema trip without it?" Alice looked around at the lines in front of the snack counters. No one gave her a second glance, and her shoulders dropped an inch. "Now, this is a national secret that you can never disclose but... I like to take a bag of Revels and tip them into the popcorn. That's right, not just the regular chocolate ones, but the toffee, the peanut *and* the coffee. I'm a rebel that way."

Sara gave Alice a slow, incredulous look. "I don't know if I can keep seeing someone who would do that. In public, no less! You forgot the orange ones, though."

"Don't knock it 'til you try it," Alice said. "I know, this is early in a relationship to be getting experimental, but that's just how I am."

"Full of surprises. Fine, you can mix your chocolate in with the popcorn, but that means I'm going to be skipping straight to wine instead of a soft drink. You brought this on yourself."

Alice was so caught up in the ritual of it all, juggling the popcorn box and their plastic wine glasses, listening to Sara relay about the last time she brought Libby to a Trolls movie in this same theatre, that she didn't think to ask again what film they were seeing. Only when Sara handed over the tickets to the teenager checking them with a torch, did Alice happen to check the screen.

Of all the things she had been expecting, the word 'chainsaw' was not even close, and judging by everything else in the title, they were in for a very violent time.

"Is this...a horror movie?" Alice said, pleased when Sara led them instinctively to the back corner of the seating. All the better not to be noticed. "As in, blood and guts and psychopaths with power tools?"

"That's a great summary!" Sara sat down. "Wait, you're okay with horror, right?"

"I—" Alice fumbled for the words. "Of course. I just expected something more like a romantic comedy?"

"Not really my scene," Sara said. "I mean, I can cry over one on a Friday night with the best of them, but when I come out to the cinema I want to really get the benefit of all the effects, you know? So you get the proper scare."

"Right. The proper scare." Alice handed Sara's wine glass to her, before downing her own drink in one gulp. "Not that a mere film would scare me."

"That's what I figured, after flying planes and all. Oh, I'm so glad we have this in common. What a great start, right?" Sara looked Alice straight in the eye, as if waiting for her to flinch.

"Right." Alice nodded, even though her jaw felt so tight that her head shouldn't move at all. Was it too late to press the panic button in her pocket and have the protection officers rush in? She was sure at least one had followed her into the cinema and would be sitting within a few rows, anyway. Ever since her teens Alice had asked to ditch them, and even when they humoured her she knew that they were still nearby, still guarding her.

Then Sara made the simple motion of taking Alice's right hand in her left, squeezing gently as the popcorn was wedged into the limited space between each of their legs. The lights dimmed as commercials started on the screen, and despite her apprehension, Alice found herself enjoying the anonymity in a room full of strangers again.

And the soft pressure of Sara's fingers helped. Really helped. Alice found herself unable to focus on anything but that, ignoring the commercials for cars and dating websites. By the time the movie trailers started, Alice had settled quite well, sinking down in the bucket seat and stretching her long legs out comfortably enough. The cinema itself seemed newly refurbished, and the room wasn't crowded, with small groups and couples spread out well across the rows.

Then the first trailer began, complete with a bloodcurdling scream. Alice jumped. Of course the previews would be for similar movies. She used her free hand to grip the armrest as flashing images promised blood, guts, and more screaming. Attractive women ran from things. Men lurked in shadows. Despite the jump cuts, the plot was obvious from even a few seconds of footage.

Alice took a deep breath.

"Looks terrible," Sara said, leaning over to whisper. "Can't wait to see it." She laughed, the sound blotted out by some kind of roar from the speakers. Alice gave a smile in return, hoping it wasn't too weak. One way or another, she was going to get through this experience.

When Sara found Alice in the foyer, she had at least overcome the urge to throw up.

"Hey," Sara said, rubbing an instinctive hand over Alice's back and shoulders. "So you're not a big fan of scary films, huh?"

"I did try, I swear."

"Oh, I saw that. You were gripping my arm so hard you almost broke the skin. The part where you whimpered like one of your horses and hid your face in my shoulder? You definitely didn't wuss out on me in there."

Alice forced a smile, although Sara's warmth was already making the whole terror situation seem far off and ridiculous. "I'm a grown woman, a few murderous tree surgeons should be bearable."

"Well, first of all, this isn't your day job. No sense of duty or obligation here. You get to like or dislike things, Alice, and not go along just to be polite."

"Ah."

"And secondly, I think this might be the first time I really get to have you, as a person. Human after all! Do you know how confident and unflappable you are all the time? That's almost as intimidating as the press following you around, or everyone knowing who you are."

Alice stared at Sara, not quite believing what she'd heard. "You…wait, you didn't think I was human?"

"I'm quite sure you are human, but you're so impressive and polished all the time that it's nice to get a glimpse of the real person underneath. One who gets flustered, or scared of gory films. I'm impressed you let me see this side of you. I promise, it's a compliment."

"Then I suppose I accept. Do I still look like I'm going to pass out?"

Sara reached out to touch Alice's cheek, her fingers gentle as she stroked the skin there for a moment. "No, you're pale but not in the fainting way. Shall we go outside?"

"Don't you want to finish the movie?" Alice gathered her remaining pride, ready to face down the rest of the gore fest.

"I'm not a sadist. My place isn't far from here, do you think you could come back for a drink? Is that even…is that weird?"

"My security will follow us, but otherwise that is more than fine with me. Unless you have a chainsaw-wielding maniac in your kitchen, in which case I might have to politely decline."

"You're safe. Unless my mother has taken up landscaping hedges without telling me, anyway. She took babysitting duty tonight."

"Then lead the way." Alice enjoyed the closeness as Sara linked her arm in Alice's, guiding her towards the front of the cinema and out into the London evening. There had been rain at some point, the pavements slick beneath their feet, but it was perfectly pleasant walking weather. Alice sent a quick text to Stuart, and sure enough a car pulled out and followed along at a respectful distance as they made their way back to Sara's.

"This is nice," Sara said. "We could be anyone, anywhere. It's not too weird for you, is it?"

"No, more of a welcome change," Alice replied. "I really am grateful for my life, but sometimes this kind of peace is just priceless. Sometimes I think I could step back, do less in public every day. But as long as I remain single, without a family like James has for example, it seems selfish to hold any of myself back. Mummy is not getting any younger either, hardly fair to leave all the work to her."

"Responsible to a fault. I must tell you, that is a nice change for me. Most people aren't interested in dating when they find out you're a single mum, and there's finding the time to even go out... I'm glad we're doing this."

"Me too." Alice saw her chance as they stepped into a quieter side street. Turning towards Sara, she placed a hand on her hip and pulled her closer. This time when they kissed it was slow and intentional, neither of them taken by surprise. Alice drank in the velvet softness of Sara's lips, so full and inviting. Their tongues grazed lightly, and Alice felt the flutter of anticipation all the way down to her toes.

"That was worth waiting for," Sara said. "You get more convincing by the minute. In your arguments about why I should date you."

"Good." Alice kissed her again, mostly because she could. They were back in motion by the time her protective detail pulled into the street, and Alice didn't recognise Sara's house until they were right outside. In her own defence, most of the houses on the street were all but identical.

Libby was already tucked up in bed, but Inès greeted them with a knowing smile. Alice had expected privacy, but Sara excused herself for a moment and dashed upstairs, leaving Alice alone with the small but formidable figure of her mother.

"Thank you for watching Libby," Alice said after the silence stretched out too long. "We both appreciate the chance to spend some time together. Although I do love spending time with Libby too, of course. I know they come as a real package deal."

"Mmmhmm." Inès filled the kettle and switched it on. "Are your men outside coming in for a drink?"

"They won't while on duty, no. I'm sure Sara explained that we're being very careful with this whole dating thing. You have my word she will be well protected the whole time."

Inès set three mugs out on the counter, but never took her eyes off Alice. Shorter than Sara, with snowy white hair, she had a particularly delicate build. Her eyes were tired but kind, impossibly dark brown as she took in every detail of Alice, right down to the baseball cap which she removed with an embarrassed little laugh.

"She's a phenomenal woman, my daughter. Doesn't waste her time on dating idiots, so you must be doing something right. But I will not see her hurt, or scared. If you are going to be around her, you find a way to keep those photo psychos away from her, hmm?"

"I will. And I will treat her right in all ways, I promise. No title exempts me from that."

"No title ever stopped someone from breaking hearts, either. But I believe you. I believe that you mean it, anyway. Tea?" It felt like there was a test in the question.

"Love a coffee, if you're having one." Alice watched as Inès reached for the cafetière, the flicker of a smile across her lips. "Just milk for me."

"Milk," Inès said with a sigh. "You English always know how to ruin a perfectly good coffee."

"Sorry." Alice almost recanted, but Inès had already poured a grudging splash of milk into the inky black coffee.

"Alors, you have a plan for all this? To show her how it's not all dangerous out there at your side?" Inès stirred the coffee and handed it over. "Because I am still surprised she agreed to it."

"I am, too. But yes, I do rather have a plan for us, including a grand gesture or two. Now one of those, I need your blessing for—may I call you Inès?"

"You may."

"Well, Inès. Let's be quick before Sara comes back down, but here's what I had in mind…"

As Alice made her excuses to go upstairs in search of Sara, Inès started on her new mission, accosting Stuart where he waited just outside the front door.

"We're really not supposed to come in, ma'am. Thank you for thinking of us."

"Nonsense," Inès said, waving her hand as though she'd never even heard of security. Alice did her best to hold back a laugh as she crept higher on the staircase. "Surely one outside is enough, *non*?"

"We prefer—"

"You come in; you eat. You take some back for your boy in the car. Everyone is happy. I cannot have guests in my home, protecting my daughter no less, and not provide some nourishment. Back in France it would be enough to make the republic fall, letting my guests go unfed."

"I suppose I am a little hungry. We don't usually eat on duty."

Alice decided to put him out of his misery. "Stuart, old boy. Please come in here and try the food. That's a direct order, my man."

She jogged up the rest of the stairs to the soundtrack of Inès' delighted laughter.

Alice encountered Sara closing the door adorned with Libby's hand-painted name, a new spring in her step at having recruited Inès for the cause of her grand surprise. Sara raised an eyebrow at Alice's sudden appearance, but without saying a word merely grabbed her by the wrist and tugged her into the next room down the hallway.

Alone at last, they fell back into kissing each other with the same enthusiasm as they had on the street earlier. Alice found herself chasing and following more than usual, Sara dictating the pace of each lingering kiss with the press of her lips and the teasing flickers of her tongue.

"We should head downstairs," Sara said with great reluctance, letting her fingers run through Alice's short hair one last time before breaking contact. "As pleasant as all this kissing is, I'm very aware of the people hanging around down there."

Alice backed her against the wall with a certain playfulness, wondering how easily she could persuade Sara to stay up here in privacy for a while longer. "Maybe they think we're playing a very involved game of Scrabble?"

"No, they don't," Sara said. "Come on, we'll have plenty more opportunities for... this. Besides, if I can convince my mum to either head home or stay over, I can get her out of the way for the rest of the evening."

"Now your plan makes sense." Alice jerked the door open. "After you."

They held hands to walk downstairs, the press of Sara's fingers against her own enough to make Alice's skin tingle. She had missed this so much without realising: the newness of a relationship where every touch was a stolen surprise or an unexpected delight. The giddiness made her step lighter and her worries fade into the background, preferring to concentrate on the sheer happiness of being around Sara.

In the kitchen Alice saw Stuart had been corralled at the table, a heaped bowl in front of him and a plate stacked high with flatbreads of some kind. He had his eyes closed as he chewed, completely blissed out.

"Girls, you should eat too. I know you won't have had anything but popcorn on your little date." Inès didn't wait for a response before fetching two more bowls. "Sara, can your friend here handle some *ghalieh mahi*?"

"Oh no," Sara said. "Best get her some rice and something a bit milder from the fridge, *Maman*. We don't want to injure her in front of her own security."

"Hey!" Alice knew when she was being mocked. "I can handle my spices. If Stuart can, I certainly can."

Stuart gave a sideways look to Inès. "No offence, ma'am, but you don't have the training."

"And you do?"

"Due respect, I'm Nigerian." Stuart took another bite to prove his point.

"You were born in Hackney!" Alice couldn't believe they had all closed ranks on her so quickly. She plucked a clean fork from the little pile on the table, scooping up a mouthful of the delicious-smelling green stew from Stuart's bowl. "Now let me show you what a cultured palate can cope with."

Sara moved towards the fridge, grabbing a bottle of beer and twisting it open. She didn't take a sip, just watched Alice as she chewed on that first forkful. The powerful flavours hit her tongue first, some definite traces of coriander and... was that *fenugreek*? Alice seemed to remember that being important in Persian dishes. Very tasty, if strong, but utterly bearable.

But as she chewed a little more the heat kicked in like a sudden, roaring flame. Peppers danced over her taste buds like lava, and Alice felt the heat rise in her face like an elevator moving up through the floors.

Oh dear God. She had made a considerable mistake.

Summoning every last bit of reserve, she didn't spit out the scorching mouthful but forced herself to swallow. Had it burned her throat? She was just glad to have banished it.

Sara handed over the open beer. "Drink. Quickly, it will help."

Although Alice's mouth seemed to be crying out for icy cold water, she accepted both the beer and the wisdom behind it, relieved when it soothed every inch of fiery surface with a few glugs from the bottle.

Gasping for breath, Alice set the bottle down with care. "Okay, fine. You may have had a point."

When everyone burst out laughing, it felt like the old days back on base. Alice joined in with them, just one of the guys again. Not a princess who needed disguises and elaborate plans just to go and watch a simple movie.

Sara wrapped an arm around Alice's waist, pulling her close and kissing her cheek. "You'll listen to me next time, won't you?"

Alice nodded. And despite the moment of panic, it had been entirely worth it.

Chapter 20

When the alarm on her phone sounded, Sara groaned but resisted the urge to throw the thing against the bedroom wall. Waking up alone, as usual, she pulled a pillow over her head and waited for the spike of morning anxiety to pass.

Then she realised: summer holidays. No work, not even the relative calm of an inset day when only teachers roamed the school. She had a pile of work waiting on her laptop as ever, but she had promised Libby they would have some genuine downtime this break. Before too long, Libby would find her breaks filled with homework and study, and it felt important to get the quality time together while they could.

Which meant, inevitably, a week in the south of France with Inès. Sara was grateful of the help, and her mother doing all the organising this time had been a godsend, even if Sara would still end up paying for most of the trip. It was worth it to get some real heat in her bones, to put some physical distance between herself and the grey buildings of the school that took up so much of her time.

Morning!

The text from Alice lit up her phone screen. Sara hadn't seen her for a week, not since their successful cinema date had wrapped up with shared meals and lots of laughter in Sara's kitchen. Then Alice had gone off in her car with Stuart and Sara had spent all her free time in the past week packing, sorting out Libby, and generally doing all the extra things that made it possible to go away at all.

Instead of typing, Sara decided to call. One good thing about Alice was that she had a way of making herself available, even if she was in the middle of some very public event. There was something in that which made Sara feel, well, a little special.

"Hello, ready to go wandering?" Alice was calling from somewhere quiet, probably still in the car.

"Ugh, sort of. For some reason my mother has been extra bossy about this trip, so I can't wait to get on the plane just so there won't be any more tasks on her endless list. I think she ended up packing most of my suitcase for me."

"Where are you off to again?"

"Near Lyon, we have some friends and family there. Not very glam by your standards, but we always have a good time."

Alice covered the phone for a moment but promptly returned. "Sounds lovely, even by my standards. Is Libby excited?"

"I can hear commotion from her room, so definitely. She's been climbing the walls since about Wednesday. I always worry she'll get bored going to the same places all the time, but so far so good. Maybe next year I'll suggest we go somewhere new, broaden those horizons a bit."

"Well, I have recommendations if you ever need them. And plenty of places to stay if you ever wanted to tag along with me."

Sara bit her lip, holding back the automatic mention of all those headlines over the years about the royals and their luxury getaways to private islands and the yachts of billionaire friends. She had seen the pictures and idly daydreamed about that kind of paradise along with everyone else, but French countryside, cheese, and wine made for a lovely break anyway. It was more than a lot of people got to experience, and Sara wasn't about to start being ungrateful now.

"I think that might be nice, at some point. Aren't a lot of your holidays working ones though?"

"Some are, some not so much. The skiing we usually do a bit of press at the start and then they leave us alone. But everyone gets some time off, that's just the law surely?"

"I should go. As much as I like talking to you, we have to get moving soon. Apparently we've booked a taxi to the airport this time, instead of getting the tube like every other trip. I think my mother has been flirting with her travel agent."

"They still have travel agents? I thought that everything was booked online these days?"

"It is when I'm the one in charge. We'd be getting the train instead of flying, as well. Anyway, I'll be on my phone as always. If you get bored. And maybe we could do something when I'm back?"

"Just a week from now?" Alice covered the phone again, the muffled sound a little louder. "Yes, that sounds good. I shall see what the schedule throws up and we can make a plan, yes?"

"Yes. Of course. Bye for now." Sara hung up just a little disappointed. It was hardly as though she expected to be the centre of Alice's universe already, but that response to another date had been a little non-committal. Surely Josephine had an idea by now of when Alice was free or not. Nobody was asking for a grand production, or even another incognito date out in London. Sara found that she'd be quite happy just driving around in the car for the chance to spend more time with Alice, something she had no intention of telling another loving soul.

"Mummy! It's holiday time!" Libby's cry made it through both of their bedroom doors and the length of the hall. Officially go time, then.

Sara got out of bed with a stretch. A shower, some breakfast, and a last-minute check of their bags before Inès arrived in a taxi. Despite the automatic urge, Sara resisted the temptation to check her email. Work was for the end of the week. They'd call if anything went really wrong without her.

Something about the gentle rocking of the black cab had Sara feeling drowsy within minutes of them driving out of her road. The endless stop-start of London traffic heading west did little to help, and at some point she completely tuned out Libby chatting in her animated way to her grandmother, and dozed off completely sitting belted into the seat.

Only when the taxi came to a stop and the door opened did Sara stir properly. She was out of the car and organising their luggage before she looked up and realised that they weren't at Gatwick.

"*Maman*? What is this?"

"We're at the airport, *non*? Come along, let's all take our own bags, Libby. Big girl like you can pull a suitcase on wheels by herself."

"I already have my backpack!" Libby turned around in a circle to show off her new one, bought especially for the trip.

"*Maman,* I thought we were flying from Gatwick."

"Ah, this is close enough. I got a good deal on the flights, didn't I?"

"A good deal means flying from Stansted, not—where is this place? It looks like a storage facility, not an airport."

For the first time, Sara started to doubt her mother's faculties. Had she been asking too much of her, with all the help to look after Libby? Or had Inès been the victim of some con artist, taking her money but providing worthless tickets?

"Well, that's private airfields for you," said Alice from somewhere behind Sara, making her quite literally jump. "Surprise?"

"What?" Sara looked from Alice to her grinning mother, then back again. "Wait, what's going on?"

"We did a surprise, Mummy! Well, Granny did, but she told me last night and I kept the secret!"

"So you're coming to France?" Sara looked at Alice, who didn't seem to have any bags of her own. She did, however, look downright gorgeous in that casual-yet-classy way only one sort of people can pull off in jeans, a smart linen shirt in pale blue, and a navy blazer worn over it.

"Not exactly," Alice replied. "You see, Inès here has been helping me with a little project. I thought we deserved a little privacy, but I didn't want to steal that from your important family time."

"This," Inès leaned into whisper, loud enough for everyone to hear, "is what the movies call a 'grand gesture.'"

"Of course, you can always tell me that this is far too much and I can head straight back to the palace. The plane would still be all yours, and you could go to France as you planned."

As much as Sara appreciated the open-hearted gesture, a little part of her wanted Alice to just commit to sweeping her off her feet. Which, Sara had to correct herself, Alice was technically doing.

"And if I say no to France, as planned?"

"You mentioned broadening horizons on the phone earlier," Alice replied. "Well, I spoke to Inès about visiting somewhere quite exclusive to see if she would be okay with it."

"*Maman*?" Sara turned to her mother, whose smile had become distinctly watery.

"You tell her," Inès said to Alice. "It's your surprise."

"Someone tell me, or we can't go anywhere!" Sara tried to keep her impatience in check but being the only one outside the secret was never her favourite.

"You wanted to know what it might be like to have some privacy, to get truly away from the public eye. It so happens there's a place we can make that happen. A little island you might have heard of, called Mustique? I hope that's okay?"

Sara had heard enough. This was no time for polite thanks or keeping things light and breezy. Her heart seemed to have grown in her chest at the sheer thoughtfulness of Alice's idea. Sara pretty much launched herself at Alice, who caught her in a hug with those reassuringly strong arms.

"Uh, a tropical paradise? Yes, of course it's okay!"

"It seemed like a nice way to get away from it all," Alice replied, lighting up when Sara answered that with a soft kiss to her lips. "But we should get going, it's a much longer flight to the Caribbean."

"You're brilliant, you know that?" Sara couldn't resist one more kiss. "Let's go."

Sara had dreamed about it often enough, usually in an overcrowded gate area waiting for a delayed budget airline flight at five in the morning, but travelling by private plane was somehow more perfect than she had imagined.

The only surprising part was that some parts still seemed quite cramped, but with only a small staff on board, they had plenty of space for the four of them. Libby took to the experience like a duck to water, sprawled out on her huge reclining seat right away and ready with her juice order as soon as the cabin crew arrived.

Inès took longer to settle, waiting to be asked at every stage and sitting rigid with her bag on her lap once she did take a seat. Before Sara could nudge her, Alice stopped by and placed a hand on Inès's shoulder, bending to whisper something Sara didn't hear. Whatever it was, it let her mother relax at last, swapping her shoes for the slippers provided and setting her bag down beside her chair.

While the others had settled into single chairs, Sara followed Alice to a more formal seating area, complete with a table between them.

"How long until we take off?" Sara eased herself into a chair.

"Oh yes, hold on," Alice said, standing up again and making a little salute gesture to one of the crew. Within what seemed like seconds, the external door was closed, the engines got louder, and the captain was asking them to fasten their seatbelts as the plane rolled into motion.

"Okay, that was pretty freaking cool," Sara said. "You're enjoying yourself, aren't you?"

"There are some perks to all this," Alice replied. "I cannot tell you how relieved I am that you like this idea. I had visions of turning up only for you to tell me that I had completely misjudged the situation. Or you would think I was being a dreadful show-off."

"I think this is one of those times where if you can do the very cool thing, you should absolutely do it. I mean, who else could pull off something like this? I just can't believe you think I'm worth this kind of generosity."

"That is something I have never doubted for a second, Sara. You are worth every minute of this, and more. I just wish I could think of more wonderful things to share with you, because believe me I want to just as much as you deserve them. Of course it helps that Annabel gave me a nudge to make a bold move. She might be the one person who understands a little what it is like to be in your shoes."

"I don't mean to be a baby about the press intrusion you know. Plenty of people go through much worse. The paparazzi do terrify me, though. I wasn't expecting that level of interest so quickly."

"People get invested. They think they own a little bit of us, and so whenever we do something different it becomes a kind of national opinion poll. I forget what it's like not to be used to that, but I have certainly never come to like it. Rather makes one feel like a piece of meat, in all honesty."

"But you can get time away from it all? Like this?"

Alice nodded, barely bracing herself as the plane picked up speed on the runway. "Exactly."

Sara gripped the armrests of her seat, much less confident. She looked over to Libby, who was practically bouncing in her seat with excitement. Any lingering doubt about accepting this new experience, so far beyond their means, evaporated at the sight of Libby thriving in it. Maybe it was acceptable to be spoiled for once, to let someone else do the organising and just enjoy being there. There was plenty of work waiting for Sara, not to mention the work of being a parent. Perhaps this was her reward.

Looking back at Alice, who had picked up a newspaper to frown at, Sara thought getting a little used to this could be allowed. She just wouldn't get carried away.

An hour or so into the flight, both Sara and Inès had succumbed to the combination of comfortable seats and an early start, dozing as the plane cut through the skies like a dart. At this point Alice would usually head into the cockpit for a word with the crew, but she saw that Libby was awake and done with whatever she had been reading.

"Excited to hit the beach, Libby?"

"Yes, thank you." She sat quite primly in her seat, and Alice made a point to get up and go over to crouch beside her.

"Everything okay?"

"Is Mustique as nice as France? Only we go to France a lot and I know how to speak to people there. Granny didn't tell me about the surprise until this morning, so I didn't have time to find out about where we're going."

"Well, I've been a few times, so just shoot with any questions you might have."

Libby looked up at her, swinging her feet back and forth as she considered. "You like my mum?"

Ah. There it was. Alice knew she had been lucky to go this long, especially with a child as precocious as Libby. But here came the moment of truth all the same.

"I do. I like her a lot, Libby. Is that okay?"

Libby shrugged. She toyed with the cover of her book, as quiet as Alice had ever seen her.

"How come we get to come on holiday too? When my friend Jade's daddy got a new boyfriend, they went on holiday but Jade had to stay with her mum. It was grown-ups only."

Alice moved into the seat next to Libby, clearly this was going to take a proper conversation. "Sometimes that's just because there's not enough money for everyone to go. Or there are some places that might not be fun for kids. Some places are really boring."

Libby scrunched her nose, not quite buying what Alice was trying to sell her. "But we were going to France, there was money for that."

"Yes, changing the plan is my fault. But I know that if I get lucky enough to be your mummy's girlfriend, then that means we spend a lot of time together too. I mean, I would like us to do that. We can go riding, or watch movies, but I wouldn't be trying to take away your time with your mum, I can promise you that."

"If you get married, will Mummy be a princess too? What about me?"

Alice held her hands up. "That's a bit far ahead for now, but my honest answer is that I have no idea. I can ask when we get home though, deal?"

"Does that mean you like me, too? I don't want Mummy to have to choose between us."

"I like you very much indeed, Libby. But your mummy would always choose you, don't worry." Alice racked her brain for a way to show all was well. "Would a hug be a good way to show that we're friends now?"

Libby nodded, jumping out of her seat to accept. Alice wrapped her arms around the small girl and laughed when barely seconds later, Libby was wriggling away. "Okay, good hug!"

Alice shook her head, watching Libby reach for her backpack and trading her book for some kind of handheld game. "Well, as long as it was a good one."

With that, Alice returned to her original seat, surprised to find sweat prickling at her hairline as if she'd just been through an interrogation. Well, at least she had survived round one.

Chapter 21

Nine hours was a long flight, even in the comfort of a private jet. By the time they freshened up before landing, Alice found herself pacing the aisle like a trapped animal. Only when the rest of the plane's passengers began to stir did she settle a little, going back to her seat and stretching out her legs, saying good morning to everyone who passed, even though they'd be landing in the evening.

"You said there was a connecting flight, Your Royal Highness?" Inès watched Sara and Libby pack up some toys and books. "Where are we landing now?"

"St Lucia, I believe. The pilots prefer that to Barbados. Mustique itself has a tiny old airport, so it's propeller plane only to land there I'm afraid."

"Are you going to fly us?" Libby stared at Alice as she asked the question. "Mummy says you can fly planes."

"I can indeed, but this is a tricky one," Alice replied. "Best left to people who do it every day. We are all pre-registered with island security of course, so don't worry about passports and all of that." She watched Sara return to her seat.

"Am I being talked about?" Sara leaned over just a little. "Libby here claims she didn't sleep at all the whole flight."

"Then who was doing all that snoring?" Alice had her hands on her hips, deadly serious. "At one point the pilot said we might have to turn back because the big loud snores were shaking the whole plane."

"I don't snore!" Libby wriggled free of her new perch on Sara's lap to stand her ground with Alice. "It must have been *Mamie*."

"Oh, this is very nice. Poor *Mamie,* right under the bus you throw me," Inès said. "I think Alice is right. You've been snoring since you were in nappies, young lady. Like a little piglet."

"Mum!" Sara had that panicked look. "You can't just...when we're talking about Princess Alice, we use the title, or Her Royal Highness, remember?"

"That was my doing, Inès is quite right to call me Alice," Alice replied, as the seatbelt light clicked on. They all took their respective seats and belted up. "Since we're all on holiday, maybe I could also have a little vacation from titles and stuffy things?"

"Oh," Sara said, her frown softening right away. "Of course. That's why you picked somewhere so private?"

"Not entirely, although it is nice to go somewhere and truly switch off for a change, especially when none of the rest of The Firm is here. Not often I get away from them entirely." Alice had more to tell them, but she was interrupted by their captain speaking.

"Your Royal Highness, ladies and gentlemen, we will shortly be landing at Hewanorra International Airport, St Lucia. If I could ask you to obey the seatbelt signs, we'll bring you down to solid ground just as fast as we can."

"I hate that we have to sit down for landing," Libby said. "It's the second-best part."

"Well, you know the best thing about a personal plane?" Alice saw the "cool aunt" opportunities coming all the time these days. Or in this case, hopefully "cool mum's girlfriend."

"What?" Libby's pout hadn't eased by a millimetre.

"We don't really have to sit down for the fun parts. Want to see the landing from the cockpit?"

Libby squealed, answer enough.

"Is it okay?" Alice turned to Sara. "We'll sit in the jump seat, and I'll keep her safe the whole time."

Sara nodded. "Just don't ask me to join you. Taking off is one thing but aiming towards the ground is more than I can watch. You remember?"

"Come on then," Alice said, releasing her own belt and taking Libby by the hand. She only had to stoop a little to lead her forward to the cabin. One sharp knock on the door and they had access. After their little chat, Alice felt confident that she was making headway with Libby and hopefully this would seal the deal. Even aside from how it would help the plans with Sara to have her daughter onside, Alice found herself hoping that Libby really did like her back. They seemed to enjoy each other's company, and while Alice had no pretentions on being a stepmother right away, she did like being around Libby just for Libby's sake. How embarrassing it would be if that feeling were not reciprocated.

"Don't suppose you want to take her down, Your Royal Highness?" Captain Alex Salah had been flying her since her teens and had written one of her letters of recommendation on joining the RAF.

"Too rusty on these beasts, alas. Reminds me I should put in some hours, though. Got room for a little one in the good seats?"

"How many times have you flown a plane, Libby?" Alex asked the question straight-faced, one professional to another.

"No times."

"Would you like to do it just now?"

"I don't think I'm allowed. Can I?"

Alice laid a reassuring hand on Libby's head as Alex winked at her. "It takes two people to land really, so the co-pilot over here will make sure everything is right. But you could be captain, if you like."

Libby didn't need telling twice. She was scrambling into the chair and staring at the controls as though she did it every day. Alice found herself smiling from ear to ear. Even outside of Sara, and the hope of being with her properly, it was impossible not to fall for Libby's charms. For so many years Alice had dismissed the idea of ever getting to be a mother, more out of self-preservation than any strong desires. Seeing the way Libby was so bright and eager to learn, so full of feelings and opinions even at such a young age, it had Alice feeling somewhere close to broody.

"Okay, Captain Libby. Let's land your first jet."

Their villa was stunning, in the Mediterranean style of sprawling white marble and tall pillars. Though they were barely throwing distance from a private beach, the grounds also boasted a huge infinity pool set in a spacious terrace overhung with palm trees.

The household staff of four lined up to greet them, and Alice was saddened that no familiar faces remained. She hadn't been out in a couple of years, and jobs like this were passed around local families, often seasonal, and subject to a high turnover. It was lovely to watch Sara's instant rapport with each of them, and the way they greeted her like one of the family in return.

"This is beautiful," Sara said, hanging back in the long hallway as Inès and Libby raced between rooms, taking in every luxurious detail and bouncing on the beds.

"I wasn't sure how close you'd want to stay, so this way everyone has privacy but nothing is too far away," Alice replied, leaning against the doorframe and giving Sara her very fondest smile, unable to hold it back. Everything about this trip felt like a logical step forward, and Alice was as eager for the next pleasant moment as she was to freeze time and appreciate each one as it came.

"I think this will work for all of us. Was it—I'm blushing like a teenager—are we in separate rooms?" Sara wasn't kidding about her blush, she looked almost sunburned across her cheeks.

"I didn't want to presume. I always take the bedroom out back—I'm a notoriously light sleeper, and when we come with a gang of friends it can get pretty rowdy. I've asked for Libby and Inès to have the connecting rooms back here, which you can see they've already found. That leaves you a choice of this bedroom in here," Alice nodded to the room behind her. "Or there's a sort of cabana out by the pool. Usually that's the worst place to get any rest, but I don't see us hosting many all-night ragers, do you?"

Sara tilted her head. "You underestimate my mother. I think I'll go with this one, since it's halfway between Libby and...out back."

That was enough to make Alice smile even more broadly. "Lucky me. I think. The important thing is we all make ourselves at home. This isn't really the kind of place with a ton to do, but I think that might be the biggest appeal. We have a chef, a well-stocked bar, and plenty of space to blow off some steam. Tennis out back, pool out front. Maybe down to the beach for some drinks and dancing in the evening?"

"In case I haven't made it clear, as gestures go this is amazing, Alice. I don't think I've ever been anywhere quite like this."

"No point in having the ability to do nice things unless you share them. Trust me, getting the best part of a week here with you is the ultimate selfish motive. And if we get some of that time just the two of us, well..."

Alice decided in that moment that the rules of back home could go hang. This was freedom, and she intended to enjoy every second of it.

She kissed Sara with just the softest of touches, a mere grazing of her lips, to test where things stood.

Sara's answer was immediate and enthusiastic, pulling Alice closer by the front of her linen shirt and kissing her with far more intent. "I think some alone time is absolutely required, yes."

"Then let's go unpack. The staff will do it if we don't get on it right away. Last one in the pool is a rotten egg?"

Sara scrunched her nose, no doubt at the childish expression. "You're on. See you there."

Alice turned around at least twice, maybe a third time, while walking away. Now she could look, she found that she didn't want to take her eyes off Sara at all.

Alice hadn't realised just how ready she was for a break. Fussing with her swimwear, she settled on the new bikini that must have been packed by Eugenia. It was more sporty than sexy, perhaps, but Alice knew she would feel comfortable in it. More appropriate for a group setting as well. She shimmied into it, taking deep breaths of sea air and leaving her suitcases open on the bed to be unpacked. While doing her own chores might be more normal for Sara, Alice had very little intention of doing the same. There was a race to the pool to win, after all.

She was almost beaten to the pool by Libby, in her bright yellow swimsuit. Fortunately, Libby had been raised sensibly and knew better than to jump in without adult supervision.

"I don't see any sunscreen, young lady," Alice said. "Should we get some from your mum?"

"I sprayed," Libby replied, quite indignant. She produced a bottle from the little bucket she was carrying, along with plastic sunglasses and a comic book. "But maybe you can make sure I got my back too?"

Alice accepted the bottle and gave her a generous top-up spray, being sure to cover her as well as Sara would expect. "Okay, let that soak in before you join me in the pool."

They were interrupted by Sara rushing past them, dropping her towel on a lounger without breaking stride and dropping straight into the clear-sided infinity pool with the grace of a ballerina. The splash almost covered Alice's indignant swearing.

"That's not very polite," Libby said.

Alice stuck her tongue out, before hurling herself into the water after Sara.

"Did you send junior out as a distraction? That's very underhanded."

"No," Sara replied, treading water and gazing around in wonder. "But I'll take any advantage I can get. Enjoy losing, I guess."

"I can't believe we're here," Alice said, swimming closer. "I really thought you had given up on this before we even got going. So thank you, for taking the chance."

"You're more than welcome. The fancy holiday isn't hurting your cause, that's for sure."

Harold, the butler, appeared at that point. "Will you be requiring drinks, Your Royal Highness?"

"I think I fancy a strawberry daiquiri. That's a real holiday drink, isn't it? Sara?"

"Same," she said, without missing a beat. "Can we have some juice for Libby? And any kind of dry white wine for my mother."

As though summoned, Inès appeared in her swimsuit and sarong, sunglasses firmly in place and a hat with a brim wider than the River Thames.

"This will do," she announced, before taking a seat on the furthest lounger and cracking open her paperback. Alice enjoyed the way Sara rolled her eyes.

"This might have been the perfect idea," Sara looked at Alice then, her expression full of promise. "Also, you look very cool when you're comfortable. Knowing the world isn't watching for a change. It's like I have my own personal Alice, and I don't want to share you."

"That can be arranged."

"I'll work it out with *Maman* and Libby, but I want to take you up on the offer to have a day or two together, just us. Maybe I am crazy, and maybe it won't be like this back home, but I'm done fighting it. Whatever happens, I'll kick myself if I don't give this a real try."

"This isn't about pressuring you—"

"No, and I don't feel that way. If a princess's charming and thoughtful ideas like this aren't good enough for me, then damn me, I am officially the problem. I mean there's high standards, then there's just being impossible."

Alice grinned all over again. There was no denying that Sara was charming, especially when she was flustered. "Then I accept your acceptance. No rush, though. Maybe we can suggest your mum and Libby take the ferry to St Vincent in a couple of days or something. Shall we just enjoy the moment?"

"Yes," Sara replied, splashing some surface water at Alice. "I'd like that."

The next two days passed in a flurry of meals, short drives, and touring the various beaches and bars of Mustique. Alice nodded at other people as they encountered them, some famous and some not, but there was no interaction beyond their happy bubble. Libby thrived on all the sunshine and activity, and each evening once she was bathed and put to bed, Alice stole an hour or three, alone by the pool or in the lush gardens with Sara.

"Shall we have cocktails?" Sara made the suggestion as she returned from her goodnights to Libby. They had opted for the pool loungers tonight, the gentle lapping of the water still inviting even at a later hour. "Mum has turned in early to watch some old movies, and Libby's asleep, so maybe we can get a bottle of something and let the staff go early."

"Anything you want," Alice replied. "And we don't have to stay out here, you know. We do have our own rooms. Lovely and cool in both of those."

Sara came to sit on the same lounger as Alice. "You have no idea how much I want to."

"That sounds rather like there's a caveat."

"I've dated around, had a few girlfriends. But if I sleep with someone, that's a commitment for me. I'm not saying I don't want to get to that stage with you, I think I've been showing you all week that I want to."

Alice laid a hand on Sara's thigh, stroking gently through the slightly crumpled cotton of her sundress. "You have seemed every bit as interested as I am, yes."

"I just need to be sure. That we stand a chance; that this can survive outside the bubble. Which is not to say we need to stop what we've been doing..." Sara trailed off without mentioning the previous evenings of languorous, tantalising kisses, reluctantly ended after an hour or two when they retreated to separate rooms. Out in public, limited though it was, they had been careful about public displays of affection, so a full day of frustrated longing was poured into those kisses and increasingly confident touches.

"Sara, for you? I am more than willing to wait. And to keep doing exactly what we've been doing." Alice didn't specify the touching that had accompanied the kisses, the wandering moments here and there as clothes shifted to reveal newly bared skin. It was clear from the hitch in Sara's breathing that she had been thinking something similar.

"Can we wait another night, until we're really alone? The arrangements are all made for Mum and Libby to overnight on St Vincent?"

Alice nodded again. "As long as you still feel comfortable doing that. I don't want you to feel like I sent them away. I'm more than happy to spend time with Libby, you know. We had a great time riding horses on the beach without you, and I think we have a future scuba diver on our hands with how quickly she took to snorkelling."

"Okay," Sara said, exhaling slowly. "I'm so glad you two are getting along. I think you know it would be a deal-breaker for me if Libby didn't want to be around you. Still, I'm sure you are used to these sophisticated, worldly women. I simply need for all this to matter. This is important. You are important to me."

"And you are important to me, both of you," Alice said. "There's no harm in doing things properly. I have a feeling that for us, it will be worth it."

"Promise?"

"Absolutely. But I still think we can have a drink in my room without getting entirely carried away." Alice stood, taking the first steps towards her room. "I won't complicate matters by pointing out that the first order of business for me is a cool shower."

Sara pursed her lips. "That would be...unfair, yes."

"There's some music I'd like to play for you, too."

Instead of words, Sara got to her feet and drew Alice close enough for one more slow, searing kiss. "Then I'm all yours."

Chapter 22

Waving Libby off was always difficult, even when Sara knew she was in safe and happy company with Inès. The nagging guilt of a single mother gnawed at Sara most of the morning, and while every rational part of her knew that she was entitled to some time for herself, to be an adult, to be a woman, it always felt like a small betrayal to hand Libby over to anyone else. Even her mother.

It was silly, but Sara also knew that the years were soon approaching when Libby wouldn't want to go everywhere with her, and she would no doubt have options with friends and school to go off and see things for herself. Sara dreaded the inevitable distance of raising a teenager instead of a sweet little girl, and she wasn't sure there was enough training in the world to overcome that natural way of things.

Libby had seemed quite thrilled that she was getting her own mini adventure, content to spend time with Inès who always verged on spoiling her. Only when Sara kissed her goodbye at the car had there been a tearful moment of Libby promising to miss her and be back soon. That brief sulk had passed in a flash, and Libby had been driven off with a smile on her face.

"How are you finding it so far then?" Alice drove the buggy with the same languid confidence she did most things, despite the rough, unmarked road and the unfamiliar route.

"Amazing. Different to anything I'd expected, but familiar at the same time? And no doubt wherever we're going will be fantastic. You've been spoiling me."

"You deserve it." Alice rested one hand on the stick after changing gear, her impressive diving-style watch glinting at her wrist as Libby's gift from the day before—a friendship bracelet bought from a chic little boutique—wrapped around it seamlessly.

"You keep telling me that," Sara said. "I'm starting to believe you."

"Then I won't mention the massages booked for when we get back." They pulled off the quiet road onto more of a bumpy track. Sara regretted the strong coffee and eggs she'd had for breakfast for a minute, but soon settled into the rhythm.

"That sounds great," Sara replied. "Don't tell Mum that's an option or she'll book someone for the rest of the time we're here. Right up to the plane."

"It's no problem if she does. I wondered... You don't mention your dad much. I know he and Inès divorced once you got into Cambridge, and that Libby calls him *Papy* but that's about it."

"Well, he's my dad I suppose. He was in my life the regular amount when I was a kid, although he worked a lot. But he hasn't been happy about some of my choices, especially without Mum to talk him round. He thought I was wrong to have Libby the way I did, and to come out after that... I think I confused him as much as I hurt him. We still do birthdays, Christmas, but I've always been closer to my mother. It's why I sort of dropped his part of my surname and just go by Marteau, since they divorced. He was offended by that, of course, but we were just tired of fighting all the time by then."

Alice nodded. "What would he think about this? About us?"

"Hmm... I don't think he'd go running to the tabloids if that's what you're asking. But he's never been exactly accepting of my lifestyle. Either the gay part or the single-mother part, as much as he is very good to Libby. She is his only granddaughter after all."

"I think my mother is disappointed to only have two. Her generation had so many siblings and cousins, we seem quite limited in numbers by comparison. I don't think Annabel has any plans for a third, though."

"They have a lovely balance as is, I don't blame her," Sara said, weighing her options before plunging in with the obvious question. "What about from you? Does she expect another grandchild or two from you?"

"Ah." Alice made a great show of watching the road ahead and checking their speed. "Sort of. She is quite a realist, though. I would like to think I still have a chance at being a mother…or at least a stepmother, in the future."

"Hmm," was all Sara would commit in response. If nothing else, it was good to know. "Now, just how private is this beach?"

"Why do you ask?"

"Because I definitely forgot my bikini top," Sara replied, which was completely untrue as she had shoved it in her bag instead of wearing it under her dress.

"The temptation begins now, doesn't it?" Alice had the decency to look properly flustered at the thought of skinny dipping.

"Oh, you bet."

Right on cue, Alice brought the buggy to a halt by a stretch of immaculate beach, hemmed in by rocks on either side. "Then let's go."

Sara stretched her arms over her head to make her point, before hopping out onto the warm sand. "Last one in…"

She squealed as Alice charged past her, both of them shedding clothes as they went. Another time Sara might have been self-conscious, but the relaxing days spent together had put a certain sway in her hips as she jogged towards the water. Was it really such a reveal after spending most of the time in not much more than a bikini or shorts?

The water was much cooler than their pool, she enjoyed the initial slap of low waves as they splashed against her knees and her thighs, until she was submerged right up to her neck. There was no hurry, just the sheer bliss of cool water against her skin. London, the harsh reality of it, all the people at every turn, felt like another lifetime. Whatever happened, this perfect interlude was something to be grateful for.

The water was as clear as in any bathtub, and the golden white sand underneath showed an array of shells and darting little fish. Time seemed to slow to a stop as she let herself bob onto her back, floating on the surface like the only person in the world. Closing her eyes for a second, she might have been a lonely castaway.

But the sea had other ideas, floating her right into Alice's path. They hadn't wandered far from shore, and the collision was a very gentle one.

Sara righted herself, all the better to take in the sight of Alice properly. The woman was unblinking under Sara's scrutiny, clearly at ease with nudity in that way public school sorts always were. Although the water skewed perspective, there was no denying the lean and fit lines of her body.

By contrast, Sara knew she was softer around the middle, her faded silver scar from having Libby mostly hidden when she was clothed. No hiding out here, though. Although she kept in shape as best she could, running around after children was really her primary form of exercise. Alice, for her part, had clearly kept up on her Olympian-level training, because she had muscles in all the right places.

"Like what you see?" Alice's grin was cheeky, but Sara thought she detected maybe a flicker of insecurity. There was no need for that. Floating closer, she wrapped her arms around Alice's neck, drawing her into a slow-burning kiss. They kept their legs in motion, enough to keep them afloat, enjoying the slip-slide motion of their bodies beneath the gentle waves.

"Very much," Sara said, although they both seemed to have forgotten the question. "This is all so beautiful, including you."

"Careful, I might start thinking you like me."

"Can't have that," Sara replied, followed up with another kiss, this one much more purposeful. Any qualms she had about getting serious with Alice had evaporated at last. They could be equals. They could respect each other. They could be together. They could have life that only belonged to them.

Maybe, just maybe, they could have it all.

Drying off on the beach, Alice marvelled quietly at how well her plan was progressing. It was possible she owed Annabel a rather large drink on their return. Or at least a hug.

Libby had warmed to Alice as she hoped, and she couldn't help but be more charmed by the girl with every passing day. Sara had overcome her reticence with no paparazzi in sight, and it felt like they were finally on that pleasant collision course to sleeping together. Not that Alice had any issue being patient about such things, but there was a constant pull somewhere deep inside her that wanted to be fully with Sara. Every time they touched or kissed it felt like a promise of more to come, and it was getting harder for Alice to cover her enthusiastic reactions to that. More than once a deep moan had escaped from her throat, and that only served to spur Sara on in whatever they might be doing in that moment.

They left the water with some reluctance, and Alice wondered how long she ought to make a show of lingering on the beach before suggesting they drive back.

"This really is a piece of paradise," Sara said, leaning back on her elbows. Despite careful sunscreen application her skin tone had darkened with long days in the sun, and she only looked more beautiful as a result. The relaxation on her face helped, seemingly a million miles from the stresses of work, commuting, and other daily concerns. "You must be enjoying the escape from all the stuffy royal duties?"

"Oh, no doubt about that. I feel a tad guilty, as always, but there will be events aplenty waiting for me on my return. I suppose a few days away is far from unreasonable. Even the toughest jobs grant some leave."

"Well, if your conditions are so tough you could always unionise," Sara said with a pointed smirk.

"Of course. I shall get right on that. Summer is a slower time anyway, the bulk of the meaningful events are in the months to come. I might be a little less available, on a day-to-day basis, but I intend to make every effort to see you as much as possible."

Sara's expression flickered with something like suspicion. "Getting your excuses in early? I suppose I should pay attention to which events are more important than I am, hmm?"

"No I—"

"I mean, I expect to rank behind say, opening a hospital...but those remembrance services, well you have those every year and there are loads of different ones. So I should have dibs on your time in November?"

"That's not funny." Alice felt her heart sink as Sara took aim at one of the parts of the job most precious to her. Of course she wouldn't understand. "Can we change the subject, please?"

"Wait, it was just a joke." Sara sat up straight, pushing her sunglasses up on top of her head. "Apparently not a funny one, but only a joke all the same."

"It's nothing. It's just...that sort of thing means a lot to me. I thought you would know better than to poke fun at it, even despite our differences."

Sara just stared for a moment. "Are you seriously getting upset over this? I just picked something at random, I wasn't trying to disrespect your beloved soldiers."

"See, there you go. My 'beloved soldiers'. You make that sound like something unimportant, something I am silly to care about. I happen to respect the fact that these people gave their lives in service to this country, and yes, they do deserve my silence and respect every year. At more than one event, as required or invited." Part of Alice knew it was an overreaction, but she couldn't bear to pedal it back just yet. "I happen to think I've been a jolly good sport about the whole 'make fun of her privilege' thing but serving in uniform was far from some little perk for me. I went up in those planes knowing I may not return. Many of my friends did not."

Sara went quiet at that, clearly contemplating her reply. "I do respect that. But you have to respect as well, that armies and navies and dropping bombs...for some of us we feel closer to those on the receiving end."

"Is that so?"

"Yes," Sara said. "Why do you sound so sceptical?"

"Do I? Well, perhaps it's because... and I do not say this lightly, but while I recognise I have a charmed life, growing up in South London with loving parents and going on to Cambridge, that hardly equates to life in a warzone. Yet you lecture me as though I had done this to you, personally. A bit rich, really."

"There you go again," Sara said, her expression stormy at best. "You can't help yourself really. For all you act like just 'one of the people', ultimately you expect everyone to see things your way. To come around to your way of thinking. All this bowing to the will of the princess stuff is why I was wary of getting involved in the first place."

"The doors have been open the whole time. Not once have I tried to prevent you walking away when you said you wanted to. And as thanks, here you are accusing me of being some colonial empire-builder, not caring for the victims of war."

Sara kicked out at the sand. "That's just my point! You're not talking about all the victims, you're simply focusing on the ones in uniform who carry the guns and drop the bombs. Perhaps I'll never know what it's like to flee an oppressive regime, but I have been an unfortunate civilian whose leaders dragged the whole country into wars I wanted no part in, and never voted for." She cleared her throat. "More than that, I've seen what that trauma does look like, when people lose their homes and have to flee. You can ask my mother if you want it first-hand."

"I confess, that is one way I hadn't thought to look at it." Alice rolled her neck a little, easing the tension from her muscles. "The two don't have to be mutually exclusive, but that is always going to be an essential part of who I am, and what I do, Sara. Is that going to be a problem for us?"

"It's not a deal-breaker," Sara said, after another agonising pause. "There are specifics we probably need to work through, but please know I would never disrespect you or the people you care about."

"I know that." Alice ran a handful of sand through her fingers. "Does that count as our first fight?"

"I believe our first fight was the day we met," Sara replied, her smile finally returning. "If you want to be accurate about it."

Alice flicked some sand in her direction. "Pedantic, but I can allow it. Still, it feels like we passed a test somehow. Besides, can lesbians really go a full week without processing?"

"It was bound to happen." Sara looked up at the shifting skies above them. "As nice as this private beach is, I can't help thinking we have a lovely empty villa waiting for us."

"You make an excellent point." Alice stood, offering a hand to help Sara up. She held on to that hand all the way back to the buggy.

Back at the villa, Sara found herself dozing just a little after her massage and shower, waiting for Alice to rejoin her. Only when she felt herself lifted from the pool lounger did she realise that Alice had arrived.

"Bugger!" Alice whispered as Sara's foot bumped one of the columns. "So much for chivalry."

Sara opened her eyes, realising she was currently in a full-on bridal carry. "Are you… carrying me to bed?"

"It seemed the polite thing to do. Give you a chance to see whether you wanted to call it an evening here, or not. Shall I let you down?"

With a nod, Sara braced herself for being back on her feet. Her hand wrapped around Alice's biceps through her shirt, and the flex of it was very pleasant.

She turned around to see where they had ended up and gasped at the sight of the room before her. It was huge, of course, white marble floors stretching out in each direction, seemingly forever. A huge four-poster bed with gauzy drapes dominated one side of the room, facing floor-to-ceiling windows that showed the beach in all its glory. The air smelled fresh, the hint of something floral on the breeze, and right behind her was the pleasing solidity of Alice, who wrapped her arms around Sara's waist from behind. She kissed Sara's neck once, twice, then nuzzled the curve of her jaw.

"Fit for a princess?"

"This is really just the pool house?"

Alice nodded.

Sara placed her hands on Alice's arms, holding them in place. "I think fit for a princess is a question for you."

"Yes, it is, and if we're talking about big scary futures, it could also be you one day. These are the perks that come with all the things we worry about. Like titles."

"Okay, I guess I see the appeal," Sara said, coming to a decision in that moment. Before it might have sent her running for her own room, but after a day of increasingly bold touches, she had no desire to be anywhere else in that moment. "It's really just us?"

"The staff are nearby, but not in the house. No interruptions unless we call for something."

"Then why don't we make the most of it?"

Alice turned Sara in her embrace, then captured her lips in a lingering soft kiss. "An offer I could never refuse, I promise you."

It was Sara who led them across the gently echoing space to the inviting bed. Time to stop denying it to herself: she was only getting in deeper, and whatever happened from there, she wanted to be with Alice.

Chapter 23

Alice swept Sara off her feet with the next kiss, holding her firmly and leveraging the height difference between them. They fell gradually onto the mattress, Alice controlling their movements until Sara was lying beneath her, trading kisses that were increasing in passion and decreasing in precision at roughly the same rate.

It already felt like it wouldn't be possible to stop kissing Sara's mouth, or the soft planes of her skin that tasted faintly of salt, and sunscreen, and just a hint of the freshness of the island air.

There was a whisper of doubt in Alice's head, that somehow they were still rushing, but it faded away with each kiss that Sara returned, open-mouthed and earnest. When she reached for Sara there was still an expectation of stopping, of being told that they should wait just a little longer, but nothing of the sort happened.

Answering a question that Alice was both too breathless and too terrified to ask, it was Sara who pushed things forward, reaching around to grab Alice's ass. It started as a simple clutching through the fabric of her linen trousers, but a moment later Sara's hand retreated. Before Alice could sigh the disappointment into their kissing, Sara's fingertips were exploring beneath that same linen, tracing feather-light lines up the back of Alice's thigh until her ass was right back in grabbing range.

Alice expected slow progress. She had been steeling herself for the prospect of fumbling touches and hesitant questions over what to do and how. Sara apparently didn't get that memo, their bodies pressing together as hands explored, and if it was tentative at all then it was surely because neither of them could bear the thought of this ending too soon.

As gorgeous as Sara's sundress was, and as flimsy as it was to the touch, Alice couldn't resist reaching for the zipper when Sara arched up off the sheets. Somehow Alice had become the blushing virgin in all this, unable to concentrate on more than one task at a time, while Sara's movements were fluid and without even a flicker of hesitation.

"Ssh." Sara breathed against Alice's cheek a moment later. "I can hear you thinking."

"I just want it to be…" Alice lost her train of thought as Sara nipped at her earlobe. "Fuck."

"Profanity," Sara replied. "And you haven't even got me naked, yet."

It was the low chuckle Alice needed, a pin in the bubble of tension that had been building, and they were both laughing when their lips meet again.

"Now, about that nakedness. I did so enjoy the sneak preview earlier," Alice said with a grin. She pulled back just far enough to turn Sara on to her front, straddling across her backside with something more like the usual regal confidence. Unzipping Sara's dress was the most tantalising reveal Alice could ever have imagined. The lines of Sara's back were exposed inch by inch, and it was only when Alice leaned forward to kiss the exposed skin, hot and eager, that she even registered the absence of a bra. "Didn't want to waste lingerie on me, huh?"

"Didn't seem much point in putting one back on after I showered," Sara said after a breathy little moan. "And then I figured, why bother with panties either? If you haven't taken the hint by now, maybe that will help?"

Alice gasped at that, and if she rolled her hips just a little against the curve of Sara's ass then, what sane person could blame her? "Consider me convinced."

Sara turned them then, using surprising upper body strength to have Alice be the one on her back. Pinning Alice's wrists above her own head, tugging slightly at her hair which must have been a wild mess already, Sara leaned to claim a slow and deliberate kiss, teasing and flickering her tongue against Alice's lips and then her tongue in turn. When Sara's mouth charted a trail across Alice's jaw and down the sensitive lines of her neck, there was no chance of holding back.

"You're, uh, taking charge?" Alice whimpered as Sara grazed her collarbone with her teeth.

"Why not?" Sara gave a defiant stare from her new position on top. "I've never been one for bowing to royalty." She sucked deliberately over the patch of tender skin where Alice's pulse was thundering like skies in the dying days of summer.

Alice wriggled her hands free for a moment, intent on touching and staking a claim for dominance, but Sara pinned her wrists again effortlessly.

"Let me. Please."

Alice could not say no.

She leaned back against the mattress and let Sara's mouth work its way over every inch of exposed skin, Alice tank top easily despatched, just like the rest of her clothing. That same deft touch resulted in one of Sara's palms, and then the other—Alice left her hands above her head, being a good girl, getting the reward—pressed against the curves of her breasts. Her nipples pebbled at the contact in the cool evening air, and they were sensitive enough for each caress to feel like a jolt of electricity all the way down to the meeting of her thighs.

The first whisper of Sara's mouth on Alice's bared breast was a dangerous moment, one that might well have exploded, but Sara pulled away again, leaving only the ghost of those velvet lips. With less control over her body, Alice might very well have come right then, embarrassing them both in the process.

Perhaps the knife-edge intensity did it, but for a moment Sara seemed thrown. That early confidence evaporated, and she knelt over Alice seeming confused.

"What is it?" Alice said.

"I just…how to choose? I want to do everything to you. All at once."

"Well, the fun part of this is whatever you don't do this time? We can pretty much start over right away…"

Sara's smile could have illuminated the entire island. She kissed Alice again, long and deep. It was a long time before they came up for air. With each passing minute, Alice only felt her arousal grow. Every time she thought she was as turned on as it was possible to be, some kiss or touch would nudge her to yet another level.

They had barely paused to catch their breath before Sara was sliding down Alice's naked body, nipping and teasing with a certain playfulness.

Alice's hips arched upwards of their own volition, and Sara seemed to take great delight in pinning her down again.

With the heel of her hand, Sara pressed against Alice's mound. It didn't take an invitation for Alice to grind against the pressure, her breath coming in sharp little pants. Before she could get used to one sensation, Sara had captured a nipple again, flicking her tongue back and forth over the hardened nub with a lot of promise for where else she might make that same motion.

When they kissed again, it was a little more frantic and there was a bumping of noses, a brief confusion over whose head should tilt which way, before they made the connection. Smiling into the kiss, Alice pulled Sara closer. No longer could her hands wait above her head, Alice needed to touch and to hold on.

"You're so... wet." Sara rested on one elbow as she ran a finger through the wetness between Alice's thighs. "All for me, hmm?"

"Yes." For once Alice had no glib remark, only the bare truth.

"I think I'll take the compliment." Sara smirked before adding a second finger, the stroking pleasant enough but sort of aimless. "Give me just a moment," she whispered, screwing her face up in concentration. This time her touch was much surer, and her fingertips slid directly over Alice's clit, making her cry out at the much-needed pressure.

Which, coincidentally, was the point where Alice decided that slow and steady was definitely best saved for round two, and if she didn't touch Sara in a more meaningful way she really might explode. Using the leverage of her thigh between Sara's legs, Alice rolled them into a more accessible position. Sara was soaked against her thigh.

"Forgive me." Alice grunted the words. "If there's a slight lack of finesse."

"To hell with finesse," Sara said.

Alice was the one to make bolder strokes with her fingers, leading the way to pressing a second, and then a third inside Sara, who moaned low and lustful the whole time. She managed to keep pace with Alice, following her example of flexing and curling fingers, their rhythms slightly syncopated but the determination the same.

"More," Alice urged, though with a gun to her head she couldn't have said more of what, exactly. Just more touching and feeling and more Sara, whose head was tilted back and practically begging Alice to kiss her neck one more time. And who was Alice not to oblige?

Being with Sara after all these months—no, years—alone was like running through a waterfall, and the rush of emotion behind the simple touches was something Alice hadn't experienced since her first few times, those furtive touches that left her so overwhelmed.

What she couldn't believe was that she had travelled the world and met women of every colour and creed, only for the one who captivated her entirely to have been just a few miles away all that time. And that they had flown halfway around the globe to allow themselves to be together. Her life had always been unusual, but Alice was beginning to think God just had one hell of a sense of humour.

"Is it—am I?" Sara seemed to be losing her confidence along with the end of her sentences, but she didn't stop working her fingers, and Alice could only nod in encouragement.

"Yes. God, yes. Just like this."

"Can we...together?" Sara met her gaze then, and something in the moment when their eyes locked was the push towards climax that Alice needed.

"So close," one of them gasped, and Alice wasn't sure which one of them admitted it first.

"Please," Alice said, ashamed at the indignity in her whining. She had seduced and charmed and asked very nicely before, but she had never been one to beg. The prospect of Sara's deft fingers making her come was enough to make Alice willing to prostrate herself and plea.

For a terrible second Alice thought she wasn't going to manage. It was the huff of satisfaction from Sara that pushed Alice over the edge, the pulsing between her thighs as stunning as the way her heart was pounding against her ribcage.

Alice fell back in relief as Sara tensed hard around her fingers.

They lay there together, breathing ragged and bodies slick with sweat. As Sara disentangled herself, falling down beside Alice, she pressed a sweet kiss to her temple. "That was gorgeous."

"So are you," Alice said, pleased with her reaction. "No regrets?"

Sara kissed her on the mouth that time, long and sweet. "Not a single one."

Chapter 24

Sara woke on their last morning in Mustique to find Libby sitting cross-legged at the bottom of the bed, reading one of her many books.

"Libs?" She had returned the day before full of excitement and stories, Inès looking a little exhausted for the first time. On instinct, Sara reached out to her side, where just a few hours before Alice had fallen asleep.

"Alice went to get a shower," Libby said, noticing the gesture. "Is she your girlfriend now?"

"It's complicated," Sara started to say, pulling herself up against the headboard. She reached for the bottled water on the nightstand, grateful to buy a few more seconds by taking a long drink.

"You always tell me before you get a girlfriend," Libby said, speaking without looking up. "Like, you ask me if it's okay first."

Sara held her tongue on that point. The two semi-serious relationships where it had come to a stage to introduce Libby might have been presented that way, but like most children, Libby wasn't really aware of all the comings and goings of Sara's adult life.

"We've been spending a lot of time with Alice, and I wanted to be sure that something was going to change before I spoke to you about it."

"So it changed already?"

Sara nodded.

"Do you like her? Like girlfriend-and-girlfriend like her?"

"I like her a lot, yes."

Libby considered that for a long, quiet moment. "Okay. But I think you're being a bit selfish, Mummy."

Sara's heart sank in her chest, as swiftly as though it had been torpedoed. "Really? Oh sweetheart, that's the last thing I wanted to be."

"I mean, it's okay that you have a girlfriend. But girlfriends break up. And when you do, that means I won't get to see Alice or go riding with her anymore, or play with Rupes and Annie. I like doing that."

"Come here," Sara said, gesturing to her daughter. Libby didn't need much encouragement to ditch the book and come clambering up the bed into Sara's open arms. "I hope that there won't be breaking up, not for a long time, maybe even never. But if anything changes, I will talk to you about it, and we'll figure it out together, okay? "

"Okay."

"Is it all right with you that I'm dating Alice? You like her don't you?" Sara had to be sure.

Libby burrowed deeper into their hug, nodding vigorously. "I think I scared Alice when I came in earlier. She fell out of bed and everything."

"I'm sure she'll forgive you." Sara must have been exhausted to sleep through so much commotion. "And don't forget, *chérie*, if anything ever changes or you don't like how things are with Alice around, you only have to tell me. I will never be mad about that. Now, shall we start getting organised? We fly home later."

"The nice people are already packing for us," Libby said, nodding to the suitcases waiting by the bedroom door. "They were in my room when I came to see you."

Oh. Sara could get used to that level of organisation.

"Right, well time for Mummy to have a shower. Meet me at the pool for breakfast?"

"One more cuddle," Libby said.

Sara was more than happy to oblige. Looking up she saw Alice watching them and smiled.

"I would absolutely love to take you home with me now," Alice said, once they were alone in the cabin of the plane. "Are you sure we have to go our separate ways?"

Libby and Inès had followed the cabin crew, their usual chatter subdued by sleepiness and creeping jet lag. Sara would usually be rushing after

Libby, but the chance for one more moment of closeness with Alice was irresistible.

"Alas, I'm back at work next week, even if the children have a while longer. I can't really ask all the grandparents to do any more babysitting than they're already doing to let me work."

"Of course."

"It helps that Libby knows we're a couple now. She always comes first, but it gives us more options when she's included too. I know, I'm lucky to have the help that I do." Sara expected Alice to swoop in with promises about how much room she had to spare, about how there would be playdates with Rupert and Anne, or other options. Maybe they were both too tired for logistics.

"Shall we?" Alice led the way to the exit and the stairs down to the tarmac. After a week in paradise, London had decided to show its greyest and rainiest evening. Typical. "That must be why they needed us off so promptly. Mother is using the plane."

Sara looked back at the frantic activity in the cabin as the crew prepared for a new passenger. Then slowly—very, painfully, slowly—she forced herself to look back across the airfield to where a convoy of sleek black cars had come to a halt, flags flapping on each of their bonnets. Gathered outside were various bustling royal employees, Sara assumed, but at their centre was the unmistakeable figure of Queen Caroline, Caroline the First, also known as Alice's mother.

Well.

"Meet the parent" hadn't exactly been on the agenda, but then Alice had just spent a week with Sara's family without even needing to be asked. It was the least Sara could do to get over herself, and get over her nerves, to meet the reigning monarch. She had just expected such an auspicious occasion to be quite a bit further down the line. And with a lot more rehearsal first.

"Oh damn, I should have brushed my hair," Sara said, frowning at the drizzle of rain that could only be making things worse.

"You look perfectly gorgeous," Alice said, with a brief hand squeeze of reassurance. "Trust me, her bark is much worse than her bite."

And oh, how Sarah wanted to believe her. Their whirlwind week had her entirely off-balance and unable to deny her growing feelings for Alice.

But the moment they returned to the real world another obstacle presented itself; Sara felt that had to be something of a bad omen.

It wasn't hard to see the changes that came over Alice as they both strode across the airfield to the hangar. Her posture straightened instantly, and a casual hand was run through her hair. Something in the line of her jaw tightened in a way Sara hadn't seen the entire week they were away. Even suntanned and casually dressed, something of that old-fashioned military bearing came over Alice as she approached the queen and her entourage of staff.

"Mummy! This is quite the welcome party."

Okay, Sara had hung in there with the best of them, and maybe it was the jet lag already at work, but something about a grown-ass woman greeting her mother the same way Libby greeted Sara had her close to cracking up. Thankfully, she held it together as Alice gave her mother a stiff little bow, before they exchanged the politest hug Sara had ever witnessed, their arms being about the only part of each body that made contact. The whole encounter barely lasted a second.

"Did you get the message? About needing the plane?"

"No, but here we are anyway. I'm sure the staff are on the ball. Mummy, I wanted you to meet someone—"

"Only your trip was not scheduled when my office checked last week. This almost caused quite a lot of chaos for my Canada trip, darling. You were supposed to be tagging along at one point."

"Right, but we agreed I had obligations here at home. Anyway, let Josephine battle that out with your secretary if needed. Right now, I would like to present someone rather special. Mother, this is Sara Marteau."

And then it was happening.

For all that Sara had been pretty chill around royalty, in palaces and private planes, it was something else entirely to have the full attention of the monarch on her, like headlights.

"Your Majesty," Sara said, dropping her hand luggage on the ground in her haste to try a curtsey. Then she remembered something about always letting them speak first. Damn.

"Ms Marteau, I trust you had a nice trip? Was the flight pleasant?"

Small talk. Great. Anyone could keep up with that. What did Sara care anyway? Hadn't she just spent weeks learning that ultimately, these people were only human?

"All lovely, thank you. And thank you for uh, the plane. And for Alice. It was such a lovely idea, to go away."

"Yes, the Princess Royal does so enjoy travelling." Was that a note of admonishment about using titles? Sara felt a distinct flutter in her chest.

"I would love to introduce my daughter, oh, and my mother!" Sara looked around for them, but they had disappeared in the crowd of cars and royal staff. "But they seem to have been spirited away already."

"I can track them down," Alice said, and took off into the throng before Sara could protest. That left her alone with Queen Caroline, whose polite, frozen smile still hadn't faltered.

"Thank you again, for letting Alice borrow the plane?" Sara tried, her voice rising into a question even though she hadn't intended it. "She surprised us all, did she mention that? I certainly wasn't expecting—"

"Ms Marteau, it is a pleasure to meet you, and I am quite sure that you have a charming family, all of whom enjoyed our hospitality in Mustique."

"We did, ma'am." Ma'am as in *ham*, closer to the American pronunciation. Had Sarah been told that, or just heard it on television at some point?

"And like summer evenings or the term of a prime minister, all things do come to an end. I believe we have laid on a car to take you all home."

"Right, I was just going to speak to Alice before—"

"That will not be necessary, hmm? Why drag these things out? Of course, one is most grateful that you have revived Alice's interest in being suitably partnered at last, but that duty falls now to the palace. To me, as her mother."

"I don't understand."

"No one expects you to, dear. In no time at all you will wonder what all the fuss was about. But one is afraid that your little adventure ends here. At least you caught the sun while you were away, such a healthy glow."

Sara took the polite rejection like a punch to the stomach. Was that a dig at her ethnicity too? She looked around for Alice, who seemed to have disappeared. Was this pre-arranged? Had everything Alice said been just to get Sara into bed? Behind that caring, serious face, was there just another player at work?

No. Not possible. Sara had looked her in the eye, had felt those lingering touches. They had talked and laughed and shared too much for it all to be a game. Right?

"With all due respect, I think I would prefer to hear that from Alice."

"That is not how things are done for us. You understand. But your car is waiting." Queen Caroline gestured to where Libby was waving from beside one of the huge black cars, waiting with its engine running. Bags were being put in the boot, and Inès was just visible in the passenger seat. "Thank you, for all that you have done. And might I remind you of the non-disclosure agreements you signed. Not to be indelicate, but one does find a timely reminder can go a long way, in case things should get emotional."

With that, the queen swept one of her signature silk scarves back over her shoulder, as though prepping herself to stride into battle. Instead, she dismissed Sara with one more glance, and started on the march across to the plane steps.

Bewildered by the sudden change, Sara looked around for Alice once more. Still no sign of her. Well, that had to be intentional. It was an airfield with only royal staff and family present, not Piccadilly Circus on a summer evening.

With nobody paying her any particular attention, Sara gathered her one small piece of luggage from the ground and walked to the car with as much dignity as she could muster. It didn't stop her expecting a shout from Alice with every step, or the tears from prickling at her eyes, but Sara didn't falter for a second. By the time she got to the car, Libby was already buckled in and waiting for a companion in the backseat.

"Isn't Alice going to say goodbye?" Libby said, eyes already droopy from being placed in a convenient napping location. "I wanted to give her my present from S'Vincent."

"She had to go and do some…" Sara settled on "…work. Don't worry about it, Libs."

"Okay, Mummy." The driver—not Stuart this time—finally got in, and before Sara could ask anything, he had punched their postcode into the visible GPS system on the dashboard. Clearly, he had his instructions.

Surrendering, Sara let her head sink back against the plush leather head rest. She should enjoy the luxury ride home because it certainly looked like being her last.

Chapter 25

THE LONDON HERALD, 10TH AUGUST

OUT OF ROYAL OFFICE?

Two separate organisations were caught short on a special guest for their events last week, and in both cases the missing patron was HRH The Princess Royal. Both are long-term patronages for her, and although one has declined to be named for this story, Redhooves Horse Sanctuary came forward to express their disappointment.

"Usually if something comes up, the palace will let us know in plenty of time or arrange for another interested member of the family to stand in. We all know the relationship the royals have with horses, and we assumed their support of our work with retired racing horses was an important cause for them."

Princess Alice has a publicly available schedule, but this is usually only shared after the fact for security reasons. Last week's has not yet been published, but a call to the palace confirmed that she was unavailable due to personal commitments. Is that royal speak for a week's annual leave? Or has the nation's hardest-working royal finally learned how to skive off?

Rumours that HRH was in fact off on a luxury break in a seaside paradise resort could not be confirmed at time of print, but summer holidays have begun for some schools if a certain teacher girlfriend had wanted to tag along.

COMPLETING THE LAST OF HER lengths for the morning, Alice pulled herself up on the side of the pool, getting her breath. She'd pushed herself for the last four or so, and while hardly an Olympic-level swimmer these days, she liked to think she still made pretty good time.

The pool, edged with black tiles but shimmering blue under the lights, was one of the few things she missed about living at the House. It was also one of the few parts of Buckingham Palace that had never been shared with the public. Tucked into the rear corner of the huge property, with Roman-style pillars and full-height translucent windows, it was the very spot where Alice and James had learned to swim, far from prying eyes or the shrieks of other children.

She smiled at the memory of her father pretending he would throw her in headfirst, only for him to jump in with her safely in his arms. From there she had learned her strokes, little water wings pinching the tops of her arms.

These days it was one of the places she still felt close to him, his sportsman's discipline and some lingering rugby injuries meant he was in the pool every day without fail. It wasn't hard to see the appeal of the peace in such a space.

She hoisted herself up onto the mosaic floor, water dripping off her as she made her way to the dressing area in the corner. Some stalls had been included in case a group wanted to change at the same time, but with the place to herself Alice had left her clothes and a towelling robe on the cabana-style chairs. To her great relief, someone had already brought in the breakfast tray, since swimming always left her ravenous.

After a quick rinse of the chlorine under the open shower, she settled down in her robe to start on the hearty meal of eggs, bacon and buttered toast. The pot of tea had been brewed to perfection, and for once she let herself enjoy every mouthful without thought of calories or how her waistline might look that day. Something about being with Sara seemed to have reawakened a deeper confidence in Alice.

That said, Sara had been pretty quiet since their return from Mustique. Alice had returned to a whirlwind of official apologies to make after press criticism of her going AWOL, but even with jet lag and getting Libby back to school, Sara had been all but silent. Her replies had been shorter than usual, if still witty, but she hadn't initiated conversation once, and it was starting to wear on Alice. Hadn't they returned on the very best of terms? Or was she being greedy by continuing to demand so much of Sara's attention?

As she finished up the second cup of tea, the china warm in her hand, Alice looked up to see Josephine hovering just outside the pool area. That in itself was unusual, and so she waved her loyal private secretary over.

"Sorry to disturb, Your Royal Highness, it's just we have a tiny schedule clash thanks to a request from Her Majesty, and I wanted to make sure you were happy with the changes before taking any action."

"I'm sure you'll do the right thing, Jos, you always do. None of us want to live in a world where I manage my own calendar, or nothing would ever be accomplished. Whatever Mummy wants will be fine."

"Only it means moving the dinner you wanted me to confirm with Sara. Which I can do, but I wasn't sure how you wanted to play cancelling one date for another."

Alice had just started to dry her hair with a towel as Josephine spoke, but that stopped her in her tracks. "Say what, now?"

"The addition from your mother's secretary is a date with Lady Susannah—"

"No, no, that is not happening. I mean, we talked about it while the Sara thing was just a cover. But I introduced them just the other day, and she knows I took her away on holiday. How can she think I'm still shopping for photogenic and dim aristos to have on my arm at the polo club?"

"Well, you are the Princess Royal..."

"And when I found myself without a regular companion, along came Sara with impeccable timing and everything else that is wonderful about her. You've met her. Why on earth would I be looking any further, unless she gives me the old heave-ho? She hasn't, has she?"

Josephine gave a knowing smile. "Not that I'm aware of, no. It is possible the wires just got crossed between offices. Let me take care of it."

"No, let me. If my mother is up to something, I really ought to nip it in the bud once and for all. It better be a mix-up, or I really am going to let her have it this time."

There was a particular shrug Josephine had perfected over her years in royal service. A very specific lift of her shoulders that didn't say "I don't care." but rather, "I think you know the answer already."

Alice was less than thrilled to see it in response to her mother's machinations. An unease crept over her as she reconsidered Sara's relative silence. "I'll head up to her apartment and clear things up before getting on with the day. I'm in London the whole time, yes?"

"Bank of England at lunch and then the Duchess of Edinburgh has requested you for her meeting about a new charity launch this afternoon. Something to do with fashion, so we'll have a change of clothes in between, pool photographers have access."

"Is that really necessary?" Alice tried not to groan out loud. Anything connected with "fashion" usually meant bright, uncomfortable clothes and more accessories than she could reasonably keep track of. That was before she contemplated the best part of an hour with Eugenia tutting at her and sighing just not quietly enough. "Never mind, I did promise. Onwards, upwards. And while I remember, do you think we could have some flowers sent to Sara at work? On my private account, of course."

"Consider it done," Josephine replied. "I'll ring ahead and let your mother know you're imminent, Your Royal Highness."

Alice waited on one of the antique chairs outside her mother's Audience Room, the same space where she met the prime minister each week, amongst other appointments. Watching a steward appear with the red despatch box containing confidential government papers, Alice tried in vain not to compare the workings of her own family to Sara's. The week spent with them in Mustique had been so enlightening, the way they'd been so comfortable and relaxed around each other. Nobody made appointments or announced themselves; spilling into each other's space was a constant occurrence throughout the day, every day. Hugs and jokes and silly stories were just part of everything they did together.

Alice had rarely been around such informal closeness, apart from when she had been very young. When her father was alive he had tried to insist on as much "normal" childhood as possible, but in his absence Queen Caroline had reverted to such a rigid form of royal life; just the way she had grown up with under Alice's grandparents. James had adapted well enough, that pressure of first-in-line always weighing on him, but Alice had always yearned for something more affectionate and relaxed.

Perhaps, if she made some real changes along the way, spending time with Sara would be the way to make that happen at long last. If ever there was a time to make an effort and shake things up, it was now. Provided, of course, her mother hadn't already married her off in some act of international diplomacy. What on Earth was the woman playing at?

"Come in!" Even through closed doors the queen's voice carried a certain authority. She entered to find that any staff in the room had already scattered, and greeted her mother with the customary kiss to the cheek and a half-hearted curtsey. Alice could hardly complain when there were only a handful of people she had to show that deference to.

"Hello, just your favourite daughter."

"And my only daughter, of course. Which helps." Queen Caroline greeted Alice with a pat on the arm, partly distracted by the stack of papers on the table, fresh from the despatch box. "What can I do for you?"

"I just came to thank you for setting up a date through Josephine, but perhaps I neglected to make things clear the other night. With Sara. And introducing you two."

"No, I understood perfectly." Queen Caroline fished her reading glasses out of her omnipresent purse and put them on to peer at the first paper on the stack. "You seem to think that you will be dating her, and that simply spurred me into action. We have to be realistic here, Alice. Don't worry, I handled it without any unpleasantness for you."

"There is nothing unrealistic about Sara," Alice replied, determined to stand her ground. "And if you had objections, not that I ever asked, the time to raise them was when I arranged a week away with her. That time has only brought us closer, thank you for asking."

Her mother looked up at the sharpness in Alice's tone, her blue eyes cool and appraising. "Is this a real line in the sand with you? Or one of your tantrums for the sake of it? Because while I admire some token resistance, the reason we all rub along so well darling, is that you tend to grumble a bit and then do your duty anyway."

"Is it a class thing? Or simply a matter of her not having a title?"

"How dare you? There is no one less classist than I. Your father—"

"Come off it, mother. We sit here in a room full of priceless antiques, with a staff of hundreds, and you claim somehow we still have the common touch?"

"A queen never loses touch with her people."

Alice scoffed. "People say we were chosen by God for these positions, but others call us parasites, a drain on the public purse. Never mind the Last Night of the Proms, *Rule Britannia* versions of history, there are still some out there who would favour the guillotine for us. And despite all that, I met someone who is willing to look past it and treat me as a person instead of my status."

The queen stood then, inhabiting every bit of her job title and barely recognisable as the mother Alice had cried on the shoulder of. "Ah. Here we go again. Time for another command performance from the woke princess."

"Since when do you know the term 'woke', Mummy?"

"You seem to think yourself better than all of us, the great royal progressive. Then why are you still living under my roof and taking the money that I secure from the government? Taxpayer money, that's how they always refer to it. Never mind that I too pay taxes, and that our combined income for tourism and whatever else far outstrips the cost of us."

Alice took a step back. "You speak about our family as though we were a troupe of performing seals. Not human beings with families and dreams of our own. Whatever duties we have to do to earn that money, we have a right to happiness as well."

"And that happiness has to look and act a certain way, or the people will deny you it. Do you want a life of being attacked in the headlines and stalked in the streets? We keep these positions through goodwill. Inviting the wrong sort of person into all this is the quickest way to turn the public against us." Caroline barely drew breath before continuing.

"If being a royal is cramping your style, Alice, you are more than welcome to give it all up. I almost did, once upon a time."

"You did not." Alice folded her arms over her chest, aware of the petulance in the gesture. "You would no sooner give up the Crown than give up breathing, and we all know it."

"You do not know every detail of my life. At one time, I thought giving up my position as heir might be the only way to keep your father. Fortunately for all of us, he proved me wrong. Still, he was happy for you to have this life and this title, Alice. Nobody knew better than him how it felt to be an outsider, but he never resented us for how we were all born."

"You really think so? When the paparazzi chased him on that damn quad bike, when he lay there with his neck broken, struggling to breathe... You really think he didn't know it was because of what he'd married into?"

Her mother stared at Alice as though she had been slapped. Not once had they ever talked so frankly about the circumstances of Cameron's death, not even in the rawest first days of their grief. But Alice had been there in the field with him, and Caroline had not.

"You do blame me. I always knew you did."

"I blame them," Alice said. "But there's only one reason why they were following us that day. Just like all the other days."

"And you want to bring your new fancy woman into all this? Hypocrisy of the finest order." Caroline picked up her papers again, mindlessly shuffling them. "This is why you should pick someone trained to the demands of this lifestyle; or remain alone."

"There is no training for this. Look at Kristina. The difference is that in other countries they don't hunt their royal families for sport. They make deals with the media, they act decently, everything that never happens here. I could have been married by now to the third in line to Norway's crown, but a few months of living here and she was miserable."

"This is simply making my point—"

"No, listen to me. What it needs is someone who has no interest in courting the attention. Who would give it all up because they never wanted it in the first place. Who would resist the urge to make a fortune selling a story because she values the privacy of a child too much. That is the kind of person Sara is, and that is why I am determined not to let her slip through my fingers. I cannot know the future, but I can certainly give this time to find out if we really are the right match."

"I suppose you will want my blessing?"

"Not yet. Although yes, eventually." Alice held her mother's steely gaze.

"You really are set on this woman? This Sara?"

"We have become close. Very close." Alice had no intention of betraying any more detail than that, but she saw the suspicion in her mother's eyes.

"And should I forbid it?"

At that, Alice had to laugh. "Mummy, one is closing in on forty. 'Forbid' is not an option."

"But you making a choice is. Between this woman and your place in the line of succession, or your income from the Crown. I could take both of those, at your request. To let you pursue a so-called ordinary life."

Stunned, it took Alice a moment to find words.

"If that was the only option, yes." Alice nodded as she said so, resolute.

"You cannot be serious. You would give up your whole life for some schoolteacher that you've known for a few months? She had very little trouble giving you up, when I put her straight on a few things at the airport."

"No," Alice said, biting her tongue at the airport revelation. Did that explain Sara's relative radio silence? Alice would bet her boots on it. "But I would give up the titles, the wealth, the money, whatever is needed, to be able to have a real chance at something. If it were to not work out, well, I have some skills. I would survive life outside the palace."

"I highly doubt that. Your dinner is booked for Friday evening, with a discreet press presence to record it. Be there. No arguments."

Alice could feel the full-blown argument just resting on her tongue, but for once she held her temper. She was not going to let her mother pull a power play on her and destroy her chances to have a happy life and family with Sara. Two could play at these games, and Alice always played to win. If that meant a little subterfuge to outwit her own mother, then Alice would do what was necessary. She knew Sara was worth it, and more. "Whatever you say, Mummy."

"Very well." With a flick of her wrist, the queen dismissed her only daughter.

Josephine was waiting in the hallway, pretending as though she hadn't been eavesdropping.

"All resolved, Your Royal Highness?"

"Not in a million years. For now, I need one of your good ideas for a first public date. Something to be seen at with Sara, where we might not be expected to speak, not yet."

"A shame Wimbledon has been and gone, or that would have been an excellent showcase. Mind you, with Elin Larsson retired it's not what it used to be. A night at the opera, perhaps?"

"Spare me," Alice replied with a groan. "I can hang in there with the best of them when a charity needs me to, but three hours of wailing in Italian is not my idea of a good time, and I suspect it will show. That gives me an idea, though."

"I can of course reserve the Royal Box wherever you go. Gives a certain privacy." Josephine practically winked as she said it.

"That... Okay, fine. And Josephine? Not a word to my mother's staff. Keep whatever she has planned in the diary for Friday, and then let the other woman know late-on that I shan't be available."

"Of course. And if I might, Princess Alice?" Josephine shuffled the papers she held in her hands.

"Yes?"

"Be careful with Sara—Ms Marteau, that is. Call in whichever favours you can to protect her. Plus, there is a child in the equation, one must never lose sight of that."

"You are so right, Jos. In fact, I need to set about making all of that secure right now. Can I count on your help?"

"Always. Where would you like to start?"

"Better call the car, I rather think. Some bridges need to be mended in person."

Chapter 26

"Nice time away, was it?"

Sara had been minding her business by the coffee machine when her boss, Dennis, came slinking across the staff room to interrupt her first peace of the day.

"Hmm?"

"Only I thought you were going to take that additional health and safety training over summer break, and then it never quite got booked. So my secretary tells me."

Sara scrambled to think what the headteacher could be referring to. The unexpected holiday change and all the romantic time spent with Alice had scrambled her organisational skills just a little.

"You mean the online course? I did that weeks ago."

"Oh. Still, you look well-rested. That won't last around here."

Sara looked around the staff room for anyone else to talk to, but as usual most of the teachers there were engrossed in their phones, their crosswords, or outright napping in their chairs. It made a pleasant change from squabbling about budget announcements or arguing about whose turn it was to supervise the school yard at lunchtime.

"I have some work I was going to get back to—"

"Mr Pritchell? Oh, and Ms Marteau! This saves me some time." Daisy was the head teacher's secretary and real seat of power in the school; she had been working there since the place was built.

"I was just going back to my office, Daisy." Sara tried to make an exit, mug firmly in hand.

"That's just it. We've had a call from the police asking if the school has a secure room they can use in about thirty minutes. I suggested they use your office, Mr Pritchell."

"Oh really?" Dennis bristled at the prospect of drama on his watch. Sara resisted the urge to roll her eyes. "Well, I shall be there, waiting, should they need any assistance."

"Actually, it's Ms Marteau I've been asked to fetch. That's who they want to meet in the secure location."

Sara gave them both a tight smile. Police requesting her presence could only be at the behest of one person—Alice. Clearly a couple of days of keeping quiet hadn't wrapped up Sara's humiliation once and for all. Was she really going to get officially dumped in front of her boss and half the staff instead?

"Very well, off you go then," Dennis said, and figuring any escape from him was a good start, Sara accompanied Daisy back to the head's office at the front of the school. The foyer was filled with trophies and fresh flowers, gleaming framed photos and certificates on every wall. Sara felt the eyes of the other office staff on her as she cut across the linoleum covered floors and hid herself successfully in the large, airy room that Dennis used to reign over them all.

When the cars arrived, Sara was surprised to see only two: one of the regulation Daimlers and a discreet protection car right behind. There was no mistaking Alice as she bounded out of her car though, heading straight for the school entrance like a Year Six who'd slept through the alarm before registration.

For one last moment, Sara considered a panic escape through the side window. Then there was a knock at the door and the urge to see Alice up close one more time defeated any such urge to salvage some pride.

"Come in."

Alice did. For once she lacked that palace polish. Her shirt was a little crumpled, and the trousers didn't match at all. Even her hair still looked a little damp, as if she hadn't bothered to dry it properly. No make-up, no jewellery beyond the omnipresent ring from her father. Sara knew first-hand that Alice never took it off, even to sleep.

"Promoted to headmistress already?" Alice shoved her hands in her pockets, standing rigid just inside the closed door instead of approaching. "You work fast."

"Borrowing the office. Apparently a secure space was needed." Sara folded her arms quite deliberately, hanging back by the window. They couldn't be further apart without one of them exiting the room. "You know, you say you don't want special treatment and then sending orders ahead like that..."

"A necessary evil. I apologise. I thought crashing into your personal office with protection officers might be a bit...public." Sara looked past Alice at that, seeing the back of an officer's head through the door pane. Of course. They were never far away.

"I can't imagine why you're here, Your Royal Highness. I really think that, all things considered, I've been making this as easy as humanly possible on you."

"Ah. About that. What exactly are we making easy?"

"I wasn't impressed that you had your mother of all people do your dirty work, but I suppose that keeps things neat. You even looked surprised to see her before you disappeared."

"I was. And there was no disappearing. I went looking for Libby and got waylaid by an equerry. When I came back, mother had boarded, and your car had already left."

Sara felt a twinkle of hope as she saw the confusion on Alice's face. "So that wasn't by design? I thought I was being ushered out of there as just the latest of your flings."

"No! What? Why would you think that? Just because we were going home separately? Oh Christ, she said something untoward, did she?"

"Your mother? Basically thanked me for my services on the mattress and ushered me off, yes. Apparently more suitable partners are already lined up for your royal self. So, you're welcome, I guess. I don't think much of you for still sleeping with me after I told you what that means to me, that I don't do that without commitment, but I guess these things don't matter to someone like you."

Alice lost her sangfroid at that last comment. Striding across the room, she took Sara by the upper arms and looked her square in the eye.

"Sara. Listen to me. Anything—*anything*—my mother said, was without my knowledge. And utterly not at my instruction. I thought you were being quiet after the intensity of a week away, or jet lag maybe. For me, absolutely nothing has changed about our plans. Or about how I feel about you."

Sara made a soft scoffing sound, lost for words in the face of Alice's sudden earnestness.

"But—"

"But what? Have I given any indication that I wanted to ditch you? Honestly, have I?"

Sara considered. Her faint headache that had been lingering seemed to fade at last, and where her eyes had felt dry all morning, now suddenly tears were threatening to spill. "No, I suppose not."

"My mother does not speak for me. She might think she does, but her plans will be dealt with in due course. All that changes is I think I want to make an official date the next thing we do, does that work? You at my side, official guest, walking the red carpet and all that tedious nonsense. Once it's in the press, it works in our favour for once."

"And you don't want to wait and see what duchess or viscountess your mother might find for you?" The fog of disappointment was fading, and Sara felt a certain lightness inside her, ready to burst through.

"Only you. Publicly, openly, and nobody else on the agenda. Interested?"

Alice was so close, her hold on Sara's biceps more of a welcome caress. What better response than to kiss her? It answered a lot of questions at once, judging by the whimper that caught in Alice's throat.

"Oh, thank God," she said as the kiss came to a reluctant end. "I really thought royal life had blown it for me this time. Mummy had me on the verge of renouncing all land and titles this morning."

Sara stopped short of a reply on hearing that. "Wait, what?"

"Worry not, no disinheritance just yet. I simply told her how important it was that I be allowed to pursue the woman that has captivated me, rather than sifting through suitable dating profiles like some kind of recruitment consultant."

"I can submit a CV if you think that will help."

"No, but you can tell me you're free Thursday for a night at the ballet. I can arrange it all—dress, shoes, stylist, car to collect you."

"Just the car for now," Sara replied. "I want to try and keep it simple a bit longer. How did you know I liked ballet? We've never discussed it."

"I took a guess, based on the prints I saw at your house. There was a book too, so I thought either a sophisticated night of dancing and champagne... or paintballing."

"That's really more of a weekend thing, but I'll hold you to that," Sara said. This time Alice kissed her, dragging Sara's bottom lip with her teeth. "Shame it's so visible in here, because I'd really love to ruin Dennis's whole year by defiling his office."

"Alas. I also have to go see Annabel about some gay charity thing. Might not hurt to get her and James on my side. They do owe us a favour, after all."

"You do that," Sara said. "But you should get going, I have a pile of work waiting and you're making me want to skip out of work for the afternoon. Which I absolutely cannot do, before you ask."

"Okay. You look gorgeous, by the way." Alice kissed her cheek this time, firm and brief. "Call me tonight?"

"Of course. I'm going to need details about Thursday."

"Let's see if I can get out of here without making a fuss, hmm?" With that Alice was across the room and out the door, halfway to the car before Sara had a chance to say another word.

Getting ready for dates with Alice was not getting less stressful as time went on. Sara was grateful to Jasmin for volunteering to share both the contents of her wardrobe and makeup tips, not to mention sleeping at the house overnight to look after Libby. The less disruption on that front, the better.

"You sure you're okay with staying over?" Sara directed the question to Jasmin, who was flipping through the books on the bedroom shelf, frowning at Sara's taste. "Only if anything changes, I need to let Mum know now before she leaves."

"Hey, I have auntie's rights to overnight babysit sometimes," Jasmin replied. "I took the morning off tomorrow as well so I can be sure to get her to school no problem, with some bonus shopping for me once she's safely dropped off. Perfect planning or what?"

Sara nodded. "I know I can trust you, Jas. Just be extra careful for people following you around or getting cameras out, please? Hopefully Libby out of context won't be recognised, but I need to know that we're all aware of these things."

Inès stood up at that. "Nonsense, they would never take interest in a child because her mother is dating the princess. You're crossing over into paranoia, Sara darling. A bit of nosy photography is not the same as a place where you are not free to move around."

"I'm not saying that," Sara replied, regretting the snappishness as soon as she said it. "I'm just doing everything I can to protect her, and all of us. When I do that, the anxiety goes away and I can just enjoy being with Alice. That's what you wanted for me, wasn't it?"

"Course it is," Jasmin said, rubbing Sara's arm. "We're all on board, Sara. Now come on, Inès, let's both of us go downstairs and let this lady have a moment to get her head on right."

Sara smiled in appreciation, closing the door behind them as they went.

Chapter 27

SARA CHECKED HER REFLECTION IN the full-length mirror one more time. She had almost thrown the damn thing out when she moved into the house, since the wooden frame had been almost falling apart, but a bit of internet-inspired salvaging had been enough to restore the beautiful old thing and make it a feature of her bedroom. She certainly didn't get as much use out of it as Libby, the true poser of the family, but at times like this being able to take in the full effect of an outfit was invaluable.

Was this how Angelina Jolie felt getting ready for the Oscars? Or Rihanna before the Met Gala? An invitation to a royal command ballet performance was exciting enough on its own, especially since it turned out to be raising money for St Sophia's Hospital Trust, the very building where Libby had been born.

Not to mention the part where Alice would be waiting for her, much to Sara's growing delight. She had tried to build up a wall around herself after a frosty reception from the queen—the actual, literal Queen of Great Britain—but after Alice had come to put things right between them, Sara had put aside the looming threat of some Lady Whomever coming in to usurp her.

Despite her every effort not to get caught up in all the royal shenanigans, that resolve was tested every time she thought of Alice's charming smile, or the way her fringe would fall out of place whenever she talked enthusiastically about something. Combine that with the impeccable manners, the easy athleticism about how she moved, and the action movie heroine traits like riding horses and flying planes, and Sara could see where all her reservations about dating had fallen away.

"You're not supposed to fall for her, girl." She shook her head at the prospect of talking to herself, but everyone else was tucked in front of the television downstairs. It felt suspiciously like freedom and added a certain fizz of tension to an already auspicious evening. Secluded resorts in far off countries were one thing, but would the night end with Sara sleeping in a palace? Or more bizarrely, a princess sleeping in this very room?

Sara had changed the sheets, to her very nicest ones, just in case. This was no time to be underprepared.

The prospect of being that close to Alice again sent a thrill through her, just in time for the ping of a text telling her the car was waiting outside. Gathering her wrap and her tiny handbag, Sara did the last-minute check for lipstick, keys, and phone.

Game on.

When she stepped outside, Sara looked for the expected glossy black car. A tiny part of her was looking forward to whizzing through London in a Bentley, or would it be one of those huge Daimlers that the queen was usually seen stepping out of? Instead, there was a rather nondescript black SUV idling in the middle of the narrow street, not that different to the cars the yummy mummy brigade drove when dropping off at Libby's school.

"Ms Marteau?" She recognised Stuart as soon as he stepped out of the passenger seat, with his immaculate black suit and white shirt, his bald head glowing deep brown under the amber streetlights. With a glint of gold at one ear, he looked every bit the city businessman as much as a professional bodyguard. Only his strong frame and serious expression gave him away. "If you could just hop in, ma'am."

"I don't really need the whole ma'am thing," Sara replied as she slipped through the open door and into the back seat, careful not to crush her dress. The toes of her satin high heels were already pinching, but she had treated herself to new ones to match the royal blue dress. "You've eaten at my house and had to put up with my mother, Stuart."

"It's protocol, ma'am. Keeps things orderly, if you don't mind. Although that was the finest chickpea stew I've had outside of my own mama's, I must admit."

"Oh, well don't let me interfere with a well-oiled machine. Are we going straight to the theatre?"

The car started to move as soon as she secured her seatbelt, and the driver made no attempt to join in their conversation. Stuart turned around from the front seat to keep talking.

"We'll rendezvous with Her Royal Highness at a nearby location, ma'am. From there you'll travel together as the royal party for the evening. We'll be in lead and follow cars either side of you."

"All this for a night at the opera, huh?"

"I believe it's the ballet, ma'am," Stuart replied.

"Thank you, Stuart. And uh…?"

"Michael, ma'am," the driver replied. "Roads are nice and clear so far."

"That's good," Sara said, and with that her stomach did its odd little somersault, the way it had walking to her first classes at Cambridge or interviewing for her current job. Just a little bit out of her element but believing it would somehow be fine. And neither of those events had had the benefit of Alice and her easy smiles waiting at the other end.

London whizzed by in a blur of orange-saturated streetlights and the brownish dark that never seemed to get all the way to black. The light pollution was something Sara rarely thought about, since she'd grown up with it. When she went away to smaller, darker places she missed the constant buzz of light and colour that felt like home.

She thought about Mustique, where she had been able to actually see the stars at night. As they approached the Thames, the only twinkling in the sky came from the top decks of red buses and the highest windows of skyscrapers.

Sara rested her forehead against the window for a moment, letting the vibration of tyres against the road pass through her, leaving a ticklish feeling in her ear. Ever since she was a kid going to and from school on the bus, it had been one of her natural comfort mechanisms. Maybe it was a way of connecting with something bigger than herself, with the hum of the city all around her. Maybe it just reduced the world down to a gentle vibration, one that warmed her a little as it passed through skin and bone and down through her body. At least the car had the benefit of a much cleaner window than the number 12 bus to Camberwell.

Another old habit persisted, and Sara held her breath as the car passed onto one of the many bridges crossing the river. Westminster Bridge? No, they were too far to the east for that, and Big Ben was too distant. Waterloo

Bridge then, heading straight into what only the signs called Theatreland, the heart of London's West End.

Only when they cleared the water and turned left onto the Strand did Sara release the breath she was holding. That was when she realised why the journey had been so smooth: they hadn't been stopping for red lights. Before she could work out how, she registered the blue flashing lights of the police car in front. Huh. Official police escort. Where had that been on all the mornings she'd been almost made late for work by roadworks or random crashes?

As they reached the famous old Savoy hotel, another London landmark that, as a local, Sara had never set foot in, they pulled into the building's underground parking. In a corner of a lower floor, the car eventually rolled to a stop.

When Sara stepped out, she saw a car waiting that was much more royal in appearance, albeit with huge windows that offered basically no privacy. She would be arriving at the theatre in a state-provided goldfish bowl. It was like an oversized version of the Popemobile—if the Popemobile had been designed for James Bond.

And standing beside it, between two plain clothes officers, was Alice. At first that was all Sara's brain would allow her to process. That same blonde hair, casually sideswept so her fringe couldn't make a break for it. Her face made up, lightly, but enough to emphasise the killer cheekbones and sculpted, strong jawline. Yes, if Sara stuck to familiar features, then her brain could absolutely keep working, keep processing.

Because when she contemplated how fine Alice looked in her outfit for the evening, Sara's brain short-circuited.

While Sara felt quite glamorous in the jewel toned dress that Jasmin had picked out for her, Alice, on the other hand, had the benefit of attending events like this a million times. Perhaps that was why she had opted for the far more dapper suit, in full black tie.

"Damn," Sara said as they came into each other's orbit at last, accepting the lingering kiss Alice placed on her cheek. Even their respective perfumes mingled nicely, a hint of sage and sandalwood in Alice's. Sara had always had a sharp nose for these things.

Blushing, Alice fussed with the crisp cuffs of her white shirt beneath the black tuxedo jacket. The tailoring had it fitted like a second skin for her, emphasising every line and curve like a pencil sketch. Those broad, capable shoulders and the long legs that let Alice tower over Sara by a few inches were impossible to miss. Sara didn't need her attention drawn anywhere else.

The car door was held open for them, and Sara settled into the backseat first, fussing with her skirts to keep anything from creasing. Only when Alice settled in next to her did she lean in for a proper kiss, a lingering promise that made Sara's toes curl a little, even inside her restrictive high heels.

"You look fantastic," Alice said as the kiss ended, resting her forehead against Sara's for a moment. "I almost don't want to waste all this on some stuffy night at the ballet."

"I was promised culture, so don't even think about it," Sara replied, ignoring her own temptation. "Josephine emailed me a handy little protocol sheet, but is there anything else I need to know before we're in the spotlight?"

"Not much. Don't smile too big, I suppose. It's hard to keep that up and then it looks like your enthusiasm is waning. Start with small smiles and pace yourself. Same with nodding and shaking hands. Conserve your energy."

Sara looked away, staring out of the window as the city rushed by. "You make it sound like running the marathon."

"Sometimes it feels like it." Alice's hand wrapped around her own, squeezing with quiet intent. "And it does not need to be a late one. We can duck out after the interval if needed."

"Oh, I'll be fine for tomorrow even if we stay to the end. I managed to get the day off."

Alice leaned across the small gap between them. "I wasn't worried about your work," she replied, and Sara felt that pleasant shiver run down her spine, like the silent trilling of a xylophone.

And before Sara could get her to elaborate on what they might achieve by leaving early, the car came to a stop and the surge of noise from a small but enthusiastic crowd rose up around them.

"Ready?" Alice stepped out of the car first, straightening her jacket and fussing with her cuffs for a moment. In low but sharp black heels, she was taller than usual, striking against the backdrop of the white metal and glass building that loomed over them. "Say the word and we'll turn this car around."

Sara looked out, the flurry of flashes waiting for her. Cheers went up from both sides. Would there ever be a better time, a friendlier welcome? Most of all, turning around meant seeing Alice only when they could sneak around or make complicated arrangements. Sara wanted all of it, the dinners and the events and the charitable causes that meant more time at Alice's side.

Realising that, she felt a bit dizzy for a moment. What else to do then, other than reaching for Alice's offered hand and stepping carefully from the car as Josephine's protocol sheet had advised. Not that Sara could inadvertently flash the press in such a long skirt, but perhaps it wasn't such a bad habit to get into.

With her hand secure in Alice's, Sara was a little startled at how swiftly they moved. Facing in each direction, she followed Alice's direction by waving to the crowd on either side. They didn't acknowledge the press directly, never quite coming to a complete stop, but they paused at strategic moments to allow the blinding wall of lights to flash over and over again.

Then just as quickly as it had begun, they were safely inside the Royal Opera House, with its spacious atrium and echoing floors. Sara had always loved the building, finding an excuse to slip inside and visit the shop or café whenever she was around Covent Garden, the way her friends had preferred the Doc Marten's store. It had been more than a year since she last attended a production there, but opera was usually a bunch of shrieking white people singing songs by old dead white guys, and that was hardly appointment viewing. Some of the contemporary dance shows were far more appealing, and the part of Sara that had wanted to be a dancer as a child retained a soft spot for all things ballet.

"Okay, the handshakes are a bit tedious but thankfully in this day and age, people are more germ-aware so it's really just the most important people in the receiving line." Alice brushed Sara's cheek with her lips as she gave the brief explanation.

"Do I need to remember all the names?"

"Only for the artistic director, she'll be keeping us company for most of the time we're here."

"Which one is she?"

"The one who looks like a superhero, but in a dress, with diamonds. Meredith Prince." Alice nodded to a tall, willowy woman surrounded by old men in black tie. "We ski together sometimes."

The pang in Sara's chest was unexpected. Jealousy? So soon?

"Your Royal Highness," Meredith had stepped forward to greet her, a kiss to each cheek. "It's been too long."

"Lovely to see you," Alice replied. "This is Sara Marteau, she's an education specialist and, of course, my date for this evening."

Sara froze at the prospect of Meredith diving in for those cheek kisses, but instead she shook Sara's hand in both of her own.

"A pleasure to meet you, Sara. I hope you enjoy the little show we've put together tonight. With Princess Alice as our patron, we've been able to do some wonderful things, particularly for the children in the academy."

"I'm sure it will be wonderful," Sara replied, the words just falling off her tongue. It felt almost natural. As soon as Meredith released her hand, Alice took it again. Was that a possessive squeeze of her fingers? Good.

Meredith introduced them to the gaggle of elderly rich men, and then to the star of that night's show, a ballerina who could barely have been twenty years old. The girl looked as if she might blow away on a breeze, but she greeted them with the practiced ease of a seasoned professional.

"Let me show you to the Royal Box," Meredith said, taking the lead. "Although I'm sure you're familiar with the way, Your Royal Highness."

"Just about, but then all the theatres blend into one after a while. Better safe than sorry," Alice replied.

"I barely made it back from Paris on time," Meredith said as they walked along the private corridor leading to the box. "The Eurostar was terribly delayed, but here I am. We have a bottle of champagne here ready for you, but can I bring anything else?"

"Champagne is just fine," Sara replied, watching the server in his smart waistcoat and white shirt rush to pop the cork and start pouring. Canapés had been laid out too, which was something of a relief.

"Then we'll leave you to enjoy the show," Meredith said, as soon as the glasses were filled. "Curtain up in just a few minutes. Thank you for being here. We so appreciate what it does for us."

"You are quite welcome," Alice replied, before turning to Sara and clinking their glasses together. "How was that?"

"With you? Completely bearable. Thank you for asking, though. I liked that not one of them looked at me funny, like I shouldn't be here."

"Of course you should be here," Alice said. "And anyone who implies otherwise would have me to answer to."

"That's very chivalrous of you."

"Chivalry comes with the title, or so I believe." Alice grinned as they took their seats. "Don't mind all the staring, it stops once the curtain rises."

"It's fine," Sara replied, although she picked a fixed spot on the wall to keep returning her gaze to, all the better to avoid eye contact with anyone staring. Mostly though, she kept her attention on Alice. "Um, about what you said in the car?"

"What did I say in the car?"

"About skipping out early, to make better use of the rest of the evening?"

"Oh. Well, yes. That can absolutely be arranged," Alice replied, her smile big and broad then. The orchestra finished tuning, and the lights started to dim. "God, I wish I could whisk you away again right now."

Sara smiled in turn as Alice gripped her thigh through the soft material of her dress.

"Patience, Your Royal Highness. We have plenty of night ahead of us."

Chapter 28

THE CAR RIDE ACROSS CENTRAL London seemed to take a small eternity, but the distance they travelled was hardly anything at all. They had made a sharp exit through a side entrance at the very end of the interval. The show had continued quite happily without them.

Alice had rarely been so pleased to see St James's Palace, although that was little to do with its impressive architecture, and more that it contained her twenty-one room apartment, a positive oasis of privacy where she could have Sara entirely to herself for the night. Some people had angled for a night just like that for as long as Alice had been old enough to be flirted with, and here Sara sat beside her like it happened every night.

She smiled at Alice, almost seeming to read her thoughts.

Any lingering doubts that Sara's head had only been turned by fancy holidays and titles evaporated in that moment; Alice could see her own desires reflected back at her in those dark-brown eyes. It was tempting to let Sara take the lead again.

And lead was exactly what Sara did, first with the skimming touch of her fingers at Alice's elbow as they were lead inside and up the first set of stairs. She led the way away from the car and the outside world, pausing only when she needed Alice to give some gentle direction with a touch at Sara's wrist.

Protocol usually dictated that Alice didn't follow anyone, but tonight she decided to compromise that most pointless of principles. She was incredibly glad she did when Sara greeted the external door of Alice's rooms by pressing Alice herself up against it and peppering kisses down the line of her neck. The last of the protection officers melted away in the hallway at that point, and it only took a twist of the doorknob to have them falling into the first reception room, one that Alice was eternally glad had been furnished with two large and comfortable antique sofas.

They were separated just long enough to kick the door closed behind them and half-walk, half-waltz towards the nearest soft surface. Sara lingered perhaps a moment too long with her lips and tongue lavishing attention on the sensitive hollow at the base of Alice's throat, but something in Alice wanted to say go on, mark me; as though a love bite somewhere so visible would be in any way appropriate for a woman of her status. Well, hell, wasn't that why high-collared shirts had been invented?

Letting Sara take the lead for a while was one thing, but Alice could never resist giving as good as she got. Where Sara had carefully pinned her hair, Alice took the initiative by running her fingers through it, scattering hair pins all over them and the floor beneath. She gathered Sara's loosened hair in her fists and tugged just a little roughly to draw Sara back up into another searing kiss.

They were both gently panting when they parted their lips anew. This was certainly more fun than any ballet could have hoped to be. Alice didn't want to be anywhere that wasn't pinned between Sara and the cushions of the sofa in that moment anyway. Especially once Sara yanked up her dress enough to let her straddle Alice's lap.

"Are we being a little impatient, darling?" Alice had to ask as Sara took Alice's face in her hands, thumbs caressing down from cheekbones to jaw in firm strokes.

"Yes. And I am past caring," Sara shot right back. When she kissed Alice again, Alice found her hands stroking Sara's bare thighs, massaging and almost tickling until one hand wandered north on the silky fabric of the dress to cup Sara's breast. "I thought I had missed my chance to ever do this again," Sara said. "At least for a few days, before you hatched your clever little plan."

"That would have been a real tragedy," Alice replied.

"Mmm." Sara said against Alice's cheek. "We are so not making it to a bed."

And she was right. She was so very right, because without warning or invitation the zip on a blue dress and on tailored black trousers were being lowered by purposeful hands. Half out of their formalwear, Alice paused to drink in the sight of Sara in her black satin bra, practically inviting Alice to trace its margins with her mouth.

So she did, and it was glorious.

Only then it got better, when Sara reached back and unhooked her own bra, which presented Alice with both bared breasts to kiss and lick… and yes, suck on, with perhaps just the hint of teeth.

Sara didn't seem to give a damn about leading anymore, especially once Alice slipped her right hand between Sara's thighs and nudged aside the wisp of fabric passing for underwear. With one fingertip Alice traced over the neat strip of curls, teasing around edges that were already slick from Sara's growing arousal: something that didn't hurt Alice's ego at all. The proof that—intentions be damned—Sara really, really still wanted them was enough to vanquish the very last doubts.

So, while Sara traced her thumbs over Alice's nipples, still trapped in the creamy lace of her bra despite her white shirt being opened, Alice was ravishing each of Sara's breasts in turn, drawing gasps and no small number of curses from Sara's mouth with every lick or fleeting nip.

That was nothing compared to the throaty moan that escaped when Alice first grazed Sara's clit, or the sharp utterance of "Fuck!" when Alice decided to hell with mere grazing and pressed her thumb down in a series of quick circles that made Sara's legs tremble against her.

While she didn't want it to be over too soon, Alice had very little self-control to call on. How could she resist, then, the cavalier impulse to slide two fingers inside? The way Sara's hips bucked in response was confirmation enough of how good an idea it was. They had all night to do these things over and over again.

"Please, Alice," Sara sighed as her head fell forward and rested on Alice's shoulder. No princess, no other titles, just the two of them completely equal in the moment. Even as her heart soared, Alice toyed with the idea of withholding, or at least making Sara think that she would, but the warmth and clenching of Sara's inner muscles around her fingers was too intoxicating to ignore. Working those two fingers in and out, in even thrusts, had Sara gasping against Alice's collarbone. Sara was almost sobbing when Alice added a third.

It was a question of angles, so Alice used the thumb of her other hand to rub Sara's clit, and it didn't take long at all before Sara tensed and then came, hard, against Alice's hands.

Alice cried out at Sara's release, and she almost fell over the edge herself—without being touched. In her focus on Sara, she had entirely pulled attention away from her own body.

"Oh," Sara said, pressing haphazard kisses against Alice's flushed chest. "You really are good at this. It wasn't some fluke on holiday. You just have to be good at everything, don't you, Alice?"

Alice pulled her fingers free and gave a little shrug, but before she could think of wiping them anywhere, Sara grabbed her wrist. When Sara smirked at her before very slowly and deliberately tasting herself on Alice's fingers, it sent a fresh wave of wanting through Alice in a surge.

"Not bad," Sara said, licking her lips. "Wanna taste?"

Another time, another woman, Alice might have said no. She might have pointed out that it was less than ladylike to lick the taste of Sara from her own fingers, but that was true of a lot of things that had already happened tonight, and nobody was buying it. Least of all herself.

So she raised her own fingers to her mouth and licked Sara's come from each one in turn.

It was enough to have Sara making a strangled little noise in her throat, and as Alice finished, Sara had her hands on Alice's shoulders, shoving her carelessly into the deepest corner of the sofa.

"I can't wait," Sara said, dropping to her knees in the only-slightly cramped space between the couch and the low coffee table.

Alice was distracted once more by the sight of Sara, mostly naked with her designer dress draped around her waist. Which was nothing compared to the distraction of Sara pulling Alice's trousers down past her knees, and then gently pushing those knees apart.

Alice did not resist, especially when Sara's mouth started travelling up Alice's inner thigh.

"Oh God," Alice groaned, because even if this scenario had haunted her dreams at various points in the past few days, she had always been able to control and dismiss it. But she didn't just want this; she desperately, unquestionably needed it.

"Well," Sara said from the floor as she pressed one finger against the silk of Alice's underwear. There was no hiding the fact that she had already soaked through it, and Sara looked just a little smug at the discovery. Those too were yanked down until they were below Alice's knees. It left her painfully aware of how close Sara was to the most private part of her, and although Alice liked sex, she had never made it a priority.

Tonight it felt like more than that, like maybe she would die if Sara left her like this, red-faced and ready to beg if needed. Sara had been special from their very first meeting, Alice knew that, but it was still a little terrifying that she could wield this power over Alice so effortlessly. When had she ever let go like this with anyone?

She stopped giving a damn at the first experimental swipe of Sara's tongue. Even if this were some kind of coup, or there would be a damning public exposure, Alice was going to go down with it. Or more accurately, Sara was. Her hands were warm as she pressed Alice's thighs further apart, and Alice thought it might just be worth it to rip a seam or two on her pooled trousers.

It was almost impossible to see Sara properly, thanks to the angle and lighting, so Alice tilted her head back and surrendered to sensation. Sara's fingers were stroking the crease at each thigh, before trailing up and over Alice's hipbones. The tingling was a maddening counterpoint to the slow exploration of Sara's tongue, which was licking and massaging over every inch of wetness, carefully avoiding the one place Alice needed it most.

Alice laughed, quietly. Of course Sara was being a tease. Right when it added to the tension most.

That was enough to make Sara pause, and she looked up with a curious expression.

"Something funny?"

"No," Alice said. It turned into a gasp as Sara's thumb pressed down suddenly on her clit. "Just keep going," she managed to instruct.

When Sara resumed that time, there was no teasing. Maybe she had seen Alice's desperation because from there Sara was firm with every movement, including the moment when that tongue—oh hell, that warm, wet, tongue that she wielded with such precision—took over from her thumb and began circling Alice's clit.

And that was it.

With that, Alice was completely gone. For a few endless seconds she was overwhelmed by the surge and crash of orgasm, since Sara held her position and sent Alice slamming into a second climax without any warning. Alice made a fist, unconsciously, and bit down on her own flesh as she climaxed. It kept her at least a little quiet, because while nobody was too close by, the rooms were hardly soundproof.

Alice had barely recovered when Sara climbed up to sort of lie on top of her. Alice's shirt was rumpled and open, but still mostly in place when Sara pressed her bare torso against it. Sara was intent on kissing Alice, letting her taste herself in some full-sensory experience.

Alice latched on to her mouth greedily, stroking and sucking until Sara was every bit as breathless as she is.

"Holy shit," Sara said when they parted, and she started easing her way back into her dress while sitting up. Alice didn't mention Sara's discarded bra, but she did zip Sara's dress the rest of the way off when she turned to ask for it.

"My thoughts exactly," Alice replied, trying to pull her own clothes off for good, lifting her backside off the seat to achieve it. Sara stood first, her discarded clothes in her arms.

"I'm tired," Sara said, but with a lopsided, fond smile. "In fact I'm so tired, you'd probably better get me to a bed right away."

"Well, I hate to disappoint but we have a bit of a hike. Downsides of living in a palace, you know."

"I don't mind stretching my legs," Sara replied. "How far can it be from your living room, anyway?"

"You'd be surprised." Shaking off her post-coital lethargy, Alice had a new spring in her step as she led the way through room after room. For once she was aware of every painting and tapestry that loomed over them, seeing the old place as though through new eyes. Was Sara regretting her decision, faced with this stark reminder of the stuffy old relics that formed so much of Alice's life?

They paused at the bedroom door, and Sara leaned in just enough to press a kiss to Alice's shoulder, where her jacket, worn as a sort of cape, had slipped to expose the crumpled white linen of her shirt. The heat surged through Alice anew.

"Okay to stay over?" Alice checked even as she ushered Sara inside. "If you need to get back for Libby, just let me know and I can call a car around."

"No, I have the whole night," Sara replied. "Not that I was being presumptuous, you know. But Jasmin jumped at the chance to stay over at ours. She works a lot, and I think she misses getting quality aunty time with Libby.

"That's right, Jasmin is her aunt, as well as your best friend."

"That's right. You two should meet, I think you'd like her. She's not dazzled by all this royalty stuff either."

Alice gestured to yet another couch in the centre of the room, right at the foot of the bed, indicating that Sara should sit. "Brandy?"

Sara nodded, and Alice went straight to the crystal decanter, pouring two generous measures.

"What does that mean—'you know'?"

"Oh, I'm sure you get it all the time. People a bit dazzled by the title and all. Please know I'm not going to bring that kind of nonsense into your life if I can help it."

"That's sweet of you," Alice said, sitting down next to Alice and handing over the wide brandy glass. "But I think I've proven that I can get people to see past all the princess stuff. *N'est-ce pas*?"

"And she speaks French, too," Sara replied, teasing just a little. She sank back against the cushions, her restless fingers trailing along Alice's thigh. "No wonder my mother likes you so much."

"Well, a few generations back my family are French. So in case there's ever a coup, we can shuffle right back over."

"Sensible. Not much explanation for why you also speak Latin, but I'm reliably informed by Annie that the reason for that is, and I'm quoting here, You're a giant nerd."

Alice took a sip of her brandy, enjoying the warmth as she swallowed it. "And yet, here you are. Quite smitten with the so-called giant nerd. What does that make *you*, Ms Marteau?"

Sara considered for a moment, swirling her drink in the glass. "Lucky," she replied, her voice so soft that Alice almost missed it. "Really, really lucky."

"Luck has nothing to do with it," Alice said, taking both their glasses and setting them on the table, before settling in close, her hand on Sara's waist as their faces drew closer. "You're making me start to believe in fate, you know. I think our paths were meant to cross."

"I'm just glad they did," Sara replied, before kissing Alice sweetly on the lips, no expectation or demand in the gentle touch. "I believe I was promised a bed, but this is certainly not it."

"This way." Alice stood, and just as she had back in Mustique, scooped Sara up bridal style, her unworn clothes falling to the floor. Her lower back gave the tiniest twinge of protest, but Alice was determined. She rounded the huge bed and realised that it was going to look so much better with two occupants instead of one person, all alone.

Chapter 29

Sara woke up with a start, light streaming into the room in a way that suggested she'd forgotten to pull the blinds down before bed. Then she squinted a little: the ceiling seemed much farther away than it should be.

Groaning softly, she rolled over and confirmed her surroundings. Heavy velvet curtains had been drawn back, letting in the early morning sunlight. The sheets covering Sara's naked body were both luxuriously soft and pretty damned heavy. She had invested in a weighted blanket for Libby the previous year, and finally Sara understood the appeal: even in unfamiliar circumstances, the heft of the sheets and blankets weighing her down brought a certain calm to the situation.

"Good morning, Sleeping Beauty," Alice said, sitting on the edge of the bed. "I made us some breakfast."

Sara shot her a suspicious look.

"Okay, I went down to the kitchens and tried to make breakfast. Which I am perfectly capable of doing, thank you very much. Only, well, it is a professional kitchen, so I was slightly in the way."

"You don't say." Sara stretched beneath the sheets, luxuriating in the way her muscles flexed and unfurled. A little twang here and there reminded her it had been quite an enthusiastic evening. "I'm not that fussy about breakfast anyway."

"Nonsense. Most important meal of the day. Come, come, I've laid it all out over here. Now, are you a browse-the-papers type? Or stick on the news and eat quietly until brains fully gear up type? I confess mine is usually dictated by how much one had to drink the previous evening."

"I could go for some news, unless the world is ending, in which case I'll default to cartoons."

"There speaks a woman who frequently loses control of the remote to her daughter."

"It's like you've been there." Sara pulled back the covers, not missing Alice's appreciative glance up and down her naked body, before reaching for the robe that had been laid out for her. Wrapping it around herself and tying the belt loosely, Sara realised it might be silk.

Damn. A girl could get used to the finer things.

Sara's socialist-voting, street-protesting, national-anthem-ignoring, child of immigrant history gave her an internal kick, like a teacher giving a warning cough for looking around in an exam. She checked her phone, realising the battery was almost done. Alice gave a knowing smile before nodding to the bedside table where a charging cable was waiting.

"I know it seems like we light the place with candles, but Josephine and her crew are really quite excellent in keeping the place kitted out." Alice led the way to a sitting area, a table and chairs rounding out two small couches in front of a fireplace. What looked like a framed painting above it transformed with a click into the morning news.

"Any preference for news?" Alice flipped through channels. "One is little biased towards Auntie Beeb, if only because the BBC usually hate us a little less than the cable news channels. Some weeks that difference is negligible, though."

"This is fine," Sara said, sitting down to a table laden with silver dish covers and heavy cutlery. The scent of a brewing pot of tea reached her nose first. Something strong and rich: Assam unless she was totally mistaken.

It was decadent to be up later than six on a weekday and having booked a rare day of leave had Sara feeling a little lazy for once. Why not take her time investigating the dishes that littered the table? Then maybe take Alice back to bed, or one of those handy sofas? Though given the luxury of everything else, the prospect of a shower was certainly calling Sara's name too. It was all faintly surreal, like an unexpected upgrade when staying in a hotel.

The newsreader droned on about some sort of tax summit, until the footage changed and Sara sat more upright on recognising the people involved.

"This morning, the Prince of Wales and his wife, Annabel, Duchess of Edinburgh, are in attendance at a primary school just across the river from their London residence. With them, Princess Anne and Prince Rupert, second and third in line to the throne, but today just ordinary schoolchildren meeting their new teachers and some classmates whom they'll be joining in the new term.

"They've gone public!" Sara clapped her hands at the sight of Anne and Rupert, both a little shy in front of the cameras. Like all other events, they didn't talk to any of the reporters, but it was adorable to watch them shaking hands with their new teachers. The adults were all lined up in a receiving line, reminding Sara of nothing so much as the day she met Alice, Libby's mini meltdown and all.

"Yes, and I believe they recorded a little something last night. Here it is." Alice had a slice of toast in one hand, barely scraped with a suggestion of marmalade. She gestured to the screen with the other.

The scene changed from the school playground to an opulent room, presumably at Kensington Palace. James and Annabel sat side by side on a plush red velvet sofa, a twin on each lap. Sara was impressed by how quietly they both accepted it: interviewer, camera, and all. Neither child squirmed even a little, but while Annie sat looking directly into the camera like her parents, Rupert studiously avoided eye contact with anyone.

"You've broken with tradition, even the one set by your own parents, Your Royal Highness," the interviewer said. "What people at home may be wondering is, why change the plan for schooling the children at this late stage? Surely these things are decided years in advance?"

"They were," James replied. "We had a plan in place from right around when the twins were born. Then of course everyone was so disrupted for more than a year, and we all had to learn the fine arts of home schooling."

"Which we very much enjoyed," Annabel added, giving Rupert a gentle hug as he sat on her knee. "We had a lot of help, of course. But now that we can head back to school full time, there were some other considerations for us, as a family."

The interviewer leaned in, coiffed brown hair and immaculate pantsuit meaning she looked the part exactly. "And what considerations were those?"

"Over the course of recent months, we've talked with doctors and educational specialists," James said, and although the words were clearly rehearsed, he seemed to be just thinking of them in the moment. "And Rupert here has a different style of learning to his sister. So although they're close and want to be schooled together, we needed to find somewhere that could help him thrive with his diagnosis."

"Rupert is autistic," Annabel picked up the thread. "That is to say, he is on the autism spectrum, and we thought for a long time about whether that was something we wanted to make public. In the end, we spoke with him about it and asked what he wanted to do.

"And although the children don't usually speak to the press, he is happy for us to talk about it, because we explained that it will help other children and families if we can be open and honest about better ways to do things. Ways that mean everyone gets to learn the way that works for them, and be relaxed and happy." James sat up straighter as he spoke, and for the first time Sara realised that was her future king. How different would the world look by the time James took over from his mother!

Alice hadn't said a word, and Sara looked across to see the silent tears rolling down her cheeks.

"Hey..." She got up and moved around the table to hug Alice around her shoulders. "This is a good thing, I promise."

"I know. I know, and I am so proud of them. I just cannot help but worry still. I think of the things that were said about me, or James, far less important things, and those have followed us our whole lives. You know there will be talk about whether Rupert is fit to be in the line of succession, all kinds of cruel things."

"Then we'll be ready and waiting with press releases or whatever, shooting down every terrible word. But maybe people will surprise you this time."

"We?"

Sara bit her lower lip, realising how presumptuous she had been. "Well, you know, if you need me. Professionally...or personally. I would be around."

Alice leaned into Sara's hug, squeezing her forearm with strong fingers. "Careful. I might start to believe you do like me."

"I think I might have given myself away on that front already."

"So much for Little Miss 'small r' republican. Kissing princesses will not go down well at the monthly anarchist meeting, will it?"

"Anarchists don't have meetings. And I'm more of a lefty feminist nightmare, in fact."

"Mustn't forget that," Alice said, pulling Sara into her lap and kissing her soundly. "Only you don't seem like much of a nightmare. Not with me, anyway. In fact, you're more of a daydream."

Sara kissed her again, and as they basked in the morning sun the day seemed endless, stretching out in front of them. "Cheesy, but I'll let it go this once. It would be nice to see Annie and Rupert again sometime. Let them know they have the extra support if they need it."

On screen, the interview had wrapped up and the newscaster was talking about the contact details for autism charities, which warmed Sara even further. This kind of public attention would have an upside after all.

"Speaking of adorable munchkins, it does seem like I have been stealing you away from Libby lately. What do you say we pick her up after school and head up to Sandringham for the weekend?"

"I have lunch plans on Sunday with Jasmin, but until then, sure. Libby will be thrilled."

"And we might even get you on a horse."

Sara gave a snorting sort of laugh. "Yeah, right."

"But before that, it's time for us to go social media official. Obviously we made the papers everywhere before they went to print late last night, and there have been shots online for hours. But what usually happens is they send me a few options and I make an official post from my account. Since this concerns both of us, I wanted to check with you which picture looks best."

"You don't have to tag me, do you?" Sara's skin got goosebumps at the thought. Alice's official accounts had followers in their millions. The friend requests alone would probably break the app if she suddenly announced Sara like that.

"Oh, no. If that becomes a thing, we would either share an account like James and Annabel, or set you up a brand-new public profile. You have everything else locked down, yes?"

Sara nodded. "Yes, between work and Libby's privacy I don't have any accounts that aren't private or locked. No public anything, anywhere. I'll be having a cull of my lists as well, weed out all the people I'm not close to before I post anything about us."

"Then we're on the same page. My preference would be this one, but look at all five." Alice handed over a tablet, then took a final bite of her toast.

Sara stared at the almost surreal images on the screen in front of her. Excellent quality, and of course no red eyes or squinting. Clearly these had been selected as the best of the bunch. And hell, she and Alice looked good together.

They kissed again as their tea started to grow cold in dainty china cups.

"Mummy!" Libby came skipping through the school gates, one strap of her rucksack dangling free, and one of her cute little hair puffs undone, the scrunchie for it nowhere in sight. Still, at least most of her uniform was still in evidence. Better than a lot of Fridays, anyway.

"Hello, trouble. All done with school and ready for the weekend?"

Libby barrelled into her with a hug. "Course I am, silly. Didn't you hear the bell while you were waiting?"

"And you're sure you didn't break lots of rules and get detention? Or maybe some extra Saturday classes?" Sara kept a straight face to tease her daughter, but Libby's indignation was instant.

"We don't have detention, Mummy!"

"Just teasing, just teasing! Now, come this way because I've got a surprise for you."

"You're not in work clothes," Libby replied, not missing a trick. "Are we going to fly again?"

"Not quite," Sara said, and when they reached the end of the school fences, instead of turning left towards the main road and the bus stops, she steered Libby right to the waiting cars in a small car park that belonged to a brand-new block of flats.

"Alice!" Libby gave a yelp and ran towards the sleek Mercedes where Alice stood beside the open driver's door, watching her surroundings from behind dark glasses. They greeted each other with a big hug that dropped Libby's bag to the ground, leaving Sara to scoop it up. She couldn't contain her grin at the sight of them so happy to see one another.

"Come on Libs, no hanging around I'm afraid. We want to get ahead of the weekend traffic."

"Are we going to see the horses?" Libby said, as Sara wrestled her into the backseat and secured the seatbelts. "I haven't got any clothes for riding!"

"I went home on the way here to get some things for the weekend," Sara told her, winking at Alice as she closed the car door and made her way around to the passenger seat.

As soon as she was situated, Alice started the engine and the other huge black car beside them roared into life as well. It was nice to have the car to themselves, but Alice was almost never allowed to go off anywhere totally unattended. Certainly not in London.

"Okay, usually the driver gets to pick the music, but Libby I think your mummy has some of your favourites on her phone. Shall we let her choose?"

"What if she chooses Baby Shark or something terrible?" Libby gave Sara a suspicious look as she asked it.

"You're right, too risky," Alice replied. She pushed a couple of buttons on the fancy console and the familiar beats of a Taylor Swift song filled the car.

"Didn't have you down for a Swiftie," Sara said, barely covering her laugh. "No opera today?"

"I contain multitudes, you know." Alice kept her eyes on the road, driving with the same easy confidence she did most things. Sara found herself distracted by the way Alice's forearms flexed and relaxed, her crisp white shirt sleeves rolled up to the elbow. "And Taylor happens to be a friend. I could have been part of the 'squad' but our schedules never quite lined up."

Sara had a vague memory of newspaper headlines and photos of Alice at some big Wembley concert a few years ago. Was that the same time, or did she just mingle with any global pop stars who happened to be passing through? All in the name of representing Great Britain, of course.

Libby's eyes were as wide as saucers in the backseat. For the first time, she had been stunned into silence.

"Is it a long drive?" Sara placed her hand over Alice's once it rested on top of the gearstick. City driving meant going up and down the gears a lot, and Sara found herself longing for the faster open roads out to the countryside. Who knew she'd been secretly waiting to join the country set all along? Maybe it was time she got around to thinking about a driving licence of her own.

"Not really. And if we hit traffic, well, you've seen what the boys in the chase car can do with their lights and sirens to keep us moving."

"A girl could get spoiled, living like this," Sara replied.

Alice shot her a cute, lopsided smile. "I certainly hope so."

Chapter 30

Alice closed her eyes for just a moment as they trotted back to the paddock, Sara perfectly balanced in front of her on Pickle, Alice's favourite mare. The saddle wasn't designed for two, so Alice had given it over to Sara as the less experienced rider, effectively riding bareback while pressed up against her and controlling the reins. It only took a light touch on a horse that knew her so well, leaving plenty of time to enjoy the gently rolling sensation of Sara in her arms.

Not that Sara was relaxed about it all, exactly. More than once Alice had passed her the reins on easy stretches, leaving her hands free to massage those tense shoulders. Each time Sara had melted a little under the touch, but the combination of being atop such a huge horse, plus watching Libby deftly potter about on a pony, brought the tension right back each time.

"How was that?" Alice brought the horse to a halt by the water troughs. She slid off with practiced ease, patting Pickle's neck as Sara took her feet out of both stirrups and swung her leg back over to dismount. A weekend's practice made a success of it, and she celebrated the safe landing by pulling Alice into a quick embrace.

"That was very cool," Sara replied once she had kissed Alice quite thoroughly. "You might make a jockey of me yet."

"I'm afraid the closest we get to racing is wearing ridiculous hats to Ascot, darling. But you'd be most welcome. And your mother would love the chance to pick out another flying saucer of a hat, I bet."

"That might be nice. All these things I thought only happened to people on television."

"Well, tag along with me and you rather become one of those people on television. Assuming that is still okay?"

Sara took Alice's hand. "Still a bit weird to think about, but definitely getting more okay with it, the more we do this kind of thing just for us, and Libby."

"It just makes me wish we had more time available. This week alone I'm in Birmingham, Manchester, something in Wales and something else way up in the Highlands. I never used to mind, and the travelling is always comfortable, but it is such a stretch of time where we could be having a long lunch, or you could be staying over."

"Are you saying lunch outranks sex, princess?"

Alice felt a tingle down her spine. "How do you do that?"

"Do what?"

"Take a title I've been hearing my whole life, like it's just part of my name, and make it sound all new? And frankly, a bit saucy."

"Saucy? What decade is this?"

"Would you really rather I tried to throw down with the lingo of the streets?"

Sara burst out laughing. "No. No, anything but that. Shall we go and see if Libby can be surgically removed from that pony yet? We need to get cleaned up and head back to see Jasmin. She was fine moving brunch to lunch, but I suspect her boss-slash-crush won't be too happy when I show up sans princess."

Alice put her arm around Sara's shoulders as they crossed the field to where Annie, Rupert, and Libby had brought their ponies in for a rest. All three were still in the saddle as Alice and Sara approached, their quiet chatter ceasing as adults drew near. Some things never changed, Alice could absolutely picture herself and James doing exactly the same as kids.

"Mummy, do we have to go?" Libby practically wrapped herself around her pony's long neck. "We see Aunty Jasmin all the time. Or maybe we can video call her? Remember when we had to do that every week?"

"It's not just about lunch, Libs. We have to get everything ready for work and school. You know Sunday is chores day."

"Aunty Alice, can't Sara borrow a housekeeper or something? Then Libby could play with us and the chores would still be done." Annie seemed quite pleased with her solution, but Alice shook her head.

"You tell me, Annie. Do your parents ever say that you can skip chores and go out to play instead?"

"Sometimes?"

"No," Rupert chimed in. "No playing until the playroom is tidy and our beds are properly made."

"See? No excuses," Sara said, nudging Alice with her hip. "Are you sure it's okay for us to have a car and a driver? I don't mind getting the train."

"Nonsense," Alice replied. "And we'll have to talk about this more, with things going public, but things like that will probably come under the old umbrella of security arrangements. You might find life easier with a person or two around to clear the way, sometimes."

"Like a bodyguard?" Libby got off her horse with great reluctance, her little feet hitting the ground hard in her riding boots. She led the pony by the reins, just as the others fell in step leading theirs, for the short walk back to the stables.

"We don't need bodyguards," Sara replied, as much to Alice as to Libby. "But I suppose I see the point. It's been a glorious weekend of ignoring the papers but I know the coverage is out there waiting for us, isn't it? People are going to know my face for sure."

Alice held back until the children were out of earshot. "I did ask Josephine to track it all. Obviously, the announcement about Rupert has taken some of the heat off us, but never underestimate the British tabloid press and its thirst for a good royal scandal or two. They are more than capable of giving too much attention to more than one story at a time. I just want you to be safe, especially when Libby is with you."

"Always so chivalrous."

"Well, I would volunteer myself, but I'm afraid my presence only adds to the problem. I could handle any paparazzi that get too close though, be assured on that."

"I'll catch up with the news on the drive back," Sara said. "And you, princess, can keep the idea of fighting photographers for my virtue out of your head. I won't have it said that I'm the bad influence who has you scrapping in the streets, yeah?"

"Go on, get yourself back indoors and get ready for lunch. Car will be here soon."

"I'm so glad we did this," Sara said, stealing one more kiss before jogging away from the stables.

Not as glad as I am, Alice thought, watching every moment of Sara's retreat.

Sunday afternoons had been reserved for games when her father was alive: cricket in the sunshine and board games when it rained, and somehow Alice and James had managed to keep hold of that time with their mother. Most weeks, anyway. Every so often a trip would require an early start, or one of them would be on a longer tour somewhere across the Commonwealth.

After Alice had seen off Sara and Libby she cleaned up and changed, even though no one in the immediate family would complain about a certain eau de stables. She headed for the Great Room, rather fancifully named for a space that contained just comfortable sofas, a huge television, and plenty of toys to keep the children occupied. With, admittedly, a priceless work of art or two hanging on the wall. The sort of detail a person forgot to notice after a while.

By the time Alice showed up, James and Annabel had beaten her to it, half-watching the kids play over their respective half-read books and a cup of tea.

"Sara get off okay?" Annabel barely looked up on asking. She seemed too engrossed in her book for real conversation.

"Yes, en route as we speak. She had some family engagement, and of course the school week starts all over again tomorrow for both of them."

"I'm surprised you brought her here," James said. "She's really no fan of the horses, you know."

"But Libby is. I even talked Sara into an unofficial lesson with me."

Annabel looked up at that. "You two are so predictable. James tried the same tactic with me."

"Excuse me, I was being a gentleman. And you might have mentioned that you'd been doing dressage since you were ten," James replied, indignant all over again.

"Well, at least you learned early on not to underestimate me. A lesson this family might take when it comes to a certain Ms Marteau."

"What do you mean?" Alice pounced on Annabel's sly smile. "Has she said something?"

"Not in particular, but I recognise something of myself in the girl. And she has that same look about her that I did, back in the early days. Where it's somewhere between being hit by a train but still being quite sure that this is the one you want. A maddening state to be in and look what it leads to." Annabel gestured to the children, her array of jewelled rings catching the light perfectly as she did so.

"Mummy will be in soon," James replied, setting his book aside. "And don't bother using me as a human shield. If she is narked about you ruining the date plan with your own media frenzy—that is one hundred percent on you."

"There's my noble big brother. A real lionheart, aren't you?" Alice said, picking up a book and putting it down again with no small amount of irritation. "Annabel, when Mummy starts on me, can I count on your support?"

"For the little that it's worth, yes." Annabel hid her frown quickly, but not well. "Although we have been getting better about listening to each other now the children are up and running a bit more."

"She will be in any moment." James got up then, starting to pace between the couches.

Alice held up her hand to cut him off. "Quit overreacting."

"You have made it quite clear you want to pursue a relationship with Sara, and your mother will respect that," Annabel said, looking to Alice and then James in turn. "And she seems quite smitten with you too, Alice. It helps that you're so good with Libby. That would be a deal-breaker for me, in her position."

"She's a great kid, it's no sacrifice on my part. And I do care for Sara, I doubt I could deny that much longer. It's bad enough I had to send them back at all. But one is aware of the cliché, and the last thing I would want is to scare them off by rushing anything."

James stopped his pacing right next to her, taking Alice by the shoulders. "Are you sure—and forgive me for being so blunt, 'Lice—are you sure that this isn't just a case of sleeping with the help to shock Mummy? Sara was technically working for us."

"What did you say?" Alice looked at the children, luckily oblivious on the far side of the room. Their presence was the only thing stopping her from launching herself at her brother with fists swinging. "I happen to care for Sara a great deal. How dare you talk about her like that? You think Dad would have wanted you to talk that way?"

"Dad loved being royalty as much as the next man. And you heard the rumours about him, so do not play the innocent with me. Mistresses, unofficial lovers, it's all part of the bloody Firm. I didn't invent it."

"But if nobody changes, then nothing ever changes," Annabel said, and Alice saw the flash of very real pain cross her expression. James hadn't, had he? Oh, that insufferable pig. "We all make our choices. And we must live with them. I think Sara would be a breath of fresh air around here, to be honest."

"Because God forbid you support me for once," James said. "There is no need to be dragging all of this out in front of family just because you are in one of your moods with me, Annabel."

"This is no mood," she replied. "I was simply reminding Alice that a happy relationship is a very valuable thing. I know you would prefer I never have an opinion of my own, but there it is."

"Guys, guys, please nobody get upset over my dating life." Alice had no idea how to un-hear the bitterness between two people she had considered really quite happy together. "We can change the subject altogether."

Any further conflict was interrupted by the arrival of Queen Caroline, whose determined stride suggested she was bringing plenty of her own.

"Alice, there you are. What on earth happened to your dinner on Friday?"

"Cancelled. I was out on Thursday, with Sara. You must have seen the coverage. We made all the papers."

"Was that supposed to be defiance? You seeing someone more suitable will make far splashier headlines. You know that's all part of the dance with those horrid little men from the tabloids. At a certain point you have to give them what they want." Caroline took up position on a couch, effortlessly presiding over the room.

"It so happens that what, or whom, I want, is Sara." Alice could see a hundred ways to back down and smooth things over; a lifetime of doing exactly that had prepared her perfectly. But if she closed her eyes and recalled the way Sara's hand seemed to fit exactly in hers, or how her smile seemed to slowly light up the room each time it spread across her face, then Alice knew she had to stand her ground at last. "James and Annabel both agree I'm making a sound choice. She helped them a great deal and was completely discreet."

"That's right," Annabel said, pulling Rupert into her arms as he wandered over for a hug. "Sara Marteau is really quite lovely. I can't imagine she would bring anything to the family but positive attention."

"Although it may look as though we go out of our way to marry commoners," James replied. "No offence, darling, but you had no titles and neither did Papa. Shouldn't one of us throw a bone to all the fourth cousins waiting in the wings?"

"That was a horrifying image, please never share that again," Caroline said. "And nobody said anything about marriage. Your sister is just bored and trying to find a little company. Even at the cost of irritating me."

"And if I did…you know, plan on something long term… There ought to be changes. Significant ones." Alice had been resisting the topic, but the thoughts seemed to come to her fully formed. A growing certainty had settled over her; she could feel it in the swing of her hips when she walked, and the way her thoughts had grown quieter when left alone.

"We talked, before, about having my own official residence. While I have never felt anything but welcome in each of your homes, and St James's does the trick for most of the time, there is something to be said for a roof of one's own. Somewhere to raise a family, whatever that might look like. And if Sara has no interest in taking things that far, then I know that is something I am looking for. Soon. Ish."

Alice caught the knowing look between her mother and Annabel. Apparently the thought of Sara not being interested was amusing to them. Alice wished she shared that level of confidence, despite all that had already happened. The whole thing seemed to teeter on a knife edge, waiting for the first big intrusion or media nastiness to tip it over into untenable.

The queen spoke up. "There is always Windsor. Oh, don't pull that face. There's nothing wrong with it."

"Not for a wedding, perhaps. But living there is a bit…you know. Like a ghost in chains rattling around the huge old place."

"Then we can have the Estates Office start looking around for something new. Surely no one can begrudge you that; three generations since the family last added anywhere to the portfolio. And it will come out of my purse, of course. No public money." Caroline pulled out her phone and stabbed at the screen a few times, presumably summoning one of her own staff. "Somewhere in commuting distance of London, then?"

"With space, yes. Somewhere easy to mark the boundaries and keep people out," James said, as though it were up to him. "Ideally somewhere they're used to having a big local landowner who calls the shots—it really cuts down on accidental trespass and all those nuisances that drive Special Branch crazy. And plenty of room for another offspring or two, eh?" James crossed the room to pull Alice into a brisk hug. "Sorry about the mistress thing," he said quiet enough that only she could hear. "I didn't realise you were so into her."

Alice gave him a smile as he ended the hug. That argument could wait for another time. "I would like to retain the option of children. Which is another thing, Mummy. The way laws stand at the moment, any stepchild or adopted child of ours would be treated quite differently. I think we should look at changing that, much as we changed the rules about girls before Annie and Rupes came along."

"You should have changed that rule before you had kids, Mummy," James replied. "That way I could have the easy life instead of 'Lice."

"No, you idiot, because you're still the eldest." Alice tossed another cushion at him just for the nickname.

"Can we please behave in front of the children? Rupert, do good children throw cushions at one another?"

"No, Granny." Rupert slipped free of his mother's embrace and came over to sit beside his grandmother instead.

"That's my boy. If they do it again, you tell them off for me, okay?"

Rupert nodded, before going back to playing with his most beloved toy train. Caroline watched him for a moment before looking up at Alice, her gaze steady but thoughtful.

"Do you love this woman?"

Alice shrugged her shoulders, buying time. If she told anyone that, it really ought to be Sara first. "I could. For the first time in a long time, I really think I could."

"Then plans will be made." Caroline made the concession with a heavy sigh, but just the slightest twinkle in her eye. "I must say, Alice. It is quite something to see you finally stand up for yourself."

"Well, perhaps it was time I found something worth standing up for." As Alice said it, she finally understood all those silly fairy tales where supposedly brave royals fought dragons or witches to save the ones they loved. In that moment, she could have conquered just about anything if being with Sara was her reward.

Chapter 31

The drive back to London seemed to fly by. Libby, exhausted by the outdoor pursuits, had resorted to napping in her booster seat. Sara used the time to catch up on some emails. Being chauffeured around certainly didn't hurt on the productivity front.

She had just replied to Jas's latest text, informing her that no royals would be coming to lunch, when Sara heard a strange popping sound, followed by a much louder bang.

Instinct kicked in.

Libby.

Sara extended her left arm, in a protective gesture over Libby's chest. Her own seatbelt pulled taut as she was thrown forward, and she felt the pressure of Libby's smaller body doing the same beneath her arm.

Brakes screeched.

A horn blasted. Somewhere outside of the car a shout rose and faded, someone still in motion.

Sara closed her eyes for just a second. Two. Had she bitten her tongue? Ow, yes. Just the tiniest nip on the edge. No blood. Good, no blood was good and—

Libby squealed. High and piercing.

Sara opened her eyes, scrabbling against the shuddering motion of the car to keep hold of her daughter. With a dull thump the car finally came to a halt.

"Ma'am, are you okay? Ma'am?" Stuart in the driver's seat still had a death grip on the wheel, but he had the grace not to look panicked as he turned around to check on them as soon as the car came to a halt on the hard shoulder. "Something hit us. Maybe just some loose stones on the road, but at least one tyre is blown."

"I don't like the sound of that," Sara said, heart still pounding. "Libby, are you okay?"

"That was scary," Libby replied, her bottom lip trembling. "Mummy..."

"You're fine, sweetheart. We're both fine."

Another thud, much louder this time. The car shook with the force of it. Sara squealed. Libby did too.

Stuart leapt into action. He was out of the car and running around to Libby's side before Sara knew what was happening. "Okay, come out this way. Come on. We need to get you to cover. There are some big rocks over here, see?" His voice was calm, but Sara saw the panic in his expression when their eyes met.

"Shouldn't we stay in the car?" Sara's question was answered by glass shattering in the driver's window. With a yelp, she let Stuart pull Libby from the car and scrambled after them, keeping low behind the car until they found shelter behind the loose boulders that lined the busy road.

Cars kept whizzing by. Sara heard her heart pounding in her chest, pulling Libby close and gently shushing her the way she had as a baby.

Stuart spoke into some kind of microphone in his sleeve, drawing a gun from a holster hidden beneath his jacket. "Shots fired. One shooter, sounds like rifle fire. I've brought both my charges to shelter but it's too open out here."

"Stuart?" Sara's head was reeling. Shots? As in guns? Had he been carrying a gun around them this whole time? Turning away from Libby but keeping hold of her hand, Sara's stomach churned so badly she had no choice but to throw up into the long grass.

"Stay here," Stuart said. "I can't wait for backup in case this idiot decides to get on the move. You're safe here, just stay covered."

Sara nodded. She had no intention of moving an inch.

"We're okay, Libs. How are you feeling?" Sara held her daughter tight, pulling back only to double check for injuries before wrapping her up in a hug again.

"Mummy, I don't like this."

The crack of gunshots filled the air again, three in rapid succession followed by one single shot. Sara's stomach flipped as she heard Stuart cry out. Another two shots rang out, then there was only the sound of cars racing by and the ragged sound of their breathing.

"Stuart?" Sara called out. "Did you get them?"

"Affirmative," Stuart said a moment later, jogging back over to them behind the rocks. His wax jacket was gone, and Sara gasped at the sight of blood spreading across the chest of his khaki-toned shirt.

"You're hurt!" Libby was the one to cry out. Sara's throat had gone dry.

"Police and ambulance are coming don't you worry," Stuart said, sitting down and using a large rock to prop himself up. "I need to put some pressure on this, can you give me a hand?"

All the first aid courses she'd been sent on hadn't prepared Sara for this scenario, but her practical mothering side kicked in pretty much right away. She rooted around in her bag, finding a silk headscarf that she was more than happy to sacrifice.

Stuart hissed in pain as she pressed down on the wound, just below his left shoulder, but he nodded in relief as it stemmed the slow trickle of blood.

"Do you think Alice will be cross we crashed her car?" Libby piped up a minute later, as Stuart continued checking the landscape, talking into his sleeve with utmost concentration.

"We didn't crash it, but no she won't be. I should probably call her, if you're sure you're okay?"

"You should definitely call her, Mummy. That's what you do with a girlfriend, duh."

"Duh, is it? Very well." Sara pulled her phone out of her pocket, surprised that her hand was perfectly steady. "Let's get this part over with."

Sara was engrossed in the very important task of helping Libby choose between a Frozen Band-Aid and a Moana one when Alice finally burst through the hospital curtain.

"We're fine, we are both fine. Two minor scratches, one on each of us. None of which required a trip to hospital, but they insisted we use the ambulance. Stuart, by the way, is a very legitimate, James Bond-level hero. I think we might owe him our lives." Sara stood up from her seat next to Libby, ruffling her daughter's hair with one hand and grabbing at

Alice's hand with the other. "Hey, what's that panicked face for? Bumps and bruises, nothing more."

"Has the doctor said so? Did they x-ray you both?"

"Alice, please. Deep breath and take a seat, okay? I get why this is difficult for you, so we're going to just breathe and sit. Breathe and sit."

For all the world it looked as though Alice was going to argue, but Sara was good at this. She rubbed her thumb over the bumpy bone in Alice's wrist, exaggerating her own breathing to keep things slow and deep. Libby, having seen the approach often enough, sat quietly until the room felt calm again.

"Sorry," Alice said, dropping her head forward and pressing it against their intertwined hands. "It was bad enough when I heard it was a random accident. I was frantic. But the thought that someone had lain in wait—that they were at least trying to hurt you or Libby… I'm not sure I can bear that."

"I only have a tiny scratch," Libby said. "Do you want a sticking plaster too, to match mine?"

"I don't think Alice needs one right now, so just keep that for her," Sara said, proud of how Libby was joining in to distract Alice from her panic. "Listen, it's just us for now but this is no private room." She indicated the blue curtain. "I don't want this to become a bad press day for you, sweetheart."

"Screw it," Alice said, accepting the hug that Libby offered her. "If they try to get in here, they really are ghouls. You should be getting discharged soon, anyway."

"Is Stuart going to be okay? The doctor said the bullet passed right through, and that was a good thing." Sara felt her stomach turn over every time her brain replayed the sound and then the moment of impact where Stuart almost fell. "And I can't tell you how brave he was, Alice. He defended us like his life depended on it, even when he was hurt."

"He's a good man. And it looks like a spot of minor surgery is all he needs, which is a relief. We'll do everything we can for his recovery, of course. Starting with a bloody big handshake from me."

"On his good arm, preferably," Sara said. "They shouldn't be long in letting us go."

"Not just yet," said an imperious voice from behind the curtain. "Special Branch have secured us all in place here for now."

The curtain drew back to reveal the queen herself.

Nobody bowed or curtsied for once, but Libby just stared, her face a perfect circle of confusion. When Queen Caroline pulled Alice into a brief hug, Sara thought of Inès with a pang. She would have to call before her mother found out about the accident from elsewhere.

"Ms Marteau," the queen said. "One owes you any number of apologies. First and foremost, I am so sorry you got a scare like this. Especially with your daughter in the car."

Sara hesitated. A polite reply would cost her nothing but equally she remembered the dismissive way she had been spoken to before. While making a good impression on Alice's family counted for a lot, Sara still had her pride.

"We were okay," Libby replied instead. Caroline looked at her, as though startled that Libby would address her directly. "Stuart totally saved us, he's like an Avenger."

"Stuart?" Caroline looked at Alice with an expression that Sara couldn't decipher. "Well. If I had known you were serious enough to give up your right-hand man to watch over them... You might have said so, Alice."

"Would you have listened?" Alice folded her arms over her chest.

"A fair point. No, the reason I rushed down here to see you both is a positive one. Special Branch inform me that the attack was not targeted at Sara and Libby here. The gunman is in surgery but before he went under his statement was that he wanted 'any royal target.' His grievances remain a mystery for now, but he seems to have been working alone."

Sara exhaled shakily on hearing that. They were safe. It hadn't been deliberate. Before she could get too emotional, Alice had come to gather her up in a hug. Sara clung on to her for dear life.

"So do you ride horses as well? Are you allowed to?" Sara overheard Libby asking. When she pulled out of Alice's embrace, she was greeted by the queen herself perched on a plastic visitor's chair, helping Libby to rebraid her hair where it had all come loose in the commotion. For the first time, Sara saw the mother and the woman behind the fearsome title. Just like with Alice, the reality did not disappoint.

"As queen, I am allowed to do almost anything I want. And I certainly do ride horses, whenever I get the chance. Sometimes I even get to do it for official events, like on my birthday."

"Oh." Libby took a moment to process. "Then perhaps next time I go riding with Rupes and Annie, you could come too. If you can keep up with us, the ponies go very fast."

"I do appreciate you coming all the way here to reassure us, Your Majesty," Sara said, before Libby had challenged their head of state to a horse race. "The main thing is that we're all going to be fine."

"I think we can dispense with formalities when in hospital, don't you? Caroline will suffice when we are in private."

Sara tried to make her mouth form the word, but her lips and tongue seemed to resist. That one was going to take some getting used to. She turned to Alice instead. "So what's this about you giving up your number one guy for me, hmm? You really are a romantic at heart."

"When it comes to you, you deserve only the best." Alice pulled her close again, pressing a brief but lovely kiss against her lips. "And as he showed today, Stuart is absolutely the best."

"Libby, would you like to come and help me get some tea?" Caroline stood, brushing off her skirt.

"Okay!" Libby took the queen by the hand and led her back towards the café area. A handful of suited men appeared from various corners to follow them.

"I think our Libby just singlehandedly won my mother's heart to our cause, surprising no one." Alice smiled for the first time since she had arrived. Alice pressed her forehead against Sara's, thumbs brushing her cheeks. "God, it makes me sick to think of you going through all that when I wasn't there to protect you."

"You're here now." It wasn't lost on Sara how Alice had said 'our' Libby. In the midst of all the chaos and panic, the one thought outside of keeping her daughter safe had been for Sara to see Alice again. The feeling of rightness as soon as Alice had taken her in her arms stirred again, and Sara knew she couldn't deny what it was for much longer. Liking Alice had been one thing, but it had become something so much deeper.

"And I am not going anywhere, until you get sick of me," Alice said.

Sara pretended to consider that offer. "Sold. Has the doctor cleared me for kissing yet, do you think?"

Alice hooked a finger in the belt loop of Sara's jeans. "Only one way to be sure."

Chapter 32

THE NEW CARS WAITING FOR them in a hidden corner of the hospital parking were built more like tanks than regular vehicles, and Alice was relieved to see her firm instructions had been followed. What she wanted to give Sara and Libby back first and foremost was their sense of security. This was the appropriate first step.

"Nice wheels," Sara said, belting Libby in and brushing hair from her forehead as she fell asleep almost right away. "She's always like this after any excitement."

"We'll talk quietly so as not to disturb her," Alice said. "But we do have a little time before it's just us at your house. It might not be unreasonable to talk about anything that's looming over us, especially because you still have your mother to reassure. Mine is thankfully headed back to the palace."

"We probably need to talk some more about how this is going to work. This was some random man, the attack was not about me or Libby...but one day it might be. Whatever protections we have, I'll need to know they're ironclad."

"Of course."

"No, Alice. Not 'of course'. It's one thing to be famous, or to be a symbol of something. I know I don't understand that. But you will never understand what these spaces are like for someone who isn't white, who doesn't look and sound quite like you do. There's also the matter of my heritage, my culture... I don't want that whitewashed completely because everyone assumes royalty is this superior British thing that I want to take over my life completely."

"Ah. When you put it like that, I understand. I think it may be past due for me to look at my staff as well. Aside from Stuart, there's a distinct lack of diversity there. Hiring people who understand things from your side can only help, right?"

Sara gave a relieved little sigh. "Yes. That's the kind of thing. Aside from all the serious things, there are immediate issues, like do I need to talk if I come to events, and how is that going to work around my job? I've been keeping up so far, but the wardrobe required for your lifestyle is very, very different to what I have available. Unless you want me to tag along to, like, Westminster Abbey in a pair of yoga pants with a slogan across the bum."

"Okay, taking all this on board," Alice said. "The best point person will be Josephine as always, but I seem to recall when James and Annabel first went official there was a sort of styling service on hand. Clothes, hair, make-up, jewellery. Everything to match whichever dress code. Is that something of a help? Eugenia does all that for me, or I wouldn't have the first clue."

Sara stared out at the London scenery as they whizzed past it. "Yes. A relief, really. Although it might take adjusting to the whole taxpayers' money issue."

"All from private funds, I assure you. We have arrangements for a lot of things."

"Then I guess it might help to get a crash course, from someone other than you, in when I sit and curtsey, and what the point of a fish knife is. I picked up a lot at university, but this is way beyond that."

"Honestly, you'll pick up most of it as you go along."

"No," Sara replied, straightening her back and squaring her shoulders again. "No, this is another one of those times where you're a little blind to reality. If you walk into some event and do the wrong handshake, or hug when you're supposed to bow, or…whatever. That's fine. Might even get you a good headline about being a regular person sort of princess. If I do it? I guarantee fifty snide articles about how 'someone of my background' would never be expected to do these things right."

Alice gave her a comforting pat on the forearm. "You're right. I apologise. And I want you to know that I will stand up for you, Sara. No one is going to ask you to look the other way or pretend these things aren't happening. It will be my honour to defend yours. But the protocol lessons?

That's one for my lady-in-waiting, then. She knows every rule back to the days of Agincourt."

"That would be a big help, thank you. I'm not afraid of learning, you know. I can respect the pomp and circumstance, the history of it. But I don't want to be splashed across the right-wing papers for wearing the wrong hat or lifting the wrong spoon, with them reporting it like I kicked a corgi, or I should know my place is with the help."

"Clearly you've been thinking about this. Forgive me for sounding too confident, but that does bode well for us." Alice nodded as the driver announced they were almost at their destination.

"Are you ever scared? About all of this? About what we could be starting?" Sara couldn't hold the thought back a moment longer, looking at Libby sleeping without a care in the world.

"Scared? I'm terrified," Alice replied. "But then I look at you and suddenly I wonder what I was ever worried about. Just like flying."

"Oh, well, I'm glad I'm easier to manage than a 747 I guess." Sara leaned across and kissed Alice on her temple, just a ticklish moment of contact. "Thank you for coming to the house. I really couldn't face a strange place tonight."

"My pleasure," Alice said.

"—And now she's what? Buying a house?" Inès stared at Sara across the kitchen table. By the time Inès had finished smothering Libby and Sara with worried hugs and kisses, Alice had excused herself upstairs to take a quick shower. Libby was back in her room having some quiet time, and Sara had no way to escape her mother's rounds of questioning as she prepared an evening feast for them. The scent of cumin filled the air and freshly sliced pomegranates were on the chopping board just inches from Sara's hand.

"A lot of it is just future planning, but things she needed to do anyway. From what Alice said though, she wants to include me in that future. That would probably mean a lot of change on our parts. And it would happen quite quickly. Am I mad to even consider this?"

"Whenever you love someone, you're always a little mad." Her mother retained that wonderful French habit of making every utterance about love seem profound, even if she had read it originally on a cereal box.

"Isn't love a little soon?"

"Is it?"

Sara felt the last denial fall away in that moment, under the scrutiny of her mother's gaze.

"I don't know. I need to be sure. I suppose I won't know for certain until I say it to Alice and she says it back. But I won't make a fool of myself. Or disrupt Libby's life over some fling."

"I know you wouldn't. I raised you better than that. But Libby is growing up fast. You're allowed a life, *chérie*. And if a princess doesn't meet your standards, I think it's possible they might be too high."

"Her being a princess is the least important thing about her," Sara replied. "In fact, it's the one thing that almost stood in our way."

"Then ignore it. If you love Alice, as a woman and a person. I think you know the answer. But rushing you or pushing you has never worked. Just don't take so long she moves along. That would be quite a waste, I think."

"And what if we go for it? If I'm some official royal girlfriend, cutting ribbons and going to dinners at the palace? What about our lives here?"

"We keep whatever parts of it we like and need. The rest? We adapt. That's what people do. London isn't like France...so I got used to something new. Just like I got used to Paris after Tehran. It was worth it, to see you thrive here. Look at what you've done Sara, and I don't mean in your dating life. You make your mother very proud."

Sara felt tears welling up, not for the first time in this bumpy day. "Thank you. What would I do without you, *Maman*?"

"Well, let's hope it's a long time before you ever find out."

Chapter 33

Waking up at Sara's for the first time was certainly a novel experience, Alice had to admit that.

Instead of an alarm, the sound of Libby yanking the curtains open—and the blast of daylight—provided the official wake-up call. The bed was comfortable, sure, but considerably smaller than the four-poster antique that Alice spent most of her nights in. Yet again, she ended up on the floor by turning too sharply. Thankfully, she'd had the presence of mind to pull on a T-shirt before falling asleep, not that Libby had lingered to see if they were awake.

Footsteps thundered up and down the stairs for the next few minutes, as Alice crawled back under the duvet to listen in horror. How was it possible that the sound could travel so well? It seemed to be both opposite and underneath them at the same time. She nudged Sara, who simply grunted and shoved her face further into her pillow.

For a moment, Alice saw an alternative life spread out before her, something she hadn't experienced since lying quietly in her bunk back in barracks. Then, in a room full of soft snores and the smell of boot polish, she had thought only of narrow possibilities: the missions she might fly and the ceremonies and medals that might come later. Would her mother present them to her? Would that be frowned upon?

This time Alice saw a different path, one where people made small talk about house prices and had a favourite coffee shop that they hit up most mornings on their commute. She pictured waiting at the school gates and booking holidays online or arguing about which type of mushrooms to buy in the supermarket. All things Alice knew about in the abstract, but that had never been part of her life.

Could she do it? Even if she stepped down from her royal position there would still be security and other concerns. What job could she realistically do? At her age there was little hope she could reenlist, and commercial flying was tough to break into. She had an inheritance, some money and investments of her own, but yet again all of that was taken care of by trusted employees.

"What are you thinking about so hard?" Sara emerged from her pillow, adorably sleep-rumpled. "I can practically hear the cogs turning."

"Just appreciating the differences," Alice replied. "And pondering the future, as one does."

"The future had better involve some bacon sandwiches and a French press," Sara said, pulling the duvet over her head. Still not a morning person, then. Alice had to applaud the fact that so far, Sara hadn't even really pretended to be. Getting up early for her was a necessary evil punctuated by blaring alarms. For Alice, it came naturally.

She slipped out of bed, more gently this time and without landing on the floor. Stealing a dressing gown, Alice wrapped herself up in the soft towelling material and tied it tightly. To the kitchen, where she could absolutely make all of Sara's dreams come true. Or at least her breakfast order.

Five minutes later, she had bribed her outgoing protection detail to fetch rolls and coffees from the nearest café, with something for each of them and the new morning detail included. After that it took simply caving to Libby's cartoon-watching requests to get her on side. By the time a sleepyhead Sara came downstairs in her pyjamas, Alice had breakfast for three laid out, right down to pouring out some orange juice.

"I could get used to this," Sara said, taking her seat and leaning across to kiss Alice. Libby pouted until she got a kiss on the cheek in turn. "Although I have a funny feeling that days here, like this, are going to be less common in the future. Libby, will you be okay staying over at the palace sometimes, or wherever Alice ends up living?"

"Will there be horses?"

"Of course," Alice replied. "Pickle will come with me, along with some of her stablemates from Sandringham. Since we'll have stables for them, I suppose one stall could be reserved for a pony."

Sara kicked Alice under the table. She should have been playing right-back for Arsenal, judging by the force of it.

"That is, a future pony. Subject to lots of completed homework, chores without complaining and some very good test scores."

Libby frowned as she looked from Alice to Sara. Deciding not to pick the argument, Libby settled for taking a hearty bite out of her bacon sandwich.

"Nice save," Sara said, before sipping her coffee with a blissful expression on her face. "We might just keep you around, Alice."

At that, Alice couldn't hide her smile.

Sara decided that she had made a terrible mistake in agreeing to this. Pins were lurking in all kinds of places that made her scared to bend or stretch, her bra straps kept sliding down her bare arms, and the small team of women who circled around her like hyenas around a felled gazelle were definitely creepy in their collective silence. She had officially exhausted her own wardrobe, Jasmin's, and her credit card limit, so Sara had relented on Alice's persistent offer to provide the necessary couture for public appearances. Since they'd been together a few months, Sara finally felt able to say yes without feeling as if she'd thrown every last principle out of the window.

She had drawn the line at tiaras, though.

"How's it going?" Alice appeared from outside the curtain. "Eugenia, thanks for coming back just to do this."

"Of course, Your Royal Highness. Delighted to help. And may I say, Ms Marteau makes a much more cooperative model than you ever have." Sara smirked just a little at Eugenia's faint praise.

The woman looked and sounded like an elderly theatrical dame, but she had a sharp eye for fashion that outstripped anything Sara could keep up with. The dress they were altering was for some dinner or other, but on a rack in the corner there were already a flurry of skirts, suits, and incredibly flattering blouses. The shoes alone would probably have paid the rest of

Sara's mortgage, but the pangs of guilt were starting to wear off with each awkward minute she spent being pinned and prodded.

"I've been thinking," Sara said, as soon as Alice came close. "About juggling work with all these commitments. People will quickly notice a pattern if I only do London and Home Counties events. Work is a good excuse, but it's still going to play as only thinking one part of the country matters. Politicians do that enough, without your branch joining in."

"Ouch, but I'm listening." Alice leaned against the one part of the wall near Sara that wasn't covered by a full-length mirror. She looked exquisite in her cream-coloured trousers, tapered at the ankle, with a contrasting blouse in a black, the subtle pattern on it matching the trousers perfectly. She had the benefit of flats too, the heel less than half-an-inch. Sara's own collection would need a few of those, because while she could strut her stuff in stilettos, she was long past the point of doing that all day, every day.

"Well, I have my master's in education as I might have mentioned."

"UCL, right? University College London? After your undergrad at Cambridge," Alice replied, with a smug little smile. "I listen when you talk, you know."

"We're not being quizzed by immigration here, but yes. Anyway, if not for Libby and the need to get cracking on my career, I would have loved to study for my PhD."

"Which would make you Dr Marteau?" Alice's eyes definitely lit up at that realisation. Sara didn't bother to hide her smirk.

The seamstresses seemed to be done, judging by how efficiently they pulled away the pinned and chalked fabric that would become a whole new evening gown.

"Could you give us a minute?" Alice never took her eyes off Sara, stood there in nothing more than lingerie and a satin slip. They quickly had the dressing room to themselves. "Are you talking about giving up your job?"

"If things progress like they have been doing then, yes, maybe a career break. But only if I replace it with something that moves me further down the line. Getting my doctorate would do that. Plus, it's much more flexible, so I could travel with you and do most of the reading on my own time."

Alice looked down at her feet for a moment. "That sounds like a big decision. Are you sure you want to change that much about your life, just to be with me?"

"As sure as you were about threatening the actual, literal queen with walking away from it all just to be allowed to see where this goes. Every day we spend together, it just seems more and more like... Well, like we're going to be doing this for a while. If you'll have me." Another time Sara might have blushed, but alone with Alice she knew there was nothing embarrassing in what she was saying.

"Have you?" Alice came over then, wrapping an arm around Sara's waist. "Of course I will. In fact, and please forgive me if this is too soon, I rather think I love you, Sara."

The signs had been there. Sara could say she saw it coming. But still, hearing the words fall from Alice's lips felt like fireworks going off in her heart.

"What a coincidence, because I'm absolutely sure I love you, too. Is that wild? I don't care if it is."

Alice kissed her, full of exuberance. Once, twice, and then the kind of kiss that blew all the numbers right out of Sara's mind. Only the presence of the seamstresses just outside stopped them from going much further.

"Well, that just leaves picking out something to wear for Annabel's event this afternoon. Ready for your first official event as my girlfriend? They might expect you to chat to a reporter or two at this one."

"As ready as I'll ever be," Sara replied. "But I'm pretty sure I can do most things, as long as you're with me."

"I can sign you up for skydiving then?" Alice couldn't hold back her grin.

"Nice try." Sara swatted her arm with a playful swipe. "Now which of these outfits screams 'fashion event'?"

"Let's get Eugenia back in," Alice said, crossing the room to do exactly that. "But you could wear a potato sack and still look gorgeous."

"This is why you're not in charge of your own wardrobe, ma'am," Eugenia said as she reentered the room. "With all due respect, of course."

Sara covered her mouth with her hand, but it did little to disguise her laugh. She was pampered, happy, and downright giddy on this new declaration of love. A fashion show with some teenagers would be no big deal at all.

When Sara pictured a fashion show run by teenagers, she'd been expecting a school hall with some tables transformed into a temporary catwalk. But Annabel had other ideas, because walking into her 'little event' was a lot like what Sara imagined walking into Fashion Week must feel like. Press were gathered behind red velvet ropes, a range of teens dressed all in black were talking into headsets, and the whole cavernous space had an air of organised chaos.

"That's the catwalk?" Sara nudged Alice with her elbow.

"Seems so. And we're right in those plum seats on the side. Front row." Alice gave an apologetic grin. "Sorry, when Annabel wants you to show up and represent for your people, she goes all out."

This was the part that was going to take Sara the longest to get used to. Just the thought of being so publicly on display, right at the white-hot centre of attention, had her chest constricting until her head felt a little loopy.

"Hey," Alice said, picking up on the sudden silence. "If this is too much, or too soon...just say the word. I can whisk us away for pizza and ice cream at any given moment."

"Please don't ever let Libby know that. Although now you mention it, some pepperoni sounds appealing."

"Weren't you thinking about going vegan?"

"I was until you reminded me pizza exists. Is there anything we should be doing to help?"

Alice waved to Annabel, who was at the centre of her most trusted staff and a few people Sara hadn't seen before. "Not today, no. We're a little early so we shake hands and do some mingling. Most of the time will be like the ballet, straight in and sit; leave before everyone else."

"Efficient, I guess." Sara slipped her arm through Alice's offered one, falling in step as though they'd been doing the rounds together for years. They soon fell into conversation with some of the prospective fashion students, their parents, and the teachers who had given so much of their own time to make it all possible. Now that Annabel had inaugurated the charity, their work could be carried on by paid staff and not just volunteers.

All too soon the big moment was upon them. Sara had visions of stumbling in her heels as they approached the sleek folding chairs that lined the runway. Overhead, rows of heavy-duty lighting had been installed, and the sound system in the huge room was playing something low and ambient until the show properly started.

Just sitting in a seat. Beside the Princess Royal and the Duchess of Edinburgh. What could possibly go wrong? Sara eyed the gaggle of photographers, mostly chatting amongst themselves while firing off some casual shots. Nothing too terrifying, then.

And then all of a sudden, the show began.

Sara was instantly captivated by the beautiful clothes the teens had created, all the more so knowing the difficult backgrounds they came from, where supplies and access to high fashion were in short supply. Sara might not have been a clothes horse herself, but she knew gorgeous and interesting when she saw it.

After a few minutes she noticed Alice's hand on her knee, alerted by the increasing flashes of cameras going off like a firework. Every time they shifted to talk to one another, or Alice leaned over to speak to Annabel, a new flurry would go off. Each time, Sara grew a little more confident and the paparazzi seemed a bit less intimidating. By the time they were on their feet, applauding the kids, Sara had almost forgotten there were any cameras in the room.

"Not bad, hmm?" Alice had been attentive and protective the entire time, something that only added to the warm and fuzzy feelings Sara carried about her these days. Confessing her love for Alice had been like reaching the summit of a mountain, and Sara couldn't help but revel in the view from the top.

"Not bad at all. Shall we run the gauntlet, then? Answer a few questions as we leave? It would give them more promotion for all that's been achieved here today."

"If you're sure?" Alice beamed at the suggestion. "It doesn't have to take long."

And it didn't, in the end. Most of the time and effort was spent on working out which journalist was yelling at them for attention. Once Sara tuned into that, giving short and simple answers was no harder than standing in front of a room full of children to teach.

"Sara, did you enjoy the show?" She could tell the direction of the reporter, if not the exact one.

"I did. Everyone worked so hard, and it looked very professional."

"Sara! Did you bring your daughter with you?"

"She has school. It's a school day." Sara hoped no one would ask why she wasn't at her own school, working. Using the leave she was entitled to for days like this had been hard. Maybe going back to study was her best route.

"Your Royal Highness! Does your mother know that you're dating a commoner? We haven't heard her blessing yet."

Alice whipped around at that, and Sara laid a placating hand on her forearm.

"My mother is a very busy woman, but if she has anything to say then you will most likely hear from her," Alice replied. "Do excuse us, we have another appointment to get to."

Sara felt herself rather dragged towards the waiting car, and only when they were safely inside did the frown on Alice's face relax.

"They don't really expect the queen to comment on whether or not we're dating, do they?" Sara leaned back as the car pulled into traffic. "I can't imagine who would care. I certainly wouldn't have, until I was the one doing it."

"Well, the monarchy is not just one big inconvenience to some people," Alice replied, withdrawing her hand from Sara's. A moment later she bowed her head, pinching the bridge of her nose. "Sorry. Sorry, I shouldn't have snapped at you. This is not remotely your fault."

"Luckily you're very forgivable," Sara replied, reaching over to pat Alice's shoulder. "At least everything else was positive. They treated us like a real couple. No gal pal nonsense of pretending we're just friends."

"Just friends wouldn't be able to do this," Alice said, turning her head to kiss the back of Sara's hand. "But you're right, we just keep going. Ready to win over a nation, including my suddenly silent mother?"

"If that's what it takes, then I suppose I am."

Chapter 34

DAILY BUGLE, 14TH JANUARY

A ROYAL CHANGE OF ADDRESS

The deed is done and the papers are finally signed. Like most millennials, it has taken HRH Princess Alice longer than previous generations to leave the family home. This is one case in which we can be sure there was a contribution from the Bank of Mum and Dad, given that her mother is one of the richest women in the world.

At her side, it is believed the world will soon see Ms Sara Marteau, and her daughter, living full-time with the Princess Royal at her newly-acquired stately home in Surrey. It is believed to boast at least thirteen bedrooms, so sleepovers at the weekend will not be a problem. With an existing staff of twenty, it is not yet known if the Palace will insist on adding their own people.

They say moving is one of the most stressful life experiences, right up there with divorce. Since the princess is yet to marry, only one of these will apply. Does domestic bliss lie ahead?

Alice had overcome some obstacles in her time: from growing up in the public eye to competing at the Olympics, but damned if some sticky brown tape wasn't about to the be the thing that finally defeated her.

"Sara? How attached are you to these plates?"

That was Sara's cue to pop her head around the kitchen door, adorably smudged with dust, her long brown hair tied up in a bandana. She was dressed for manual work, in cropped jeans and a tank top that had been stretched out, a few tiny holes around its seams. Her skin had a sheen of sweat from all the packing-based exertion, and it took considerable self-control on Alice's part not to knock all the damn plates on the floor and lift Sara up on the kitchen counter in their place.

"They're not family heirlooms, if that's what you're asking? Why?"

"If there's one thing I can confidently say we have plenty of, it's crockery. Would you be okay with these going into storage as well?"

Sara stood in the doorway fully then, hands on her hips. It made the tank top ride up over her stomach a little. Alice licked her lips, pushing up the sleeves on her denim shirt a little higher past her elbows.

"Doesn't it sort of feel like all my stuff is going into storage? I'm all for combining resources, but it's already weird for me to be moving in with someone so early on."

"It has been months, darling. In lesbian terms, we've basically been playing hard to get by not sharing a postcode after the second date. But you're right. I'll mark this box as kitchen, then."

"Dining room," Sara corrected. "You need to follow the list that the office gave us. I'm almost done with my clothes, and I want to have Libby's things sorted into piles. If she goes through each individual possession we'll be here for another year. I've already bagged up things she's grown out of or didn't like in the first place."

Alice stood up, wincing as her knees groaned. The dreaded brown tape had stuck to her sensible black cargo trousers, and she resisted the urge to play with the pockets some more. She hadn't worn anything so practical since the RAF, and the temptation to hunt around for small tools and other things she had brought remained high. It was important to her that Sara saw the pampered princess could muck in and help as well as anyone.

Jasmin appeared beside Sara then.

"How. Many. Books. Can one woman have?" She pushed past Sara with a groan, helping herself to one of the chilled beers sitting on the counter. "I thought Libby was bad with her comics, but that cupboard under the stairs is like the British Library. Just when you think you've seen every book in existence, boom! Here's another half-broken bookcase filled with two Bibles, half of Terry Pratchett's Discworld series, and a seriously out-of-date copy of What to Expect When You're Expecting."

Alice looked to Sara in accusation. "Do you have a book problem?"

"It's not a problem! I read a lot, and quickly! So maybe I raid the charity shops every now and then. It keeps my brain occupied. And you, Jas, can stop showing me up in front of my girlfriend any time you like."

"Oh no," Alice replied, helping herself to a beer and clinking the bottle against Jasmin's. "We already have a deal for all your embarrassing university stories. Any hope of loyalty is gone, gone, gone."

Jasmin grinned, giving a little shrug of her shoulders. "What can I say? She's very persuasive, this princess of yours. She can't pack for shit, but don't worry. I'll go around after her and make sure none of the boxes collapse."

"Hey!" Alice gave her a playful shove for that, not missing the delighted smile on Sara's face as her girlfriend and best friend got on so well. "Now how long until Inès brings Libby back? At least *she's* genuinely on my side."

"You keep telling yourself that," Sara replied, wrapping an arm around Alice's waist and pulling her in for a beer-tinged kiss. "Thank you for helping us pack, by the way."

"The least I could do. Thanks for moving in with me. I love you, you know that?"

"I had heard a rumour, yes."

"Okay, enough already," Jasmin said, throwing in a gagging noise for good measure. "Have some respect for those of us still trying to melt our difficult bosses."

"You should have invited her to the packing party. She could have finally met Alice," Sara said.

"I might have forgotten to mention she'd be here," Jasmin replied with a big grin. "Serves Kathleen right for making me work overtime on my birthday."

"Sounds complicated." Alice pulled the tape off her trousers, frowning at how much of it was stuck to her again already.

"Not as complicated as falling for a princess," Jasmin replied, with a little snort of laughter into her beer bottle.

"Worth it, though." Sara finally let go of Alice, but the ghost of her touch lingered as they went back to packing up the house.

"Alice! You startled me!" Caroline did seem genuinely shocked to see her, but Alice had asked the equerry not to announce that she was waiting. There was a distinct impression in recent weeks that the queen had been avoiding her only daughter, despite the initial thawing back at the hospital with Sara.

Ever since Alice had settled on a new home—a leafy estate with a phenomenal old house at its centre, just twenty miles from central London—it seemed her mother had been less available to her than ever. Even the paperwork for the house had been handled directly by staff, Alice getting no chance to discuss it with Queen Caroline outside of a couple of brief phone calls to get the details right.

It still felt peculiar to be a homeowner in her own right, after a lifetime of residing in palaces and other public-owned properties. The fact of Sara and Libby coming too—with Inès at least part of the time—made the whole prospect just a smidge less terrifying. Had it been just down to Alice to rattle around the halls with only staff for company, she might never have made the leap. As it was, she had retained her apartment at St James's for official business, something the papers had already been grumbling about.

"I do apologise for the startling, but then some might say your behaviour lately has bordered on avoidance, Mummy."

Caroline gave a little scoff, before sitting heavily in the ornate armchair by the fireplace. She kicked off her shoes, a sure sign of a long day, and leaned back against the cushions with her eyes closed. "I am sorry, darling. My intention was not to shut you out."

"Then what was it? Here I am, officially dating someone, moving in together even, and still no public statement from you. As far as the world knows, you might not even be aware that this is all happening. Did I not make myself clear about my intentions with Sara?"

"No, you did." Caroline pulled a cushion into her lap, fussing with the intricate stitching of the tapestry on it. "And one must confess to rather struggling since then."

"With what? With Sara?"

Caroline shook her head. "With missing your father. Is that not the most ludicrous thing you ever heard? After all these years, to be struck down again by grief."

"No. No, of course you still miss him. We all do." Alice came closer, kneeling down beside her mother's chair and taking her hand. "My happiness was never supposed to be at the expense of yours."

"And nor should it be," Caroline replied, sniffing just a little before sitting up straighter. "I had a similar glitch when James got serious about Annabel, but it does pass. I confess I had my doubts about this girl of yours, but the word from every corner is that she is doing a smashing job at your side. And that little girl of hers is just the sweetest child. I understand the move is imminent?"

"The new house is just about ready for us, yes. Some parts will be off-limits for decoration, but the protection team really are anxious to have us under one roof. Sara's home is a nightmare for them, all those houses in a row like that."

"And of course the press need to hear from me. One shall issue a statement, and of course a photo call as one of your very first visitors to the new home. Assuming an invitation still stands?"

Alice stood up again then. "You know it does. And there's nothing to stop you seeking out a new companion, Mummy. Has it not been long enough alone?"

"That is absolutely the last thing we ought to be talking about. Now, was the lack of public acceptance the only reason you came chasing after me? We never have you here at the House these days."

Alice rocked back and forth on her heels for a second, looking around the room. She had made a decision before setting off for Buckingham Palace, but did it stand now, in the face of what they had just discussed, mother to daughter?

Yes, Alice had to assume that it did.

"Do you remember when James and Annabel decided to get married? All the discussions and decisions, the planning and the details? How every decision had to be recorded, right down to the colour of the hymn sheets?"

Queen Caroline nodded, her eyes narrowing just a fraction. Someone who knew her less than Alice might not even have noticed.

"Well, if someone wanted to avoid that level of fuss, but also wanted a favour regarding access to the royal jewel collection...while one is more than happy to go for a brand-new piece, we do have rather a few stones stashed away."

"Traditionally, a royal bride-to-be would be brought in to meet with the royal jeweller, presented with an array of options. Is that what we are talking about, Alice?"

"Not just yet, but one has learned in this life that it is best to be prepared. These things can take some time to work out."

"What about you? What ring will you wear to show an engagement?"

Alice wiggled the index finger with her father's ring. "Thought this might do, if the sentiment of it all can be excused."

"Well." Caroline stood then, shorter than her daughter but a slightly intimidating presence as ever, even without her heels. "Only one thing for it, in the name of making a wonderful pair."

She gave a long, wistful look at her left hand, before twisting the large diamond ring and its matching wedding band free. The band was quickly replaced, but the ring was placed into Alice's waiting palm as soon as she extended her hand.

"But Mummy—"

"Ours was a happy marriage. I think it time we used that to bless another union, don't you? Oh, we can have it boxed up. A little presentation please, dear daughter."

"And if it needs to be sized?"

"Then so be it. That ring is yours now, to do with as you wish. You father would think it proper, just as I do."

Alice grabbed her mother and pulled her into a hug before they could think better of it. "Thank you. Thank you."

"Make a lifetime of happiness with it, yes?"

Alice nodded, wiping an errant tear as they ended their cuddle. "I will. I promise."

Chapter 35

DINNER AT A PALACE WAS somehow everything Sara expected, and still nothing as she had ever imagined. Her first time had been three hours of frozen terror, barely able to keep a smile on her face. With a few months of practice, it was starting to feel like just another regular way to have dinner.

But even with Alice at her side, every time she was introduced to someone new, Sara felt a flutter inside her chest; a panicked butterfly trying to escape the constraints of muscle and bone. Sara had a list of names and titles committed to memory in the same way as she usually retained the names on a class register, but she soon picked up on the vague but warm way Alice greeted everyone. To be met by a princess was to seem like the first time, but also like encountering an old friend all at once.

"Have I mentioned how beautiful you look tonight?" Alice smiled as they both sipped at champagne from delicate flutes.

The waves of introductions were over, and Alice had directed them to a quiet corner as they waited to be called into dinner. James and Annabel had tried a similar approach, but he had been cornered by the prime minister, an odious oaf of a man that no amount of polite society could bring Sara to respect. The man couldn't even brush his hair properly, well, what little real hair he had left. Sara had opened her mind and her principles to the idea of constitutional monarchy, but she still absolutely drew the line at professional politicians.

"You might have mentioned it, yes." Sara looked down at the deep purple silk of her gown, cinched and pinched in all the right places by Eugenia's crack team of seamstresses. Not since the birds in Snow White had such a wonderful feat of sewing been part of Sara's life. The accompanying shoes pinched a little around the toes—black patent stiletto heels that made Sara reconsider her commitment to femme—but catching sight of herself in a mirror that probably dated back to the Tudors, Sara had to admit that the overall effect was worth it. This was how she looked now, this was just what she did: dressing up nicely for grand occasions of state. Including this State Dinner for the Turkish President and his wife.

The room held over a hundred guests, all in white tie regalia. A large number of the men were in military dress, medals gleaming at their chests. Alice had opted for her 'dress blues', the ceremonial version of the Air Force uniform. Sara found her curiosity piqued. "Later, will you tell me what each of those medals are for?"

"Some are just symbolic you know. Because of the various honorary positions and... yes, okay. I would like that." Alice smiled before looking back at the other guests. They had failed to talk much about her time in the military since their last squabble about it, so Sara filed that away as a good sign.

"Josephine reminded me earlier that it's Trooping of the Colour next week? Which one is that again?"

"Queen's official birthday," Alice replied, with a nod to her mother. "And one of our most official outings of the year. Short of a wedding—someone else's wedding—it's the best way to mark you as royal family official. So to speak."

"I don't think I've ever watched it before," Sara said. "Is that terrible?"

"Suspect it was not your kind of thing, darling. But there is one catch: Mummy, James, and I all ride in the parade itself. So you'll be in the stand behind where Mummy accepts all her salutes, with Annabel and the aunties and so on. I get to come and join you when the riding part is done, of course, but you'll be flying sort of solo for the first time. Ready for that?"

Sara took a long sip of champagne, draining her glass. "As I'll ever be."

ROYAL COMMUNICATIONS

Statement from Her Majesty, Queen Caroline I, 17th June

As confirmed by her own office, my only daughter, the Princess Royal, has embarked on a new romantic relationship. As her mother I am delighted that Princess Alice has found a partner as accomplished and respected as Ms Sara Marteau, an educational specialist of south London.

Per palace rules, we will not be commenting further on the private lives of the queen's children, other than to wish them every success and happiness in their future lives.

ENDS

The evening had passed almost without incident when Sara noticed the queen bearing down on her from across the room. They had been a polite distance apart at dinner, so Sara had managed to avoid talking to her for most of the evening. Apparently, her luck had just run out.

"Ms Marteau, how lovely you look."

"Thank you, Your Majesty. Please, call me Sara. And that dress is just stunning." Sara wasn't lying, the creamy white dress overlaid in sparkling crystals was a work of art. While Queen Caroline had a more petite build than Alice, there was a certain similarity in how they carried themselves. Looking around for her erstwhile date, Sara saw Alice in conversation with the prime minister this time. Damn, no escape was worth talking to that man.

"Are you enjoying the event, Sara?"

"Very much. Thank you for inviting me." Sara hated small talk at the best of times, but this was bordering on excruciating. "And thank you for the statement. About, you know, us."

"It was overdue. You seem to be making my daughter very happy. Long may that continue."

"As long as she'll have me, yes," Sara replied. "Will you come to visit us at the new house?"

Queen Caroline nodded and gave a little wave across the room to the Turkish ambassador. "Oh yes. Diplomacy calls right now, but just you two try and keep me away."

As they had been so often, palace staff were Sara's saviour at the Trooping of the Colour. While James and Alice rode around behind their mother on terribly huge and impressive horses, Sara much preferred her seat in the stands.

Every time the event moved on or she was expected to face a certain way, a member of staff would steer her or whisper the correct instruction just in time. Sara refused to think about the television cameras, beaming her image all over the world. The real-life crowds were more than enough to be getting on with, their cheers and flag-waving beyond anything Sara had experienced before.

The whole family gathered together on the balcony at Buckingham Palace to watch the Red Arrows fly in formation overhead. The children rejoined them for this part, with Libby following alongside Rupert and Annie as though they had always done it. Sara was proud to take her hand as they all moved into their respective family groups. As soon as Alice came into sight, Sara felt about three pounds lighter on her feet. It helped that Alice made a beeline straight for her and Libby, that magnetic pull between them as strong as ever.

Cheers went up from the crowd as all three senior members of the family took up their places, with Queen Caroline at the centre. Ordinarily these events were stuffy, like photographs brought to life in slow motion, but today the rules had definitely been relaxed. Caroline held Rupert up in her arms as they waved to the crowd together, and Anne was lifted up on Annabel's shoulders, making her taller than James.

Sara tried the waving, but every so often would picture herself from outside her body and her arm would drop in sheer self-consciousness, clutching Libby's shoulder instead. "I can't believe any of them care that I'm here right now," she said, when Alice shot her a questioning look.

"That reminds me," Alice said. "Josephine inflicted some of the post on me this week."

"Not being paying your bills again?"

"Ha. Ha. Here, you should see this one. It's addressed to both of us."

"Here?" Sara looked around. "Won't they wonder what I'm doing?"

"I'll distract them, with Libby's help." Alice stepped partly in front of her, affording a little privacy. She bent forward to ask Libby something, and moments later Libby was up on Alice's shoulders, squealing in delight to reach the same heights as Annie. "Go on."

Sara stepped just inside the open French windows and unfolded the pale blue sheet of paper and glanced at the writing. Definitely someone younger, possibly into their early teens. Written small, as though to keep it all on one page, it took a moment for Sara's eyes to adjust.

Dear Princess Alice and Sara,

I am writing because I saw you both on television again today. You were opening something at a hospital with a big ribbon. My dad asked who that woman was standing with the princess, and my mum told him that Sara is your girlfriend.

I thought my dad would be cross about that, or not like that the princess has a girlfriend. Instead, he said, "Well good for her, she looks like a nice girl." I didn't know he thought like that.

Because I was so surprised, I didn't even think about it, I just told both my parents there and then that I think I might be gay too, because I like girls and not boys. They didn't shout or get upset. They said they loved me just the same, and that I could go out with anyone I liked.

I think they understand better because of you, and because they can see that being queer is a good thing if it's okay for the royal family to do as well. I'm not scared anymore of what people might think of me.

Thank you,

Poppy O'Hara (age 13)

Sara was glad her mascara was waterproof. She hadn't stood a chance in the face of that message. Wiping away tears with the linen handkerchief in her bag, she took a deep breath before turning back to Alice. "That was not remotely fair."

"Are you okay, Mummy?" Libby skipped over to hug Sara as soon as Alice set her down.

"Well, I cannot have you thinking that your presence here is unimportant. If nothing else, it is incredibly important to me. And this Poppy. And who knows how many others."

"You win." Sara waved to the crowd again, to a fresh round of cheers. "But I know those are not the only kinds of letters we get."

"The only kind that matter," Alice replied. "We do not pay attention to the other kind. Now do you see why this is so good? Apart from the fact that I love you quite madly, of course? We get to be everything that we never saw growing up. That counts for so much."

"You're right," Sara said. "You're so right."

Queen Caroline drifted over to them. "All okay here? Alice, did you make Sara cry?"

"No!" Sara jumped in to reply. "Well, in a good way. She showed me a nice letter."

"Ah, very well dear. I thought she had been up to something." Caroline patted Sara on the shoulder, before exchanging pointed looks with her daughter.

"Come along, Libby," Caroline said. "Let's go get some cake before Anne and Rupert eat all of it." She offered a hand that Libby took just as soon as Sara had released her. Alice wrapped her arm around Sara as they watched Caroline settle on a high-backed sofa inside, her three grandchildren playing at her feet and chattering back and forth.

When they were alone again, Sara turned to Alice. "You know, that's the second time I've seen your mother without her engagement ring. Still wearing her wedding band, but no big split-your-lip diamond."

"That sounds like you've been casing the joint," Alice replied with a grin. "I'm sure these things need to be professionally cleaned and whatnot. Or maybe she was mugged and forgot to tell us. But I'd say the jewellers is a good guess."

"Oh, is that a good guess?" Sara pressed into Alice's side, accepting an arm around her shoulders. "Well, that's a relief."

"One is so glad you're relieved."

"If it were anywhere else. In, say, someone's pocket. Ready for a fresh proposal, as it were, then that might be okay too."

Alice didn't reply, but Sara saw the deliberate way she swallowed.

"That sort of question would be an easy one to say yes to, just for the record. Not that anyone is asking yet, but still."

That was enough to get a beaming smile from Alice, who pretended it was for the crowd's benefit.

"And who says I would? I would have to ask Libby for permission, and that's just for starters."

"She's easily bought. You know her price."

"A pony," Alice replied. "But there's some would say talk like that is rushing things. Even moving into a big house, those places can feel terribly small if you argue often. Staff lurking everywhere, not enough privacy. It wears on a person. On couples."

Sara took a moment to consider. "So we'll cope. It's what people do."

"And if it's ever too much…" Alice trailed off.

"I know. You'll give it all up and we'll move to Croydon. Don't think I don't appreciate the gesture. Anyway. No one is asking, remember?"

"Right." Alice patted the breast pocket of her jacket. "Not just yet."

As the crowd's attention fell on them again, Sara could hear the calls for them to kiss. They had been quite careful about PDAs whenever they were out, but in that moment Sara was ready to shout about their love from the rooftops.

Or at least the balcony of the palace.

Slowly but surely, Alice leaned in and kissed Sara softly on the lips. More cheers resounded, before the unmistakeable sounds of jets filled the air. "I'm so glad you're here at my side."

"Turns out there isn't anywhere I'd rather be."

Other Books from Ylva Publishing

www.ylva-publishing.com

A Roll in the Hay

Lola Keeley

ISBN: 978-3-96324-355-4
Length: 185 pages (66,000 words)

Veterinarian Tess has quit the city and her cheating girlfriend for a new life in a Scottish village. On day one, she has a run-in with stuck-up Lady Karlson who tries to boss Tess around as if she owns the whole town... which she sort of does. But could there be something more to the constant, rising tension between the warring pair?

An enemies-to-lovers lesbian romance about making your own path.

Never Say Never

Rachael Sommers

ISBN: 978-3-96324-429-2
Length: 220 pages (75,000 words)

Ambitious Camila might have lost her marriage but she doesn't need love to build a TV empire and raise her young son. What she does need is a nanny.

Enter Emily—bright, naive, and new to New York City. Emily is everything Camila is not and that's not all that's unsettling.

Surely she can't be falling for the nanny?

An age-gap, opposites-attract lesbian romance with a puddle of melted ice queen.

Up on the Roof

A.L. Brooks

ISBN: 978-3-95533-988-3
Length: 245 pages (88,000 words)

When a storm wreaks havoc on bookish Lena's well-ordered world, her laid-back new neighbor, Megan, offers her a room. The trouble is they've been clashing since the day they met. How can they now live under the same roof? Making it worse is the inexplicable pull between them that seems hard to resist. A fun, awkward, and sweet British romance about the power of opposites attracting.

A Heart This Big

Cheyenne Blue

ISBN: 978-3-96324-202-1
Length: 253 pages (89,000 words)

Country girl Nina loves to offer city kids a taste of rural life at Banksia Farm. When a lawsuit threatens, she needs help to avoid losing the farm.

Enter lawyer Leigh, who doesn't have time for small, unpaid cases or rural visits that wreck her cool—and her clothes. Still, warm-hearted Nina and her challenging daughter are awfully hard to say no to.

A captivating opposites-attract lesbian romance.

About Lola Keeley

Lola Keeley is a writer and coder. After moving to London to pursue her love of theatre, she later wound up living every five-year-old's dream of being a train driver on the London Underground. She has since emerged, blinking into the sunlight, to find herself writing books. She now lives in Edinburgh, Scotland, with her wife and four cats.

CONNECT WITH LOLA

Website: www.lolakeeley.co.uk

E-Mail:divalola@gmail.com

Her Royal Happiness

ISBN: 978-3-96324-601-2

Available in e-book and paperback formats.

Published by Ylva Publishing, legal entity of Ylva Verlag, e.Kfr.

Ylva Verlag, e.Kfr.
Owner: Astrid Ohletz
Am Kirschgarten 2
65830 Kriftel
Germany

www.ylva-publishing.com

First edition: 2022

Credits
Edited by C.S. Conrad and Sheena Billet
Cover Design and Print Layout by Streetlight Graphics